PENGUIN
T

KU-165-264

Patrick Dillon was born in London in 1962. He lives in Kennington, London, where he runs a successful architectural practice. *Truth* is his first novel and his second, *Lies*, has recently been published by Michael Joseph.

# TRUTH

**PATRICK DILLON**

PENGUIN BOOKS

## PENGUIN BOOKS

Published by the Penguin Group
Penguin Books Ltd, 27 Wrights Lane, London W8 5TZ, England
Penguin Books USA Inc., 375 Hudson Street, New York, New York 10014, USA
Penguin Books Australia Ltd, Ringwood, Victoria, Australia
Penguin Books Canada Ltd, 10 Alcorn Avenue, Toronto, Ontario, Canada M4V 3B2
Penguin Books (NZ) Ltd, 182–190 Wairau Road, Auckland 10, New Zealand

Penguin Books Ltd, Registered Offices: Harmondsworth, Middlesex, England

First published by Michael Joseph 1996
Published in Penguin Books 1997
1 3 5 7 9 10 8 6 4 2

Extract from *Brewer's Dictionary of 20th-Century Phrase and Fable*, published by Cassell plc,
copyright © Market House Books Limited 1991, by permission.

Extract from 'Caravan' by Duke Ellington, Irving Mills and Juan Tizol, copyright © 1937
and 1988 by Exclusive Publications Inc. Sole agents for the UK, British Commonwealth
(excluding Canada), the continent of Europe including Scandinavian territories and South
Africa: J. R. Lafleur & Son Ltd. Reprinted by permission of Boosey & Hawkes Music
Publishers Ltd.

Extract from 'Round Midnight' by Thelonious Monk and Cootie Williams, copyright ©
1944 Advance Music Corp., USA, Warner Chappell Music Ltd, London W1Y 3FA.
Reproduced by permission of International Music Publications Ltd.

The moral right of the author has been asserted

This novel is a work of fiction. Names, characters, places and incidents are either the
product of the author's imagination or used fictionally. Any resemblance to actual events or
persons, living or dead, is entirely coincidental.

Printed in England by Clays Ltd, St Ives plc

**truth**   In jazz slang, music that is regarded as being of the highest quality and communicating the essence of something

*Brewer's Twentieth Century Phrase and Fable*

The last time I'd seen Joe Bates he was wearing a peaked cap and a grey suit and leaning against a dark green Rolls-Royce with shaded windows. Maybe he'd wanted people to think the Roller belonged to him, or maybe he'd thought it would fall over if he walked away. Today he was wearing a denim jacket with three holes in it and something that looked like a black scarf but wasn't. It spread all over the pavement around his head, as if he'd wanted to use it as a cushion.

He was lying with his head by a row of parked cars and his feet by a brick shed full of dustbins. Beyond the parked cars was an expanse of paving and a dead tree with someone's initials carved on the bark. Tower blocks looked down at him from every side. It wasn't the sort of place you'd choose to die in, but Joe Bates hadn't been given the choice.

I said, 'Who found him?'

Cayman nodded towards a fat man sitting on a wall at the back of the pavement. The man's face was the colour of old paint and there was a pool of vomit on his shoes.

'Time?'

'Six.'

'What was he doing?'

'Walking the dog.'

I said, 'Where's the dog?'

No one knew where the dog was.

I bent down and examined Joe Bates. From the front he looked as if he'd just felt tired and lain down for a nap, except the parking lot between two tower blocks was a funny place to take a nap and his eyes were open. He had handsome eyes, model's eyes, and a long handsome face to go with them. If it wasn't for the three holes in the back of his neck you could have put him on the front of a magazine.

Cayman said, 'His name's Joe Bates, sir. He lived in one of the blocks. They must have got him on his way home.'

I didn't say anything.

'There's every chance he's got a record,' Cayman went on, 'living round here. We can check it back at the station.'

'He didn't have a record,' I said.

Cayman looked at me in surprise.

'They let him off.'

'Did you know him, sir?'

I said, 'He was a friend of Hill's.'

A man in uniform got out of one of the cars parked behind the ambulance at the kerb. He came towards us, stooped down and started to draw a chalk line around Joe Bates's body.

'How was he killed, Sergeant?'

'Three bullets,' Cayman said. 'One in the neck, two a bit lower down. The damage to his head must have been when he fell over.'

There was a pause. Cayman was looking at me as if I was supposed to give him a prize for working that out by himself.

I said, 'Did anyone hear anything?'

We both looked up at the towers. Above us were tiers of access decks. The parapets were lined with kids' faces staring down at us in silence. As far as they were concerned, it was just another show, better than a crazy old woman, not as good as a fire. The faces had the cruel look of spectators at a circus.

Cayman said, 'We've done the two far towers. We'll be through any time.'

'That's too slow.'

'I'm doing the best I can, sir. I –'

He was about to tell me something about too few officers covering too much ground. I cut him off. 'All right.'

'Anything else you want, Chief Inspector?' Cayman's voice was tight.

'No.'

'All right, then.' He wasn't looking at me.

'You can send anyone back who isn't needed,' I said. 'Get an incident room set up. You'd better stay here with me.'

He grimaced and went over towards one of the police vans. Cayman was ten years older than me and two rungs back down the ladder. The last time we'd worked together that hadn't mattered. We were never going to like each other but at least he'd respected me. That was before Hill.

I watched the policemen coming back from the two further towers. I didn't think they'd have learnt anything, and I didn't think they'd learn anything in the low-rise blocks either side of where Joe Bates lay. In Chelsea we'd have had neighbours running out of the front doors to tell us what they saw, or heard, or dreamed. Round here people kept the doors closed and televisions turned up high. If they heard shooting they turned the volume up even higher to drown it out.

A white car drove up to the kerb with its light flashing. Three more uniformed men got out. Cayman spoke to them and they spread out, one to each of the stair towers on the nearest blocks. There was a stampede of children's feet. Suddenly the access decks were deserted.

Cayman said, 'How much do you know about him, sir?'

I sighed. 'Do you remember Paddy Moran?'

Cayman didn't say anything. I knew he remembered Paddy Moran.

I said, 'Bates was driving the car when Hill killed him.'

'That was your case, wasn't it, sir?' Cayman knew it was my case.

'Bates has been following Hill round for years,' I went on. 'I don't know what else Hill used him for. Some time back he was charged for splitting open Tim McCreedy's knuckles with a monkey wrench. GBH. They let him off.'

'Why?'

'Hill paid for the lawyer,' I said.

There was a pause.

Cayman said, 'Who would have killed him?' He nodded towards what was lying on the pavement.

'Who do you think?'

'Would Hill do this to one of his own friends?'

I said, 'Hill doesn't have any friends.'

There were people coming out of the flats now on their way to work. Some of them walked past with dead eyes and some of them wound up against the barrier staring, as if we'd staged the whole thing just to cheer them up. One of them, a little braver than the others, came across the pavement towards us. He was an ordinary man in the sort of coat you wouldn't remember anywhere.

Cayman looked at him and said, 'Back, please.'

'What's happened?' The man's eyes were glued to Joe Bates's outflung hand.

'There's been an incident. Could you get back, please, sir.'

'What sort of an incident?'

'Somebody's dead,' Cayman said flatly.

'Dead?' The man nodded vaguely as if he'd heard somewhere about people dying but couldn't remember where. 'Was he killed?' He already knew the answer to that. If Joe Bates had died of a heart attack there wouldn't be two vanloads of policemen crawling all over the estate.

Cayman snapped, 'Back, mate. Behind the line. Now.'

There was a gleam in the man's eye. Dead was boring but killing woke something up in him. The animal knowledge that one day, if he got tired of working and watching TV, fucking, voting or drinking soapy beer out of tins, he might just kill someone himself – or get himself killed by someone. And that felt like a relief. His focus skewed over the body. He almost looked as if he was laughing.

He said, 'Shot, was he? Or was it a knife?'

Cayman shouted, 'Everyone back *now*. Get behind the line and stay there. And that includes you.'

The man turned and trotted back towards the line: the line that keeps all of us in and thoughts of murder out, that keeps us working and drinking soapy beer and still not killing anybody.

Cayman said, 'Fucking vultures. Sorry, sir.'

The fat man at the back of the pavement stood up. His

4

belly was hanging out of the top of his trousers and his mouth was open.

He said, 'Do I have to stay?' It sounded like his tongue had suddenly become too big.

I looked at him. A trickle of grey sick clung to his collar. For a moment I almost felt sorry for him. He was just an ordinary man who loved his dog and didn't like finding dead people on his morning walk. He had swollen tears running down his fat cheeks and was staring at me with a heartbroken look as if there was anything I could say that was going to make things right.

'Has anyone taken his statement yet?'

'No, sir.'

'Why the hell not?'

'There hasn't been time.'

'Make time. Do it now.'

Cayman's lips tightened but he didn't answer back. He called two policemen over and spoke to them. They lifted the man up by the shoulders and carried him towards a car.

They needn't have bothered. I could have written his statement for him:

One morning I was going for a walk near where I live. I was thinking about my breakfast, and whether to get the car serviced, and what the teacher said about my boy's homework, when suddenly I saw a man lying on the pavement. It seemed to me strange that he wasn't moving and that blood was coming out of a hole in his head. Then I started screaming. After that I stopped screaming and was sick. I am making this statement in a state of what the doctors call shock. Next week I will be talking about it too much, and the week after my family will be bored, but I still won't be able to sleep without seeing dead people. The only dead person I saw before was my grandmother who was eighty years old and had no hole in her head. Signed . . .

It would only tell us what we already knew: that somebody had killed Joe Bates in a council estate just off Kennington Lane. But because we were policemen we wouldn't believe it was true until we'd typed it out on a form and lost it in some filing cabinet. In six months' time we'd find the fat man again and put him in court, and he'd testify that he was indeed whoever he said he was and he'd seen the dead man with his own eyes, but he still couldn't sleep at night and his wife had now left him because she didn't like him talking about dead people, particularly just before breakfast.

I watched them help the fat man into a car and drive him off towards the station. Cayman was still hovering about, watching the policemen move along the access decks.

'Do we know anything else about Bates, sir? Was he still working for Hill?'

'I don't know. He used to make money on fashion shoots until he found out he could make more money hanging round Hill. The past few months he's been working as a chauffeur. He was supposed to be going straight.'

'What about Hill – what's he been doing since Paddy Moran?' Cayman wouldn't meet my eye.

I said, 'Killing people.'

Somebody's radio squealed, spat static and said something about a road accident at the Elephant and Castle. A blue Astra drove up behind the ambulance and a small man got out holding a silver photographic case. The rows of kids' faces were back on the access decks.

The small man came up to us, unlocked the case and started screwing together an aluminium tripod. He had a leathery, sly face and patter that was so old and smooth he couldn't even hear himself say it any more.

'Lovely day for a picture.' He didn't laugh; nor did anyone else. He screwed the camera into the top of the tripod and pointed it at Joe Bates.

'Any sign of a gun?' I asked Cayman.

'Not yet, sir. If he's got any sense he'll have dropped it in the river by now.'

I nodded. 'We'd better go through the bins. Keep them cordoned off until forensic give us something to go on.'

It was a routine, as pointless and automatic as checking the tower blocks.

Cayman turned to talk to a policeman standing behind us.

The photographer was peering through his camera at Bates's body. He said, 'Smile for the birdy.' Nobody laughed.

'We've got his wife down at the station,' Cayman said, turning back to me.

'Clare,' I said.

'You know her, sir?'

'I interviewed her in the Moran investigation.'

'What's she like?'

'Better than him,' I said. 'She thought he was innocent. I didn't know they lived here.'

'Number twenty-nine.' He pointed towards the block nearest us.

'Have you taken a statement yet?'

'We were waiting for you.' His voice was tight.

I said, 'Was she in a state?'

'Quiet, they said. She's got a kid – two years old. Bloody hard.'

I said, 'Isn't it?'

The photographer snapped his tripod shut. Two men in green overalls who'd been lounging against their ambulance came to life. They pulled a stretcher out of the back and carried it over to where Bates lay.

I looked round. The morning traffic was snarled up behind us on Kennington Lane. Faces looked down from the top deck of a stationary bus. Something to tell them about at work: a blanket with a man's hand sticking out of it. Something to think about in the middle of the night, and make them get up and check that the doors were locked and the gas switched off. Police vans, a crowd of people, a shape under the blanket that was at the same time familiar and as strange as anything ever could be; the same shape their husband made under the blanket at night. I wondered how many of them had seen somebody dead before. A woman with thick forearms leaned on the access deck above us and peered down as if she was looking into a pit.

I said, 'Wait a minute.'

I stooped, and rolled Joe Bates over on to his side. His head sagged to one side and came to rest. The handsome blue eyes stared past me through hooded lids. His sneering, hard man's mouth was an ugly purple line split by teeth. Stubble covered his jawline and cheeks. Joe Bates needed a shave but he wasn't going to get one.

I felt in his pockets. In the side pocket of the jacket there was a Rolls-Royce key ring with two doorkeys and the keys to a car. I found a half-pack of Marlboro in the other side pocket along with a cheap lighter and another key, not on a ring. I gave all the keys to Cayman and told him to try them on Bates's front door. Then I rolled Bates over on to his side again and felt his back pockets. One of them was empty.

From the other I pulled out a roll of green banknotes tied up with a rubber band.

One of the stretcher men whistled. He was going to say something, then caught my eye and didn't.

The notes were fifties. I started to count through them. The stretcher men picked Joe Bates up and lifted him on to the stretcher. His body was stiff, as if he didn't want to go wherever it was they were taking him. His head dropped back, bumping once on the pavement.

I was still thumbing through the notes when Cayman came back.

'The two Chubbs open his front door, sir. The separate one . . .' He shrugged. 'Doesn't seem to belong. Maybe it was from his office.'

There was a roar of car engines starting up behind us. One by one they were pulling away from the kerb. The photographer drove off; the ambulance gave one shriek of its siren, to move the kids, and nosed its way towards Kennington Lane.

Cayman said, 'Are we quite sure it wasn't just a mugging, sir?'

I opened out the roll of banknotes for him.

Cayman whistled. 'Keep him in fags for a bit.'

I didn't laugh. 'We need to find Hill.'

We turned towards the car. One of the policemen who'd been knocking on doors was waiting for us.

'Old lady in thirty-six,' he said. 'Light sleeper. Heard three shots about one o'clock. Thought it was the television. Then she heard a motorbike drive off.'

'Immediately?'

'She said immediately.'

'Is she making it up?'

The policeman shrugged.

'A motorbike,' I said.

Cayman said, 'Not Yardies. They use four wheels.'

I looked at him. 'Bring her in for a statement.'

We got into the car, slamming doors. Behind us two policemen were unrolling red plastic tape across the pavement. There are 150 murders a year in London and most of them start something like this, with two coppers unrolling red tape across a pavement. The kids were still looking down from the access decks, staring at the chalk mark where Bates had been lying, as if it was about to get up and walk away. An old drunk was staggering around beyond the cordon, shooting people with his forefinger and laughing. Like I said, it wasn't the sort of place you'd choose to die in. But Joe Bates hadn't been given the choice.

## 2

We interviewed Clare Bates in a narrow room on the top floor of Kennington police station. The room had a low ceiling, a dark grey carpet which was scuffed under the chairs, and a grille over the window. Through the grille you could see part of a park and a row of shops. Even halfway through the morning the fluorescent lights in the ceiling were switched on. You wouldn't have called the room comfortable, but most people who were brought there were beyond the sort of comfort that wallpaper can give. A poster on the wall advertised Neighbourhood Watch to people for whom it was already too late. This was where you came if you'd just been robbed, raped, assaulted in the street, or if somebody had found your husband with three holes in his neck on a pavement off Kennington Lane.

Clare Bates didn't look as if she ought to be going through this. She was a slim woman in her twenties with trusting grey eyes and a wide forehead. Her hair was tied back in a black ribbon. She looked too nice to be married to Joe Bates in the first place, too nice to be living where she lived. She smelled of clean laundry. She was pretty but not sexy; the kind of girl you'd expect to see working at a charity fair or picking up her kid from school, not sitting in a dingy police interview room, talking about who might have shot her husband.

She was looking at me with a wounded expression. By now she had been crying so long she'd run out of tears. Her eyes were like washed-out grey skies after rain.

I said, 'What do you mean he didn't have any enemies? He was a criminal, wasn't he? Criminals always have enemies.'

Behind me Cayman shuffled restlessly from foot to foot.

Clare Bates opened her mouth to say something. Two narrow blue creases appeared across her forehead; then her face puckered up like a kid's and she started crying again.

I leaned forward towards her trembling blonde head. 'Joe had been hanging around with Hill for four years,' I said. 'You're telling me they never argued?'

'He didn't see Hill any more.' Her voice was firmer than I expected. There was just one jump in it, then she got it under control.

'How can you know that?'

'I know.'

'Because he told you?'

'Because he didn't.'

I said, 'What about Paddy Moran? Twelve months ago Hill and your husband were standing trial together for murder, now you say they hardly knew each other. You expect us to believe that?'

'They were let off,' she said. 'You know they were. Anyway, Joe was only accused of driving the car.'

'And that makes him a nice guy?'

She looked up at me. Something had hardened in her eyes, like ice hardening over water. With one hand she tucked a strand of blonde hair behind her ear. Her lips were trembling. 'You were like this before,' she said. 'Don't you ever treat people decently?'

A woman police constable came in with three cups of coffee. She put them down on the table. She looked anxiously at Clare Bates, then at me. I nodded towards the door.

When she had gone Cayman said, 'Take us through it again, love. In your own time. When did he come home?'

She sighed. 'About half past seven.' She'd said it all before. 'I'd just put Patrick down.'

'Did Joe always work on a Sunday?'

'Sometimes. It wasn't unusual.'

'Did he tell you what he'd been doing?'

'Driving Sir John.' She brought out the title with a little flourish of self-importance.

'That's the guy he was working for?'

She nodded. 'Sir John Penny.'

'Who is he?'

She frowned. She said, 'He's important, a politician. He's very influential.'

'Influential with who?'

She didn't answer that. There was a pause, then I said, 'Did he say where they went?'

'Joe didn't talk about work.'

'What happened when he came home?'

'Nothing,' she said. 'We talked.'

'What about?'

'I don't know.' She sounded irritated. 'Patrick . . . What does anyone talk about?'

'Did you argue?'

'Then?'

'Ever.'

'No more than anyone else.'

Cayman asked, 'What about supper . . . did he eat?'

'He wasn't hungry. He changed and went out again. I'd eaten earlier.'

'Where was he going?'

'He didn't say.'

'Did he often go out alone?'

'He had a lot of friends.'

'What sort of friends?' I asked.

She looked at me coldly. 'All sorts,' she said.

'Did you think he was going straight?'

'He was.'

I said, 'You wish.'

Clare Bates's hands had fisted into balls on the table. The knuckles were white. She said jerkily, 'My husband has just been killed . . .' She couldn't go on. There was a long silence. Outside someone walked along the corridor whistling a tune I couldn't make out.

'Tell me about Hill,' I said.

She swallowed. 'What about him?'

'How often did your husband see him?'

'He didn't see him any more.'

'Since when?'

'Last year.'

'After Paddy Moran got killed?'

'After they were let off,' she said.

'Is that because you made him promise not to?'

'That . . . and other things . . .' She stopped herself and looked down at her hands.

'What other things?'

Clare seemed to be examining her fingers very closely. 'Me,' she said.

There was a pause.

I said, 'Go on.'

'Hill made a pass at me. Joe told him he mustn't come round any more.'

'What sort of a pass?'

The two blue creases came back across her forehead. She broke out, 'For God's sake!'

'It's all right, love.' Cayman stepped forward to the table. He didn't look at me. 'We'll talk about something else, all right? What time did your husband go out last night?'

Clare's hand strayed up to a plain gold chain round her neck. I found myself wondering if she bought her own clothes, or if Joe had bought them for her. She was stylish, in a girl-next-door kind of way. Not flashy, but as stylish as you can get from High Street stores, as stylish as anyone was where she lived.

'I'm not sure,' she said. 'About eight o'clock.'

'Why didn't you go with him?'

'I had to look after Patrick.'

'And that was the last you heard from him?'

'Until this morning.' There was a pause before she said it. I could see her swallowing.

'What did you do?' I asked. 'Last night.'

'I watched television . . . I don't know. Spoke to my mum. Patrick woke up a few times.'

'Does your mother live nearby?'

'We spoke on the phone.'

'Weren't you worried about Joe?'

13

'Of course I was.' She looked up at me through wondering, hurt eyes.

'Did he often stay out late?'

'No . . .' She hesitated.

'Sometimes?' put in Cayman.

'He liked drinking with the lads.'

'Where did he go when he stayed out?'

'It was only once or twice. He stayed with friends.' There was distress in her voice. 'That's normal, isn't it? He'd sleep on the floor.'

She looked beseechingly up at Cayman, as if she wanted him to tell her their life had been normal and that made up for the fact most people's husbands don't end up lying dead on the pavement outside their home. I wondered if that was what kept her going: the desire to be normal in a place where normal was hard, and ugly, and usually had an unhappy ending.

Cayman nodded soothingly.

'What about money?' I asked. 'Did he have money when he went out?'

'I didn't ask.'

'Who did the housekeeping?' Cayman said.

'I did.'

'Do you work?'

'No. We only have what Joe makes. Three-fifty a week.'

'That's good money for a chauffeur.'

'He was good at his job.'

'Did they pay him cash?'

She looked bewildered. 'Yes.'

'When?'

'On Friday night. He gave me the housekeeping straighta-way. Why are you asking all this?'

'How much was the housekeeping?'

'Two hundred.' She shook her head. 'We didn't spend half of it – I put what was left over in the Halifax.' A sensible girl trying to do the best thing by her kid. 'I was trying to save.'

'So he had over a hundred on Friday night?' I asked.

'It was usually gone by Sunday. Joe always went out

14

Saturday night – for a curry. And he'd stand drinks for his mates.'

'So how come he had twelve hundred pounds in his pocket this morning?' I said.

Clare Bates kept staring at me. She didn't know what to say. Her grey eyes were bewildered.

Cayman said, 'Did you often see him with a lot of money?'

Her lips said no, but no sound came out.

'Are you sure?'

She swallowed again. There was soft white skin under her chin which moved when she swallowed. Suddenly she looked tired. Not angry any more, or shocked, or hurt; just tired.

'I'm sure.'

'Do you have any idea where the money would have come from?'

She shook her head.

There was no sound outside. The three coffee cups were sitting untouched on the table. Clare Bates picked one up and sipped from it. There were purplish rings under her eyes.

Cayman said gently, 'How long were you married, love?'

'Four years. Just over.'

'How old's your boy?'

'Nearly two.'

'That's a nice age,' he said.

'How did you meet Joe?' I asked.

She shrugged. 'I don't remember. At my mum's pub, I think.'

'She runs a pub?'

'The Blue Corner.'

'It's up in Southwark,' Cayman said to me.

'Did you know him a long time before you married?'

'Three years.'

'What happened when he was charged with smashing up McCreedy's hand?'

She didn't look at me. She was too tired to be angry again. 'I made him promise to be careful . . .' She paused. 'Not to see Hill again.'

15

I said quietly, 'He lied to you. He was still seeing Hill. Where else would he get twelve hundred pounds?'

Clare looked at me dumbly. Her lips moved. She said, 'I want to stop now.'

Cayman opened the door and went out.

When he was gone I said, 'When did Hill make the pass at you?'

'Just before the trial. He's done it before.'

'What do you mean?'

'We knew each other as kids. He was always chasing after me. It made Joe furious.'

'What happened this time?'

She shook her head.

'Go on.'

She took a deep breath. 'He was drunk. He asked me . . .' All I could see was the top of her head. 'He asked me to go to bed with him.'

'What did you say?' I asked.

Clare Bates looked up. She was crying again, the tears spilling out on to her cheeks.

'You're a horrible man,' she whispered.

The door opened. Cayman came back in with the policewoman. The woman put her arm round Clare's shoulder and helped her up. She didn't look at me.

Cayman said, 'All right, love. That's all for now.'

The policewoman helped Clare Bates out.

Back in my office Cayman put his notebook down on the desk. He didn't look at me.

He said, 'You bastard.'

Through the thin partition we could hear someone typing and someone else dictating a report. The voice was a high sing-song, a Jamaican voice. We heard doors slamming, people going in and out. I looked at Cayman's plain, shocked face. I wanted to tell him it wasn't me that was unfair, or cruel, or insensitive. Outside, in the estates of South London, the junkies were sweating in the crack dens, or waiting under the podiums of the South Bank begging for the money to shoot up. It wasn't me that was unfair. I wanted to tell him that until all the Joe Bateses were dead and all the Hills were locked up it would go on just the same, and that mattered more than one woman crying in a police interview room. It wasn't my fault. If he wanted someone to blame he should go higher up than me.

I looked over Cayman's shoulder. The office was a tiny cupboard just wide enough for a desk and filing cabinet. It felt like any other office except it didn't have any photographs of wives and children, or postcards from Spain, or joke mugs. It didn't have anything except the tools of the job: a desk, a phone, a police-issue lamp with chipped enamel. On the wall was a pinboard covered in typed memos I hadn't read. In one corner of it I'd pinned the only personal thing I had in the room: a photograph of Miles Davis, the one they'd used for the cover of *Milestones*. I used to look at it while I typed up reports, my old typewriter hammering out the details of deaths and assaults, of what people saw and what they suffered. Miles sat on a chair, cradling his horn in one hand. His brown eyes stared straight out at the camera. The green shirt he wore was open at the neck. I knew that album by heart: I could pick up the melody from any track on it and let it wash briefly through the office while I flexed my fingers. I used to do that while the reports piled up in the intray: statements of witnesses, photographs. We all need some way to keep ourselves sane.

I looked at the photograph now. Miles stared back at me. His eyes seemed to hold a kind of challenge.

I said, 'Joe Bates hung around with Hill. Hill's tied up in this.'

'It's no reason to treat her rough.'

'She'll survive.'

He said, 'You know what you are? You're a bastard.'

'Listen.' I swung round towards him. He was standing on the other side of the desk with his hands hanging by his sides. 'Bates is up to here with Hill. Someone kills Bates. Whoever it was, Hill is mixed up in it – I'd put money that he did it himself. Either way, it gives us something to go on. That's all that matters.'

'People matter.' His chin quivered self-righteously. Next door the typing had stopped. Someone was laughing, a high monotonous laugh.

I said, 'They're not our business.' I got up. 'Let's go.'

Cayman didn't move. He looked angry and scared at the same time. The combination pinched his eyebrows together as if he was squinting at me. There was something wrong with the colour of his face.

He said, 'I want to register this. I'm going to put in a report.'

'You can do whatever you damn well like.'

'You can't . . . It's not right to . . .' His eyebrows went up. 'You have to treat people right.'

'Are you talking about Clare Bates,' I said, 'or you?'

Cayman winced. 'You *are* a bastard.'

It started as a shout and ended as the kind of whisper that wants to be a shout. A door opened somewhere in the outer office. Cayman clenched one fist. Someone was shuffling papers in the far corner of the room; neither of us looked round. The door opened and closed again.

Cayman said quietly, 'It was all right before. No one likes a Smart Alec but we put up with it. You respect a man who gets the job done. I'm damned if I'm going to take it these days.'

'You think that's what it means, getting your sergeant's exam?'

Cayman flushed. He said, 'I wasn't talking about that. I meant, since Paddy Moran.'

There was dead silence in the room.

I said, 'You're on the edge, Cayman.'

'I don't care. Someone's got to say it. If I have to work with you . . . Did you know we were all joking in the CID room, hoping we wouldn't be put on your team? People used to want to be on your team. You used to get the job done.'

I kept my voice as cold as I could. I said, 'There isn't anything else to say.'

We stared at each other through a glass wall of rank. Cayman's expression had a stupid sense of injustice. He was the sort of copper, normally, who'd do what he was told. Now he'd drawn a line and was trying to stand up to it.

Quietly I said, 'We need a car. Go and get a car.'

'I'm going to put in a complaint.'

'You do what you like. I'm telling you to get a car.' I wasn't looking at him any more.

Cayman's voice asked where we were going. It sounded subdued. I was digging in the drawer of my desk.

I said, 'We're going to find Hill.'

## 3

I couldn't remember the time before Hill any more. There must have been a time when I'd never even heard his name, but I couldn't remember how that had felt. These days his mocking face seemed to have been living with me for ever. In my dreams it looked like the faces police frogmen fish out of the river: bloated, unnaturally white, with eyes the colour of seaweed. Women always said they found him attractive. That might have been the remains of his looks – Hill had been a handsome boy once. More likely it was because he was a child whom no one had ever taught where to stop, and some women found that hard to resist. Matthew Hill did what he liked and expected people to like him for it. He'd got his face by staying up too late for too long, sleeping with too many women, drinking in too many places, anywhere from Mayfair nightclubs to crack dens on the wrong side of the river. When he was with you his eyes crawled over your skin like two green lizards.

The wrong side of the river was where Hill's father, Dick, had come from. He hadn't stayed there long: these days he lived in a flat on Park Lane, dealt in property, and had nothing to show for twenty years on the Old Kent Road except his accent. Hill could have gone on from there. Ten thousand pounds of education a year had bought him the right voice, the right friends, everything he needed to settle on the right side of town. But the right side of town was too polite for him. Hill preferred the bad-smelling side that his father had paid a fortune to wash off. He liked tatty pubs and seedy parties, tarts with too much make-up and voices that could cut glass, and he didn't give a damn what anyone thought of him. The police had started picking him up for drugs offences when he was still in his teens. He got off with the sort of fines he could scrape out of his glove compartment and went back to Mayfair. No one realized then that Hill was ambitious. A year or so later he was stopped at Heathrow with ten ounces of heroin in his Gucci suitcase.

Putting Hill in prison was like leaving a kid in a sweet shop. He met a nice crowd of housebreakers and dealers, professionals all of them, who soon realized that Hill was not only smarter than them, and richer, but didn't have so many scruples. Hill liked meeting people like that and he liked boasting about it afterwards. When he came out he was a celebrity both sides of the river.

He spent the next few years playing with that fame: that was how he ended up looking the way he did. He put his finger in protection rackets, and in drugs, and fenced stolen goods in the South London markets. At the same time he was starting to dabble in his father's property firm. It didn't mean he was settling down. He went on getting into trouble, getting arrested for it and somehow getting out again. One day early in 1989 a down-and-out called Paddy Moran made the mistake of bedding down in a doorway on Bermondsey Street that happened to be on Hill's way home. Hill was in a mean mood about something – we had witnesses who told us that. He'd been drinking all evening and boasting about how he was going to hurt somebody. Moran should have chosen another doorway, or maybe had a different face. Hill had given him plenty of time to regret that. There must have been a moment when Paddy Moran had realized this wasn't going to be just another beating and the expression that came on his face then stayed on it. It was still there in the police morgue the next day. By the time Hill had finished with him the old man had eighteen stab wounds in his head and chest, his legs had been broken, and his hands cut off at the wrists.

Someone – someone who knew him – had seen Hill's blond-white head running away down Bermondsey Street and getting into a car. We spent half a year building the case around that, and all the circumstantial evidence a jury could dream of. Just before the trial Hill hired the most expensive lawyer in London, and our eyewitness paid off the mortgage on her home. When the time came to give her evidence she couldn't remember anything except a black woman walking in the opposite direction.

I'd lived over the last day of the trial so often I could do it in my sleep. Hill's lawyer was a short man with grey hair escaping from under his wig. He played the jury like an old ham on a music-hall stage; you could see he'd beaten them by the way their eyes followed him. Hill had been given a haircut and a new suit and told to laugh at all the judge's jokes. The judge liked that. He didn't like me. He didn't like the way I got angry at Hill's lawyer, or the way I interrupted one of his jokes. When the jury went out I felt something cold start to grow at the bottom of my stomach. It didn't take them long to make up their minds.

Hill was acquitted of all charges. I could still recall the tone of the foreman's voice without even trying: 'Not guilty . . . Not guilty.' The foreman had a narrow face and hair smoothed down with hair oil. When the judge asked him for the verdicts he grinned like a kid who knew he'd got all the right answers.

Hill had celebrated with a cocaine binge in a nightclub off Berkeley Square, then opened a bar called Babylon in the Southwark Bridge Road. The bar was his little piece of Mayfair in South London, and it filled up with the sort of people he liked. The Moran case had changed Hill. Before he'd been mad and bad; now he was dangerous as well, and he liked it. He liked the flicker in men's eyes when they met him and he liked what women saw when he walked into a room. The acquittal had also proved to him that nothing was going to touch him. Since the day he walked out of court Hill had been living in a different city to everybody else. He floated above the pavements that everyone else walked along, because he'd killed a man and no one had touched him for it.

After the Moran case I went back to the grind of police work, but it didn't feel the same. The old lags – people like

Cayman – said it was all part of the game, but that wasn't a game I knew how to play. We'd tracked a murderer down and he'd walked free out of court. It wasn't only Hill who was changed by it.

It was just past twelve o'clock. If Hill wanted to run we were too late anyway; if he wanted to tough it out we knew where to find him.

In the car park behind the police station we piled into an unmarked blue Escort and headed towards the Southwark Bridge Road.

## 4

The lunchtime crowd at Babylon was two black guys in fake Armani suits and a thirty-something hunched over his drink with his mouth open. His eyes had the shocked look of junkies' eyes, as if they'd seen things no one else had and couldn't forget it. Behind the bar a young barman was fishing in his mouth with a toothpick. He didn't have much else to do. No one was talking. Outside buses were roaring past on their way across river to the City. The barman's eyes followed them through the plate-glass windows like a drunk watching someone else's glass.

Babylon had a blond wood floor, lights made out of bent coathangers, and walls done in some paint effect that looked like the inside of a smoker's lungs. The stainless-steel fridges behind the bar were full of designer lager. It was a nice effect, but it was in the wrong place. Babylon needed a roomful of Soho advertising executives and people who said they worked in the movies. Instead, it had two sharp boys from Brixton on their way up and a junkie on his way down. Someone should have told Hill he was putting his money in the wrong place.

The barman's eyes came alive when Cayman and I walked in. Inside, the room was deeper than it looked from the street. There was a sofa at the back and some armchairs under a big gilt mirror with candles on it. The bearded man sitting on the sofa didn't look like a customer. His eyes turned suspiciously towards us as we went up to the bar.

'Hello, gentlemen.' The barman's voice was Australian. He was a handsome kid with short-cropped blond hair and sideburns. He had a gold earring in one ear.

I said, 'Is Hill here?'

'Who wants him?'

'I do.'

We stared at each other for a moment. I was better at it than him.

He started playing with the beer mats on the bar. 'Sorry, fellas. I haven't seen him today.' His tone was soothing. He was used to dealing with people who talked tough.

'When did you see him?'

'Last night.'

'What time?'

The two suits were watching us. Their eyes had narrowed.

The barman said, 'What can I get you fellows to drink?'

'I'm a policeman,' I said.

The barman raised his chin slightly. The bearded man at the back had got up and was watching us uncertainly, the way bouncers do when they haven't worked out who to punch.

I took out my ID and spread it for him. The barman's eyes flickered from the ID back to my face, then to a door marked 'Private' behind the bar.

'Where's Hill?'

'I told you, he's not here.'

'So where is he?'

'I don't know,' the barman said.

'He runs this place, doesn't he?'

'He owns it.'

'What's the difference?'

'I don't know.'

'What do you know?'

He shrugged. He still had his fingers spread out on the steel top of the bar. His blond hair fell in a girlish lock over his forehead. He didn't look tough enough to be working for Hill, but maybe Hill counted him as decoration, like the blond wood and the bent coathangers.

'What's your name?'

'Harry.'

'Your other name.'

'Freeman. Harry Freeman.'

'Got a work permit, Harry?'

He nodded uncertainly.

'How long have you been over here?'

'Six months.'

The tough at the back of the room was chewing on his jaws.

'What time does Hill normally come in?'

'About now.' Harry's eyes flickered towards the door. 'He might be at his dad's office.'

'What time do you open?'

'Midday.'

'Is he usually here?'

'I suppose.' He shrugged.

'Did he tell you he was going to be late?'

'No. Say, what's this about, fellas?'

With one hand I raised the hatch across the bar and ducked under it. I opened the door marked 'Private'. The barman's voice bleated behind me. Inside was an office with a leather executive chair, a Habitat desk and a girlie calendar pinned up by the window. The window had a grille across it.

The barman followed us in. I spun him round by the shoulder and said, 'Sit down.'

Harry's eyes were shocked. He opened his mouth to protest, then sat down carefully like a kid trying out the teacher's desk at school.

'I've got to mind the bar.'

'Fuck the bar.'

He flinched as if I'd hit him. Cayman shut the door and leaned against it.

'Listen, fellas . . .'

'What are you scared of, Harry?'

'I'm not scared.'

'You're acting scared.'

'I'm sorry.'

'What are you sorry about?'

'I'm . . .' His eyes groped. 'I'm not.'

'You're not what?'

He opened his mouth but the right thing didn't want to come out. 'I don't know,' he said.

'Were you working last night?'

'Yes.'

'How busy was it?'

'It was a Sunday night.'

'I know that. I asked how busy it was.'

He shrugged. 'I don't know. A dozen people all night. Quiet.'

'What sort of people?'

'Just . . . people.'

'Was Hill here?'

'Yes.'

'What time did he come in?'

'Just after nine.'

'Alone?'

'Yes. I mean . . . he was alone then.'

'Who was he with later?'

'A couple of guys. Drinking.'

'Who were they?'

Harry looked from me to Cayman and back again. He gulped. 'I don't know . . . One of them was . . .' Harry raised one hand and drew a circle with it. 'A tall guy. Dark hair. He'd been in before. Fellow called Joe Bates.'

I stood up from the desk. Dark stains had appeared under the arms of Harry's white shirt.

'Joe Bates,' I said.

'That's right.' Harry nodded eagerly, as if the right answer was going to get him out in one piece.

I said, 'What time did Joe Bates come in?'

'Not long after Mr Hill.'

'Did they often drink together? Were they friends?'

'Quite often . . . I don't know. Often enough.'

'So they must have been friends.'

'Not the way they were talking last night,' Harry said.

There was a pause. Harry's eyes flickered towards Cayman then back to me.

I said, 'Did they have an argument?'

'You bet.' Harry's eyes were round.

I perched on the edge of the table and stared down at his innocent, clean-shaven face. 'They had a fight,' I said quietly.

'I wouldn't call it a fight. A row, more like.'

After another pause I said, 'Do you know what it was about?'

Harry shook his head.

I slapped my open palm down on the table-top. 'Didn't you hear anything?'

Harry jumped. He stammered, 'I don't know, fellas, they were . . . they were at a table.'

'Didn't you bring them drinks?'

'I guess so . . .' His face had lost its colour. It looked like a ventriloquist's doll: white cheeks, red lips and dark rings about the eyes.

'So what were they talking about?'

Cayman said, 'Were they drunk?'

'Joe Bates was drunk when he came in. Hill was . . .' He shrugged. 'So-so.'

'Looking for trouble?'

'Joe Bates was.'

I said, 'Are you looking for trouble, Harry? We can find some for you if you want it.'

'No!' He shot an agonized glance at the door. 'Look . . .' He was having trouble stopping his lips from trembling. His voice was a whine. 'Just tell me what it's about . . .'

'You tell us.'

'I ought to talk to Mr Hill.'

'You're talking to us.'

'It's just . . .'

I raised one finger and brought it down on the edge of table. Harry started as if I'd cracked a whip. His thin face was twisted. He said, 'I heard . . .' He stopped and swallowed. I kept my eyes on him. 'I heard them talking when Joe Bates went to the toilet. Hill and the other guy. Hill said . . . "He's got it coming." That was all. I don't know what it was about. Look . . .' His eyes stared wildly at us. 'They were drunk, all right?'

28

I sat back. '"He's got it coming",' I repeated slowly.

Harry's voice was hardly more than a whisper. 'That's right.'

Cayman said, 'Who was this other man? Are you sure you hadn't seen him before?'

'Never.'

'Did he leave with the other two?'

'Before. Hill and Bates went on drinking.'

'Until what time?'

He closed his eyes. 'Until we closed.'

'What time was that?'

'About midnight. Half past, maybe.'

'And they left together?'

'No.' He shook his head. Sweat was darkening his hair. 'Hill stayed on to do the till.'

'For how long?' Cayman's voice was sharp.

'An hour, I guess.'

There was a long silence.

I said, 'How do you know it was an hour?'

'I guess I . . .' His voice was failing. 'I guess I looked at my watch.'

'You're not sure, then. It could have been earlier.'

'I don't think so.'

'Hill could have left just . . .' I tried to work it out in my head. 'Say fifteen minutes after Bates. Twenty minutes. Yes?'

He shook his head. 'I don't think so,' he repeated.

I wiped the back of my hand across my mouth and regarded him. His face was as still as if it had been carved out of wood, frozen by fear.

'Had you been drinking?' I asked.

Cayman drew his breath in sharply. Harry blinked nervously.

'Go on. Had you had a drink?'

'Just . . . one or two, I guess.'

'One or two what?'

'Vodkas.'

I nodded slowly. 'Vodkas,' I said. 'You'd been drinking

29

one or two vodkas and you're not sure whether you looked at your watch.'

He kept his frightened eyes on me.

I put my face close to his and whispered, 'You were so fucking pissed you didn't even know your own name.'

Harry whimpered.

'What time did Hill leave the bar?' I said.

'I don't know.'

'It could have been any time — isn't that right? It could have been a quarter to one and you wouldn't have known the difference.'

I could only see the top of Harry's head, now. His shoulders were shaking. His head moved up and down.

I stood up. 'Take him in for a statement.'

Cayman came over from the door and put his hand under Harry's arm. Outside, the bar was almost empty. The two black guys had disappeared; the junkie was contemplating terrors at the bottom of his ashtray.

I said to the bouncer, 'Have you seen the owner today?'

He shook his head. His eyes were on Harry. 'What's he done?'

'Work permit.'

'Are you looking for Mr Hill?'

I said, 'No.'

There was no point letting Hill know we were already looking for him. We left the bouncer looking puzzled, which was what he was best at. Outside Cayman put his hand on Harry's head and forced him into the back seat of the car.

I said, 'Take him back to the station and get down a statement. Make sure he says what he just told us. I'll be back about three. I want a search call out on Hill.'

'Where are you going?'

I looked at him. Cayman's face was a mask. He said 'What about the others? You've got a team, remember. A murder squad. What are they supposed to do — play cards?'

I said, 'I've already put some of them on assignments.'

'And the rest?'

'I'll leave that to you, Sergeant.'

'Where are you going?'
I said, 'To see Sir John Penny.'
I started walking towards the bridge.

## 5

Sir John Penny lived at the eastern edge of Belgravia, so close to Buckingham Palace he could have lobbed his coronet over the garden wall. There were big cars parked along each pavement. A Filipino woman was on her hands and knees outside the next door along, scrubbing the marble step. There was no one else in the street.

The number of Penny's house was painted on the two big columns that held up the porch. Behind them was a front door wide enough to drive your Rolls-Royce through. I rang the bell and waited. I didn't have to wait for long. There were footsteps and the door opened. A woman in a housecoat looked out at me. She looked Spanish.

'Yes, please?'

'Is this John Penny's house?'

'Yes.'

'I want to see him. I'm from the police.'

Her eyes narrowed. 'What's it about, please?'

I said, 'Bates, his chauffeur.'

'Is Bates in trouble?'

I had the feeling she would have liked Bates to be in trouble.

I said, 'It depends what you call trouble. Someone killed him last night.'

Her eyes went round and one hand went up to her mouth. 'Dead?'

'As dead as you'd want to be.'

She didn't understand that. She looked at me for a moment, then looked behind her into the hall. 'I'll see if he's in. Wait, please.'

She tried to shut the door on me but I was already halfway inside. The woman grimaced and closed the door behind me. 'Wait here.'

The hall was silent with the kind of dead silence that must have had the place to itself for a long time. A grandfather clock counted out time for anyone who was interested; two high-backed chairs stood to attention against the far wall. Ancestors looked down at me from the walls as if they knew I wasn't supposed to be there and in their day they'd have known what to do about it.

'This way, please.' The Spanish woman was standing on the half-landing, her hands on her hips.

My feet didn't make any noise on the stair carpet. Nothing made any noise except the grandfather clock. It was the sort of place you whisper in, so as not to frighten the furniture.

The door on the first landing stood half open. The Spanish woman pointed to it and nodded. She didn't say anything.

I found myself in a tall gloomy room full of books, hunting prints and dark furniture. There were thick curtains across the windows. I couldn't hear traffic. In front of the window was a mahogany desk with a man sitting behind it. He was a big man with a craggy, forbidding face and a domed forehead with grey hair receding from it. His jaws were clamped shut. The hooked nose belonged to some Roman emperor, or a 1930s dictator. He looked as if his favourite game would be shouting orders at soldiers the wrong side of a parade ground.

The man wasn't looking at me. His gaze was fixed grimly at a point somewhere along the skirting board. His hands were clamped so tightly on the arms of his chair that the bones showed white.

I waited for Sir John Penny to say something. He didn't.

I tried a cough. It was the kind of discreet cough that ordinary people have been trying on people like Penny for centuries, the sort of cough a dachshund might give a mastiff if he wanted to get the mastiff's attention.

Penny's jaws worked a little and his eyes flickered towards mine. His eyes were a pallid blue, slightly watery. They blinked at me, recoiled, and fastened on the floor behind me, as if some dog had walked in with me and he was trying to remember the dog's name. A slight frown creased his forehead.

I walked forward into the room. On Penny's desk was an old-fashioned telephone, a blotter and three pens set out in a row, nothing else. As I reached the desk his frown switched to the pens, as if they were the ones trying to mess up his morning.

I said, 'Mr Penny?'

Penny shifted suddenly in his chair. His jaw jutted out aggressively, as if he was about to tear a strip off some insubordinate junior lieutenant. I braced myself.

A high, reedy voice said, 'Ye-es.'

It was a tentative voice, the voice of an ageing clergyman, not a field marshal. The words came out too loud, and unsteady, as if Penny had misjudged the top step and fallen forward into a room full of people. He shot me a startled look and the craggy face melted into the apologetic half-grin of a truant schoolboy.

From that close I could smell the brandy on his breath.

I pulled back a chair and sat down.

I said, 'My name is Detective Chief Inspector Havilland. I'm here about Bates, your chauffeur. Did the maid tell you about Bates?'

The grin disappeared. Penny's mask was back in place. He frowned seriously, the way a magistrate would frown at a kid who'd been caught joyriding.

He said vaguely, 'Bates . . . Yes, what's happened to Bates? He didn't come this morning.'

'Was he supposed to come?'

'Nine o'clock.' The pallid blue eyes shot me another look. 'The usual time.'

I said, 'Bates won't be coming today.'

'Tomorrow?' Penny's voice trembled.

'Not ever. Bates is dead.'

It took a moment to sink in.

He said, '*Dead? Bates is dead?*' His eyes were uncertain.

'He died last night,' I said. 'I'm sorry.'

The look Penny turned towards me was scared. His fingers fluttered on the arms of the chair.

'But . . . how? Why? I don't understand.'

I said, 'Somebody killed him.'

Panic rose up Penny's cheeks. His eyes started blinking uncontrollably. He broke out 'Oh my God . . . my *God* . . .'

He lumbered up from the desk and over to a drinks cabinet in the bookshelf. I heard a bottle jarring on the rim of a glass. I didn't watch. I looked at the picture over the fireplace. It was a print of a hunting dog with a small animal between its teeth.

When Penny turned back to the desk he wasn't holding the glass. His face was set again. Breeding and five star cognac had done their job.

'He had a family, didn't he? A wife and a child. We must do something for them.'

I said, 'I'm trying to find out where Bates went before he was killed. Maybe you can help me. Did you see him yesterday?'

Penny frowned. 'I believe I did.'

'You mean you're not sure?'

'I . . . Yes, he picked me up here. I had meetings.'

'Was that usual on a Sunday?'

That question was too hard for him. 'I don't believe it was.' The frown was stuck on Penny's face like an odd weight that he couldn't get rid of.

I leaned forward. 'We need your help, Sir John. You can tell us where Bates went yesterday. Before he was murdered.'

He didn't like me saying murdered. He looked up at me and the panic flickered back into his face. 'Who would kill a chap like Bates?' he said. 'He was just an ordinary chap.'

'We don't know that yet.'

'Will you catch them?'

'We'll try.'

'Of course you will.' For some reason it seemed to reassure him. 'Of course you will.'

35

'Bates came to pick you up yesterday,' I prompted him. 'Do you remember what time that was?'

'It was after lunch.'

'Where did he take you?'

'Oh . . . I don't know. To meetings.' He set his jaw. 'I'm a busy man.'

'Of course you are,' I said. 'What kind of meetings?'

'I don't understand.'

'Who were the meetings with?'

Penny shifted uneasily in his chair. His eyes moved towards the door. He said, 'I'm afraid I can't tell you that.'

'Why not?'

'I . . . I don't remember.'

'You don't remember who the meetings were with, or you don't remember why you can't tell me?'

He opened his mouth then shut it again.

I said, 'They can't have been very successful meetings if you don't remember who they were with.'

'I suppose not.' He tried to laugh, but the laugh wouldn't join in. He frowned. Very seriously he said, 'Did you know I'm in politics? I'm on the Council.' I remembered Clare Bates telling me that. 'The Police Committee.'

He might have meant it as a warning, but the warning died halfway across the carpet.

I said, 'Were you going to political meetings yesterday?'

Penny said formally, 'I beg your pardon. I can't add anything to what I've already said.'

That was the longest sentence he'd said all week. He blinked at the desk. His lower jaw jutted out. I watched him for a moment, rocking gently back and forward in his chair. His eyes were focused somewhere below the desk-top.

'All right,' I said. 'Tell me about Bates. How long did he work for you?'

Penny screwed up his eyes. 'A year?' He made it into a question.

'Were you satisfied with him?'

'I don't know . . . I suppose I was.' There was something bothering him.

'What was the problem?'

'He drank sometimes . . . once.' Penny's eyes were stuck halfway up my tie. 'I had to dismiss him.'

There was a pause.

'So how come you took him back?'

'Oh . . .' Penny's hand fluttered off the arm of the chair and settled again. 'He apologized. It never happened again, you know. And he had a family. It can be awfully hard for these chaps to get jobs, you know.'

Penny had been brought up to look after the servants; it would be one of the codes that governed his life. There were probably so many codes in his life that no room was left for anything else; anything except drink, and the hunting prints, and the grandfather clock ticking in the hall downstairs.

Very quietly I said, 'Where did Bates take you yesterday?'

John Penny's face screwed up like a child refusing to eat something. He said petulantly, 'I'm a busy man. I have a lot of meetings. Business contacts. Politics.'

'It would help if you told us, Sir John.'

He fidgeted, but didn't say anything. His gaze ran along the skirting behind me like a small animal looking for somewhere to hide.

I said, 'Tell me about your business.'

'I'm a company director.'

'What's the company?'

'There are several.' He waved one hand vaguely. I could guess what kind of a director he was: a stuffed shirt wheeled out to impress visiting foreigners and to give speeches to the staff; a title on the letterhead and the face to go with it. I wondered if John Penny knew when he was being used.

I said, 'Where did Bates take you yesterday?'

There was a long silence. When he answered Penny's voice was reluctant, like a small boy being led towards big waves. 'I don't understand. Does it make any difference?'

'Probably not.'

'I would prefer . . . Some matters are confidential.' Penny's voice wavered and died.

He fingered the edge of the desk-top. I wondered if he was

trying to tell me something. Maybe there were no politicians or business contacts; perhaps his meetings were at a small house somewhere in Maida Vale with a mistress waiting in it for John Penny to come and visit her. Maybe that was what he was scared of. I tried to imagine the mistress: a quiet woman, probably, not glamorous. A quiet woman in a house with no ancestral portraits and no grandfather clock, who'd listen to his dull stories of school and the army, and fill his glass without complaining.

If that was the truth, I didn't want to take it away from him.

I said, 'Just tell me what area you were in, and what time you came back. We'll leave it at that.'

Penny shot me a grateful look. 'Mayfair. We were in Mayfair.'

'All afternoon?'

He nodded.

'What time did you get back?'

'About five o'clock,' he said. 'Dri –' He stopped. He was about to say drinks time, but for John Penny any time was drinks time.

I sighed. 'Just a few more things. Did Bates have any problems?'

'Problems?' He frowned as if he didn't know chauffeurs had problems. 'I don't think so.'

'Can you think of any reason why he might have got into trouble? Did he seem worried about anything?'

'Not that I noticed, no.'

'Where did you keep the car?' I asked.

'In Waterloo. Near where Bates lives. A garage.'

'Does it have a name?'

He frowned. 'I don't remember.'

I said, 'How did Bates get the job? Do you remember that?'

'I believe he was recommended to me.'

'Who by?'

'A business contact of mine.' He looked mildly at me. 'A man called Hill.'

I said sharply, '*Hill?*'

'Yes.' Penny's eyes wavered away. 'I'm a director of his father's company. I've known Dick Hill for twenty years.'

There was a long silence.

I said, 'Did you know Joe Bates was a friend of his son? They were drinking together just before Bates was murdered.'

The big man behind the desk seemed to sag. His mouth came open. His hands jumped on the arms of the chair as if they needed to run away but couldn't.

He said 'Good *God*.' His voice was a whisper.

'Did Bates never talk to you about Matthew Hill?'

'Never.'

'What about Hill himself?'

'I thought . . .' His face was an unhealthy yellow colour. 'He said Bates had been recommended by a friend.'

'You didn't know they were close?'

Penny shook his head slowly. His eyes looked drained, as if someone had pulled out a plug at the back of his head and inside was a whirlpool of disappearing thoughts.

It wasn't hard to guess why he was so scared. If Bates had taken him to see his mistress, then Matthew Hill knew all about it. I would have been scared myself.

I stood up. Penny was on autopilot now. He didn't get up when I opened the door.

I said, 'I'm sorry to have taken so much of your time.'

There was no answer from behind the desk. John Penny was staring at the carpet behind my feet again, as if the dog had come back in but he still couldn't remember its name. As soon as I'd gone Penny would be back at the drinks cabinet, trying to do something about the muddle inside his head. Outside the grandfather clock whirred and began to strike. I didn't want to keep him from his medicine. I closed the door and started walking down the long stair-case.

'Excuse me.'

A woman was waiting in a doorway on the half-landing. She had thick grey hair piled up on top of her head and cheeks that were red from spending too much time out of doors.

'You're the policeman, aren't you?'

'That's right.'

'There was a call for you. Mr Hill, my husband's business partner. He wanted to talk to you. I said you were both busy.'

I looked at her. 'Thank you.'

'You can use the telephone if you want.'

'That's all right.'

The woman had something else to say. Her hands were clasping and unclasping in front of her cardigan.

'I'm sorry about my husband. He . . . He isn't always like this.'

I said, 'You mean he doesn't always drink?'

One hand flew to her throat. 'That's horrid.'

I shrugged. 'Is that what you meant?'

'No. I mean . . . he's worried about something. He hasn't been sleeping.'

I kept walking down the stairs. I said, 'It doesn't matter.'

'Is it true Bates has been killed?'

'Yes.'

'Johnny doesn't know anything about it, does he?'

'No,' I said. 'I was just asking some routine questions. We need to know where Bates was.'

'Did my husband tell you?'

I stopped and looked back up at her. I wondered whether the grey-haired woman knew anything about her husband's mistress, and what she would do if Hill brought it out.

'Enough. He was killed later in the evening anyway. It doesn't have anything to do with this.'

'A murder. It's horrid.'

I said, 'Isn't it?'

The Spanish woman had appeared from somewhere and was holding the door open. Penny's wife didn't say anything else. She stood in the doorway with her hand to her throat while I went out.

Dick Hill ran his property business from a double-fronted Georgian house behind Park Lane. A small brass plaque on the door said 'Hill Properties'. There was no other sign. The hallway had too much marble floor, an abstract sculpture and a plastic receptionist with teeth. The receptionist was looking down the hallway. A little welcoming smile appeared on her face every time someone passed the door.

I said, 'Is Matthew Hill here?'

'He isn't in today.' The voice was classless, without personality. It sounded like a voice on a telephone. 'Are you from the police?'

'Why?'

'They were here earlier.'

Cayman had been finding things for the squad to do.

'Were you expecting him in?'

'Not until tomorrow.'

I said, 'I'd like to see his father. He left a message for me.'

'Do you have an appointment?' The question came out mechanically, as if someone had pulled a string in her back.

'Tell him it's about John Penny's chauffeur, Bates.'

'That's what the other men said.' Her face switched from bright to concerned. 'Nothing's wrong is it?'

'Very wrong,' I told her. 'Someone killed him last night.'

Without the smile she looked like a nice girl from typing school that someone had smeared in make-up and zipped into a hundred-pound suit. Her mouth went into a circle and her hand fluttered over her neck.

She said, 'Oh my *God*.'

Her accent had slipped. I asked her how I could find Dick Hill and she pointed crimson fingernails at the stairs. I left her staring at the door of the reception.

The stairs were covered with oak panelling. There was a maroon carpet with the Hill Properties logo woven into the border. Two young men in suits were talking money on the landing. At the second floor I found a door marked 'Chairman'. I knocked and a woman's voice told me to come in. The voice was low and intimate, as if we were sharing a private joke or were about to go to bed together.

I found the voice sitting behind a desk with a typewriter on it. There was no paper in the typewriter. The voice had dark golden hair, an expensive tan and a cream two-piece suit that someone must have made for her.

'Can I help you?'

I said, 'My name's Havilland. I heard Dick Hill wanted to see me.'

'Mr Havilland. Of course.' She stood up and stuck her hand out as if we'd just been introduced at a cocktail party. 'Mary Fane. I'm his assistant.'

Mary Fane had a strong, humorous face with high cheekbones and sloping temples. She didn't look like anybody's secretary. She gave me half a smile, as if I'd only get the other half if I behaved myself. Her eyes were the colour of something rare and expensive.

'I hope there isn't a problem.' She said it chidingly. I didn't answer. I didn't know what she called a problem.

'Is Mr Hill in?'

She smiled again. 'I'll tell him you're here.'

She went over to a door at the far side of the office, knocked, then opened it without waiting for an answer. The room on the other side was big even for a property tycoon. At a desk half a mile away a small neat man was sitting over some drawings with a man in a blue suit standing over him. The man in the blue suit had a harassed expression on his face, as if he spent too much time standing next to property tycoons.

I followed Mary Fane into the office. She didn't like me

doing that. She looked over her shoulder and said, 'I'm sorry, Mr Hill. There's a Mr Havilland to see you.'

Dick Hill looked older than I remembered. He had a brown, wizened face, the face of a market trader or a bookie who'd made good. For a moment he stared at me, then he turned to the man in the blue suit.

'Sorry, Alex. Do you mind?' His voice was South London; he'd never managed to lose that. It was a sharp voice which clipped the ends off words as if he didn't have time for them, like someone snipping the ends off cigars.

Alex did mind but there wasn't a lot he could do about it. He rolled the drawings up and stormed out past me with a look that said we were all conspiring against genius. I heard the door close behind him. Mary Fane was still in the room.

Dick Hill stood up. He had quick, neat movements. Stiff white hair was brushed back from his forehead. He was dressed with too much care: a fancy tie, the knot held in place by a flashy gold pin. His suit was expensive. He moved restlessly, constantly, as if he had more energy than he could ever use up by making money.

'Detective Inspector Havilland, isn't it?'

I said, 'Chief Inspector, if you're trying to flatter me.'

Dick Hill's handshake was brief and firm, like the clip of a pair of scissors. His eyes stayed warily on my face.

I said, 'You've heard about Joe Bates?'

'Why else would I want to see you?'

'How did you know I was at John Penny's place?'

He shrugged. 'Stands to reason, doesn't it? Chap gets killed, you go to see his boss. Besides, one of the coppers told me.'

I said, 'You *have* been busy.'

Dick Hill didn't smile. He put his head on one side and looked at me. His expression wasn't hostile or helpful; it wasn't anything.

'Tell me what happened,' he said.

'Haven't you got something to tell me?'

He frowned. 'I don't understand.'

'I thought you wanted to make a statement.'

'You're a clever kid, aren't you?' he said. 'I remember that from before. You were a right clever boy.'

'Why did you want to see me, Mr Hill?'

He didn't answer straightaway. He turned back to his desk and fiddled for a cigar.

Without looking up at me he said, 'I heard you were looking for Mattie. For my boy. They called up from his restaurant.'

'Is that what you call it?' I said. 'Have you ever been there?'

Dick Hill ignored me. 'I hear a chap's dead and I hear you're looking for Mattie. You put two and two together, don't you?'

I sat down across the desk from him. Dick Hill's face was hard.

'Then your blokes come here asking for him.' He leaned forward across the desk. 'You're after him again, aren't you? You made a fool of yourself last time and now you want your own back. Blasted coppers never give up. You're going to say he kills his own mates, now. You're going to pin this chap's murder on Mattie.'

There was silence in the room. Mary Fane moved suddenly. Her face still held the same amused smile, as if we had all been working out a practical joke to play on a friend of hers. She said, 'I'll get some coffee, shall I?'

Dick Hill didn't respond. His eyes were still on my face.

I said, 'If your son killed Joe Bates he'll have to pay for it.'

'He didn't.'

'That's not what it looks like.'

Dick Hill was tapping the end of the cigar on the desk. 'Shall I tell you what it looks like from here? I think you've been planning this since the moment he walked free.'

I stood up. 'Is that what you wanted to tell me?'

'I'm telling you ... He didn't have anything to do with this, my son. You leave him alone. That's what I'm telling you.'

'How do you know?'

'He wouldn't have. Not Mattie.'

'Do you know where he is?'

'I know where he was last night.'

'Where?' I said.

'With me.' The old man's face was taut. 'He was with me all evening.'

Slowly I sat down again. I said, 'You could get yourself into trouble.'

The old man didn't move.

'How well did you know Joe Bates?'

'Who's Joe Bates?'

'The chap who was killed,' I said.

'I didn't.'

'You knew he was a friend of your son's.'

He shrugged. 'Mattie's got a lot of friends. I don't remember Bates. Do you?' The question was directed at Mary Fane.

The woman gave a distant smile. 'I might remember the face.'

'Come on,' I said. 'How could you forget him? He was driving the car when Mattie killed Paddy Moran.'

There was a long silence. Dick Hill's cigar was halted in mid-air, six inches above the desk-top. For a moment I thought he was smiling at me. Then I realized he wasn't looking at me at all. He was looking over my shoulder at Mary Fane. His expression was soft, the expression of an old man looking at a beautiful woman.

'I was right, wasn't I?' He was talking to himself, or to Mary Fane. 'He's going to try and pin it on my boy.'

I said, 'Your boy was seen drinking with Bates ten minutes before he died. They were arguing. People saw them.' Dick Hill shook his head. The curious smile stayed on his face. 'They were in his bar . . . his restaurant. We've got the barman's statement they were arguing. Your son left ten minutes after Joe Bates. Half an hour later he was dead.'

Dick Hill shook his head suddenly. 'He didn't have anything to do with it. I'm telling you. He was with me.'

'What time?'

'Last night.'

I shook my head. 'Last night he was fighting with Joe Bates. We've got a witness.'

'You had witnesses last time.' The old man's voice was scornful. 'Blasted cops can always rig up a witness.'

'And you can always buy them off,' I said. 'Just like last time. Like when your son killed Paddy Moran.'

Dick Hill's face didn't change colour. It went very still. 'You can't say that.'

'Why not?'

'Because it's a lie. They found him innocent, remember? In a court of law.'

I said, 'That doesn't make it a lie.'

Mary Fane moved suddenly and began collecting coffee cups on to a tray on the side of the desk. She didn't look at either of us.

I said, 'Why would Bates have been arguing with your son?'

'I wouldn't know.'

'Did they have business together?'

'I don't know.'

'How did Bates get the job driving for John Penny?'

He said, 'Why should I know that?'

'You might have got him the job.'

He shook his head. 'Maybe Mattie did it. He's good to his mates, Mattie. He looks after them.'

'Penny didn't know that. He didn't know his chauffeur was a friend of your son's. When I told him he looked scared. Why would that be?'

'Scared?'

'All right, confused.'

Mary Fane said, 'Sir John has a lot on his plate.'

'How long have you known him?' I said to Dick Hill.

'John Penny? More than twenty years. He's a friend of mine.'

'I thought he was one of your directors.'

'He's both. That's the way we do business here.'

'Is she a friend of yours, too?' I nodded towards Mary Fane.

'Yes, as a matter of fact.' Dick Hill's face was soft again.

'My right-hand woman. Don't know what I'd do without Mary.'

The woman in the cream suit smiled. It was the sort of smile you'd give a child who'd said something clever.

'How much time does John Penny spend here?' I asked.

'You don't need to know that.'

'I'm asking it.'

Dick Hill swung suddenly forward over the desk. Through clenched teeth he said, 'I don't want to say anything else. I know what you're up to now. That's all I wanted.'

I didn't get up. I said drily, 'I'm trying to piece together Joe Bates's movements yesterday, Mr Hill. Perhaps you can help. He took John Penny out yesterday afternoon to make some visits. Penny remembers they were business meetings but he doesn't remember who they were with. He's confused about it. Maybe you can help all of us.'

'No.'

'When did you last see him?'

'Not for a week or more.'

'Is that usual?'

'Usual enough.'

'He didn't come to see you yesterday afternoon?'

'No.'

I said, 'How long has Penny been a drunk?'

Mary Fane's smile twitched as if there was a bad smell in the room. Dick Hill sat back suddenly in his chair. Very quietly he said, 'Don't you dare talk like that. Not about a friend of mine.'

There was a long silence. The man behind the desk was staring past me. I remembered him at his son's trial: an old man sitting in the public gallery surrounded by pressmen and the vultures who wanted to know what a real murderer looked like. He'd been there every morning before nine and didn't leave until the court rose. I wondered how much else he'd suffered for his son's sake. Maybe all fathers have to love their sons and it's just bad luck if you end up having to love someone like Matthew Hill. I wondered what had gone through his head when they read out what his son had done

47

to Paddy Moran. He'd told himself that it wasn't true because it was easier for him to lie to himself than to believe his son had lied: that was what love did to people.

I said, 'Do you know where your son is, Mr Hill?'

He shook his head.

'Why isn't he here? He works here, doesn't he?'

'He doesn't come in every day.'

'How often does he come in?'

'That's none of your business.'

'When did you last see him?'

He stood up. 'I don't believe I can help you any further, Chief Inspector.'

I said, 'Why would your son have been arguing with Joe Bates?'

'I don't believe they were arguing.' There was anger in his voice. 'Joe Bates was his mate – you said so yourself. It's another set-up, just like the last one. I knew you'd try to get your own back.'

I said, 'Your son killed Paddy Moran and you know it. This time he's gone too far. We won't make the same mistake again.' I said it louder than I'd meant to.

Dick Hill's face was beyond anger. Now he just looked old and hurt. 'Mattie always told me he didn't do it. If my boy tells me something, it's the truth. I brought him up to tell the truth.'

'Joe Bates was lucky,' I said. 'Shot in the back and no one cut his hands off. When Mattie killed Paddy Moran it was for fun.'

Mary Fane was staring into the middle distance as if she was alone in the room. She might not have heard a word we'd said.

Dick Hill said quietly, 'Someone ought to do something about you.'

I stood up and walked towards the door. Mary Fane followed me out into the outer office. She gave me a brief smile, as if we both knew it had been a good party. She said, 'I'm sorry about Bates.'

'Do you remember him?'

'I know who you mean.'

She stood coolly behind the desk, fingers resting lightly on the empty in-tray.

'What do you do for him?' I asked suddenly, nodding towards the office door.

'I'm Mr Hill's assistant.'

'Do you come to all his meetings?'

'Most of them. Mr Hill likes to have my opinion afterwards.'

I said, 'You're very lucky.'

'I think so.'

She smiled dismissively and pulled open one of the desk drawers. It didn't look as if there was anything in it.

Downstairs the receptionist was still crying. She was doing her best but her lips didn't have any shape to them. I told her I was sorry about Bates too and walked out into the Mayfair sunlight.

## 7

The head of Area Four CID had an office two doors down from mine but about twice the size. It was battered but comfortable, a bit like Mason. The back of the desk was covered with photographs in little perspex frames: a middle-aged woman with a red face; a sulky boy with acne; a spaniel puppy. That was Mason's family. Scattered across the desk there was an old-fashioned telephone, some dog-eared police files and a mug that said, 'My son went to New York and all I got was this lousy mug'. Mason was sipping from the mug.

He said, 'I'm not getting my fingers burned over this again.'

Mason was a small man with a kind face and wrinkles around his eyes. He'd been going bald for years without ever quite getting there. He had grey eyes that twinkled when he talked to everyone else except me. Everyone else thought Mason was a treasure.

He said, 'Run over it again, will you?'

I sighed. 'Joe Bates was killed about one o'clock this morning by three shots to the back of the neck. A gang killing. He was a driver who's been in with Hill for years. Some time ago he was charged with GBH to Tim McCreedy. He got let off. He was charged with Matthew Hill over Paddy Moran – he was driving the car, remember? Last night he was seen arguing with Hill –'

'Have we got an autopsy report?' Mason interrupted.

I gave him the autopsy report. He read it slowly, then turned back to the beginning and read it again. I looked at a picture of the red-faced woman playing with the spaniel's ears.

'Three shot wounds,' Mason said thoughtfully. 'Only one of them fatal.'

'That's right.'

'Have you found the gun?'

'We're still looking. He'll have taken it away if he had any sense.'

'Who?'

I tried to be patient. I said, 'The guy who killed him.'

Mason thought some more. I looked at the upside-down cover of a report in his in-tray. There was a sandwich box sitting under Mason's chair. I guessed it had been packed that morning by the red-faced woman, with another box to go off with the sulky youngster to his college or office. Mason's heart wasn't chasing villains any more, it was playing Happy Families in Wimbledon.

Mason read, ' "Time of death, one o'clock".' He looked up at me. 'Any witnesses?'

'An old woman who lived in the flats. She heard a bike drive off around one. She might have heard some shots.'

'That all?'

'No one ever hears anything.'

'It is funny, though. Three gunshots. This isn't Los Angeles. You'd have thought someone else would have heard it.'

I said, 'We don't have to prove whether he was shot or not. He's got three holes in the back of his neck.'

Mason put down the report and looked at me. The grey eyes didn't twinkle. He said, 'You're an arrogant sod, did you know that?'

I kept staring at him. I didn't say anything.

'Go on.'

'Bates got home from work about seven-thirty. An ordinary day's work, nothing unusual. He changed and went out for a drink with his mates. That wasn't unusual either. About nine-fifteen he turned up at a bar called Babylon in Southwark Bridge Road. He was already quite drunk. Babylon is owned by Hill. The barman there saw Bates and Hill talking. They were with another guy who doesn't matter. Everybody saw them arguing –'

51

Mason waved the autopsy report. He said, 'You're going to tell me Hill did it.'

'They talked for about three hours,' I went on. 'They were both drunk. Everyone heard them arguing. Halfway through Bates went out to the toilet. The barman overheard Hill saying to the other guy that he had it coming to him. By half past twelve Hill and Bates were the only people left in the bar –'

'How well did Bates know Hill?' Mason interrupted.

'I told you, he smashed up McCreedy's fingers for him.'

'That was never pinned on Hill.'

'We both know he paid for it.'

'He was cleared.' Mason was frowning. 'The courts cleared him.'

There was a long pause. Then I said, 'Joe Bates was driving the car when Paddy Moran was killed.'

Mason picked up his mug and read the writing on it. He smiled fondly, thinking about something else. Then he put the mug down again. He said, 'This isn't a vendetta, Havilland. It's a murder investigation.' His voice was mild.

'About twelve-thirty,' I said, 'Bates left the bar. Hill left immediately after him. Everyone had seen them arguing. Bates was shot a mile away at one o'clock. What else do you want?'

'Nothing. As long as it sticks.'

'He didn't turn up at the bar today. Or at his father's office. That was unusual. We may be too late already.'

Mason fiddled with his pen. 'You really want to get him, don't you?'

'I did get him.'

Mason shook his head.

'You know I did.'

'He was acquitted.'

'We both know how.'

'That's justice, Havilland.'

I said, 'Paddy Moran was a down-and-out Irishman with a drink problem and nowhere to live. Hill had a public-school accent and the best lawyer money can buy. Where's the justice in that?'

'He was let off by a jury.'

'On a majority decision.'

'It was still a jury.'

I said, 'He bought them and you damn well know it.'

Mason put down the mug. He looked me full in the eye. His eyes had brown flecks in them, like rust stains on metal. 'That's not the point,' he said.

'What is the point?'

Mason sighed. 'You take me through this every time, don't you? Why can't you just do the job like everyone else?'

I didn't say anything.

'The point is we made our case. We gave it to the courts. What happens after that is none of our business. I've seen plenty of decisions in my time that I didn't like, decisions I didn't think were right. But it's not my job to say so. We're not dealing in justice, Havilland, we're dealing in truth. We find out the truth, serve it up to the courts and if they're too blind to see it, then we shrug our shoulders and start again. If it's justice you want to make, then you're in the wrong job.'

'Paddy Moran's dead,' I said. 'And Hill's still out on the streets. Are you telling me that's right?'

'I'm not telling you it's anything. It's what happened. It's life. It's better a few Hills out on the streets than one of them locked up for something he didn't do. That's the way things work, Havilland. If you cross that line . . .' He shrugged.

I said, 'So how do you deal with the Hills. With the ones who buy their way through the net?'

'I don't, because that's not my job. We're only policemen, Havilland. We're not gods, or saints, or even politicians. I've been a policeman for thirty-two years. That's enough to make anyone humble. You're not there to make the world a better place, you're there to help old ladies across the road and sweep up the mess after a robbery. And now and again you catch a Hill and he *is* sent down, and that's nice. But I've seen coppers who thought they were bigger than that, thought what they were doing was more important, and they all went bad. We're not the law, we're just a part of the law, the messy part at the bottom, and the less we think about what goes on over our heads the better. Partly because it's not our business and partly because there's not a damn thing we can do about it. The sooner you learn that the better.'

Very quietly I said, 'I think you're wrong.'

Mason looked at me. His eyes didn't twinkle. 'To be perfectly honest, I don't give a damn what you think.'

There was silence in the office. From a radio next door we heard the time pips for the six o'clock news.

Mason ran one hand over his eyes. He said, 'Anyway, it's past history.'

'Not to me.'

'That's your problem.' He looked at me coldly. 'I had Bob Cayman in here earlier. You know what he wanted? He didn't want to work for you any more. Said, Why should he put up with you sneering at him in front of the other coppers. I said I knew what he meant.'

'What did you tell him?' I kept my voice hard.

'I said it wouldn't be for long.' Mason looked tired. 'We've got a team here, Havilland. You always thought you were smarter than everyone else but it didn't matter before. It doesn't do any harm to have one officer with a few brains. I don't like what the Moran case did to you.'

I didn't say anything. I didn't like what it had done to me either, but I didn't have anything to say about it.

He leaned forward over the desk. 'It's in the past, all right? You need to pull your team together, get on with the job. All right?'

I said, 'What about Hill?'

'You don't have enough to convict him.'

'Not with a jury like Paddy Moran's.'

'Not with any jury.'

'Maybe he'll confess.'

Mason laughed. 'Maybe he'll walk into the station and ask us to put the cuffs on him.'

I tried to keep my voice steady. I said, 'Hill and Bates were seen quarrelling. Twenty minutes later Bates is dead. We've got enough for a warrant.'

Mason was playing with the mug again. He nodded wearily. 'What do you want from me?'

'I want support to pick him up and agreement from the other areas.'

'Where do you think you'll find him?'

I said, 'Hill has two apartments, one in Mayfair, the other in Lambeth. The Mayfair flat's his main home. The other he uses to take girls to, ones he doesn't want to be seen with in Mayfair.'

'You've done your homework.'

'He's also got a house in Docklands but it's let to somebody else. He's never lived there. I've had a man watching the bar all day, and the club where he goes in the afternoon. He hasn't shown up at either. The chances are he's already gone to ground – in that case he'll be somewhere in this area but it'll take time to find him. If he doesn't know how close we are then we can pick him up at home tonight. But I'll need men to cover both addresses.'

Mason paused. Then he nodded. 'Call Bert Morris,' he said. 'Tell him it's all right. Go on.'

I got up and made for the door. Just before I got there Mason's voice said, 'You've done all right, George. It's a good day's work.'

I went out and shut the door behind me. I couldn't think of anything worth saying.

## 8

Hill's flat was halfway up South Audley Street in a block lived in by foreigners, film companies and rich people's grandmothers. In the thirties it would have been called modern. None of the inhabitants liked it enough to live there all year round. There was only one light showing on the street side. It wasn't Hill's.

Cayman crushed his cigarette in the ashtray and said, 'We could be wrong. He could be at his fuckpad in Lambeth.'

He pressed a switch on his radio and talked into it. The radio talked back.

I said, 'Any sign of him?'

'Not a dicky-bird.'

A street-sweeper turned into South Audley Street. It worked noisily past the parked Porsches and Jaguars like an old butler pushing drinks at a society ball. The tarmac reflected orange streetlights behind it. Next to us a shop sign read: 'SLOANES CHEM ST'. There was a green neon cross in the shop window and a picture of a model waxing legs that didn't need waxing. The other shops were dark. There were hardly any passers-by. Most of the residents of South Audley Street were lying by swimming pools in Los Angeles.

'Time?'

'Late.'

'What's the time?' I repeated.

'Twenty to eleven, sir.'

I said, 'Thank you.'

Out of the corner of my eye I watched Cayman chewing his lip resentfully. When I came out of college Cayman had already been pushing a beat for ten years. He'd reached sergeant at forty, and now he was taking orders from a man ten years younger than him who'd been drinking in student bars while he walked up and down Kennington Road in the rain. In the past that never seemed to matter. It mattered now.

A taxi drew up outside Hill's block. A young man got out. He was wearing a high-collared overcoat that looked European. He paid the taxi and started walking down the street, towards Piccadilly.

Cayman said, 'Does he own the flat or rent it?'

'His money but it's in a company name. A tax dodge.'

'His father's company?'

'Yes.'

The young man had disappeared. From Park Lane we could just hear the roar of traffic, the noise of a city settling in for the night. The sky was a lurid orange.

'Last time I did this –' Cayman stopped. For a moment he'd forgotten that he didn't like me any more. In a different voice he went on, 'We spent all night freezing our balls off on a fire escape while the villain was locked up in the cells. He'd turned himself in that afternoon and they forgot to tell us.'

'That's funny,' I said.

Out of the corner of my eye I saw Cayman's hands grip the steering wheel. The hands disappeared and I heard him fumbling in his pockets. There was the flare of a lighter, then cigarette smoke filled the car.

'Are you sure it was him, sir?' Cayman asked.

'Who?'

'Hill who killed Bates.'

'What do you think?'

There was a pause. Then he said, 'Yes.'

I didn't say anything. A blue Escort van was sliding past the row of parked cars, the driver craning over the wheel to see street numbers. It stopped two doors down from Hill's. The driver got out, opened the back and pulled out a long parcel wrapped in brown paper.

'Funny time for a delivery.'

Cayman said, 'Funny shape for a pizza.'

The driver went up to a doorway next to a dry cleaner's shop. He rang a bell. After a moment someone opened the door and took in the parcel. Cayman let out his breath.

'Check Lambeth again.'

The radio squealed twice and gave a burst of static. Cayman's voice said 'Hello, Charlie. Anything going on? Over.' The radio squealed again.

Cayman sighed and said, 'He'll have gone to ground if he's got any sense.'

'Hill doesn't think he needs to.'

'He needs to this time.'

'He needed to last time but he didn't.'

'Last time he got off.'

I didn't say anything.

'Where did you get him last time?'

'Drinking in a pub in Peckham.'

'Did he resist?'

'He gave me his lawyer's phone number.'

Cayman shook his head.

'It wasn't only the lawyer,' I said. 'For the time he was killing Paddy Moran there were eight men who swore he was drinking with them in a wine bar on Borough High Street. One of them was a magistrate.'

'What about this time?'

'This time it'll be different.'

Cayman crushed his cigarette into the ashtray. It gave off a sour smell of used smoke that dried the back of my mouth. Outside we heard footsteps on the pavement, then a voice talking. A man and woman came into sight, walking fast down the pavement. They were in evening dress. The man was talking and gesticulating; the woman looked bored. He laughed at something he'd said, a high, girlish laugh that sounded too loud in the deserted street. The woman kept walking. They passed out of sight.

Nothing else was moving.

Cayman said, 'I never understood about Hill.'

'What do you mean?'

'All of this.' Cayman pointed towards the sleeping apartment block. 'Why does he hang around in South London if he's got this?'

I said, 'Hill's a poor little rich boy. His daddy brought him up with money, sent him to public school, bought him the flat. Part of the time he goes with it – that's the Mayfair Hill. But there are things he can't do up here. Maybe he doesn't like the people enough. Maybe he can't forget his father started out as a trader on the Old Kent Road. That's why the rest of the time he's hanging out in Southwark and Lambeth with crack dealers. That's why he started Babylon.'

'Jekyll and Hyde,' said Cayman.

'No. He doesn't bother to conceal it. He likes showing off expensive clothes in South London and he likes boasting to his rich friends about the seedy characters he knows. They think it's glamorous. The trial was the best month of his life.'

Cayman sighed. He fumbled in his pocket and brought out the packet of cigarettes again. He said 'Some people are –'

I put a hand on his sleeve. A taxi was drawing up outside Hill's block.

Cayman sat frozen with the unlit cigarette in his hands. A man and a woman got out of the taxi. The woman stumbled a little and wrapped her coat about her. She looked slightly drunk. The man turned back to pay. Streetlights shone on a thatch of hair so blond it was almost silver.

I whispered, 'Hill.'

We waited in silence. The taxi drove off and we could see him clearly, pushing his wallet back into his jacket pocket. The streetlight turned his eyes into dark shadows. He took the woman's arm and she laughed shrilly, swaying on stiletto heels. They went to the door, opened it and disappeared inside.

I said, 'Five minutes.'

Cayman was busy with the radio. He spoke into it, and it answered with a burst of static followed by a muffled affirmative.

'Ready, sir.'

'All right.'

I swung open the door of the car. The May night was colder than it looked and sent a shiver up the back of my neck. I pushed the door to without shutting it and crossed the street. Cayman was behind me. To one side of the doorway was a long row of bells in an Art Deco brass plate. I rang the one marked 'Night Porter'. After two rings a door opened at the end of the hall and a man shuffled out. He was an old man in shirtsleeves and soft slippers that were trodden down at the back. He wasn't in a hurry. He shuffled down the hall, unlocked the door and said, 'Yes?'

I showed him my ID. He took my wrist to steady it and read the ID with his eyes screwed up. He had a broad forehead and deep-set eyes. His arms were too long for his body, like the arms of a gorilla.

'What do you want?'

'We're arresting a resident of this block. Until we come down I want the door locked and no one else admitted. A policeman will stay with you. Keep the lift at the ground floor. Do you understand?'

He grunted and nodded. He didn't look impressed.

Four uniformed policemen had come in behind us. I nodded to the first three and they followed us up the stairs. The stairs had fading seventies decorations: gold mirrors; plastic flowers on the landings. They smelled of furniture polish. The doors we passed had foreign names on them; no sound came from behind them. At the second floor we spread out. I rang the bell. There was a shrill squeak of laughter inside.

'Who is it?' A girl's voice, drunk.

I rang again. There was a rattle of chains and the door opened a crack.

Cayman leaned his shoulder against it and slammed it back against the wall.

The girl was retreating down the hall in front of us with her mouth open, screaming. She was naked except for pearl earrings and a man's face towel which she tried to keep in front of her. Her eyes were round holes in a face smeared with lipstick. Behind her a door opened. Hill was standing in the corridor, white hair curling from his torso. He was holding a gun. His lips were drawn back over brown uneven teeth, like a dog's lips.

Cayman shouted, 'Police.' He pushed me to one side and ran towards Hill. The girl doubled up on to her knees with a sob. Uniforms filled the hallway. Over their heads I could see Hill's hands in the air, still holding the gun. There were shouts and the sound of someone swearing. Hill's hand dropped the gun.

I said, 'All right, it's over.'

The girl was crouched on the floor with her face in her hands and hair spread over the carpet. Her back was trembling.

I pushed past the policemen. They had Hill face to the wall with his arms twisted behind his back. One side of his face was pressed up against the wallpaper; his free eye stared mockingly at me.

He spoke through clenched teeth. 'Enjoying yourselves?'

I took a step forward and slammed my hand into the back of his head. Blood flowered over the wallpaper.

'Stand him back.'

The policemen pulled him off the wall. A trickle of blood ran from one corner of his mouth.

'What about the girl?' Cayman asked.

'Get rid of her.'

Hill said, 'You want to beat me up in peace?'

He moved a fraction of a second too late, and the policemen on either side didn't let him move far enough. Hill coughed and looked up at me through green eyes that kept their truculent, half-mocking expression. There was a sheen of blood under his nose.

One of the policemen lifted the girl by the shoulders. She stayed doubled up, fighting to cover herself.

He said, 'Come on, miss.'

With a squirm she shook herself free and scampered into the bedroom, slamming the door behind her.

'Follow her.'

The copper raised his eyebrows and pushed open the door. We heard an angry, high-pitched wailing from inside.

61

The blood was staining Hill's teeth. He said, 'What have you dreamed up this time?'

I stared into his green eyes. They were fringed by disconcerting white lashes the same colour as his hair. His face had filled out since I last saw him, swollen at the jowls and chin. He didn't look scared.

I nodded towards the door at the end of the corridor. Cayman opened it and the policemen manhandled Hill into a big low-ceilinged sitting room with leather sofas against the walls. In the middle of the floor was a white fluffy rug with a pair of stockings lying on it. Seduction music came from a stereo in the corner. I crossed the room and switched off the music. Cayman pushed Hill back into one of the sofas.

He wiped the back of his hand across his bloody nose and examined the results. Hill had delicate white hands like the hands of a child, incongruous. If you'd only seen his hands you'd have thought Hill was an angel.

'They make them tougher than they used to.' His voice was mocking.

'Save it.'

He looked up at me. 'Go on, then. What is it this time?'

I said, 'Have you got a licence for that gun?'

Hill opened his mouth and gave a contemptuous laugh.

'Who have you got to be afraid of?' I asked. 'Who did you think I was, Paddy Moran's brother?'

Hill turned and spat deliberately on to the white leather of the sofa. His spittle made an obscene red mark on the cushion.

'Who's Paddy Moran?'

I said, 'The old man you killed last year. Have you forgotten already? How many have you killed since then?'

He laughed at me, showing his blood-stained teeth. 'I forgot,' he said.

I turned away. I either had to turn away or hit him again. He was too like the Hill I had dreamed of: mocking, contemptuous, beyond my reach.

With my back to him, I said, 'Where were you last night?'

'What time?'

'Late.'

'I don't remember,' he drawled.

I swung round. He was sprawled across the sofa with his head back. White hair sprouted from his chest and shoulders.

'See if this helps,' I said. 'You were drinking in Southwark Bridge Road with Joe Bates. You had an argument with him. He left at closing time. Now tell me what happened next.'

Hill's eyes were alert suddenly. He said, 'What's happened to Joe Bates?'

'Started to remember yet?'

Hill didn't say anything. His head moved slowly sideways but he kept his eyes on me. His hands twitched on the sofa.

'All right,' I said. 'We'll start again. Where were you last night? Let's say ten o'clock.'

Hill's lips moved slowly. 'I want to call my lawyer.'

'Why? We haven't pulled you in for anything yet.'

He laughed, a nasty, dirty laugh that made you want to wash your hands. 'You never did learn to play by the rules, did you?'

Cayman took a step towards me. He said, 'Answer the Chief Inspector.'

Hill shrugged. He kept his eyes on me. 'I was in my bar, Babylon.'

'You know it,' I said to Cayman. 'It's the one with the empty till and a crack market in the men's toilet.'

'What's happened to Joe Bates?'

'Why do you ask us? We weren't there. You can tell us all about it.'

Hill shook his head. 'What's this about?' His eyes were the colour of green marble.

I put my face close to him.

I said, 'You're under arrest for murder.'

I could hardly get the words out. Something pounded in my chest as I went through the caution. Hill's swollen face swam in front of me. I forced myself to stand up and look at Cayman.

'Pull the place to pieces. I'll take him back to the station.'

'Do you want help, sir?' Cayman was looking oddly at me.

'No. Join me when you're ready.' I turned back towards him. 'Be thorough, understand? When you're finished I want this place to look like a Salvation Army refuge.'

Hill laughed his ugly laugh. I turned and walked out of the door. Behind me I could hear the policemen wrestling him up off the sofa.

The girl was standing in the hallway dressed in a black coat. Her face was shocked and hung over, her make-up smeared, her eyes scared. Under bright light she didn't look older than seventeen. Downstairs the night porter was peering out of his office door. I ignored him and walked out into the cool street. A car was waiting. South Audley Street didn't seem to have noticed the fuss: there was no crowd. Behind me Hill's head shone white under the streetlights. The policemen pushed it down and forced him on to the back seat.

I slammed the door on him myself.

## 9

Under fluorescent lights Hill's skin was the blue-white colour of turned milk. The blood had dried to a brown stain under his nose. We sat either side of the table in the interview room.

'You got to the bar around nine o'clock,' I said. 'Yes? Are you going to make me go through it again?'

'Have you called my lawyer?' His shoulders were tense.

I said, 'The number was busy.'

'At eleven o'clock at night? Do me a favour.'

'We'll keep trying,' I said.

He scowled. His fingers lay motionless on top of the table, like dead worms.

The room was bare. There was nothing in it except for the table and our chairs.

Hill said, 'What happened to your friend?'

'He'll be here soon.'

'I want my rights.'

'What about Paddy Moran's rights?' I said. 'And I don't mean last rites.'

Hill said, 'That's funny.'

A siren went past on the Kennington Road. Hill shifted uneasily in his seat.

'You were in Babylon all last night,' I said, 'drinking with Joe Bates. You were seen arguing together. At half past twelve Bates left the bar. You followed him.'

Hill shook his head.

'You followed him,' I went on. 'You were carrying a .38 calibre handgun. Just outside the entrance to his block you caught up with him, and killed him with three shots in the back at point blank range. That's what happened.' There was a pause. I said, 'Isn't it?'

Hill's green eyes stared at me. His tongue appeared for a moment between his crooked teeth. He didn't say anything.

'Was it about his wife?' I said. 'Or something else?' I pushed my chair back from the table. 'Let's say it was his wife. You'd made a pass at her, she'd told you where to put it. Bates started giving you a hard time about that, so you decided to get him out of the way.' I leaned forward towards him. 'It's as good as anything, isn't it?'

Hill raised one hand slowly to his lips and chewed on a finger.

I said, 'We can play this any way you want to. That's my story. See if you can come up with a better one.'

Hill said, 'I want to make a phone call.'

'Later.'

'Now.'

I shook my head. 'What are you in such a hurry about? You've got a whole lifetime in front of you.'

His green eyes narrowed, as if he was calculating something. 'I was in the bar,' he said.

'That's more like it.' I nodded. 'What time did you get there?'

'I thought you knew all that.'

'I want to hear it from you.'

He drew in air through his teeth. 'About nine.'

'Where had you been before?'

'With friends. A bar in Jermyn Street.'

'Very smart,' I said. 'Have these friends got names?'

He said some names.

'So by the time you got to Babylon you were already drunk.'

'Why are you asking me? Haven't you written it already?'

'Like I said, I want it from your own mouth.'

'What if I don't sing the right song?'

'You will,' I said. 'You walked into Babylon about nine o'clock. Was Bates there already?'

He shook his head. 'He came in later.'

66

'What state was he in?'

'The usual.'

'Meaning?'

'Pissed.'

'Was he aggressive?'

'Not to me.'

'Who was he aggressive to?'

'He was looking for trouble from the other customers.'

I said, 'You mean there was another customer?'

Hill ran the tip of his tongue over his lips. 'He was looking for trouble so I bought him a drink and took him to a table in the corner.'

'Had you arranged to meet him?'

'No.'

'At what point did you decide to kill him?'

Hill's fingers bunched on the table top. He didn't reply.

'Tell me about Clare Bates,' I said. 'How long have you known her?'

'We were kids together.'

'She's the wrong side of the river, isn't she?'

'Before Dad made his money.' He gave me a sickly, false smile. 'We used to play together.'

'That's sweet,' I said. 'She told me you'd never been able to leave her alone. What did you think when she married Joe Bates?'

He shook his head. I leaned towards him.

'Or did you know when you were out of your class?'

His eyes were green slits.

'Joe Bates,' I said. 'John Penny's chauffeur.' I shook my head. 'That must have hurt.'

'He wasn't working for Penny then,' Hill said. 'Anyway, it didn't matter to me. She could do what she liked.'

He had himself under control, but it wasn't easy.

'It didn't stop you trying again, did it?'

He shrugged.

'What did she say?'

He smiled suddenly, showing all his dirty teeth. 'She told me to fuck off,' he said.

'Sensible girl.'

'She's soft.'

'Did Joe know about it?'

'Yes.'

'Is that what you were arguing about last night?'

He was looking at me sideways. 'Partly.'

'What was the other part?'

Hill shook his head.

I leaned my elbows on the table and propped my chin on my hands. 'Did you often argue about that?'

'Joe was a drunk. He argued about a lot of things.'

'Did you ever fight?'

He shook his head. 'He wouldn't have dared.'

'Do anything you told him, would he?'

He didn't say anything.

'What else did he do for you? Was it just Paddy Moran or have there been other jobs since?'

'I don't know what you mean.' He smiled. 'Joe Bates was at a bingo hall in Streatham the night Paddy Moran died. Weren't you at the trial?'

I slammed my fist down on the table. Hill didn't move his fingers. Suddenly the room seemed very cold.

I said, 'Don't play any fucking games with me.'

There was a pause. Hill's face looked like a death-mask, expressionless, chalky white.

'Who was the other man you were talking to?' I asked.

'I don't remember another man.'

'Harry does.'

'You don't want to listen to Harry.'

'Why not?'

'He's a pansy,' Hill said.

'He says you were talking with Bates and another guy he didn't recognize.'

Hill put a finger in his mouth and bit once at the nail. 'Someone else came up to us. I don't know who he was.'

'Harry says you talked for a long time. He heard some of it.'

'I hadn't seen him before. Someone had told him it was my place.'

'What was his name?'

'He didn't say.'

'What did you talk about?'

'He said he liked the bar.'

'You're lying,' I said.

Hill's head turned to one side. He gave me a truculent, schoolkid's grin.

'Harry brought you a round of drinks while Bates was in the toilet. He overheard you talking to the other guy. You know what he heard you saying?'

Hill's grin was frozen on his face, as if someone had made him up that way.

I leaned towards him. 'You said, "He's got it coming . . ."'

Hill shook his head. 'Get my lawyer.'

I stood up and walked over to the window. It was blocked with a thick security grille, to stop Irish terrorists getting in and everyone else getting out. Through the grille I could see a thin strip of the shops opposite, the legs of two beat coppers measuring out the pavement.

I said, 'How did you meet Joe Bates?'

'I've known him for years.'

'That's not an answer.'

'He drives for John Penny.'

'It was you who introduced them.'

Hill shrugged. 'I met him in a pub.'

'Which pub?'

'The Blue Corner. He's a regular.'

'Is that Clare's mother's place?'

He nodded.

'And you started using him as a driver.'

'Sometimes.'

'Why did you need a driver?'

'I can't drive,' he said.

'Did he know you were going to kill Paddy Moran?'

Hill smiled. He didn't say anything.

'Did he know you were going to kill him?'

There was a long pause. I turned back towards him. He was hunched over the table.

'Forensic have tested your gun,' I said. 'It's the same one Bates was shot with. You could save yourself some trouble.'

He shook his head. 'There hasn't been time.'

I regarded him for a moment. Then I said, 'How come Clare Bates's mother is running a pub?'

'It used to be her old man's.'

'Tough life for a woman.'

'She's a tough woman.'

'What happened to her old man?'

'He died.'

'What of?'

'Old age.'

'How old was he?'

Hill smiled again. 'Forty-six,' he said.

'You knew him?'

'He was a friend of my father's.'

I said, 'Why did you put Bates in to drive for Penny? Was he spying for you?'

'I don't know what you mean.'

'What else were you arguing with Bates about last night?'

'Nothing in particular.'

I said quietly, 'You don't have a fucking chance and you know it. Why not do yourself a favour?'

I came back across the room and sat down again. Hill's forehead was a slime of sweat.

'I'd lent him some money.'

'What for?'

'To buy a car. Six months ago.'

'How much?'

He shrugged. 'Two grand.'

'Did he pay it back?'

'No.'

'And that's what you were arguing about?'

'Yes.'

'When was he due to repay it?'

'New Year.'

'What were you going to do about it?'

'I told him he had a month.'

70

'Then what?'

Hill ran his tongue over his lips. 'Then I'd ask him again.'

I said, 'Bates had money on him when he died. More than a grand. Was that anything to do with it?'

He flicked his eyebrows up. 'I didn't know he was carrying money.'

'Why didn't you take it off him?'

'I told you, I didn't know he had it.'

'You could have searched him.'

Hill smiled. 'Nice try,' he said.

'Do you always lend money to people?'

'Some people.'

'People who have something on you?'

'People I like.'

I sat back in my chair. I said, 'I went to see John Penny this morning.'

Hill's eyes watched me.

'What does your father use him for?'

'He's one of our directors. I told you.'

'How much do you do for the business?'

'It's where I work.'

'Every day?'

'Some days.'

'Do you have shares in it?'

He nodded cautiously.

'Penny seemed nervous,' I said. 'Do you know what that's about?'

Hill looked at me. Eventually he said, 'Penny's always nervous.'

'Does your father know what you get up to round here?'

'Leave my father out of it.'

That was a raw nerve. I leaned forward again.

'What did your father say about Paddy Moran?'

'He said I didn't do it. I was let off, wasn't I?'

'Did he pay for the lawyer?'

Hill's fingers were tensed on the table-top, as if he was trying to grip hold of it. He didn't say anything.

'He must be pretty sore,' I said. 'Gives you money. Sends

you to a nice school. And the next thing he hears you're getting yourself in trouble down in Southwark. He sounded pretty sore when I met him this morning.'

Hill's eyes were looking murder at me. I stood up suddenly and came round behind his chair. The silver hairs on his collar were damp with sweat. I saw his shoulders tense. I bent down and put my mouth close to his ear.

'You killed Joe Bates,' I whispered. 'We've got you this time. The sooner you confess, the easier it'll be for everybody.'

There was compete silence in the interview room. Slowly the back of Hill's head moved from left to right.

## 10

For reading, Mason wore half-moon spectacles that made him look like someone's grandfather. The clock behind his desk said half past midnight. There was a brown crust around the rim of the joke mug from New York.

Mason put down the sheet of typewritten paper he had been reading from.

He said, 'I'd have put money that he wouldn't crack.'

He took off the glasses and folded them up on his desk. His eyes were tired; tired of late nights at the station when he should have been at home with the red-faced woman and the sulky boy; tired of reports; tired of confessions to things that shouldn't ever have happened.

He repeated, 'I'd have put money on it.'

With one hand he rubbed his eyes, leaving them red-rimmed. The top button of his shirt was undone.

'He'd reached the end of the road,' I said. 'He realized it.'

'I wish more of them would realize it.'

Mason picked up the typewritten statement form again. He read:

I pulled out the gun and shot him three times. He went down the first time, but I kept shooting. It was because of his wife. He damned well deserved it . . .

He looked at me. 'It's all we need, George. He's given us the whole works. There's no way he's getting out of this one.'

He yawned, a middle-aged man who couldn't take the late nights any more.

I said, 'When will he be able to go down?'

'Not tomorrow. Wednesday if I get this in first thing.'

'Will you?'

Mason laughed. 'In a hurry?'

'I want to see him locked up.'

'So do a lot of people.'

'I've been waiting long enough.'

'Yes,' Mason said. He sighed. 'You deserve it.'

He looked at the sheet of paper for a moment without speaking. Then he said, 'We ought to find that other witness.'

'The guy who heard him threatening Bates? We'll find him.'

'It would be as well.'

Mason stood up and started buttoning his shirt. He yawned again.

'You've done well, George. Bloody well.'

'Thank you, sir.'

'Be taking over my job soon.' His smile was tired, but it was a smile.

'I don't know about that, sir.'

'Come on, George. You're as ambitious as all hell. I'm not complaining about it.'

'No, sir.'

He turned and picked up the jacket from the back of his chair. 'I still don't know how you got it out of him.'

'We were on to him faster than he thought,' I said. 'He should have started covering up straight away.'

'Speed is everything,' said Mason. 'Isn't that what they teach you in police college?' He broke off in a yawn and started pushing his arms into his jacket. 'I don't know about you, I need my bed. It's all right for you youngsters.'

I stood up. Mason packed his sandwich box into a leather briefcase and picked it up. He was waiting for me to go but I wanted him to say something else first. He knew it, too. His grey eyes almost twinkled.

'OK, I'll admit it. You were right.'

I stood up.

'Going to celebrate?' he asked.

He smiled indulgently and went out of the room in front of me.

In the outer office a tired-looking woman was stabbing at a typewriter. Cayman was standing over his desk, shuffling papers.

I went up to Cayman and said, 'Drink?'

He shook his head. He didn't look at me.

'Why not?'

'I just called my wife,' he said.

'Quick one. It's not every day –'

'No.' His voice was funny.

I looked around the office. The desks were littered with plastic cups, sandwich wrappers, files vomiting papers over the floor. A black woman in a housecoat was dropping plastic cups into a bin liner. This was it: this was where the overflow of London's anger and hatred came to be collected, filed, tamed. A shabby room with memos sellotaped to the walls.

I said to Cayman, 'It's on me.'

'Another time.' He picked up his briefcase.

The black woman came over to his desk. She said, 'Are these dead?'

Cayman nodded. She picked up two plastic cups and dropped them in the bin liner. The ID card slapped against her breast when she bent over.

Cayman said, 'I'll see you tomorrow.'

He picked up his case and walked out. The tired-looking woman pulled the page out of her typewriter with a noise like a saw rasping.

I called across the room, 'Drink, Helen?'

She shook her head without answering, picked up a clean page and fed it into the top of the machine. Her fingers were black from the carbon paper.

'I'll see you tomorrow, then.'

Downstairs the noise of voices and laughter came through the door to the canteen. I pushed the door open. Inside there was loud talk and the smell of grease. Someone was banging plates together. At the counter was a queue of men in zipper jackets and uniform pullovers. I joined the end of it. It took a long time to move forward.

The woman behind the counter said, 'What can I do for you, sir?'

I was the only person she called sir. Her face was impassive.

I ordered a coffee and stood there wondering what to do with it. At a table behind me some coppers were talking football results over platefuls of chips. Beyond them was a table with two CID men at it.

I walked towards them and said, 'May I?'

They didn't say no. One of them buried his face in his cup.

There was a pause. I said, 'We got Hill today.' My voice didn't sound right.

One of the CID men screwed up his eyes and looked at something on the far side of the room.

The other said, 'I heard.' His voice was flat.

'He killed Joe Bates. Confessed to it an hour ago.'

'That's good.'

Another pause. I couldn't think what else to say.

The first man looked at his friend and said, 'Anyway, I told him he'd never make it to the coast, not in that old banger. Didn't even get to fucking Croydon.'

He laughed unevenly. His friend laughed with him. I looked at the brown ring of coffee halfway down my cup.

'Why were they going to Brighton anyway?'

'Playing a gig there. My mate plays in a band. Drummer.' He slanted his eyes maliciously towards me. 'You don't like that sort of music, do you, George? You're a jazz man.'

I said, 'That's right.'

'Fucking Miles Davis.'

The coffee tasted of burned mud. His friend said mildly, 'I don't mind a bit of jazz.'

'It's poof's music.'

I looked away.

'It's what college boys listen to, isn't it? College boys and fucking poofs.'

I stood up. I said to the second man, 'I ought to go.' My cup was still half full.

'Been a long day, has it?'

I didn't answer. The canteen was crowded. People didn't get out of my way, they just weren't there when I walked towards them. The swing doors opened in front of me. Outside it was cold. A high-pitched voice filled the lobby. A woman with no tights and her hair in a scarf was leaning over the desk, trying to describe her cat. The young copper on duty was saying, 'She's called Lineker. Does she answer to her name?'

I went up to the desk and said, 'Anyone going north?'

The copper didn't smile at me. 'I'll see.'

He disappeared into the inner office. After a moment he came out and said, 'Jack's going up to North Ken, if that's any good. Five minutes.'

I told him I'd wait. A drunk was dozing on the bench under posters exhorting people to keep their doors and windows locked and stay off drugs. I waited until a voice from the inner office told me Jack was parked round the back.

The police car was too hot and smelled of chips. Jack was talking into the radio. He didn't pay any attention to me. We crossed the river at Lambeth Bridge and headed on towards Hyde Park. Victoria Street was deserted. Jack hummed a tune faintly under his breath.

'Can you take me all the way home?' I asked.

The driver shrugged.

I said, 'We got Hill today.'

'I heard.'

Cars were circling slowly around Hyde Park Corner: cars on their way back from parties or the pub; cars taking people home. Jack switched on the light and gunned up Park Lane. A heavy smell of leaves and rotting grass drifted in through the open window.

When we were just past Marble Arch, I said, 'Don't take me home. I'll get out.'

'Here?'

'Take this right.'

He swung the car across the oncoming traffic and dropped me where I pointed, alongside a row of stuccoed houses with shops under them. I got out of the car and leaned over. 'Thanks for the lift.'

Jack didn't say anything. I watched his tail-lights to the end of the street.

## 11

Beside me was a railing with a gap in it and steps leading down to a basement. Music was coming out through the basement door. The guy leaning against the door had eyes which hated everybody. He didn't move back when I pushed past him. Inside the door was a long room full of smoke and the noise of people shouting at other people who were too drunk to understand what they said. On a stage at the far end a band was playing jazz. There were five of them: rhythm, sax, trumpet, and a girl singing. The girl had a tired face and not enough make-up to hide how pale she looked. I went towards the bar. The barman was keeping nervous eyes on a black guy in a fur coat who was chatting up a white girl who didn't want it. When he saw me his eyes went dead.

I said, 'When will Mary be free?'

He said 'She won't be, for you.'

I took a glass of whisky and sat down at a table in the corner. The place was only half full. People mouthed words at each other across ashtrays and dirty glasses. Two men were embracing on a bench against the wall. The band were playing 'Caravan'.

> Night and stars above that shine so bright,
> The mystery of their fading light
> That shines upon our caravan

None of the audience was listening. Mary was singing with her eyes closed, leaning on the music, not the crowd. I'd never heard her sing it before. The insistent rhythm shuffled out into the room. I closed my eyes and listened. It was a song I'd always associated with triumph. I remembered playing it the day they passed me out of police college with the highest grades they'd ever had. I played it again when they promoted me; and when I got the job in Kennington. It should have been the right song for a night like this: Hill behind bars, an old ghost exorcised. I wondered why Mary had chosen to sing it tonight.

It was nearly one o'clock. The set would end soon. I looked at the ring of whisky in my glass. For some reason my mind went back to the first time I'd ever heard 'Caravan'. I would have been thirteen years old, a boy lying on his bed in a country town in the Midlands. The record had been in the box of 78s Ralph and I had found in the attic, among my father's things. We had taken them down to the gramophone and listened – for the first of many times – to Duke Ellington, Glenn Miller, Bix Beiderbecke. I didn't know how to describe the music, or what it made me feel. The best I could say was that it didn't come from Leicester or any place I'd ever been. We went through the stack, then went back to the top and started again. We had never seen our father play them, but even so the music made us talk about him.

Ralph told me stories about how he died: 'There were five of them. In stocking masks. He took them on single-handed.'

After a while I got confused about what was true and what Ralph had made up. All I could remember was a man with kind eyes who didn't play jazz. My mother never wanted to talk about him. She said he'd just been found in the street with his wallet gone, victim of a mugging which got out of control. I had dreams about men with no faces and my father's body lying in the gutter. The dreams were soaked in jazz music.

It was a long time since I had thought about my father. At the time of the Moran trial I had dreamed about him every night: lying still in a street with the dawn coming up. His face came from a photograph my mother kept on her chest of drawers: I was too young really to remember him.

I watched the sax player on stage fight through a solo with too many notes in it. Mary was sipping water over by the speaker stacks.

Throughout our childhood my brother and I had done everything together: our father's death made us closer. We bought records, caught the train to a jazz concert in Birmingham, scored weak grass off a man in a record shop near the station. We'd fought about who was better, Duke Ellington or Count Basie. When we weren't talking about music we were sitting on the top bunk, looking out over the market place, and planning how we were going to set the world to rights. The two of us were a team who could achieve anything. Ralph was going to be a doctor and save lives. And I came home one day and told him I wanted to join the police. I'd thought Ralph could understand anything.

'It's a waste.'

'What of?'

'You've got a brain, for God's sake.'

For the first time I had discovered something I couldn't explain to him. I wanted to say something about doing my bit, something about straightening out a world with too many wrinkles in it. Instead, I'd made a stupid joke about liking the uniform. Not long after that Ralph had gone to college, discovered the Rolling Stones and come back with hair down to his shoulders. From that day on the link between us had started to change. When I went up to visit he talked about his wife and children. When I told him about Hill's acquittal he had said how sorry he was, but I knew from his voice that he didn't really understand. He'd sold his jazz records because there wasn't space in the attic.

I opened my eyes. 'Caravan' had turned into fuzzy soul music coming from the speaker stacks either side of the stage. The band had gone. A man in a T-shirt was standing on the stage coiling up electrical cable. I took another sip of the whisky. Tonight I should have been feeling triumph; instead, the bitter taste of the whisky seemed to be tainting everything. I wondered what Ralph would think of me if he could see me now. What would Mary think? I felt like a child who'd thrown a match into a petrol drum and was waiting for the explosion.

I got up and walked towards the stage. On one side was a

swing door. I pushed through it and found myself in a corridor full of instrument cases. Voices came from a door on the left. A man walked out carrying a big drum case. He saw me, stopped, and half turned back towards the door, then he shrugged and walked off down the corridor without saying anything. I went up to the door. Behind it was a small locker room full of metal cupboards. The single bare bulb looked bright after the bar.

Mary was talking to a man in a red T-shirt and shades. She caught sight of me before he'd stopped talking and her smile went stiff around the edges.

She said, 'Sorry, Charlie. It's someone to see me. It won't take long.'

Charlie looked at me and turned his back without saying anything. He packed the pieces of his sax into a black instrument case and walked out, shutting the door behind him.

Mary sat down and started to fish in her bag for a packet of cigarettes.

I said, 'I thought you gave up.' My voice sounded wrong.

'There are a lot of things you give up.' She shook out a match and the room was filled with the smell of old fires. 'How have you been, George?'

I shrugged.

'Busy?'

I said, 'Quite busy.'

'Did you hear the show?'

'The end of it.'

'It was crap.' She took the cigarette out of her mouth and sighed smoke. '*I* was crap.'

'You weren't.'

'You used to tell me if I was.'

'Does John?'

'John doesn't like jazz. He likes . . .' she shrugged. 'Other things.'

'Such as?'

She said, 'Stop it, George.'

There was silence for a moment.

Mary said 'You *have* been busy.'

I didn't say anything.

'You look it. It always shows.' She blew out smoke. 'You should take more care of yourself.'

'I needed to talk to you,' I said.

'Not again.' There were exasperated lines around her mouth. 'There's no point, George. We've said everything. What's the point?'

'That's not what I wanted to talk about,' I said.

'What else is there?'

She meant, what else is there for two people to talk about when they've spent three years living together, and when one of them has betrayed the other. Nothing else ever seems quite as interesting.

I said, 'I'm in trouble.'

There was a long silence. Mary dug in her bag for another cigarette but she didn't light it.

She said, 'Maybe I'm not the right person to help you.'

'You don't know what it is.'

'Whatever it is . . . Oh, for God's sake, George.' When she looked up at me there were tears in her eyes. She whispered, 'I want you to be happy, OK? I said that.'

There was a long silence. Outside music was jarring off the walls of the club. Inside were rows of grey lockers, the smell of Mary's cigarette.

She said, 'It was a terrible gig. We didn't have time . . .' She grimaced. 'It was my fault.'

I didn't say anything. Ash fell off the end of her cigarette.

'John's coming for me,' she said.

'Soon?'

She looked up. There was a narrow crease between her brows. She said, 'Fuck, you *are* in a mess.'

I wasn't looking at her any more. I was looking at the floor next to her feet.

'I told you,' I said. 'I'm in trouble.'

'What kind of trouble?' She sounded wary.

I said, 'You remember Hill?' I hadn't pictured it like this.

'You think I'd forget him?'

'We arrested him today.'

'Again?' Her voice was ironic.

'For murder. He killed someone. The guy he stood trial with before.'

Mary looked at me through wary grey eyes. 'So that's good, isn't it?'

Very quietly I said, 'I forged the confession.'

For a long time she didn't say anything. Outside they were playing jazz music, something I didn't recognize. Inside was the smell of smoke, the cold lightbulb, and rows of metal doors.

Then Mary said, 'I don't believe you.'

'What?'

'I don't believe you. It's a trick or . . . something. You wouldn't do that. Not you. I remember what you used to say about . . . people who did things like that.' She whispered, 'Not you, George.'

I said, 'Yes, me.'

'Why?' She sounded angry.

'To be sure of getting him.'

There was a sudden rustle of the plastic bag.

'I can't take you like this, George. You used to be so . . . sure of yourself, you know? You were so full of yourself. It was really . . .' She paused. Her voice came from a distance, as if she wasn't looking at me. 'Sexy, God help me. I can't understand you like this.'

'I need help. I want to talk to you.'

'You want to fuck me.' Her voice quivered at the end. 'You want someone to fuck so you come to me. Telling some stupid story.'

'No.'

The door at the end of the corridor banged and loud jazz blew through it. A man's voice called, 'What's up, honey?'

'Nothing.'

'Will you be long?'

Mary didn't answer. I lifted my head.

She said, 'You're angry now.'

I didn't say anything to that, either.

'Sit down, George. I'm sorry. I'm angry about the show.'

'I shouldn't have bothered you,' I said.

'Why are you doing this?'

'Doing what?'

'I don't know.'

She crossed her arms and buried her face in her hand. She was still wearing her stage clothes: a black dress, badly cut, and jewellery that someone else had given her.

'I can't believe this. You'd never have done . . . this.'

'I did.'

'What's happened to you?'

What had happened to me? I didn't even want to think about that.

'Before, it was . . . You wouldn't even have thought of it.'

'No.'

'So why now?'

'I told you. To make sure he –'

'Who gives a damn whether Hill goes down or not? There's only . . . one of him. What does it matter?'

I said, 'You know it matters.'

'Not this much. You've let the whole thing eat you away. If it hadn't been for that . . .'

She didn't have to finish. If it hadn't been for that we might be married by now, arguing not this way but the way married people argue; we would be happy.

'You didn't have to let it change you,' she went on.

I said, 'There are a lot of things that didn't have to happen. You didn't have to walk out. You didn't have to go off with John.'

Her chin snapped up. 'I thought you wanted my help!'

'I do.'

'So . . . Anyway, I *did* have to. I *did*. No one could have put up with you mooning around the flat feeling sorry for yourself. And not saying anything. For Christ's sake, George, you hardly ever spoke. For six months.' There was a pause. 'All right, so I . . .'

I stood up. I didn't want to go over it again. I'd come because I didn't have anywhere else to go, not to work over the various ways we'd betrayed each other.

'Where are you going?'

I said, 'I'm going.'

'George . . .'

A man was leaning against the swing door, holding it open. He had heavy cheeks and the hair was receding from his temples. He blinked when he saw who it was. Up on stage the man in the T-shirt was tearing electrical tape off the floor. Only a few tables were still full. The black guy in the fur coat was leaning against the bar by himself.

The barman didn't look at me as I went past.

## 12

At home there was a light winking on the answerphone. I pressed the button and Ralph's voice spoke to me. His voice was the same as always: indulgent, joking. He still didn't know about it. For a moment I was tempted to call up and tell him – tell him what I'd done, and the way I'd betrayed everything we'd talked about as children. I'd never had a secret from him before. But one phone call wouldn't have been enough. I didn't just want to hear his voice; I wanted him to climb down off the top bunk and take control, the way he had when we were kids. I wanted him to tell me what to do.

I stripped off and lay down on the bed. I didn't think I would sleep. I wondered what Hill was thinking about. I wondered what Paddy Moran's brother was thinking about in his working man's digs in Kilburn. The thought of Paddy Moran was a help. I tried to remember the look on his face when we got to him. It had shock in it, and pain, but mostly it was full of amazement: amazement that after the poverty and drink, after the cold nights out of doors, life had still kept one up its sleeve for him. I remembered the voice of the jury foreman, the tremor with which he'd held the paper he was reading from and the sick weight which hit the bottom of my stomach when I heard his words: '*Not guilty . . . Not guilty.*'

I tried to think of the last trial. Somehow it made it better if I kept remembering that I'd had no choice. I pictured Hill standing in the dock like a kid waiting for a prize at speech day. His lawyer had asked him questions in a quiet, confiding voice, the way you'd speak to a sick uncle. When I went up into the witness stand I tried to catch his eye. I wanted to say to him, 'You know Hill did this. We all know it. Why are you trying to help him?' My mouth had been dry. I knew I was getting the answers wrong. I knew that if I only had time to think, I could see past the traps he set, straighten it all out, make things clear. I had got angry; the judge had rebuked me. His eye, looking coldly at me along the bench, had something final in it. That was when I knew we were going to lose.

The evening after the verdict I hadn't gone home. When I did go home Mary was sitting on the sofa. She'd been crying and she started crying again when she saw me. I hadn't known how to tell her I'd failed at something. That was what it felt like. Hill was free and it was my fault. After years of winning whatever I tried I hadn't known how to admit that even to myself.

Mary had said, 'Why didn't you come home? What's happened?'

I should have told her about it then, but it made me angry that she asked. I went into the kitchen.

'George?'

I said, 'Work. Something came up.'

'Has the trial finished yet?'

I was drinking glasses of water at the sink.

'Has it?'

'No.'

I didn't say anything else. I drank more water, rolled into bed and slept all day. Our relationship died sometime while I was sleeping. We kept dragging its corpse about with us for a long time, like two people pulling a reluctant dog along the pavement. Sometimes I wondered if people noticed it was dead. Maybe they could smell it, or see its corpse hanging from our shoulders. We kept living together, going out, eating meals. We even made love with the corpse lying in bed next to us, and both of us pretending we were alone. There was nothing we could do to bring it back to life.

It was a week before Mary found out from the newspapers that Hill was free. She behaved as if I'd told her a lie, when all I'd done was bury something I didn't know how to talk about.

'You should have told me.'

'It's none of your business.'

'What's that supposed to mean?'

At night I dreamed I was a child again. I was lying in bed at home and dreaming child's dreams: my father's funeral, his face bending over me. I was in a city filled with empty streets and the sound of footsteps running way from me. Awake, I saw the street where an early milkman had found Paddy Moran's body, rolled it over and seen the empty stumps in his coat sleeves. No one at work spoke to me about Paddy Moran, or about Hill.

At home Mary fought a losing battle against silence.

'I'm going to move out, George.'

'You must do what you want.'

A pause.

'I'm seeing someone else, if you want to know.' Her voice was unnatural. 'Maybe you don't care anyway.'

'Does it mean anything?' I could hear the whine in my own voice.

'Everything means something.' Another pause, like the widening of sea between two icebergs. We were in the same room and we could hardly hear each other. 'I told you. I'm moving out. I've had enough, George.'

I said, 'I thought we were happy.'

'We were happy.'

'So?'

'We aren't any more.'

Mary was putting on her overcoat. 'I'll come for my things in a couple of days.'

'We should talk.'

'It's too late, George.'

I said, 'Why?' I didn't like myself. I was only saying it because I was scared.

'Because it is.'

'Is it my fault?'

She said, 'I told you. I'm seeing someone else.'

Two days later I had come home and the flat didn't recognize me: cold walls; empty shelves; her address on the back of an envelope by the door. She'd left two pints of milk in the fridge. Mary was waiting for a friend to pick up the last of her things.

I said, 'You left the curtains.'

A friend of hers had made the curtains.

'Why would I want the fucking curtains?'

They didn't look cheerful any more. They looked like make-up after a party, or Christmas decorations halfway into February. It had only taken two days to dismantle three years of living together.

I turned over in bed. Something else turned over with me. It was the knowledge of what I'd done, the knowledge of that bogus confession locked in the drawer of Mason's desk. I had managed to extinguish one demon, but at what price? The price was lying alongside me, breathing loud in my ear. Maybe I would never be free again.

I gripped the sheet with my hands. It was too late for regrets now. Tomorrow Mason would question me and I would have to respond straight, fighting my corner. I would have to repeat what Hill had said, stare Cayman down, keep my nerve.

For a moment I almost wished that I could go back. I could take a taxi to the station, break into Mason's office and tear the confession up. But Mason had seen it already. He had congratulated me on it. It was with me now, part of me; something I couldn't undo or wrestle off my back. It was too late to go back.

I wondered what chance I had of getting away with it. The canteen had already guessed. I thought of Cayman's tired face: 'Another time'; of Helen Rodber's brusque shake of the head when I suggested a drink. They all knew. It didn't matter that others had done the same thing. They didn't like me and now they had a reason not to. If any of them disliked me enough, then word would leak out and I would be finished. I winced at the risks I was taking. Why had I done it? Because otherwise Hill's face would never have gone away. There would have been another trial, another jury, another 1989. Another foreman would smile up at the bench. '*Not Guilty.*' Hill would have floated out of reach again, his white face bobbing like a painted balloon. I would have had to go on living with it.

I told myself that there was no other way. Mason wanted Hill locked up, too: he would be on my side. I told myself that Hill was a killer; he had killed Paddy Moran and he had killed Joe Bates. I told myself that what I was doing was better justice than had been done to Hill last time. A lot of the night went in arguments like that. I piled them up around me like a kid building sand ramparts on the beach. Sometimes I believed them, and sometimes I just lay there with my eyes shut. I thought about Hill's face and I thought about the sheet of paper in Mason's desk. It was a long time before I drifted off to sleep.

When the phone rang I was dreaming of a courtroom. I was in the dock. The lawyer questioning me was just a wig without a face. A thatch of white hair was escaping from under the wig . . .

I looked at the alarm clock. It was just after three o'clock.

The voice was a woman's, cultivated, precise. She said, 'Are you investigating Joe Bates's murder?'

I tried to say something. My mouth was too dry. I was still trapped in my dream.

The voice said, 'You arrested the wrong man. If I were you, I'd ask Fred James about it.'

My voice was a croak. I tried to say, 'Who's Fred James?'

There was a click. The line went dead.

## 13

Mason's voice was thick with fatigue. He couldn't take the late nights any more. In the office next door somebody was singing.

'So who the hell *is* Fred James?' He sounded irritable.

'I don't know.'

'Well, why the bloody hell don't you know? It's your case, isn't it?'

'Yes, sir.'

'Well, then.'

Mason looked again at the slip of paper he was holding. He threw it down on the desk with a snort of disgust. I picked it up.

It was a sheet of ordinary white photocopy paper. On it was taped a photograph of Joe Bates in his chauffeur's uniform. Underneath there was a strip of plastic printout from a child's labelling machine.

The printout read: 'ASK FRED JAMES.'

'Well?'

I shook my head.

Mason snorted again. 'You know Hill's denying he ever confessed?'

I didn't say anything.

'Well?'

'What did you expect?' I said. 'Last night we took him by surprise. He didn't have time to think it out.'

'His lawyer's making some bad noises.'

'Let him.'

Mason's grey eyes were troubled. I leaned forward over the desk. 'We've got to expect this,' I said. 'Hill will swear till he's blue in the face he didn't make that confession. You know what he's like. He'll use his lawyer. We've got to be ready for that, too.'

Mason said, 'And then this . . .' He nodded towards the paper lying on the desk between us.

He still didn't look at me. He wasn't looking at me when he said, 'He did make that confession, didn't he?'

'What are you suggesting?' I made my voice hard.

'Did you record it?'

I shook my head.

'Why not?' Mason sounded exasperated. 'You know what the code of practice says.'

I said, 'There wasn't a machine available.'

'They'll use that. A murder case with no tape of the confession? Next year we won't even be able to bring it to court – when the new regulations come in. It's hard enough without a tape as it is.'

'It's my word against his.'

'Was anyone else there?'

'No. Cayman was going through his place. They found ammunition there . . . more banknotes. The same as the ones we found on Bates.'

Mason said, 'You should have got someone else to witness it, at least. They'll use that, too.'

'Let them.'

He picked up the sheet of paper and repeated, 'And then this . . .' Irritation flared up suddenly in his tired face. He said, 'I want you to go from one end of this case to the other and back again. We don't take any chances. If there's an angle to it you don't know about, you go out and find it. If Joe Bates sneezed ten minutes before he died I want a memo on it.'

'Yes, sir.'

'Someone's sending us an anonymous tip-off about Fred James and we don't even know who Fred James is. For Christ's sake!'

'Hill confessed,' I said.

'All right, he confessed. If you say so. And as soon as we get into court his lawyer will tear that confession into little pieces. No damn witness, for Christ's sake! That's why we should be taping everything. Then he'll put Fred . . . this Fred James in the box and we won't even know what to ask him! We won't know who he is! I thought you wanted to nail Hill good and proper this time!'

'I do.'

'Well, then.' He puffed out his cheeks and blew out a sigh. 'Find Fred James,' he said. 'Find him and find out what's he's got to do with it. Find out who sent this. Find out what's going on.'

'It could be a nutter,' I said. 'It could be nothing to do with it at all. Someone with a grudge against Fred James. Or else Hill's behind it himself.'

Mason's grey rust-flecked eyes swivelled towards me. The skin was wrinkled around them like the skin of an old lizard. 'In that case it won't hurt to find out, will it?'

I said, 'No.'

'Do you have anything else on at the moment?'

'No.'

'Well, then.'

After a pause he said, 'If it's a red herring let's find out it's a red herring. Let's eliminate it. Let's get at the truth.'

My throat was dry. 'Is that all?'

'No.' Mason picked up the paper again. He studied Joe Bates's face. 'The only thing you want is to get Hill behind bars, isn't it?'

'It's where he belongs.'

'Well, the best way to do it is to rule out everything else that's possible. You understand?'

'Of course.'

'If we leave any loose ends his lawyer will tie them all together in knots and we'll be back where we started.'

'We've got a confession,' I said.

'No, we don't, not if he denies he ever made it. You can't give a man like Hill that much space.'

'This is as close as we'll ever get. Isn't it my word against his?'

Mason's eyes flicked away from mine. He picked up the

paper again. 'I don't like this, Havilland,' he said. 'Why would someone send us this? Hardly anyone even knows Hill's been taken in. He hasn't even been bloody committed yet. And someone's telling us to look somewhere else. I hate it.'

'Yes, sir.'

'Are you going to follow it up?'

I nodded.

'*Who's Fred James?*' He said it slowly, almost angrily.

'I told you, I don't know.'

Mason shook his head. 'I'll tell you who he is. He's someone someone else thinks killed Joe Bates. And you never even bloody heard of him!'

The singing stopped next door. There was a sudden burst of laughter and a woman's voice imitating a police siren.

'The aim of this is simple, Havilland. We don't want to get Hill. We don't want to save the police embarrassment. If Fred James killed Joe Bates, we charge Fred James. That's all that matters.'

'That's not going to happen,' I said. 'Hill confessed.'

'Yes.'

He didn't sound like it made anything better.

Mason put the paper into his in-tray, then took it out again. 'Do you read the newspapers?' he asked.

I told him I did.

'You can see what's going on. West Midlands, the Guildford Four. They're after us, Havilland. There's nothing they like better than the sight of policemen with shit on their faces. And it's not going to happen here.' He looked old. 'You're going to find this Fred James and you're going to rule him out. Or in. I don't care which, just find out what he's got to do with it.'

There was a knock on the door. A policewoman in uniform came in. She said, 'Second post.'

She put a pile of papers down on the desk. On the top was a sheet of plain white A4 with two strips of plastic printout stuck to it. Mason picked up the sheet and looked at it. Without a word he passed it across the desk to me and got up from his chair. The two strips of printout were stuck end to end, running up the length of the page.

They read: 'FRED JAMES FUCKS CLARE BATES.'

'Well?'

I didn't say anything. The blood was pumping in my ears. I could hear the woman's voice on the telephone: 'Are you investigating Joe Bates's murder?' I saw Joe Bates's handsome face pillowed on a black scarf as if he'd drifted off to sleep. 'ASK FRED JAMES.'

Mason was scratching the back of his leg through his trouser pocket. Without turning round he said, 'You did talk to Clare Bates, at least?'

'Yes.'

'Did she mention a Fred James?'

'No.'

'What did she say?'

'Nothing much. What time he came home, what time he left.'

'What was she like?'

I tried to think what Clare Bates was like: a pretty, tired face with wide-apart grey eyes, hair tied back in a ribbon. I remembered the soft fold of skin under her chin.

'She's a nice girl. I don't think she has anything to do with this.'

'I didn't say she did. But I'll tell you . . .' He pointed at the desk without turning round. 'Someone doesn't think she's a nice girl.'

There was a pause.

'Hill had been chasing her,' I said. 'That may be what's behind the whole thing. In that case it wouldn't be surprising if Hill's people are trying to drag her into it.'

'Is that what you think this is about?'

'Yes.'

Mason swung round. 'I hope you're right,' he said quietly.

For a moment we stood looking at each other. There was no more triumph or fellow-feeling in the way he looked at me, just suspicion.

He jerked his head towards the door. 'Get on with it.'

I stood up. Mason's back didn't say anything to me. I walked out of the office and closed the door behind me.

The talk in the outer office stopped.

The woman who had been laughing turned away from her companion and started opening files on her desk. Someone else was suddenly deep in a document, moving his lips to show how interested he was. Somebody slapped the top of the photocopier shut and it began to whine.

There was a dry taste in my throat. I went over to Cayman's desk. Cayman was packing photos into his briefcase.

'What are you doing?'

My voice sounded too loud. I could feel backs listening to me.

Cayman didn't look at me. 'I only came in to tidy up. My mother's ill.'

'Your mother died two years ago.'

'My wife's mother.'

I said, 'You're a fucking awful liar.'

The guy by the photocopier started whistling.

Cayman flushed. He didn't say anything. He kept putting his things into the briefcase.

'Have you got permission?'

He jerked his head towards Mason's door.

'When are you coming back?'

'I'm not. I got accepted for that course.'

His voice was quiet but determined. He wouldn't look at me.

'It doesn't start until June.'

'I'm taking leave.' He raised his face suddenly and looked at me from a distance, as if there was a thick sheet of glass between us. 'I'm owed a week from last year. He signed it this morning.'

I nearly said something, but there was nothing to say. I turned away. The guy from the photocopier was bending over the woman, whispering something in her ear. Her shoulders were shaking; she was trying not to laugh out loud.

I picked up the letter with Joe Bates's photograph on it and walked towards the photocopier. The man next to it had a big pile of documents on the trolley beside him. He looked at the wall. His face said he knew I was there.

I said, 'May I?'

The machine whined and flashed a bar of white light under his hands. He raised the lid, swept up the sheet and replaced it with another from the pile next to him. He kept staring at the wall as if it was the wall he didn't want to talk to. The machine started to whine again.

I said, 'Excuse me, Constable.'

Something flickered in his eyes but that was all. He stabbed a red button and the machine fell silent. In the silence he raised the lid, took out his document and stood back against the wall.

I said, 'Thank you.'

Nobody else in the room was talking. I made my copy and walked back to my office. As I shut the door behind me I heard the talk start up again.

## 14

Rain had washed Joe Bates's body off the pavement. Someone had cut the red police tape, which hung limply from a lamp post. The old drunk was sitting with his back against a parked car, muttering to himself.

The inside of the stair tower smelled of urine. At each landing I saw rows of doors stretching off along the access decks. The Bateses' flat was on the second floor. Two kids ran away when they saw me coming. From the deck I could look down at where Joe Bates had been killed. From that height you could still faintly make out the outline of a man's legs. There was a white stain on the pavement where the blood had been scrubbed away with bleach. I wondered whose job that was.

Beyond the pavement and the parked cars another access deck looked across at me. A woman was sweeping outside her front door. She jumped back inside when she saw me watching, and slammed the door shut. The tower blocks on the edge of the estate glinted in the sunshine.

With a shock I realized that I was looking forward to seeing Clare Bates. I wasn't sure why. Maybe because two days ago we were both living straightforward lives – not happy perhaps, but straightforward enough. And now Joe Bates's death had pushed us both over a cliff's edge. There was something clean about Clare; something honest and uncomplicated. Most of the people I met were lying to me and the others were telling me too much truth, more than anyone ought to hear. Clare Bates was just a straightforward girl in a bad situation; someone who didn't deserve to be there; someone who'd probably find their way out in the end.

Maybe I was getting like Mason. Maybe I'd been a policeman too long.

The Bateses' flat had a mahogany Georgian-style door with a brass knocker that someone bothered to polish and brass numbers above it. There were flowers in the kitchen window.

I rang the bell. Inside I heard footsteps, then the sound of locks being opened.

She was wearing a white knitted top over black trousers, and holding a green butcher's apron. I guessed that she'd taken the apron off to answer the door. She didn't look as if she'd had a lot of sleep. When she saw me her eyes lost their friendly look. For some reason I felt disappointed.

'Yes?'

'I'm sorry to bother you, Mrs Bates. I've got some questions to ask you.'

'I thought I answered all your questions.'

'Something else has come up. Do you mind?'

'Oh . . .' She rubbed the back of her hand across her forehead. 'Of course not.'

The front hall was narrow, with a carry-cot on the floor. She led me through into a living room with long windows on to a balcony at the back.

I'd been into places like that before and I knew what they were supposed to look like: the peeling brown wallpaper and the smell of old food, the unwashed plates scattered around a television set in the middle of the floor. The Bateses' living room was different. It had polished floorboards, a white rug and two modern sofas upholstered in blue and white stripes. There was more of the blue material around the windows. The walls were covered with a yellow paint effect that came out of Sunday magazines. Blue and white flowers stood on a side table, filling the room with their scent.

Clare stooped to pick up some children's toys from the rug.

I said, 'You've got a nice place. You've made it nice.'

Clare looked surprised. 'Oh . . . Thank you.'

'Did you have a designer?'

'Don't be silly.'

'What do you mean?'

'It's only a council flat.'

She turned and took the toys out of the room. Sun was pouring in through the long windows at the back. It looked like somewhere you'd shoot an advert for washing powder: the same kind of taste, the same kind of perfection that isn't quite real. The ideas came from Sunday magazine lifestyle features. It wasn't a room which expressed any personality. Instead, it expressed a yearning: to be living somewhere else, in a house somewhere which didn't have tower blocks looking down at it, and kids racing past the front door, and people being killed on the pavement outside; a yearning to escape from South London, to join the nice people in the tree-lined streets where the police were on your side; a yearning for security.

She came back into the room.

'Did Joe do it? The DIY?'

'No. It was me.'

'Did he help you?'

She shook her head. 'He wasn't interested.'

'Where did you find the time?'

'It was before we had Patrick, most of it. I had all the time in the world then.'

'You ought to set up a business.'

It was hardly a joke and she wasn't into jokes anyway. Not from me.

I said, 'Where's Patrick?'

'He's out with his gran.'

She wasn't wearing any make-up, I noticed, or hardly any. There was the same simple gold chain around her neck.

'Can I get you some coffee, Inspector?'

'Thank you.'

I sat down. I heard her moving around in the kitchen. I could imagine the kitchen.

Clare came back and sat down on the other sofa, as far away from me as she could get. She folded her arms. 'What is it that's come up?' she said.

'Some details I want to check.'

'I thought we went over it all yesterday.' She sighed. 'Go on, then.'

'What time did Joe come home on Sunday?'

'Half past seven.'

'Did he stay for dinner?'

'He went straight out. I told you all this.'

'He didn't tell you where he was going?'

'No.'

'Did you have any ideas?'

'The pub,' she said. 'There wasn't any mystery about it.'

'Which pub did he drink in?'

'My mum's. The Blue Corner.'

'That's a funny name,' I said.

'It's a fight pub. My dad ran a gym.'

'Do they still have boxing there?'

'Yes.'

'Where else did Joe drink?'

Clare got up. She went round behind me and began to fiddle with some things on the side table. Her voice said, 'I don't know. Wherever he had friends.'

'Hill's bar?'

'So you tell me. I didn't know that.'

I left a pause. So far all I'd done was put off asking the next question, but I couldn't put it off for ever. I kept my voice as light as possible.

I said, 'Who's Fred James?'

There was a long pause. No answer came.

I was about to turn round when Clare's voice came from the kitchen. 'Do you take sugar?'

She was standing in the doorway holding a sugar bowl.

Maybe she really hadn't heard. I told her no sugar and waited until she came back with two cups and put them down on the coffee table. She bent down over the cups, stirring one of them.

Without looking at me she said, 'I'm sorry, you were asking something.' Her voice sounded normal enough.

I said, 'Who's Fred James?'

She sat down and swept the hair back from her forehead.
'A friend of ours. Why?'

'A friend of Joe's?'

'Both of ours.'

'Does he live near here?'

'He lives in Tower Bridge Road. With his mum. He runs
an antique shop.'

'How well do you know him?'

'Why do you ask?'

I felt like a child wading into a cold sea with his parents
urging him on from the shore. I wished someone would
tell me I didn't have to go on. I wished I could go back to
Mason and tell him that Fred James never existed, that
Joe Bates never existed, that I'd spent a nice morning sitting
in a sunlit living room talking to a nice girl over a cup of
coffee.

But there was no way of avoiding it.

'Are you having an affair with him?' I made my voice
hard.

She sipped her coffee. Over the rim of the cup she looked
at the kitchen door, then she put the cup down and looked at
the window.

'Yes.'

There was a long silence. We could hear kids' voices down
on the roadway outside.

I took another step into the cold water.

'Did Joe know?'

She didn't answer. Suddenly I realized she was crying.

I tried to say something but she waved a hand at me. I
thought of the plastic strip running up the sheet of white
paper: 'FRED JAMES FUCKS CLARE BATES.' It hadn't even
crossed my mind that it might be true.

'You would have found out sooner or later.'

'Did Joe know?'

'Of course not.'

'How long had it been going on?' I asked.

'About a year.'

'Had it started when I last met you?'

'During the trial? That's when it did start. I thought Joe was guilty. I thought we were finished.'

There was a pause.

'How did you meet him?' I asked.

'Oh . . . in his shop.' She wiped the back of her hand across her eyes. 'I used to buy things off him.'

'Did anyone else know?'

'Only my mum.'

She pressed her mouth shut, closed her eyes and took in a deep breath through her nostrils. Her chest rose and fell. She sat like that for a moment, with her eyes shut and her legs drawn up under her on the sofa.

I said, 'Was it serious?'

She shrugged. 'What's serious?'

'Were there any others?'

I didn't want there to have been others.

Her face screwed up in disgust. 'I didn't mean it like that,' she said. 'I meant . . . Oh, I don't know whether it's serious.'

After a pause I said, 'Why?'

I didn't just mean, Why had she fallen for Fred James. I meant, Why did this have to have come up, Why couldn't Joe Bates's body wash smoothly off the pavement and Hill go to prison without a hitch. I was almost angry with her.

Clare looked down and rested her temples on her hand.

'You shouldn't think I like myself for it,' she said. 'Just when Joe was going through the trial, and everything. I was supposed to be standing by him.'

'He didn't deserve it.'

'No.' She looked at me, her grey eyes still full of tears. 'You don't know half of it.'

'Had there been problems before?'

'Problems!' She took a deep breath. 'He used to drink. When he drank he wasn't like . . . himself. He turned into a bully. I was scared of him.'

'Did he hit you?'

She nodded. The white skin under her chin moved as she swallowed.

I said, 'Often?'

'Once is enough.'

'But it wasn't only once.'

She shook her head.

'Why didn't you leave him?'

'I couldn't. Because of Patrick. And it wasn't bad . . . I mean, a lot of people put up with worse.' She wiped her nose with her forefinger. 'My mum used to put up with worse.'

'And then Fred James came along.'

Once again I was inching forward into cold waves. I could hear the woman's voice on the telephone, her clearly enunciated syllables: 'Ask Fred James about it.'

'Fred was nice,' she said simply. 'He was a cut above Joe. He's . . . a gentleman.'

'A refuge?'

She nodded. 'It took a long time before it started. Then Joe looked like he was going to jail. It looked as if he'd done something . . . horrible. And I thought, Why should I put up with this any more? I'm still young. Fred was so kind to me.'

'Did he ever ask you to leave Joe for him?'

'He knew I wouldn't. Not after Joe got off.'

'How often do you see him?' I asked.

'A couple of times a week.'

'Do you go round to his place?'

She shook her head. 'Stop it.'

I said, 'Had you been arguing with Joe the night he was killed?'

'Not that night. He was drunk, but he didn't want to stay in the house. He went out.'

'He didn't tell you where?'

'I told you.'

'What did you feel when you heard he was dead?'

Suddenly her shoulders were shaking. She said, 'Excuse me . . .'

She went out of the room half running, with her hand over her mouth.

I sat for a while, looking round at the tasteful soap-advert room. I heard a tap running in the bathroom. All this was a cover flung over a life she didn't want to own up to. The painted walls, the blue curtains, the rug – she must have put them all together and dreamed that she was a real person living in a real house just like this; instead of another battered wife on a council estate. It was a brave try, you had to say that. She had climbed her ladder and painted the ceiling, dreaming all the time that the fairy-tale would come true and a smiling husband would walk in through the front door – just like in the adverts – pat the dog on the head and give her his trousers to wash. I wondered what Fred James looked like, whether he had white teeth and rumpled brown hair and the sort of laugh you only heard in the adverts.

I got up and looked at the pictures on the wall. They were photographic reproductions of Victorian prints: *The Village Wedding*, *The Awakening Conscience*. I wondered what I was going to hear when I did, finally, ask Fred James.

Clare Bates came back into the room. 'I'm sorry,' she said. 'That was stupid of me.'

'It's not surprising you're upset.' I sounded like a social worker.

She shrugged. 'You've got a right to know.' She sat down in the same corner of the sofa. 'When I met Joe,' she said, 'I was only nineteen. I was living with my mum above the pub. I hated it. Every night I'd go to sleep with the sound of men fighting underneath my bedroom. I used to dream of running away. Joe was different in those days. He was very good-looking . . . It sounds stupid now, I thought that meant he must be good.' She laughed bitterly.

I said, 'You're not the first person to make that mistake.'

'I didn't question anything. And he always had money. He seemed to want the same things I wanted. Getting married was a chance to go up in the world, to get settled . . .'

Her voice trailed off. I thought she was going to go on but she didn't.

'When did he start to hurt you?' I prompted.

'A few months after we married.' She smiled suddenly. 'You should have seen our wedding . . .' She fell silent.

'Go on.'

'I kept finding excuses for him, to start with. I kept telling myself it was just a one-off, that it was worries about work, or . . . And he kept saying sorry and that it wouldn't happen again. I always believed him. You always do.'

'Did Patrick make a difference?'

'For a time.' She sighed. 'Then it started again. We were almost living separate lives by the end . . .'

Two people living separate lives in a perfect flat with rag-rolled walls and framed pictures.

'What would he have done if he'd found out?' I asked.

'I don't like to think.'

'Did you worry about it?'

'The whole time.'

'Would Fred have protected you?'

Her face swung towards me. She said, 'Fred doesn't have anything to do with this, if that's what you mean.'

'It's what people will think.'

'Fred wouldn't hurt a soul,' she said. Her voice was soft. 'He's a gentle man.'

I wanted to believe that. I said, 'Where can I find him?'

Her eyes searched my face. 'You're going to arrest him, aren't you?'

I sighed. 'We shouldn't have to,' I said. 'Hill confessed last night. I shouldn't be telling you this. He was seen arguing with Joe . . . You've got to keep that quiet, for now.'

'Hill!'

'Does that surprise you?'

'I suppose not.'

I leaned forward suddenly. 'Did you ever hear him threaten Joe?' I asked. 'Or the other way round. Did Joe ever say he'd pick a fight with Hill?'

'I don't think so . . . No. I didn't know they were even seeing each other.' She said it bitterly.

'But it doesn't surprise you?'

She shook her head. 'Not with Hill. Nothing would surprise me.'

'All right,' I said. 'But Fred doesn't have anything to worry about – do you see?'

She gave me a sudden smile, the first I'd ever seen from

her. Her face was relaxed. 'Thank you for telling me that. It's the first time it's felt . . . Oh, I don't know. As if someone's on my side.'

'Where can I find him?'

'In the Tower Bridge Road. Fred James Antiques.'

'Have you seen him since?' I asked.

'I didn't want to. I don't know what to say.'

The doorbell rang suddenly, shrilly.

'Could that be him now?'

'No, it's my mum.'

She got up and went out into the hall. From where I was sitting I saw her open the door. Outside I could see a pushchair and a woman who looked like an older version of Clare. Clare glanced over her shoulder, then went out on to the deck and pulled the door to behind her. I heard them talking outside. After a moment they came back in, manoeuvring the pushchair into the narrow hallway.

Clare said, 'This is my mother. Chief Inspector Havilland.'

Close to, the older woman didn't look like Clare. Her hair was the same, and she had the same wide-apart eyes, but her eyes held the hard expression of someone who had been through it and come out the other side. She must have been about forty – probably she'd had Clare when she was only a kid. She needed the heavy eye make-up she was wearing. Her clothes hugged her body. Either she was a manhunter, or she was fighting age with everything she could find.

'Jill Cowans. Pleased to meet you, Chief Inspector.'

There was more South London in her voice than in Clare's. There was a faint note of innuendo in it, too. That may just have been habit.

'Have you found the bloke who killed Joe, yet?'

'We think so.'

'Was it a mugger?'

'I can't go into detail.'

'You should have more coppers on the beat. It's not safe on these estates. When I was a girl you couldn't go out of doors without falling over a copper.' Her voice was accusing.

I said, 'Things were probably different when you were a girl.'

Her eyes blazed at me.

Clare was stooping over the pushchair. The child kicked and gurgled.

'Patrick needs his rest, Mum.'

I looked at Clare's hands deftly undoing buckles. 'You've been very helpful, Mrs Bates,' I said.

She didn't raise her head. Suddenly I stooped down, took hold of her wrist and moved it away from the child's face.

Just under his left ear, on the hairline, was a purple bruise. It might have been a week old.

I said, 'Who else did Joe beat?'

'It wasn't him.' Clare's voice was angry. 'He wasn't like that. Patrick fell out of his cot. He doesn't sleep well.'

'Fucking coppers.' Her mother's voice was ugly.

I walked out on to the access deck; the Georgian front door closed behind me. On the pavement below two kids were kicking a satchel, keeping it away from a third child who was wailing with his mouth wide open. The drunk was picking at the waste cans. Somewhere a car engine was revving angrily; somewhere Fred James was waiting to see me. I didn't want to see him: I didn't want to walk any further into that cold sea; I didn't want him to tell me that he had killed Joe Bates and that Hill had been miles away, leaning over the counter in his bar. I felt like a child watching the tide creep towards his sandcastle.

There was nothing that I could do to save it.

## 15

I started walking back along Kennington Road. I ought to have gone to Mason and told him what I had just found out. Or else I should have gone to Tower Bridge Road and asked Fred James questions that were now overdue. Instead, on an impulse, I turned left, heading for the railway arches.

A goods train was waiting on signals above the road. Underneath it the arches curved round towards Waterloo Station. Outside the first, a group of bikers was sitting on the kerb drinking out of polystyrene cups. Their jackets advertised a courier service. At five-thirty they'd take the jackets off and be warriors of the road again; for the moment they were mercenaries. The next arch along was empty. The third was blocked by cars parked haphazardly across the pavement. There was no sign over the door. I picked my way between a rusty Escort and a Honda with no doors. Immediately inside the opening a sixties Jaguar was jacked up with a lightbulb clipped to the edge of the bonnet. The arch smelled of wet brick and motor oil. Somewhere a radio was playing.

To the left of the entrance was a glass kiosk, the glass obscured by the backs of bills. I pushed open the door and the radio got louder. Inside was a desk covered in papers, a girlie calendar and an old car seat with a man sitting on it. He had a sandwich bag open on his knees. When I came in he stared at me through thick glasses and kept chewing.

'Tony.'

The man swallowed and said, 'Hello, George.'

His voice was deep and terse. He took another bite of his sandwich. The bread was stained with oily fingerprints.

'Whose is the Jag?' I said.

'Pile of shit . . . Belongs to a lady. I told her not to buy it.'

'What's wrong? The engine?'

He chewed for a while, then said, 'Why do you care? You don't even have a car.'

'Maybe I'll get one one day.'

'I wouldn't bother. I don't. Take the bus.'

I pushed some old paper cups to one side and perched on the edge of the desk. Tony crumpled up the sandwich bag and threw it on to the desk.

'No one needs 'em. Not just for living round town. If you're going out of town, travelling a lot, it's different. I wouldn't have one, not for . . . anything. Used to. If I could have back all the money I spent on motors . . .'

He stood up, brushed crumbs off his trousers and walked out of the office. I followed him. He took the bulb off the edge of the Jaguar's bonnet and held it low down inside the engine.

He said, 'What do you want, anyway?'

'I'm looking for a garage. Somewhere round here. Takes care of Rollers, smart stuff.'

'I don't do smart stuff.' Tony showed teeth through the oil stains and laughed a deep, fat laugh that stopped abruptly when he bent back into the engine. 'Why?'

'A car I'm trying to find.'

'Does Mary still have that 2CV?'

I said, 'I'm not seeing Mary any more.'

'Pity.'

Tony lifted his head out of the engine. He didn't look at me. In one hand he was holding a metal cylinder blackened with oil. He said, 'I told her. I said, the drive shaft's cracked. I can pack it, might last a year. If you want to waste your money it's your business.' Without pausing he went on, 'There's a place up the road. Valet service, garages them at night. They pay through the nose. It's a good business to be in.'

'How do I find it?'

'Go to the end and turn in under the railway. It's in the arches on the other side.'

I said, 'Thanks, Tony.'

'No problem.' He clipped the light back to the edge of the bonnet. 'Shame about Mary,' he said. 'She was a nice girl. I expect she'll still need servicing.' He laughed the fat laugh again.

'I expect so.'

'All right.'

On my way out I turned round. 'Do you know the name of that garage?'

Tony looked up at me from the Jag's engine. He smiled. '"Fucking Smart Motors for People with Too Much Fucking Money,"' he said.

I found 'The Belgrave Auto Centre' where Tony had said it was, underneath the arches and behind a screen of plate glass and artificial plants. A receptionist with lacquered blonde hair asked if she could help me. I said I was from the police but she smiled anyway.

'Do you keep a car here for Sir John Penny? The driver's name was Joe Bates. Lived near here.'

She told me I'd have to speak to Maurice about that. I waited until a small man came out of a door behind the reception. He was wearing a blue coat with 'Belgrave Autos' embroidered in fancy writing on the chest.

'Yes?'

I said, 'I'm looking for a car belonging to a man called John Penny. I'm from the police.'

Maurice scowled. 'What makes you think it's here?'

'I know it's somewhere round here.'

Through the open door in the partition I could see men fussing over the bonnets of large cars.

He nodded. 'We keep Penny.'

'Can I see it?'

Maurice shrugged and led me through the door in the partition. Behind it light glinted on polished bonnets and windscreens. A man was flicking a duster over the car roofs. The place smelled of wax, like a new car showroom.

I said, 'When did it last go out?'

'Sunday, would have been. I wasn't in. Hasn't been out the last two days. Don't know why.'

He screwed up his eyes and peered at me. 'Is the chauffeur in trouble?'

'Should he be?'

Maurice shrugged. 'Only asking.'

'Did you know him?'

'No more than anyone else.'

'What made you think he might be in trouble?'

'Looked the type.'

He led me through cars to the far corner. Inside the cars were leather seats, phones, the sweet-smelling capsules in which their owners hurried from house to boardroom, to Council meetings or concerts. The money they paid for these cars wasn't for style or machinery; it was for the six inches of privilege it put between them and the street outside, for the tinted windows, for the air conditioning that saved them breathing the same fumes as everyone else.

Penny's car was parked up against the wall of the garage, a big green Rolls-Royce with buff seats. It had an ordinary number plate: Penny had money, but it was a different kind of money. Just behind it a man in a chauffeur's uniform was leaning against a pillar smoking.

Maurice nodded towards the car. 'That's Penny.'

'Has he kept it here long?'

'Long enough.'

I said, 'More than a year?'

Maurice looked at me. 'A long time.'

'How long had Bates been driving for him?'

'Why don't you ask him?'

'I'm asking you.'

The small man shrugged.

'Is it open?' I asked.

'Try it.'

The driver's side door opened. Inside the car smelled of cigars, slightly stale. A red light on the dashboard winked at me.

Maurice was standing by the side of the car, watching me through the windscreen.

'What time did you say the car came back on Sunday?' I asked.

'I don't know. I wasn't here.'

'Who was here?'

'Jack does Sundays.'

'Is Jack here now?'

Maurice nodded.

I said, 'Go and ask Jack. I want to know what time the car left and when it came back.'

Maurice thought for a moment, then nodded and disappeared between the parked cars. I bent back into the Rolls-Royce. There wasn't much in it that told me anything, except that Penny had plenty of cash, and that plenty of cash bought you walnut dashboards, silent clocks and deep carpeting for your feet. The glove compartments were empty. I ran my fingers under the seats and came up with a cheap cigarette lighter and an advertising flyer from some magazine. This wasn't the sort of car that filled up with crisp packets and old Coke tins.

In the dashboard was a hatch set into the walnut. I turned the handle and it dropped down. Inside was a pile of papers in a leather wallet: car documents; service history; a letter from Belgrave Autos. Underneath that was a brown envelope with no writing on it. I opened the envelope and pulled out a wad of receipts from service stations. Idly I looked through them. Mostly they were from a Texaco station on Kennington Road: Joe Bates must have filled the car up on his way home, or else the garage did it. A few were from motorway service stations. They seemed to go back just for the last three months. I was about to put them back in the envelope when something about the top one, the most recent, made me look at it again. I took it out of the pile and slipped it into my pocket, then folded the rest back into the envelope and put it back where I had found it.

A voice behind me said, 'Have you got a warrant?'

I swung round. The chauffeur who'd been smoking against the wall was standing right by the car door, grinning.

'Only kidding,' he said. The voice was Irish. 'Are you from the police?'

I closed the compartment door and snapped the catch shut.

'I could tell, the way you were searching it. They wouldn't let you do that if you weren't from the police. Not here. Is someone in trouble?'

I said, 'What's your name?'

'Dennis. I drive for one of the other fellows here.' He nodded towards the far side of the garage. He had a red, sunburned face. He looked like he'd have been more comfortable on a building site than under a peaked cap. 'Be taking it out in a minute. It's a Merc. I'd sooner have a Merc any day, more guts to it. These things are pretty but out on a motorway you're better in a Merc. Grand cars.'

I got out of the car and shut the door behind me. The door made an expensive noise when it shut.

'I wouldn't know,' I said. 'I don't know anything about cars.'

'Good for touring, too. You wouldn't want to make a long trip in a Roller.' The chauffeur dropped his cigarette and ground it out with his foot. 'So who's in trouble? Is he dead?'

'Who?'

'The old man.' He shrugged. 'The guy who owns the car.'

'How do you know he's an old man?'

'They're all old men.' He laughed.

I said, 'No, it's the chauffeur.'

'What was his name?'

'Joe Bates. Did you know him?'

He frowned. 'I know some of the fellows here. We come in different times. Was he a big fellow, looked like a . . . a movie star or something?'

'That's him.'

'Sure. I saw him taking this car out, when I think about it. Didn't know his name.'

'When did you see him last?' I asked.

'Wouldn't know.' The chauffeur had lost interest. He was watching Maurice picking his way towards us across the garage floor. 'So he'll be wanting another driver, will he? The old fellow. If this Bates is in trouble.'

'Maybe.'

'The brother's looking for a job. Had a job, but the fellow moved abroad. Grand driver, as well, the brother. Take a car over anything. Mercs, Rollers. Smart-looking man, too. He'd be the fellow for a job like this.' He swivelled his eyes back towards me. 'You'll tell him, will you?'

'Tell who?'

'The fellow who owns this. If he's looking for a new driver. Tell him Peter Miller's the man for him. He can get hold of him through the garage.' He nodded, gave a tug on his cap and sauntered off towards the back doors just as Maurice came up.

Maurice didn't seem to have got any happier. He jerked his head towards the chauffeur. 'What was he bothering you with?'

'Nothing that matters. Did you find out about the car?'

Maurice was looking at me suspiciously. 'Out all Sunday afternoon. Like you said.'

'I asked what time. The time it went out and what time it came back in.'

'Went out just after lunch.' He shrugged. 'Half past one.'

That fitted what Penny had told me.

'And it came back?'

Maurice squinted at me. 'Middle of the evening. Just after seven.'

I said, 'Seven o'clock?'

'Just after.'

'Is he sure about that?'

Maurice shrugged again. 'I only asked him what you said.'

I looked at him for a moment. He had a pinched, sullen face, the face of a man who's spent too much time polishing other people's cars.

'Do the drivers ever use these cars for themselves?' I asked. 'After they've finished for the day?'

'Why?'

'To impress their girlfriends . . . A night on the town. Any reason. Before they bring them back here.'

He shook his head. 'More than their job's worth.'

'Joe Bates wouldn't have done that?'

'None of them would.' He squinted at me. 'What's he done?

I looked at him.

'Will the car be going out soon?' he asked.

'Not with Joe Bates,' I said.

Outside, the secretary was staring past artificial plants and plate glass at two kids wrestling with a ball against the opposite kerb. Joe Bates had come there every morning, slid into the big green car and driven north, over the river, to Penny's life in Mayfair and Chelsea. On Sunday he'd done just the same thing, the same way he always had. He'd driven Penny around, filled the car up with petrol, dropped it back to the garage. Then he'd changed his clothes and gone out to meet Hill and get murdered on the pavement outside his flat.

I wondered if he'd known, that Sunday afternoon, that Hill wanted to pick a fight with him – or whether he'd been planning to start a fight himself. Maybe he'd thought about that while he waited for Penny, or thought about his wife at home. If it came to that, I wondered what Clare Bates had been doing all afternoon. Maybe she hadn't been at home at all, but with Fred James. I found it hard to imagine that. Or perhaps Fred James was by himself somewhere, planning to kill his lover's husband. I could imagine that, but I didn't want to.

Maybe nobody had been doing, that Sunday afternoon, exactly what they told me they'd been doing – not even John Penny.

## 16

The Blue Corner stood at a junction half a mile south of Southwark Bridge, where one rundown high street ran into another and left behind a strip of pavement, two newsagents and an old black guy in a funny hat.

The guy in the hat ranted at me as I approached the pub. He told me I was liar, a cheat and a sinner and it was only a matter of time before God struck me down. I knew all of that already. I didn't give him any money for it.

The Blue Corner was a big old-fashioned public house with blue paint peeling off the stucco on the ground floor. There were some wooden tables outside and a blackboard propped against the wall. The board said: '8.30 Jimmy Mulligan vs Thomas "Dark Destroyer" Briggs Sold Out'. Through a window above the door I could see the rope around a boxing ring. The windows were thick with dirt. The pub sign showed two old-style fighters with bare fists shaping up in front of something that was either a tree or a green skyrocket. Some gold writing above the door had dulled to a dirty beige.

Inside, the Blue Corner was almost empty. Two silent old men were propped against the wall. At the bar there was a big man in a tracksuit with a shaven head and no neck. He was drinking orange juice. The towel over his shoulder was dark with sweat. A boy was going from table to table with a broom, pushing crisp packets out of sight. From somewhere in the back I could hear a hoover.

I went up to the boy and asked where I'd find Jill Cowans. He had two earrings, acne, and hair greased into curls on his forehead. He pointed towards a door next to the bar.

It opened on to a narrow staircase. There was a closed door on the first landing. From behind it came the sound of someone grunting and a leather glove slapping rhythmically into a punchbag. A high-pitched voice was droning monotonously, 'Get under it, boy. Get under it.' I went on up to a landing under a dirty skylight. Beyond the landing was a corridor with a brown carpet and half a dozen doors. The door at the end was not quite closed.

I paused, not knowing what to do.

A voice from behind the door at the end called, 'I'm in here.'

I walked along the corridor and pushed the door open.

The room was large and untidy, with clothes littering the floor. Net curtains hung drunkenly across the grimy windows.

Jill Cowans was lying sprawled out on a bed against the back wall, with her legs and arms spreadeagled. She was naked. Her breasts stood out very white against the blanket. Black hair tufted from between her legs.

She looked at me. Her eyes were disappointed. She said, 'I don't want to fuck *you*.'

She said it with the stress on the 'you', like she did want to fuck somebody.

Without concern she pulled the sheet over her and sat up against the pillows, drawing up her knees. She reached for a cigarette.

I wondered who she'd been expecting.

'What do you want?' Her voice was neutral, neither hostile nor encouraging.

I walked forward into the room. 'I want to ask you some questions.'

She blew smoke and shook out the match. 'Sit down.'

I looked around. The floor was covered with a mess of clothes. They were jumbled together anyhow: dirty knickers, dresses, a motorbike helmet. The wardrobe door hung open. A table in the corner was covered with open make-up bottles and full ashtrays. There were bills and lists sellotaped to the mirror above it.

She said, 'On the bed.'

I sat on the bed.

'You want to ask me about Joe Bates?'

I said, 'Did you know he used to beat your daughter?'

I'd wanted to shock her but she didn't look shocked.

'Everybody knew.'

'Did anyone do anything about it?'

'What can you do?' She drew on her cigarette. 'Men are like that. You probably do it yourself, dear.'

I looked at her. The sheet was drawn tight across her breasts. There was a white halter mark around her neck.

'Do you have a girlfriend?' she asked.

I didn't say anything.

'How old are you, anyway?'

I said, 'What about your husband? Did he beat you?'

'He's dead.' She said it with finality.

'Who killed him?'

'Did I say anyone killed him?'

'No. Hill told me he died young.'

'A lot of people die young.'

'How long ago was that?'

'Ten years.'

'Was it his pub?'

'It was in the family.'

'What did he die of?'

'What does anyone die of?' She said it as if that was an answer.

The tough talking might have been an act. I wondered what she had been like before her husband died.

Jill Cowans blew out smoke and said, 'This is getting morbid, dear. What do you want to know about Joe?'

'Hill was seen arguing with Joe on Sunday night,' I said. 'What would that have been about?'

'Women or money. What's it ever about?'

'Which?'

'Could have been either, with them.'

'Hill told me he'd lent Joe money.'

She snorted. 'Hill didn't lend him anything. It was an advance.'

'An advance on what?'

'Joe used to sell coke for him.' Her hands rested on her knees with the cigarette between two fingers. Her nails were painted dark red. She said it quite calmly, as if she'd told me Joe sold used cars.

'Who to?'

'People who wanted it.'

'Anyone?'

'Rich people who wanted it.'

'Is that where he got his money from?'

'Of course.'

I said, 'Did Clare know?'

'Clare's a child.' Her voice was half contemptuous, half protective.

'When we found him,' I said, 'there was twelve hundred pounds in his pocket. In cash. Would that have been drug money?'

'What do you think?'

'Why did you never tell her?' I asked.

'Why spoil it?' She lifted the cigarette and studied the end of it. 'Clare doesn't like to look at things that don't fit in.'

'Did Joe Bates fit in?'

'To start with.'

'What happened?'

She looked at me. 'She found out he was a bastard.'

'How long did it take?' I asked.

'As long as it took for him to get bored of her.'

'Did he sleep around?'

'Of course he did.' She might as well have said, 'He's a man.'

'Did Clare know?'

'Probably.'

'You mean she didn't want to face up to it.'

Jill shrugged.

I said, 'Hill's confessed to killing him. Does that surprise you?'

'No.' She reached over and stubbed out the cigarette. 'Clare told me. Anyway, it's not exactly a shock.'

'Isn't it?'

'He's been chasing Clare as long as I remember. Joe always hated that.'

'Had they fought about it before?'

'Argued.' Her eyes were on my face, appraising me. 'I once heard Joe say he'd get him for it.'

I froze. Jill was watching me. I wondered if she knew what she might just have given me: the evidence to convince Mason, to back up Hill's confession.

'When was that?' I said.

'A couple of weeks ago.'

'Could you remember the date?'

'Fucking coppers.' She laughed. 'It was the night we had the Leroy Wilkins fight, if that's any help. I can dig the date out for you. He was sitting in the saloon bar. Didn't know I was behind him.'

I said, 'So you think Joe could have had a go at him? Picked a fight?'

'Why not?'

'Would you testify to that?'

'You mean, would I stand up in court with it or would I take Hill's shilling?' She laughed mockingly. 'No. I'd come through with it.'

'You used to know him as a kid,' I said, 'didn't you? That's what he told me. Said you were an old friend of his father's.'

Jill's face clouded. 'That was a long time ago. Longer than I want to think about. Things change.' She looked up at me suddenly. 'You should have seen him them – sweet little boy with golden hair. That was before his dad went posh.'

'What happened between Hill and Clare?'

'He wanted her to sleep with him. She turned him down. It wasn't the first time.'

'When did it happen?'

'A few months ago. Didn't make Hill give up. Hill doesn't give up. Joe was furious about it.'

'How do you know?'

'People told me.'

'Do you know him well?'

She shook her head. 'Not any more. His dad used to drink here. Before he went over the river.'

I said, 'What's he like?'

'Dick's all right. It's the boy you need to watch.'

'You don't need to tell me that,' I said.

'No.' She blew smoke out through her nostrils. 'I don't suppose I do. Had him up last year, didn't they?'

'Yes.'

'Have anything to do with it yourself?'

I said, 'A little. What did Dick Hill think about it?'

'Oh . . .' She snorted. 'Didn't believe a word of it. His boy? Innocent as a lamb.' She laughed. 'You see what you want to, don't you? When it's your own kids.'

'Does he still think that?'

'Ask him, why don't you?'

'How often do you see him?' I said.

'Not much. Not any more. Used to, one time, before he got smart. We were like that, once, Dickie and me. Friend of my old man.'

I said, 'I'd have thought he was older.'

Her eyes went hard. 'He is older.'

'What was he like?' I asked. 'Before he made money. Was he like Hill is now?'

'Dickie? No!' She made a face. 'Not Dickie. He was a charmer. Still is, if it comes to that.'

'Was he straight?'

'As straight as anyone.' She shrugged. 'How straight can you be down the Old Kent Road? Not if you want to leave it. Dickie always knew he was going somewhere.'

'Was he tied up in anything?'

'Nothing he couldn't get himself out of.'

I said, 'Why don't you see him any more? Did you argue?'

'Why do you think?' I waited for her to go on. She looked at me through smoke. 'Dickie could buy me a hundred times over. You don't stay friends when it's like that.' She shrugged. 'Good luck to him.'

'Was there a bust-up? Something to do with Clare and Hill?'

Jill looked at me coldly. 'We just don't see each other.' She ground the cigarette out into a pile of butt-ends on the ashtray. 'I'd still help him if he wanted anything.' She laughed. 'Not that Dickie Hill would ever need my help.'

'Would you go to him?'

'For help?' She looked at me sideways. 'Not if the house was on fire and he had the bucket. That would kill it for good.'

There was a pause.

'How did Joe know that Hill had made a pass at Clare?' I asked.

'Hill never bothered to hide it. What was Joe going to do?' She snorted again. 'Hill had him by the balls. He owed him everything – his job, his dosh. What was he going to do?'

'Did Joe talk about it?'

'Joe always talked.'

I said, 'The night Bates was killed, did he come in here?'

'As usual.'

'Clare thought he'd stopped drinking.'

'That's what she wanted to think.' Again her voice had that half-contemptuous, half-protective note in it.

'What time did he come in?'

'About eight-thirty.'

'How far gone was he?'

'He wasn't. He didn't waste any time, though.'

'Did he become . . . abusive?'

'No more than usual.'

'You didn't like him,' I said.

Jill laughed and stubbed her butt out in an ashtray by the bed. The ashtray was already overflowing. 'You're a smart one, aren't you, dear?'

I said, 'Tell me about Fred James.'

She looked at me. Her eyes were challenging.

'My daughter's fucking him.' It was as if she was forcing herself to speak coldly about Clare, the tough act of a woman who wanted to hide how much she cared about her child. 'You knew that. She told you this morning.'

'Tell me about him.'

'Fred James? He's a wimp.'

'Was he good to her?'

'If you mean good in bed, I don't know. I haven't been to bed with him.'

'Why not?' I asked. 'What's the matter with him?'

She stopped in the act of pulling out another cigarette and looked at me.

'Fucking copper,' she said.

She pulled out the cigarette and reached for the matches.

'You didn't like him either.'

'Fred's all right.'

'Could he have killed Joe?'

She made a face. 'No way.'

'Why not?'

'I told you. He's a wimp.'

'Even with a gun?'

'He wouldn't have known what to do with it.'

I said, 'Does he know Hill?'

'Everyone round here knows Hill.'

'More than everyone?'

'You'd better ask him.'

'Will I find him at the antique shop?'

She laughed. 'Antique shop, my foot,' she said. 'It's a junk shop, dear. Fred James is a rag-and-bone man in a fancy suit. Don't let him fool you.'

'I won't. Did he sell things for Hill?'

'What do you mean?'

I said, 'Was he a fence?'

Her eyes were hard all of a sudden. 'I wouldn't know that.'

'You seem to know everything else.'

She drew smoke in through clenched teeth. Her eyes narrowed. For the first time she'd forgotten that she was naked. Up until then the knowledge of it had come off her like a scent.

Without removing the cigarette she said, 'He trades in Bermondsey Market. You know what the business is like.'

'Why are you trying to protect him?'

'He's my daughter's man.'

I stood up abruptly and looked down at her.

Jill leaned forward off the pillows. She kept the sheet tight across her breasts. She said, 'Fred James was paying protection to a friend of Hill's. That's how he knew him.'

I nodded and kept looking at her, a tough woman in a tough world who'd had to get used to looking after herself.

I said, 'What about you? Do you pay Hill protection as well?'

For a moment she looked her age. The make-up was just on the surface. Underneath it was a fighter tougher than any of the pumped-up men in her gym. Her mouth was a scarlet line.

She said, 'I've got my own protection.'

I turned towards the door. She was smoking normally again.

'You can come back sometime if you like,' she said casually. 'My paper said something about a blue-eyed man.' She laughed. The laugh turned the invitation into a joke, but it didn't quite close the door. Maybe it was a trick she'd learnt to save herself from rejection, a trick she'd learnt when her body began to soften and the face looking back at her in the mirror began to need more make-up.

The door on the first-floor landing was open. Through it I could see punchbags, mattresses, a pair of rings. A black guy was standing just inside the door, watching me come downstairs. He was over six foot, with a barrel chest and the narrow waist of a dancer. He was wearing a blue tracksuit with the sleeves rolled up over massive forearms. His eyes were mean.

I said, 'Good luck against Jimmy Mulligan.'

He said, 'I am Jimmy Mulligan.'

I could feel him watching me all the way down to the bar. Like she said, Jill Cowans had her own protection.

## 17

There was a crowd outside Fred James's antique shop. They were watching two firemen in yellow boots reel a hose into the back of a fire engine. Two other fire engines were pulled up behind it. The pavement and street were wet. Police cars with lights flashing had been drawn up across the street both sides of the shop to stop the traffic. One of the policemen was arguing with a group of kids behind the cordon.

Smoke was still coming out of the shop window, a sour smoke that filled the whole street and dried the back of your mouth. The shop sign was hanging down from one corner, Fred James's name almost obscured by soot. Smoke had scorched the brickwork between the open windows and above the door. In the first-floor windows firemen's heads were moving around. There was the sound of a hose and a cloud of white steam drifted suddenly out of the left-hand window, rose lazily into the air, dissolved.

Fred James Antiques appeared to have gone out of business.

A few pieces of charred furniture were sitting on the pavement outside. They hadn't saved much: a row of forlorn dining chairs, a low sofa with the upholstery blackened, a couple of standard lamps. An old woman was sitting on one of the dining chairs, talking to a fireman.

I walked up to the cordon. One of the policemen recognized me and nodded. My heart was pounding. The tide had crept still further up the beach. It was lapping at the walls of my sandcastle now, sapping away the walls faster than I could build them up again. My anonymous informant had been right about one thing already: Clare Bates's affair with Fred

James. She had told me to ask Fred James about Bates's death; now it didn't look as if she'd waited for me to ask.

'When did this happen?'

I was answered by a small boy in glasses. His eyes were wild with excitement. He said, 'It was a-*mazing*. There was flames everywhere. Shooting out the windows and . . . smoke and . . .'

The policeman said, 'Emergency call about one o'clock, sir. Too late to save the shop. Lucky it didn't spread next door.'

At one o'clock I'd been in the garage where Penny kept his car.

The policeman said, 'You'll find Detective Chief Superintendent Mason inside, sir.'

He said it as if that ought to cheer me up.

I ducked under the cordon and walked across the wet roadway towards the shop. The crowd watched me. Close to, the smell from the shop was almost overpowering. Damp soot was mixed with the musty smell of old furniture, wet brick, sodden upholstery. It was a thick, corrupt smell that caught on the back of the throat like something you couldn't make yourself swallow. It came out of the shop like the filthy breath of a tramp. The paint had blistered on the frames of the windows and wept long streaks of yellow resin. Broken glass filled the entrance.

Inside I stepped over glass and piles of blackened debris. The heat of the fire was gone: it was as cold as an underground cave. A foul, damp wind blew through the shop. There was hardly any light to see by. The ceiling and walls were black, the walls streaked with moisture. Ruined furniture was piled up on either side. The furniture was calcified: fragile black chairs and charcoal tables. I was walking on glass and a spongy mess of carpet and wet books. I trod on something larger and stooped to pick it up: it was a Victorian china doll with blue eyes and yellow hair, its dress singed at the edges. I dropped it and wiped my hand on my coat.

A torch swung towards me from the back of the shop. I

saw white teeth grinning underneath it. A fireman said, 'Mr Mason's upstairs if you want him, sir.'

'Is the owner up there?'

'No.' He kept tramping towards the door. 'They got him out. And the old lady, too.'

I went towards the door he had come from. There was a staircase behind it. The handrail was gone and the treads were sagging. A yellow hose snaked its way up between blackened bannisters. I could hear voices upstairs.

The first floor must have been used as part of the shop. The destruction was the same as downstairs but this time I could see it clearly in the light from broken windows. Mason was standing in the middle of the room, next to a tall man with a lugubrious face and child's lips that stuck out in a pout. The tall man was carrying a black document folder under one arm. Uniformed policemen were nosing around the room, searching the debris on the floor.

'Where the hell have you been?' Mason's voice was angry.

I didn't say anything.

'Good of you to come along. You only missed the start by a couple of hours.'

I ignored that. 'How did it start?'

'You'd better ask her,' Mason said.

He pointed to a thin woman with grey hair who was scraping soot off the walls and smearing it into a polythene bag. A young man was standing behind her with a clipboard.

'Quick off the mark,' I commented.

'More than I could say for you.'

The lugubrious character opened his mouth and gave a single short laugh through his baby lips.

I said, 'Why is he here?'

'I've asked Detective Superintendent Rose to help you with the investigation.'

Something tensed up inside me. I tried to keep my voice under control.

I said, 'This is my case.'

'A fat lot you've been doing about it.'

'I'll give you my report later, sir.'

'I'll look forward to that,' Mason said drily.

I took a step towards him. I could feel the other police-men listening. 'Who's in charge of the investigation?' I asked.

'You are.'

'He's senior to me.'

'So you'll have a wise head to give you advice.'

I said, 'Why didn't you consult me?'

Mason's grey eyes were cold. 'You weren't there to be consulted.'

There was a crash from the back of the room and a policeman cursed. A voice called, 'The floor's gone over here.'

'Where's Fred James?' I said.

'That's what I asked you at nine o'clock this morning.'

I started to say something but Rose interrupted me. 'He's back at the station.'

'Did he have anything to say?'

'He was in shock. His mother was asleep upstairs. They only just got her out.'

'Will we be able to question him?'

Mason said furiously, 'If you'd got to him earlier on –'

'All right,' I said. 'But I didn't. I was following another line.'

'I told you to follow this one.'

I said, 'I don't think this is helpful.'

'You're telling me it isn't.'

We looked away from each other simultaneously. The policemen were making a small stack of objects by the window. The grey-haired woman was talking to her assistant in a clear, precise voice.

'Could it have been an accident?' I asked.

'What do you think?'

I shrugged. 'Is there any reason for it not to be?'

'We're tipped off to look for Fred James during a murder investigation,' said Mason. 'Then Fred James's shop is burned out and his old mother nearly killed. And he thinks it might be an accident.'

Rose opened his baby lips again and gave the same short laugh.

I said, 'All right. What's your idea?'

'Maybe there was something he wanted to get rid of.'

'His mother?'

Mason looked at me. 'Maybe that *was* an accident,' he said. 'Or maybe he didn't have much time. Maybe he thought she was safe.'

'Maybe she set fire to it herself,' I said. 'Maybe it was a suicide attempt.'

'I don't like sarcasm, Havilland.'

'I don't like having people drafted in over my head.'

'Too bad.'

'Besides,' I said, 'the murder investigation is closed. Or did you forget that Hill confessed?'

Mason looked at me. 'No,' he said. 'I hadn't forgotten. Have you forgotten that he's denied he ever signed it?'

Rose opened his mouth and said, 'This isn't an angle we can ignore.' His voice was as gloomy as his face.

I didn't say anything. I couldn't think of a reason why we should ignore it except for Hill's confession, and that was only a reason for me.

Mason shook his head and sighed. 'Let's get back to the station. What time can you let us have something, Lucy?'

'Not before tomorrow morning.' The grey-haired woman's voice was brisk. She didn't turn round.

Rose and I followed Mason downstairs and outside on to the pavement. The crowd was still staring at the shop as if it might burst into flames again. Two of the fire engines had disappeared. One lane of traffic was creeping past the police cars.

We got into Mason's car. Rose sat in front. The back of his head was flat, with coarse red ears sticking out from it.

As levelly as I could, I said, 'I want to speak with you privately, sir.'

'There'll be time for that later.'

'When?'

'After we've interviewed James.'

We stopped in traffic on the New Kent Road and the driver cursed under his breath.

I said, 'Is *he* going to be there?'

I made it as offensive as I could. I didn't want Rose to start thinking I liked him.

'Detective Superintendent Rose has been assigned to your murder squad.'

'I object to that,' I said. There was something cold inside me, as if the sea had broken in and was slowly drowning me from within. I kept my voice steady. 'Can you give me any reason?'

Mason was slumped in the corner of the car. The skin was creased around his eyes. He looked tired. 'Save it, Havilland.'

Rose's thick ears were burning red. In the wing mirror I could see his hands clenched into fists on his lap.

I said, 'Is he a real policeman?'

Mason didn't look out of the window.

'You're close to the wind, Havilland. Bloody close.'

'Fred James was paying protection to Hill,' I said. 'Did anyone tell you that?'

Mason sighed. 'If Hill killed Joe Bates, why would he burn out the shop of someone who had nothing to do with it?'

'Why would anybody?'

'Exactly. The only person who might would be James himself. Particularly when he realized he was going to be taken in.'

'How could he have known that?'

'He could have been tipped off.'

'By?'

'I don't know. Maybe by the same person who tipped us off.'

'That wouldn't make any sense.'

'It doesn't make sense either way.'

'So what do we do?'

'We do what they suggested,' Mason snapped. 'We do what you should have done six hours ago. We ask Fred James.'

## 18

Fred James was a delicate-looking man with a pretty face and a mass of soft brown hair. He had large eyes which looked nervously about the room when they brought him in, as if he was expecting to see instruments of torture. He was wearing the bottom half of an expensive blue suit and carrying the jacket. His shirt was smudged with soot.

Rose was standing by the table, chewing on his baby lips. James tried a smile on him but it fell way short. The smile was a reflex: his eyes were shocked beyond smiling. I wondered how far that smile had got him before; it looked as if it got a lot of use. Maybe it had sold junk repros as valuable antiques; maybe it had got him out of Hills threats; maybe it had got him into Clare's bed. I tried to imagine him with Clare but I found I didn't enjoy it. He had a gigolo's wide lips and a girlish waist. He looked as if he'd fall over if you sneezed at him.

James sat down. His eyes were wide and colourless. They held no expression at all except fear and shock. On one cheek there was a nasty brownish mark, just turning into a bruise.

'How did you get that?' Mason pointed to it.

'The . . . the guys in the cells.'

His voice was a feminine whisper. With enough charm shaken into it, it might have sounded nice.

'Why did they do it?'

'They said . . .' James's voice broke off in a sob.

We could all guess the kind of things they'd said.

Mason sat down opposite James. He kept his eyes on James's face. He spoke in a tired voice, as if we all wanted to get it over and we knew he was going to help us.

'What's your name?'

'Fred James.'

'Full name.'

'William Frederick.'

'Date of birth.'

'First of October, 1963.'

'Address.'

'Fifty-eight, Tower Bridge Road.'

'You lived above the shop?'

'With my mother.'

'Is your mother all right?'

'She's with friends.' James's large eyes were fixed on Mason.

'We're going to ask you some questions, Fred.'

'About the fire?'

'And some other things. What do you know about a man called Joe Bates?'

'I know his wife.' His Adam's apple jerked up when he talked.

'How well?'

He looked at Rose. Rose was fishing in a packet of cigarettes.

Fred James said, 'Can I have a cigarette?'

Mason looked at Rose and nodded. Rose handed him a cigarette and lit it for him. James pulled smoke down into his lungs and coughed. He wiped the back of his hand over his mouth.

I said, 'You're having an affair with her, aren't you?'

'No.'

'She thinks so.'

'I . . .' He took another drag on the cigarette. I thought his eyes were more alert. 'It was a fling,' he said at last.

'She's not that sort of girl.'

He waved one hand vaguely. 'A few times . . .'

I said, 'When did you last see her?'

He looked at Rose as if Rose was going to whisper him the answer. Rose didn't say anything. Fred James shook his head like the question was too hard for him.

Mason asked gently, 'What were you doing on Sunday evening?'

'Which Sunday?'

'Last Sunday.'

'I don't remember.'

'It wasn't that long ago.'

'I . . . I was at home. With my mother.' His voice wobbled when he said 'mother'. It was like a high-wire artist suddenly losing his balance, then picking it up again.

'Did you go out at all?'

'No.'

Rose moistened his lips and said, 'I thought you went to see Clare Bates.'

'No, I didn't.'

He sounded like a kid lying to the teacher. I saw Mason catch Rose's eye. They'd planned this beforehand, planned all of it and cut me out.

Mason said, 'Who burned your shop down?'

'It was an accident.'

'How do you know?'

He wasn't sure of the answer to that. His eyes flickered.

Mason said softly, 'We'll get the lab reports tomorrow. You can't hide it these days. Those boys can look down a microscope and tell what sort of match you used.'

'I . . . I didn't.'

Rose said, 'Look what we found.'

He stepped forward to the table, took a gun out of his pocket and laid it down in front of Fred James.

James's eyes widened. He stared at it.

It was an ordinary handgun with a chipped metal handle. A .38.

'In the rubble,' said Mason. 'Our boys can find a needle in the proverbial. Arson never was a good way to hide things.' He said arson like it was something we'd all accepted.

James's eyes were fixed on the object in front of him. They held a mixture of horror and fascination. It was like the way a kid would look at a gun.

I moistened my lips and tried to swallow. I didn't want my voice to give anything away. I said, 'When did Hill's friends last collect protection from you?'

Mason cut me short. He said, 'There's time enough for that. Tell me about the gun, Fred.'

Fred James shook his head. 'I never saw it before.'

'It was in your shop.'

Rose said, 'Doesn't look like an antique.'

'I kept it there for safety.'

'I thought you never saw it before.'

'I . . .' He swung round suddenly and looked at me. He had a thin face with a straight nose in it. He would have been a handsome guy but he was shaking too hard for me to see him properly.

Mason said, 'Tell us about shooting Joe Bates.'

James's eyes wandered off my face. He seemed to have lost track of where he was.

'We found it in the office,' Rose said. 'Underneath your chest of drawers. Same calibre as the one that killed Joe.'

'Would have been easier to drop it in the river,' said Mason conversationally. 'Unless you had something else to hide. Did you have something else to hide, Fred?'

Mason and Rose had taken on the playground bully tone policemen use when they know they're in control.

I said, 'How come you didn't get your mother out first?'

A gasping sound came from James's mouth. Mason shot me an angry look. He leaned over the table and spoke very rapidly. 'You went over to Clare Bates's place about midnight, didn't you? You waited for Joe to come back. When he came past you jumped out and pulled the gun on him. That's right, isn't it, Fred?'

No sound came from Fred James. His head had dropped almost to the table.

Rose said, 'Save yourself trouble if you owned up. We're going to charge you anyway.'

It was a two-man act and I wasn't part of it. I was a spectator. I felt like I ought to be cheering them on, but I wasn't in the mood for cheering.

There was a long, long pause. When Fred James's voice came, it was almost too quiet to hear.

'If someone starts something with you, then it's not killing, is it?'

'What do you mean, Fred?'

'If someone pulls a gun on you ... unprovoked. And there's a fight ... Well, then, it's just manslaughter, right?'

'Did he pull a gun on you?'

Fred James's eyes were fixed intently on Mason's, almost as if he was trying to seduce him. He had long, delicate eyelashes like a girl's.

'Yes.' He nodded several times. 'I didn't know he was carrying it, see? Do you see?'

We'd all seen this before. He'd given up; it was all about to come out.

Mason said gently, 'Tell us from the start.'

Fred James looked down at the ground. His hands were trembling.

'I didn't mean to kill him,' he said at last. 'You do believe that, don't you?' His voice was South London all of a sudden. The layers of smoothness and charm had peeled away like flaking varnish, and left Fred James back where he started: the small pretty kid on his knees in the playground with three big boys standing around him.

'But you did kill him?'

Mason's voice. Again, there was a pause.

'Yes ... No. I was just trying to keep the gun away from me. That's not killing somebody, is it? Not if it's not your fault.'

'Tell us from the start.'

Mason was watching him like a patient hunter waiting for the prey to inch closer to the trap.

'I just wanted to have it out with him – you see? To talk to him about it. I didn't know he'd be carrying a gun. I wanted to talk to him about the way he treated Clare.'

He looked up suddenly. He was speaking to Mason alone. Rose and I might as well not have been there. His voice was stronger now. He had got into his stride. He might have been back in the shop, selling a line to some customer who had just walked in. He was willing us to believe him.

'Clare didn't know I was going to. She wouldn't have let me. She didn't want Joe to know anything. But I tell you ...' He shook his head. 'If you'd seen what she went through. I was just going to tell him to knock it off. I didn't want to see him with his mates around so I waited near his home. Understand?'

'Go on. You waited by his home. Where did you wait?'

He frowned. 'Outside. In the alley. It was hours before he came along. I thought he might get rough but ... I didn't know he'd have a gun on him.' His eyes were shocked again.

'Were you carrying anything?' Rose interrupted. 'Quite a risk to take with a man like Bates.'

'I only wanted to talk to him.'

'All right,' Mason said. 'Go on.'

'I almost missed him when he came past. He was walking quickly with his hands in his coat pockets ... like this. I jumped out and called after him ... I told him to wait a minute because I wanted a word with him.'

There was a pause. It took all of my strength just to keep my face immobile.

'And then?' Rose prompted.

'When he saw me he went ape. He was drunk – really drunk like I hadn't seen him before. He came running towards me and took a swing at me. He had his hands round my neck. I could feel something in his pocket ... I didn't know what it was.' He broke off with a sob.

'Did he pull the gun on you?'

'That's when I realized. I thought I was going to ... die.' He brought it out with a gulp. 'We were struggling. It seemed like it went on for hours. Suddenly there was a bang ...'

He stopped. He had both hands in the air, trying to describe the scene.

'It must have gone off. He must have got his hand on it and it went off. All of a sudden Joe went limp. His knees gave under him. I didn't understand at first. I kept hitting him. Then he fell over . . .' James stopped abruptly. He took a pull of the cigarette. A long tail of ash fell on his fingers. There was silence in the interview room.

'What happened next?' Mason said quietly.

James's voice was weak again, as if the effort of confession had exhausted him. 'I don't remember. I remember being at home. I hid the gun in the office.'

Rose said, 'How many shots went off?'

'I . . . I don't know.' He looked nervously up at Rose. 'Two? I don't remember.'

'Did you talk to Clare that evening?'

'No. She doesn't know I did it.'

'Did you tell anybody you did it?'

'No. Only you.'

There was silence. Suddenly I realized that Mason was looking at me. I stared him back, but I couldn't have spoken.

Rose said, 'Will you sign that if we write it out for you, Fred?'

His shoulders drooped. He whispered, 'Do I have to?'

'It'll be easier for you if you do.'

'What'll they charge me with?'

'We don't know that yet, Fred.'

He looked at Mason. 'It wasn't murder,' he said. 'Honest to God, it wasn't murder. I didn't kill him. Sometimes you don't even go to jail for manslaughter, do you? They let you off . . .' His voice tailed off.

'Will you help us write it out?'

'Yes.' You could almost see his spirit ebbing away.

'And sign it?'

There was a pause. 'I want a lawyer.' His voice had faded almost to a whisper again, like when he had first come in.

Mason pushed back his chair. He said, 'Get him a lawyer.'

## 19

I followed Mason upstairs to his office. We passed a lot of people on the stairs but nobody wanted to look me in the eye.

He led me into the office, put his case down on the desk and shut the door. I didn't sit down.

Mason said, 'A day ago nobody knew who killed Joe Bates, now we've got murderers coming out of our damned ears. What do you have to say to that?'

I didn't have anything to say to that.

He sat down and hunched over his desk.

'You're all wrong, Havilland. I knew it from the first day you walked in. I should have got rid of you then, except you were the blasted star pupil and I couldn't touch you.'

I didn't say anything. There wasn't anything to say. All I could do was wait for it to finish.

'I was building a team here,' Mason went on. 'Do you know what that means? A team. A group of lads who'll work together, and trust each other ... who know what they're about. But you didn't want that, did you? You wanted to do it your own way. When did I ever see you down in the canteen? You're a loner and there's no room for loners in my patch.'

I said, 'There's more than one way of doing things.'

I should have kept my mouth shut. Mason looked sharply at me.

'No, there isn't,' he said. 'There's a straight way and a crooked way. You chose crooked.'

'I don't know what you mean.'

His rusted grey eyes were cold, unyielding.

He said, 'Don't play with me.'

His hands were clasped above the desk.

'When I joined the force,' Mason said, 'being a policeman was simple. You caught a villain, handed him over to the lawyers, then went back and caught some more. We didn't think we were anything except coppers doing a decent day's work. What's wrong with that? Why isn't that good enough for you?' He was getting into his stride now. His voice was rising. 'If we couldn't get the evidence we let them go. If they got lucky in the courts we waited till the next time. You probably think I'm old-fashioned, is that it?'

I didn't say anything.

He shouted, 'Is that it?'

'No, sir.'

'In twenty years the only bent copper I met was a fellow who turned the blind eye because they were blackmailing him for being a pansy. Now you only have to open the blasted newspaper and it looks like we're all in league with the villains. Do you think I like that? Do you think it's good for the police? I don't pretend to know what you're doing in this outfit . . . Whatever it is, is it doing it any good?'

My head was beginning to swim.

'Were there any witnesses to Hill's confession?' he snapped.

'No.'

'Isn't that funny.'

He slammed his hand down on the surface of the desk. There was a long silence.

Very quietly he said, 'I think you wrote it for him.'

There was no sound at all in the office. There might have been nothing in the room except Mason's angry eyes staring at me.

He said, 'Did you?'

More silence. My mouth felt as if it was full of dust.

'Yes,' I said.

The word lay on top of the silence, as if the silence was something solid that stopped it from fading away.

Mason's voice, when it came, was full of disgust. 'I hate a

bent copper.' There were angry lines around his mouth and eyes.

I said, 'I still think Hill did it.'

'Fred James doesn't think so. Fred James thinks he did it.'

I didn't say anything.

'Well?'

'I don't believe him.'

'You don't believe him!' Mason laughed bitterly. 'That's flipping rich, that is . . .' He leaned towards me over the desk. 'Anyway, it's not the point, is it? You rigged a confession. All the hours we put in trying to keep a lid on this area, trying to talk people into going straight, and a blasted copper starts to cheat the system. I could –'

He didn't tell me what he could do. He didn't have to.

'How long have you been in this squad?' he asked.

'Four years.'

'So how many other confessions have you rigged? What else is in the closet? What are we going to find when we go through your files?'

'Nothing,' I said. 'Good convictions. Nothing else.'

'Oh . . .' He laughed again. 'You're all indignant now. How could anyone suggest George Havilland broke the rules . . . Do you know what that sounds like, coming from you?'

I didn't say anything.

'Well?'

I said, 'This is the first time. There isn't anything else.'

'Why?' He almost shouted the question.

'To make sure he didn't get out of it again,' I said. 'Like Paddy Moran. Like every other time we've ever put our fingers on him. Is that what you want?'

'It's better than this!' Mason's eyes blazed at me. 'It's better than bent coppers taking the law into their own hands and . . . using it to fight feuds . . .'

'It's not a feud.'

'So what would you call it?'

'Hill did it,' I said. 'He killed Paddy Moran and he killed Joe Bates. If we have to bend the rules to make sure he pays for it, then –' I broke off.

142

'Then it's all right?'

'I don't know,' I said.

'If you break the rules then you're no better than he is. You understand? That's all there is to it.'

'No,' I said. 'Not if it means he gets away with it again.'

'And you'll do whatever you need to achieve that?'

'Within reason, yes.'

'Except the trouble is,' said Mason, 'that this time it wasn't him who did it. It was Fred James. You fucked up.'

I took a deep breath.

'Fred James killed him,' Mason went on. 'And you're left waving a false confession and bullshitting me about how Hill deserved it anyway. Do you know what you sound like? Hill could have gone down for life.'

'He would have deserved it.'

'That's not for you to say,' said Mason. He rubbed his eyes with both hands. 'Or me. Hill didn't do this and you know it. Don't even bother denying it.'

'So you want him out on the streets?'

'That's where he belongs. Until he does something real.'

I said, 'You mean, until he finds another Paddy Moran?'

'If need be, yes.'

'Isn't that a bit hard on the Paddy Morans?'

'So what's the alternative?' Mason was angry again. 'Just tell me that. Who decides who stays in and who goes out? You? Don't make me laugh, you're a fucking bent copper. What do you know about justice? You thought you were the one who chose, and you were wrong.'

I didn't say anything.

Mason sighed. 'I could throw you to the wolves,' he said. 'The press would eat you for breakfast – do you know that? What do you think your face would look like on the front page? Detective Chief Inspector Havilland – *former* Chief Inspector Havilland – seen entering court . . . You know the only reason I don't do that? Because it would hurt the rest of us. It would hurt Cayman, and Rose, and me. It would hurt all the straight coppers who work hard, and keep their noses clean, and who just about keep this city from falling into the hands of the villains. That's the only reason. You understand? The only reason there is.'

He got up and turned to the window. Outside the traffic snarled along Kennington Road. There was the distant sound of a siren.

He said, 'I'm putting you on suspension. I'll decide what to do with you later.'

I wanted to answer that, but no answer would have been good enough. The tide had come in; my sandcastle was in ruins.

Mason turned and looked out of the window. 'Get out,' he said.

I took a deep breath. 'What about Hill?'

Mason said, 'He was released an hour ago.'

## 20

I walked out into the main office. Everything seemed to be running in slow motion, as if the room was filling up with green water and we were all floating in it. Backs were turned to me in slow motion; the conversation came from far away, from somewhere under the sea. I went to my office. There was nothing in it that mattered to me. From the pinboard I took down the photograph of Miles Davis and put it in my pocket. I opened and closed the top drawer. There was nothing in it I needed. Through the door I was dimly aware that the outer room was emptying, as if everyone in it was being drawn away by a tide that didn't touch me. Doors banged in the corridor outside.

The desk officer glanced quickly at me when I came downstairs, then buried his face in the report book.

Outside it was raining, a steady downpour like a second flood. I hesitated for a moment, then turned right. People stared at me as they brushed past. I felt a cold wind blowing through my coat. Suddenly I was vulnerable; I was one of them. A shoulder barged into me and someone cursed. I looked at the passing faces: men and women; a pensioner leaning on her shopping basket; a child towed along by a dog. I felt as if I'd spent my life standing on a bridge and now someone had pushed me over into the current below. It tugged at me, pulled me under, froze my arms and legs. I was just one of them, an ordinary sinner with a bad conscience walking along a pavement in South London. Late commuters passed me, hurrying towards the trains. At the lights two kids were washing windscreens from a bucket of dirty water. I kept walking towards Waterloo. There were crowds spilling out from a bar under the arches: tramps and idlers, men in suits who didn't want to go home to their wives. The ground shook as a train rumbled overhead.

I crossed The Cut, passed a brightly lit theatre, turned right beyond it. Babylon was crowded, a garish crowd spilling out on to the pavement. There were men with thick necks and tans, girls dressed up with elaborate hairdos and too much make-up. They were drinking bottles of beer and cocktails the colour of boiled sweets. The talk was loud, fast and hysterical. Inside the bar, music was thumping from loudspeakers. I pushed my way through the crowd, and dug out a space at the bar. Harry was working the other end. Another barman, a man with gypsy looks and a ponytail, was spraying tonic water out of a hose.

'Where's Hill?' I had to shout it.

'He's not in tonight.'

He dropped the hose and hurried back along the bar. I stood there dazed. It hadn't crossed my mind that Hill might not be there. I couldn't understand it. I had come to find Hill and he wasn't there. I felt as if I had been climbing up a staircase and missed the top step.

The man next to me was a tall black guy in a hound's-tooth suit and a tie pin. He was holding a fifty-pound note to attract the barmen's attention.

He snapped the fifty down on the counter and said, 'Mother-fucking slow sons of bitches.'

He said it too loud; some heads turned. Harry punched the till and came running. When he saw me his face went dead. I kept my eyes on his face while he took the order. He brought the drinks and put change down on the counter in a white saucer.

'Where's Hill?' I said.

Harry said, 'No way.' His voice was jumpy.

'Where is he?'

'I should never have talked to you.'

I said, 'Why, what did he do to you?' I had to shout over the noise of the music.

He gave a twisted smile and his eyes filled up with tears.

A tanned man in a white T-shirt elbowed in next to me. 'Bacardi and coke, mate. Two of 'em.'

I nodded at Harry and he turned round to get the order. His face was tense. When he was done he turned back to me.

'Now you tell me where Hill is.'

'He's not here.'

'When's he coming back?'

'Don't know.'

'Have you seen him?'

'Don't know.'

He was standing with both hands on the counter. I leaned over and put my elbow across the back of his fingers, putting all my weight behind it. His mouth snapped open but no sound came out.

'What time was he here?'

'About four-thirty.' His voice was a gasp of pain.

'Did he say where he was going?'

Harry shook his head.

'You're going to tell me some more about Sunday night.'

He nodded, begging me to take the weight off. I released his hand and he rubbed the crushed fingers.

'Get me a whisky.'

He got me a whisky. It tasted thick and warm, and the noise of the bar began to recede. The other barman was shooting odd glances at us.

I said, 'Who was the third guy Hill and Joe Bates were talking to on Sunday night?'

'I told you, I don't know.'

'Describe him.'

'Middle-aged. Big fellow, brown hair. He had a plummy voice.'

'Did you hear a name?'

'No.'

'All right. How did he arrive?'

'I didn't see. A cab, I think.'

'A black cab?'

'I think so.'

'What about when he left?'

Harry shrugged. 'He just left. Car must have come for him.'

'What type of car?'

'I don't know.' He was starting to back away from me.

I said, 'Get me another of these.'

He filled it up halfway and dropped a cube of ice into it.

'If you see Hill,' I said, 'you won't tell him what I said. That's better for both of us.'

He shook his head. His eyes were bitter with the humiliation of someone who knew he was easy to hurt.

I said, 'You shouldn't be working here.'

'You shouldn't be drinking.'

I picked my glass up and turned away from the bar. The bouncer had spotted me. His eyes followed me as I pushed my way to the back of the room but he didn't make a move. A girl with straight blonde hair was standing by herself near the sofa, swaying slightly.

I said, 'Do you know where the phone is?'

She tilted her head towards a door in the corner. It was a stainless steel door with a porthole. I pushed through it and found myself in a black-painted corridor. A black guy with a belly was standing half inside the door to the men's toilet. He was talking to somebody inside who I couldn't see. He sized me up, then kept on talking. From one pocket he took out a wad of cash and passed it to the man inside.

I didn't let him catch my eye. I walked to the phone, picked it up and dialled a number. It rang four times, then there was a click. The voice on the machine was Clare's. She sounded cool and matter-of-fact, unlike the noise inside my head. I hung up, dialled again and got the machine again. I didn't leave a message.

Above the phone was an advertisement for a minicab company. On impulse I picked up the phone again and dialled the number.

A voice said, 'South London Cabs.'

I said, 'I'm calling from Babylon, a bar on Southwark Bridge Road. I had a cab from here on Sunday night. I think I left something in it.'

The voice said, 'What's your name?'

'You didn't have my name. Harry called the cab for me.'

'What time was it?'

'About eleven.'

'Wait a minute, please.'

I waited. The black guy in the toilet doorway had stopped talking and was watching me. He was still holding money in his hands.

'Hello?'

'Yes?'

'We did make a pick-up from Babylon at that time but there was nothing left in the car. What was it you lost?'

I said, 'Nothing important. It was a scarf. Can you do something else for me?'

'Go ahead.'

'I want a cab tomorrow morning. The same driver. Ten o'clock.'

'Does it have to be the same driver?'

'He had an honest face,' I said.

I gave her my name and address and hung up. I walked towards the men's toilet.

'Excuse me.'

The fat guy's eyes went mean. He pressed himself back against the doorframe but didn't step aside. I squeezed past him. There was nobody inside, but one of the cubicle doors was shut. The urinal was a sheet of white glass with water trickling down in. I kept my eye on the fat guy's reflection. He didn't make a move. The whisky was buzzing inside my head. It hadn't made me feel any better but at least Mason's face had blurred at the edges and his voice had receded. The fat guy's body swayed in the curtain of water. I tried to remember what I was there for. To see Hill, of course. Hill's thatch of white hair appeared in front of me. I zipped up my flies and turned towards the door. The fat guy was still watching me. He pushed himself back against the door-frame.

I said, 'What's the matter, can't you make up your mind whether you want to go or not?'

Outside the bouncer was waiting for me. His eyes were flat and hard. 'What are you doing here?'

'Enjoying myself like everybody else.'

His mouth made a single movement. 'Out.'

'Of course, not everyone's enjoying themselves,' I said. 'Some people are working.' I jerked my head towards the toilets.

The girl with the long blonde hair was watching us. She had a serene meaningless smile, like she wanted us both to be happy.

'Out.'

He was moving in on me, his chest stuck out the way he'd been taught when he was boxing. I didn't step back.

I said, 'Didn't Hill tell you not to hit policemen?'

'You're not on duty.'

He pointed to the empty glass I was holding.

His eyes were flat and hard. Suddenly I didn't have the stomach for it. The room seemed too crowded, too loud, too small. Hard voices were shouting at me. The blonde girl rocked on her feet. I wasn't a policeman anymore, I was down in the bear pit, down there with Hill and the rest of them. Behind the bouncer's shoulder I could see Harry watching us. I shoved the bouncer to one side and started walking before he could regain his balance. He followed me. He wanted everyone to see me going without a fight, but I didn't care any more. The guy in the hound's-tooth suit was standing by the door talking to a white girl in a leather mini-skirt. I pushed past him and walked out into the rain.

## 21

Clare Bates looked surprised but she managed not to slam the door in my face. I thought that was a good sign.

'Can I come in?'

She had to think about that one, but in the end she stepped back into the hallway and let me past. There was a single small furrow between her eyebrows. I didn't know what it meant.

I said, 'I tried to call earlier.'

'I was with my mum.'

'I met your mum.'

'She told me.'

The whisky wanted to give me away. It kept jumping about in my throat, trying to get out and tell Clare that I wasn't there to ask questions about her husband or to chat about her mother: I was there because there was nowhere else on earth I could go except a flat which didn't recognize me any more; and because, for some reason which I didn't want to think about too closely, I had caught myself trying to work out excuses to see her again. I was there because that was the only place I'd been in months which didn't smell of fear, or greed, or evil; because I couldn't forget her wounded look when I bullied her at the station – although I saw a lot of wounded looks – and because she was clean and honest, and I'd forgotten what it was like being with someone like that. The whisky wanted to tell her that even though I looked like a suspended policeman with drink on his breath and an axe hanging over his head, I could actually be quite pleasant, and underneath it all there'd been a human being, once, although we'd lost touch a long time ago. It wanted to ask her for help.

I said, 'Do you mind if we sit down?'

'Of course.'

She led me into the living room. It looked the same as it had earlier except for the pushchair parked in one corner. A book was lying opened out on the coffee table.

'You were reading.'

'Oh . . . yes.'

'I'm sorry to disturb you.'

Quite soon I'd have to start using sentences longer than five words, and saying things that meant something. The whisky was still making suggestions but I wasn't far enough gone to listen to it.

'Have you eaten?'

'I ate with my mum. I'm sorry, can I get you something?'

I said, 'Thank you. A coffee.'

She went into the kitchen. I picked up the book. It was a romantic novel, something about a secretary falling in love with her boss, or a frog turning into a prince. She'd probably had enough of princes who turned into drunken thugs with three bullets in their neck on a pavement outside the front door of the castle.

Clare appeared in the kitchen door. 'I didn't know policemen stayed on duty so late.'

'I'm not on duty.'

The half-smile — maybe it was no more than a quarter-smile — disappeared from her face. She went back into the kitchen and I heard her banging teaspoons.

She came back in with two cups of coffee and sat down in the middle of the other sofa. That was one cushion closer than last time.

'I'm afraid it's decaff,' she said. 'I don't keep real.'

Was that the way she'd responded to Joe Bates when he forced his way into the flat, drunk and incoherent? Talk trivialities, talk wallpaper, talk decaff. Pretend that everything's normal. Hope the prince doesn't turn into a thug in front of your very eyes.

I said, 'I'm not on duty because they suspended me this afternoon.'

She sipped coffee to save herself from having to look at me.

'Why?' Her voice was small and cold.

'I think Hill killed your husband. Hill's good at getting off things. After Paddy Moran . . .' I stopped. I'd almost forgotten her husband had been involved in that as well. I said, 'Hill did kill Moran. I think Joe was involved in it as well. Maybe you know that, too.' She didn't say anything. I went on: 'He used money to buy half the jury and paid a lawyer to sweet-talk the other half. That's how he was let off. I didn't want that to happen again so I wrote a confession for him. When Fred James confessed they found out about it.'

I looked at her. She wasn't looking at me.

'You did know about Fred's confession?'

Her head moved slowly up and down. 'I heard his shop burned down. I was trying to find out where he was.'

There was a long silence. Slowly Clare's face emptied of everything. It was like someone smoothing out a sheet. She came out looking tired, older, more like her mother. Her grey eyes stayed on my face.

'Were you surprised?'

'Surprised? God . . .!'

I closed my eyes. 'I mean . . . Did you think he could have done it?'

'He said he did.' Her eyes were confused. Suddenly she shook her head. 'I don't understand.'

'Fred confessed to it. But there are things in his confession that don't make any sense. I think someone might have forced him to.'

'So why would he say he did?'

'I don't know yet.'

Clare's eyes wandered off my face and looked around the room. She whispered 'Poor Fred.'

I said gently, 'They'll let you see him if you want to.'

She shook her head.

'I can get a message to him.'

She thought for a moment, then shook her head again. There was a long silence.

I said, 'Could Fred have killed Joe? You told me before that he was too gentle to hurt anybody.'

'No . . . I don't know. I don't know anything any more.'

She covered her eyes with one hand. I sat forward in my chair.

'I don't think he did,' I said. 'I really believe that. If it's any comfort.'

'Thank you.' Her voice was numb.

There was a pause.

'What about the police?' she asked. 'I mean . . . the other policemen . . .'

She looked embarrassed.

'It's OK,' I said. 'The real police. I don't know. At the moment they're still patting themselves on the back about Fred's confession. There's a chance they'll start to see the holes for themselves, but they probably won't want to. They've already let Hill out.'

'He's free?'

'I wanted to warn you about that. There's a chance he'll come here.'

Clare said, 'Oh God.'

'Could you go to your mother's for a few days?'

'I'd rather stay here.'

'I'll give you my number. If anything happens, don't just call the police, call me as well. Even if he just rings up.'

'Yes.'

There was a pen lying on the table. I wrote my number on the fly-leaf of her book, then put my name after it in case she'd forgotten it.

'Will you do that?'

'Yes. Thank you.' She got up suddenly. 'I'm sorry, I need a drink. What about you? I suppose you're allowed to now . . .'

It was nice of her to pretend she hadn't smelled the whisky. I said I needed a drink too and from somewhere in the kitchen she brought out a bottle of white wine and two glasses. It didn't taste of much after the whisky, but it was cold and soft, and Mason's face became a little more blurred.

With a bit of effort I might even be able to push him under the surface.

Clare got back on the sofa and curled her legs up under her. She'd reached my end of the sofa.

'What will you do,' I asked, 'if Fred's let out?'

Clare looked at me. 'My husband's been killed and my ex-boyfriend's in prison for killing him. I . . . I don't even dare to think about the future any more.'

'Ex-boyfriend?' I said sharply.

Clare wasn't looking at me. She held the wine glass by its stem and revolved it slowly between her fingers. She didn't say anything.

'I didn't know it had finished,' I said.

'It's been coming to an end for a long time now.'

'You didn't tell me that yesterday.'

She shrugged. 'There wasn't any reason to tell you.'

'It could help him. If they knew.'

'I hadn't even told Fred yet.'

'Told him what?'

'Oh . . . that it was over. I decided a long time ago.' She gave a bitter smile. 'It seems a long time. Last week.'

'How would he have taken it?'

'He wouldn't have been angry or anything, if that's what you mean. Fred wasn't like that.'

I noticed she was using the past tense.

I said, 'You ought to tell them it was finishing. It might just help him.'

'Maybe.'

'What . . .?' I began, then I realized I didn't have a question, at least not one I could ask her then. The things I wanted to know were too big. I said 'Why wasn't it working?'

'Because it started wrong. If something starts wrong you can never put it right. It stays with you. I'd always have felt guilty about Fred, even if he does get out of all this. Even if he didn't . . . kill Joe.'

The last two words were too much. She turned her face away.

'Please . . .'

'No.' She put her hand out. 'I'll be OK. Can we talk about something else? Tell me . . .' She turned her face back towards me. Her eyes were tight shut. 'Did you really make up Hill's confession? I can't believe that.'

'Yes.'

'Why?' she asked.

'I told you.'

'Is that a good enough reason?'

'No.'

'I can't imagine you doing that.'

It was the first personal thing she'd said to me, the first time she seemed to have noticed me as something other than the law. Maybe it was the wine, or maybe it was because I wasn't the law any more.

I said, 'A year ago I couldn't have imagined myself. The trouble with being a policeman is you spend too much time with criminals.'

'How long have you been a policeman?'

'Are you really interested?'

'It's better than . . . talking about anything else. If you don't mind.'

'Ten years,' I said. 'I've been in this job for four.'

She took a sip of her wine. She was only half listening to what I was saying.

'That's a long time. What does it do to your home life?'

What had it done to my home life?

I thought of the friends I hadn't made the effort to keep up with, the evenings I'd come home late and fallen into bed. I thought of the holidays I hadn't taken and the parties I'd been too tired to go to.

I thought about times when everyone was talking about their jobs and I was smiling because you can't tell your friends about the Asian kid's face after four skinheads jumped him; or the tramp you found who didn't have a face at all any more; or the woman whose husband used to beat her in front of the children until one night she stuck a corkscrew through the side of his head and dialled 999 herself and cried when the ambulancemen told her he would make it. They lived in a different city, and cities are built on the common illusion of security. So you don't tell them anything, you keep it inside. And gradually the phone stops ringing, and you stop seeing them.

I thought about Mary, who even before Hill had started to resent the evenings alone and the anger that used to walk into the flat with me.

I didn't want to tell Clare about that empty flat, the kitchen with the empty cupboards, the bare walls which no longer had Mary's pictures on them. I didn't want to think about it myself.

I said, 'It isn't easy. There's too much that you can't share. That's why most policemen spend all their time with other policemen.'

'You mean, nobody else understands?'

'Partly that. And partly you don't want to have to tell other people about it.'

'If I was married to a policeman I'd want to know.'

'No, you wouldn't.'

'Anyway, doesn't it make it easier to share it?'

I thought of the photographs on Mason's desk: the red-faced woman and the garden in Wimbledon.

'For some people. Maybe they're the ones who last longest. I could never bear to.'

'Why not?'

'Because you don't want to hurt people you care about.'

'Why would it hurt them?'

'It would hurt them to know what's going on. And what you're doing every day. If they cared about you.'

She said, 'I suppose that means you aren't married.'

'I nearly was.'

'What happened?'

'She found someone else.'

'That's not fair.'

'It was my fault.'

'Why?'

'It was after the Moran case. Things changed. I changed.'

'Then it's Hill's fault . . .' She stopped. One hand had flown to her mouth. She was blushing.

She said, 'I'm sorry. I'm being inquisitive.'

'That's all right.' I didn't mind her being inquisitive.

'What do you do to take your mind off it?'

'Listen to music. Jazz.'

'I don't know anything about jazz. Why that?'

I didn't answer for a moment. Why jazz? I saw a man lying in a street, somewhere in a Midlands town. By a chain of thought she couldn't have followed, I said, 'How old were you when your father died?'

She frowned. 'Sixteen. Why?'

'I just wondered.'

'Poor Dad. I wish he was here now.'

'Were you close to him?'

'I don't know. I felt as if I was. Even if . . . A father, it's not a gap you can fill.'

I didn't say anything.

'We're getting morbid.' She closed her eyes. When she opened them again she looked worn out. 'I'm sorry, I . . . I'm tired now. I suppose it's the wine.'

She looked at me dispassionately. We'd both of us done things we shouldn't have and neither of us knew how to escape from them. One strand of her hair had come loose and was hanging over her forehead. Suddenly I realized that she was crying. I opened my mouth. I was going to say something stupid, or else the whisky was.

Clare turned her face away. She said, 'Please . . .'

I stood up. The room veered away to the left but I managed to keep up with it.

I said, 'I'm sorry. I shouldn't have come.'

It wasn't what I meant but I didn't know how to say what I meant.

'That's all right. I'm glad you came . . . It's better when there's someone to talk to.'

She didn't look up at me. The glass hung down from her fingers. There was a damp stain on the rug. I couldn't think of anything else that might comfort her.

I hesitated for a moment, then crossed the room quietly and let myself out.

## 22

The access decks of the estate were lit up in a dim orange glare that showed rows of doors, the silent stair towers, no people. The tower blocks loomed above them, a few lights still shining on the upper floors. It felt like being in a prison. A sickly glare shone back from the pavement, which was still greasy after the rain.

There was no light on the stairs. I made my way down by feel, one hand on the cold, damp brick, the other out in front of my face. There was a smell of urine. Outside a cold wind was blowing. It carried with it the smell of wet roads, of silent brick houses, of the empty forecourts of filling stations. London at night. As I came out on to Kennington Lane I stopped for a moment and leaned against the wall. I felt as if I had already walked a hundred miles. My legs wanted to stop there, to fold up on the pavement like an old tramp's and wait for dawn. The lights of passing cars dazzled me.

I had to think hard to work out which way to go. Somewhere behind me in the darkness Clare was preparing for bed, tidying the flat, trying not to think about anything. I pushed myself off the wall and turned up Kennington Road. The smell of wet leaves plucked at me from the gardens along one side. Behind them tall houses reared up, their windows curtained and blank. I wondered what time it was. To pull my left wrist from my pocket felt like too much effort. Ahead of me the pavement was a narrow thread, trees on one side, gardens on the other. By concentrating hard I managed to keep it running in a straight line. Any lapse of concentration and it would start writhing, swelling like a river in flood, breaking into pieces. The end of it would rear up and crack like a whip: I would be hurled into the dark, wet roadway.

I watched my shadow stretching in front of me until it broke up and a new, hard shadow was chasing me from behind. Voices were ringing in my ears. Mason's voice: 'I'm putting you on suspension.' Clare Bates's voice, and the voice of Fred James confessing to murder. A streetlamp clicked out ahead of me and the ribbon of pavement was cut. I heard my footsteps stamping beneath me as if they were trying to keep the stones down. I was in an unreal world where truth no longer seemed to indicate any direction; it had come loose from its moorings, was drifting, waiting for any of us to claim it.

My footsteps echoed back from the garden walls like the footsteps of a stranger. Was that my shadow, or the shadow of some distorted creature clinging to my back? In my ears I could hear a faint droning. Maybe it was the traffic; or the crowd in Babylon; or the crackle of flames through Fred James's old furniture. I could still see the contempt in Mason's eyes. As far as he was concerned I was finished: I had forfeited any trust I ever possessed. His eyes hung in front of me, two streetlights casting shadows both sides of me. I wondered if I was ever going to make it home. Perhaps I should just give up, settle down in a dark gap between lights and wait for someone to find me. They would shake my shoulder in the morning, shout to make themselves heard above the roar of traffic.

I shook my head. I had almost fallen asleep as I walked.

I waited alone at the bus stop. When the bus came it was almost empty. The conductor swayed at the back, dozing, little snatches of melody escaping from his lips. Opposite me there was a middle-aged black woman in a hat. Her eyes snapped away whenever I looked at her. Suddenly I realized what I must look like. I was every late traveller's nightmare: the mad guy, the one who talks to you, or follows you home from the tube. The one who tears apart your cocoon of anonymity. The black woman stared rigidly over my shoulder. Her eyes were full of the fear which lives in all city dwellers always: that anyone who isn't for you is against you; that it might, it just might, happen to you. Her whole body was tense. The conductor hummed, crooning away the fear, crooning to keep himself awake. Outside London drifted past like a dark sea that we were floating on: waves of houses, junctions, the sudden rise and fall of the river.

I leaned forward and said, 'Do you go up to Marble Arch?'

The conductor looked at me. He nodded without interrupting his crooning. The woman opposite had relaxed: I was as lost as she was.

I got off at the top of Bayswater Road and began walking towards my flat. I was cold now and my head hurt. I didn't want to think any more, I just wanted to get to bed. A few cars passed. The park, on my left, was dark.

I crossed over and turned up my street. When I reached my steps the light clicked on.

It didn't need to. There was enough light coming out through the open front door.

I stopped dead. Somewhere in my head bells started jangling. My brain wouldn't connect. The key was in my pocket; how could the door be open?

Slowly, as quietly as I could, I went down the steps and pushed the door wide. There was a noise in the front room. I couldn't see anything through the window: the curtains were drawn. I went into the hallway and opened the door to the living room.

It looked as if it had been at the centre of an earthquake.

There wasn't much to destroy in there, but it had been destroyed. Records lay broken all over the floor; the sofa had been overturned; mangled hi-fi equipment was spread over everything as if someone had disembowelled an electric animal. The walls were smeared with red paint, a crude drawing of a prick, my name.

Hill was standing in the middle of the chaos. His eyes were bright with pleasure. Behind him the bearded bouncer from Babylon was standing with his back to me. He had a razor in one hand. With it he was slicing an X across CDs. He did it deftly, efficiently, tossing each ruined disk into the mess on the floor.

Hill said, to no one in particular, 'He's a jazz fan. He likes jazz music.'

The bearded guy laughed as if that was funny.

I leaned against the wall. Adrenaline had cleared my head. I kept my eyes on Hill's.

'A bent copper who likes jazz music.' He said it louder and louder, until by the last word he was shouting.

I tried to keep my voice cool. 'Who were you with in the bar on Sunday night?'

It was the first thing that came into my head.

Hill frowned. He hadn't been expecting a question. 'What?'

I said it again. I had to keep my voice cool.

The bearded guy turned round. He snapped the razor shut and slipped it into his pocket. He looked at me as if I wasn't human at all, just something for him to punch.

'I don't think he was a stranger,' I said. 'You were talking with him for a long time. And Bates. Both of you behaved like you knew him.'

Hill stepped towards me. He kept coming until his cold eyes were only inches from my face. I stared him down. He was shorter than me. His white-blond hair smelled of oil.

Suddenly I found myself on my knees, coughing. The carpet had flecks of blue in it I had never noticed before. Hill's shoes were in front of my face.

I tried to get a grip around his knees with my left arm and pull him over. Something heavy cracked into my ribs. It did the same thing again and got my kidneys. I coughed and let go of Hill, rolling over to protect my head. Records crunched underneath me. From a long way off I heard Hill's voice: 'Don't mark him.' Somebody laughed. Somebody thought that was funny. There was another sharp pain in my stomach and then my shoulder was wrenched back.

Hill's face was floating inches above me. It was disembodied, bloated, a grotesque white head hanging in the air like a diseased moon.

He said, 'You thought you could put me away for good,

didn't you? Fit me up for a fucking murder. I'm going to drag you through hell for that.'

His lips worked and he spat in my face, blinding me. I rolled away, trying to get my arms about my head. The other man's boot was thudding into my ribs quickly now, without stopping. Through the cracks in my fingers I saw Hill's feet. There was a sudden blinding light in my head.

I was listening to a sound like someone hitting a bass drum loud and slow. It was the start of a big band track, a dance song. I was in a nightclub with bright lights in the ceiling. The Duke Ellington band was up on stage. Duke was there himself, wearing a white tailcoat, sitting at a white piano. He was counting time with one hand. The bass drum beat louder and music suddenly filled the room, punchy brass chords soaring to a wild crescendo. 'Mood Indigo'. The trumpeter rose for a solo.

Then everything went black.

## 23

Life came back like water oozing across mud at the turn of a
tide. I seemed to be in some kind of grey cavern. Rocks dug
into my ribs and my mouth was full of seaweed. Maybe I'd
been washed up there. Maybe there'd been a shipwreck and I
was Robinson Crusoe. Maybe I'd died. There was a sound of
hammering. I tried to work out whether it was inside my
head, or out in the cave. Maybe someone was making a boat
for me to escape in. With an effort I opened my eyes.

A pile of books. Broken records. The corner of a doorway.
The doorway looked too big, towering above me. This must
be what doorways looked like if you were a small animal.

At the foot of the doorway, I noticed, there was a severed
hand. It was a man's hand and its fingernails were crusted
with blood. I wondered whose hand it was. He must have
been in a fight before they cut it off. The signet ring on the
little finger said GH. I hoped GH was getting by all right
without his hand. If it had a signet ring, I thought, it must be
a left hand. I was proud of working that out. With any luck
GH was right-handed. I hoped so, for his sake.

My thoughts wandered. The hammering was still going on
somewhere in the distance. There didn't seem to be anything
I could do to make it stop.

The sight of the hand made me wonder what had happened
to my own hands. If I could find them, then I could pick up
the severed hand on the carpet and give it back to GH. He'd
be grateful for that. Suddenly I imagined the feel of that inert
flesh, the fingernails crusted with someone else's blood. The
thought of it made my stomach heave: my mouth filled
abruptly with a thin residue that tasted of tar. I heard a

groaning sound – maybe that was GH looking for his hand. I tried to call to him but nothing would come out. The hammering went on. Somebody must be hammering at the door to the cave. I wondered why they bothered. There wasn't anybody alive in here.

My mouth seemed to be full of something wet. I opened it and felt a scorching sensation on my right wrist. That was a shock to me: I didn't know I had any wrists. I didn't know I had anything at all. Now I thought about it, new parts of me were coming to life every moment. The hot, wet sensation seemed to have unleashed currents which scorched through my body, discovering legs, shoulders, nerves. My new limbs writhed like snakes with fresh skins that hadn't yet hardened. My whole body was a mass of jangling nerve-ends, searing pains. Desperately I wished that I could put it all back to sleep again, go back to the way I had been before.

Suddenly I wondered if I was being tortured. At this very moment there must be a huge electric voltage twisting my muscles. Maybe I'd passed out in the middle of the torture and they'd been waiting for me to come round.

I had to stop them. I had to confess.

I tried to remember what it was I had to confess. I could remember a body lying on a pavement. It was a man's body in a denim jacket and I'd shot him three times. I could remember putting the gun against his neck and pulling the trigger. I hadn't liked the way he jolted. After he'd fallen I'd drawn a chalk line around him to make sure he didn't come back to life. I had to tell them I'd done it, then maybe they'd turn off the current.

I opened my mouth and heard the moaning sound again. It was like wind on a cavern's mouth; I couldn't utter a word. Now I realized what they'd done. It was a torturer's joke: they'd gagged my mouth, then told me to confess. If they only knew how much I wanted to confess! Tears of frustration scorched my cheek. They were acid tears, acid like the taste in my mouth. I wanted to brush them away, but I couldn't. I didn't have anything to brush them away with.

That made me wonder again what had happened to my hands.

I froze. The pain had not stopped but I had worse terrors to occupy me. The hand in front of me had moved.

It moved slowly and haltingly, like a wounded animal. The fingers twitched. It was coming towards me.

I stared at it in horror. Dragging, as if it was very heavy, it crept towards me, then rolled suddenly over so that I could see the crust of blood under the nails.

I knew what it wanted to do to me. It wanted to force its fingers down my throat and choke me so that I could never confess at all. I tried to scream. The hand moved another inch closer. I had to get away now, or I would never have another chance. With an effort that felt like tearing the skin from my own flesh, I rolled over onto my back. The hand fell away from me; I lay there panting.

I lay there for a long time. The ceiling of my living room blurred, then came back into focus. I could feel my chest heave, sucking in draughts of air. I could remember where I was, now, and who I was. Hill had been in the flat. He had been waiting for me in the flat and had done this to me. I remembered his face looming over me, his lips moistening to spit into my face.

The hammering sound was still going on. Someone was at the front door. I had to get up.

I clenched my teeth and rolled into a sitting position. I wouldn't say I enjoyed it, but at least the room was the right way up. There was a mess of broken records underneath me. The room looked as if someone had picked up the whole building, shaken it like a dolls' house and put it back down again. I didn't want to think about that yet. I wanted to stop whoever it was making that noise on the door.

Using the doorframe, I managed to pull myself up on to my feet. I closed my eyes and felt my way towards the bathroom. The floor underneath me felt crooked. Something in my stomach was trying to fight its way out. I felt cold china under my hands just in time and vomited into the basin.

When I stood up the room had straightened itself out. The face looking back at me out of the mirror was a corpse's face. There were no marks on it: I wondered what it had died of. I ran cold water and splashed it over me, not caring where it went. It did nothing for the pain but my head was starting to clear. I felt as if someone had driven over my legs with a steamroller. The fingers of my left hand were numb. Cupping my hands together I let clear water run into them and drank, again and again. The taste of tar was still there but at least I had the use of my tongue.

The corpse in the mirror opened its mouth and said, 'All right.'

The hammering on the door continued.

I splashed my face one more time, then turned and limped back down the hall, taking short steps. I got to the door just as it started to bend under another assault.

The man on the doorstep was a weedy-looking black guy in a leather raincoat. He was wearing a huge floppy cap made of artificial fur.

He said, 'You takes your time, don't you?'

He said that before taking in who he was talking to. It wasn't every day he had a corpse answer the door. His eyes widened and flicked past me into the flat, as if whatever it was that had done this to me might still be in there. His nose wrinkled up in disgust.

I said, 'You'd better come in.'

He opened his mouth to protest but nothing came out. He followed me into the living room and stopped in the doorway, bug-eyed.

'You have a party?' he said.

He had a voice like a kid's voice, high-pitched and drawling.

'No.'

He shook his head. 'Some people.' He stared at the smash of records on the floor. 'You *must*-a had a party.'

I left him staring, and went into the kitchen to make coffee. While it was brewing I got the shower running cold, pulled my clothes off and stepped under it. It felt like being whipped with barbed wire. From the neck down my body was a relief map of bruises. It had valleys, mountain ranges, wide deserts. Hill and his friend had known how to do their job. In a few days I'd be back to normal with nothing permanently damaged except the two organs they cared most about: my pride and my nerve.

I pulled on clean clothes, poured a cup of coffee and took it back into the living room.

The taxi-driver was peering suspiciously around him. 'I nearly give up,' he said. 'Twenty minutes I was knockin'. Called the office, they said you asked for me special.' He looked at me accusingly. 'You ain't him.'

'What do you mean?' I said.

'They told me you was the guy I picked up Sunday. You ain't him.'

I took a sip of my coffee.

'Weren't this address, either. I told 'em.'

'What was the address?'

'You bein' funny?'

'No.'

'He weren't nothin' like you,' he said.

'What was he like?'

He looked around the ruined room again. 'Told 'em he liked my driving.'

I put down the empty cup. 'What was he like?' I repeated.

His eyes narrowed. 'Why you say that? Why you ring 'em up and say you was him?'

I didn't say anything.

'That's funny, man. Why you do that?'

'I wanted to ask you some questions about him,' I said.

'What kinda questions?'

'Where you took him. What he looked like.'

He shook his head slowly. 'I don't answer no questions.'

His face was full of suspicion: suspicion of white people, of people who asked questions, of people who looked like corpses.

I reached into my pocket and took out a ten-pound note. I held it out to him. He stared at it.

'Go on. Take it.'

He shook his head.

'I'm not going to get you into trouble,' I said wearily. 'I just want to ask a few questions about the man you picked up on Sunday night. I'll pay you for it.'

'I got another call to pick up.'

'It can wait.'

He shook his head. 'Uh-uh.'

I went up to him and pushed the banknote into the pocket of his leather coat. 'There. I'll make it easy for you.'

He wouldn't have taken it, but he wasn't going to give it back either.

'What did he look like?' I said. 'Was he my height? Taller?'

The driver thought for a minute. 'He was white,' he said. He put some venom into it.

'Keep going.'

His eyes flicked away from me, remembering. 'Pretty big guy,' he said at last.

'My age?'

'Older.'

'Did you get a name?'

He shook his head.

'Where did you take him?' I asked.

His eyes narrowed. I got out another tenner and handed it out to him. He took it this time, and folded it away in his pocket. 'Took him home.'

'Did you go straight home from the bar?'

'Uh-huh.'

'Where was home?'

The fake fur cap tilted back towards the door.

'Near here.'

'Which street?' I said patiently.

'No way.'

'You took the money,' I said.

'I get myself into trouble.'

'You'll get yourself into trouble with me if you don't tell me.'

He didn't say anything.

'You want me to ring up your office and say I didn't like your driving?'

He thought about it. 'You wouldn't do that.'

'Want to risk it?'

His eyes registered uncertainty. 'Why you want to know?' he asked suspiciously.

'That doesn't matter. Just tell me where you took him.'

His face was sulky now. 'Big house near here.'

'Which street?'

'Don't remember.'

'Yes, you do.'

He made a face. 'Somerset Gardens.'

'That's better. Which number was the house?'

'Don't remember.'

I took out another banknote and held it up in front of him.

His hand reached towards it, then fell back. He shook his head. 'Don't remember.'

'All right,' I said. 'What time did you get there?'

''Bout midnight. He din' give me no tip.'

I said, 'That was stupid of him.'

'Said my car smell of cigarettes.'

'Some people,' I said.

I picked up my jacket.

He frowned. 'You wanna go somewhere?'

'You're a taxi-driver, aren't you?'

He led me out to his car, a shabby brown Toyota double-parked outside the steps. Daylight hurt my eyes but the pain in my body was subsiding to background noise.

'Where you wanna go?'

I said, 'Take me where you took him. Somerset Gardens.'

'Oh no.'

'There's nothing to worry about,' I said patiently. 'All you have to do is find the house and leave me there.'

I took the ten-pound note out of my pocket and held it up. This time he took it out of my hand.

## 24

Somerset Gardens was ten minutes' drive from my own flat, in the quiet, wealthy squares east of Lancaster Gate. It was a part of London inhabited only by rich foreigners and English people who'd just become rich: people who had plenty of money but hadn't learnt where they were supposed to spend it. The houses looked old but weren't, just like the fortunes inside them. Behind neo-Georgian façades was everything the 1950s had counted a mod con. Flashy cars were parked nose-down in the drive-ins.

The taxi-driver pulled up halfway along and pointed to a house across the street. There was a dark green Porsche outside with mud on its tyres. Behind it, squeezed up against the garage doors, was a big motorbike under a rain cover.

I paid him off, then slowly climbed the steps and rang a doorbell. I didn't have to wait long. The man who opened the door had a smooth face and long eyelashes. He might have been North African. In one hand he was carrying a pair of garden shears.

'Yes, sir?'

I said, 'I'm from Hill.'

His soft eyes were impassive. 'Bates?'

'Bates is dead.'

He thought for a moment, then said, 'Come in.'

The hall was quiet. It looked a bit like John Penny's hall, except that everything in it was as fake as the house. The floor had been polished up to look old. On the left was a repro sideboard with a portrait of someone else's ancestor above it. The grandfather clock at the end said half past ten, but I didn't believe it.

The clock whirred and chimed, a single brassy note.

The butler said, 'Mrs Poole is upstairs.' He had a faint accent.

Still holding the shears he led me up the stairs and showed me into a big drawing room at the front. It was too tidy, with the tidiness of people who've bought everything they can think of but didn't have enough things when they started out – people who spend their money on servants, not on sprawling estates in Wiltshire with leaking roofs and farms that made no money. It was as if a foreign designer had tried to do a version of Penny's house. It looked about the same, but it was a lie. Everything in that room had been bought within the last five years, introduced to each other and told to behave as if they'd known each other for ever. They weren't possessions, they were extras.

I didn't notice the woman at first. She was sitting absolutely still on the sofa, her back straight, her face gazing in front of her. When I coughed she didn't move. She was tall, in her forties, with a pile of unconvincing golden hair. Her face was heavily made up. She sat staring at the empty armchair with her head cocked, as if someone in it was telling her a story.

I coughed again. There was still no response. The butler was smiling.

I walked round so that the woman could see me. She didn't see me. Her eyes were gazing emptily across the room. They were big, and blue, and empty. They hung emptily in her face like vacant blue skies over islands no one had yet discovered.

Suddenly she moistened her lips. She had a face like a puppet's face, stretched and made up to look like the face of a beautiful woman. A small pink tongue showed for a moment and disappeared.

She said, 'Hello, Mr Bates.' Her voice was a sing-song, like a child reciting a nursery rhyme.

'I'm not Bates,' I said.

I drew up a chair and sat down. The butler went out.

The woman's eyes were trying to focus. Slowly she turned her head, keeping it level as if she had something balanced on top of it. She looked at me as if I was a hundred miles away. I should have told her it was she who was too far away. I was in the only place I could be.

'Have you got something for me?' She sounded like a kid begging for sweeties.

'Maybe.'

She pouted. A small frown appeared between her eyebrows, as if someone had painted it on.

I said, 'When did Bates come here last? Do you remember?'

The frown deepened. Clouds gathered in her eyes.

'Sunday,' she said clearly.

'That's good. Did he bring you something then?'

She thought for a moment, then nodded. The frown cleared. 'But it's all gone now. That's why you've come.'

I pulled the chair in closer. 'Did Bates come to see you often?'

She frowned again. She said haughtily, 'Don't be impertinent.'

'I'm only trying to help,' I said. 'I want to be as nice to you as Bates was. You don't want me to go away, do you?'

'Oh no!' One hand flew up to her mouth.

'Well, then.'

She smiled vaguely, like a child asked to smile for a photograph. She had forgotten the question.

'How often did Bates come?'

'Often.' She nodded seriously, then remembered whatever it was she had balanced on her head and abruptly raised her chin.

'Twice a week . . . three times a week?'

'Whenever I needed him.'

'What time did he come on Sunday?'

'I didn't see him.'

'Why not?'

'I was in bed. I was sick.'

'Did he come to see you?'

Her face changed. Again she put on the haughty voice. 'You're a very impertinent man.'

'I know that,' I said apologetically.

She wrinkled up her nose in disgust. 'You are quite revolting,' she said decidedly.

I stood up. 'Well,' I said. 'In that case . . .'

'Oh no!' She held out her hands to me. 'I didn't mean that. You will stay – won't you?'

She sounded like a society hostess pressing her guests not to leave early. It was as if her voice wasn't properly connected to anything any more. It was like a CD jumping tracks through all the manners she'd ever adopted in the past.

I sat down again.

'Can I have it now?' she said winningly.

'In a minute. I want to know more about Bates first.'

She looked puzzled. 'Where is Mr Bates?'

'He couldn't come,' I said. 'He's got a new job. He moved away.'

'I don't understand.' There was a rising note of hysteria in her voice. Her hands were fluttering over her lap again. 'I don't under*stand*.'

'He went away.' I made my voice loud enough to force hers down. 'I came instead of him. Hill sent me.'

There was an abrupt silence. A polite smile settled on her face.

She said, 'Can I have it now?'

'Were you very sick on Sunday?' I asked.

'I was in bed.'

'What time did Bates come?'

'He didn't. He gave it to Auguste. Auguste brought it to me. Sir John was visiting downstairs.'

'Do you mean Sir John Penny?'

'Of course I do. He was talking to Gerry.'

'That's your husband?'

She laughed suddenly, a high brittle laugh. 'They had a fight.'

'Is that right?'

'Yes.' She nodded eagerly. 'They were shouting. I could hear them.'

'John Penny and your husband?'

'It was awful.'

'What did you hear?' I asked.

'Oh . . .' She shook her head. 'Men's things.'

'Money?'

'You'd have to ask Gerry about that.'

There was a creak of the floor behind me.

'What,' said a voice, 'would you have to ask Gerry about?'

I swung round. A man was standing in the doorway.

He was well-built, athletic, with broad shoulders and a barrel chest. The jacket of an expensive suit was slung over one shoulder. His brown hair was expensively cut, his brown face tanned and too healthy, the face of a man who knew he was attractive. For some reason it made me think of an animal's face: the same look that's almost an expression until you realize it doesn't mean anything at all. A briefcase was on the floor next to him.

'Who are you?' he said peremptorily.

His wife was taking short, nervous breaths, like someone about to dive underwater. Her eyes were scared.

I didn't stand up. I said, 'Hill sent me.'

'Why did you come up here?'

'Why not?'

'You don't come upstairs,' he said. 'Hill should have told you that.'

'Auguste showed me up,' I said.

'I'll speak to him.'

He stood back, ostentatiously making room for me to get out. I didn't move.

'I was having a nice chat with your wife,' I said.

He didn't say anything.

'You'd better go now,' she whispered. She was leaning towards me as if he wouldn't be able to hear. 'Gerry doesn't like me having visitors.' She sat back and smiled blandly about the room.

'Why's that?' I asked. 'Doesn't he like people having parties without him?'

I stood up and went out of the room. The man closed the door behind me and followed me downstairs.

In the hallway he said, 'What are you doing here?'

'I told you, Hill sent me.'

'Why?'

'I'm Penny's new driver. He needs one after what happened to Bates.'

'I don't know about that.'

'No reason why you should,' I said.

'Did you bring her anything?'

I shook my head. 'I just wanted to introduce myself.'

He looked at me. His brown eyes were hard and meaningless, like an animal's eyes.

'Get out,' he said. He said it dismissively, the way he'd get rid of a waiter.

I turned away. I walked slowly down the front steps into the street of fake houses. No one did anything to stop me.

I wondered whether Penny knew what Bates got up to while he was in his political meetings. I wondered whether that was what he and Gerry Poole had been arguing about on Sunday afternoon.

Most of all, I wondered what Poole had been doing in Babylon the night Joe Bates was killed.

## 25

The same Spanish woman opened the door to John Penny's house. She was wearing the same housecoat, but this time she didn't ask me for my name.

She said, 'We've been expecting you.'

I didn't understand that. She left me waiting in the silent hallway and disappeared upstairs, swaying her hips. I stood in front of the grandfather clock and tried not to think about what Hill had done to me the night before. There were plenty of things I didn't want to think about. I didn't want to think about what Mason would say if he heard I was still calling myself a policeman. I didn't want to think about Fred James, or what Clare Bates would feel about me after my visit the night before.

There were footsteps on the stairs. I followed the Spanish woman up to the first landing. Next to the study door was another. She knocked on that door, then opened it and ushered me in.

I found myself in a big, formal drawing room with full length windows framed by heavy curtains. There was too much furniture, a big fireplace, some old-fashioned bookshelves. The tables were covered with photographs of children and dogs. John Penny was not in the room.

In front of the fireplace was a long sofa. Penny's wife was sitting at one end of it. She was holding a glass in one hand and staring ahead of her with a rigid expression. Behind her stood a lanky man in a grey flannel suit. He had one hand on the woman's shoulder and was gazing sorrowfully down at the top of her head.

I stopped in the doorway. It looked as if I'd just interrupted a proposal of marriage.

Penny's wife put down her glass, nearly missing the edge of the table. Her eyes were bright, empty, only half focused. She said, 'Elizabeth Penny. We met the other day.'

The man squeezed her shoulder and made a soothing noise between his teeth.

The steel-grey hair was piled up on top of her head. She was wearing a white blouse that looked vaguely sporting, as if she'd just come in from riding a horse.

'I wanted to see your husband,' I said.

All of a sudden her face crumpled. She didn't look as if she'd had any practice crying. She did it awkwardly, making noises like a small animal caught in a trap.

The man turned his face towards me for the first time. It was a long, melancholy face with half-moon eyebrows and too much chin. He said, 'Is this some kind of a ghastly joke?'

I felt stupid, as if I'd come in halfway through a film and couldn't pick up the plot. I took a few steps into the room and tried to look as if I knew what was going on.

'Maria said you were from the police.' He had the precise, fastidious voice of a schoolteacher or country vicar.

I said, 'I was here the other day, asking Sir John some questions about Bates's murder. There were some loose ends to clear up.'

Elizabeth Penny gave a gasp and rolled her face back into the tall man's hand. Her shoulders were shaking.

The man straightened himself up. He put one hand on the top of Elizabeth Penny's head. He said, 'I regard this as a disgrace.'

Elizabeth Penny stopped crying abruptly. It was as if she had suddenly remembered whatever they told her in the nursery about not letting anything show.

'I regard this as a disgrace,' the man repeated. 'Sir John Penny died earlier this morning. Do you understand? I shall certainly complain to your superiors.'

'It's all right, Jackie,' Elizabeth Penny said. Her voice was calmer than I would have expected. 'It's all right.' She turned to me. 'We thought you must have come to ask some more questions. The other officers have only just left.'

I said, 'I'm sorry. I haven't been at the station. No one had told me.'

'Well you bloody well know now, don't you?' The man's voice was spiteful.

'It's not his fault, Jackie,' Elizabeth Penny said. 'It's a mistake, don't you see?' She turned to me. 'Why did you come to see my husband?'

'To ask him some more about Joe Bates.'

'Oh yes.' She frowned. 'Bates. He died, didn't he?'

I didn't say anything.

'I'm sorry, I probably can't help with any of that. I didn't really know Bates.' Suddenly she pointed to a chair. 'Won't you sit down?'

I sat down. I needed to.

'What were the police doing here?' I asked. 'What's happened to your husband?'

'Oh . . .' She looked blank. 'I'm so sorry, I don't remember your name.'

I told her my name.

'How silly of me.' She pointed at the man next to her. 'This is Dr Royce. He's an old friend of the family. Our family doctor.'

The man grunted at me.

'The police came to tell me. My husband died in an accident. One of his building sites. They found his body this morning. He was a property developer – of course you know that.'

'What was he doing on the building site?' I asked.

'He went out to a meeting last night.' She shrugged. 'He must have gone on to the site and lost his footing on the scaffold.'

She said it dispassionately, almost as if she was talking about somebody else's husband. I looked at her ruddy, country-woman's face. It was as if death was just one of those things, like riding accidents or the death of a horse. This was the kind of crisis she'd spent her whole life being trained for.

She knew what to do. You mix a stiff gin and tonic, or two if that helps; you call the family doctor; you send telegrams to the children's schools. You don't cry in front of strangers or servants. Any crying can be done afterwards, upstairs.

'Who found him?' I asked.

'The contractor's men. Scotty . . . he's the foreman. They call him Scotty. When he came in to work this morning.'

My mind was trying to catch up but it couldn't move fast enough. I said, 'I still don't understand. He went to a meeting at the site last night? Who was with him?'

'Nobody.' She shook her head. 'He'd gone out to a meeting. They think he must have gone to the site afterwards.'

'In the middle of the night?' I asked. 'Why would your husband have gone to a building site at night?'

'We don't know.' She shrugged. 'Johnny loved visiting his sites. It was the part he loved best. He got on with the men so well . . . you see?'

'But at night? Had he done that before?'

Royce gave a snort of disgust. 'They've been over all this. The other men who were here. Do you have to make it worse for her?'

'He's only doing his job, Jackie. I don't mind. Really.'

Royce grunted, picked up Elizabeth Penny's empty glass from the edge of the table and stalked over to a drinks cabinet in the corner. Without turning round he said, 'I think I'll have one to keep you company.'

I didn't think it was his first.

I frowned. 'Who was the meeting with?'

'A business colleague. His name's Hill. Johnny's a director of his company.'

'Dick Hill?'

'Yes.' She didn't manage to hide her dislike.

'Does he know what happened?'

'He said the meeting never took place. It's all very odd. He said . . . I'm sure Johnny said he was going out to a meeting.'

'When did you speak to Dick Hill?

'Last night. When my husband didn't come back I rang

up. I thought they must be sitting up late. That happened sometimes, when they had company business to discuss.'

Royce came back with a glass and put it in her hand. Elizabeth Penny took it, then licked a finger where it had spilled over the edge. That was the first time she'd moved since I came in.

I said, 'So Dick Hill and your husband had a meeting last night which never took place. This morning your husband's body was found on one of their building sites.'

Royce said, 'That's what it looks like. Of course, it's early days.' His voice carried a doctor's meaningless reassurance.

'He must have slipped on the scaffold,' Elizabeth Penny said.

It wasn't hard to imagine why John Penny might have slipped.

'Had your husband done anything like this before – gone out to a site late at night?'

'My husband was a very busy man.' She sounded proud.

I remembered Penny sitting behind his empty desk: a man busy trying to clear up the mess inside himself.

'Weren't you worried when he didn't come back?'

'Of course she was bloody worried,' Royce interrupted.

'I called everybody. Nobody knew where he was. I even thought of calling the police.' Her forehead puckered. 'I wish I had now. One doesn't want to make a fuss, does one?'

'Steady on, old girl.' Royce's hand was back on Elizabeth Penny's head again, kneading the hair. Half of his drink was already gone.

I said, 'You told me the other day that your husband was worried. Could this be something to do with it?'

I put it as gently as I could. Elizabeth Penny's blue eyes stared right back at me.

Royce said, 'For God's *sake!*'

'If you are suggesting that my husband may have taken his own life . . .' She stopped and looked abruptly down at her glass.

Royce said, 'Johnny wasn't that sort of man.'

'They never are,' I said.

Royce blinked. 'Bloody hell. I thought I'd seen it all, now I . . . Bloody hell!'

'Stop it, Jackie.'

'I won't stop it.' His face was an unhealthy liver colour. His long chin was jutting out towards me. 'He comes here and starts abusing the memory of –'

I cut in drily: 'Whether he did anything or not, that's what it looks like and a lot of other people are going to think so too. It's better you face it now.'

'You don't understand,' Elizabeth Penny said. 'Johnny was a happy man. He wouldn't even have *dreamed* . . . Besides, we have children. Johnny didn't run away from things.'

I remembered the man sitting behind the desk in the study next door. It had seemed to me that John Penny was running away as fast as he could from everything in sight. He hadn't looked the way happy men are supposed to look.

I said, 'Did he ever tell you what was worrying him?'

'No.' She shook her head. 'I don't know that he was really worried. He just wasn't sleeping as well as usual. Johnny was always a heavy sleeper.'

'Were there any money problems, anything like that?'

'That question is quite out of order,' said Royce primly.

I said, 'What about emotional troubles? Something in his private life?'

'For God's sake!' Royce exploded.

When she spoke, Elizabeth Penny's voice had shrunk to something so cold and hard it had almost lost its accent. 'If you'd known him you wouldn't ask that question.'

'I didn't know him.'

'There are still *some* men. Men who aren't always . . . who don't always . . . John would *never* . . .' Her voice rose to a squeak and died. She put one hand over her eyes.

Royce said, 'Frankly, I think you've asked enough questions for now, don't you?'

I turned away and walked over to the desk in the corner. Behind me I could hear Elizabeth Penny talking to the doctor in a voice that was half a whisper and half a shriek. I heard: 'You should *never* . . . one shouldn't *ever* . . .' The doctor's voice rumbled inaudibly. I didn't know if she was telling the truth. On the desk was a sheet of letter paper half covered by an opened bank statement. The date, in copperplate writing, was the day before. I slid back the statement. *Dear Gerald . . .*' I glanced behind me. The doctor had sat down next to Elizabeth Penny. His head was close to hers. *I am writing in reference to the proposals you made to me at our recent meeting.* That was as far as he'd got. Maybe he'd started the letter before going out to meet Dick Hill and falling off a scaffold to his death. I pushed the bank statement back over the letter and turned round.

I said, 'I'm sorry if the question distressed you.'

Royce said pompously, 'I must ask you to leave the house.'

'It won't only be me who asks questions like that,' I said. 'When I spoke to your husband on Monday he wouldn't tell me where he'd been the day before. To be honest, I assumed he must have been visiting . . .' I paused. 'A friend. If there's anything like that you ought to be ready for it.' I was talking to Elizabeth Penny.

She said to the fireplace, 'There isn't anything like that.'

There was a long silence. I should have left straightaway, but I had too much to lose.

To break the silence I said, 'How well do you know Dick Hill?'

'Very little.' Her tone was dismissive.

'What did you think of him?'

'Frankly, I thought he was common.'

'Did you socialize with him?'

Royce snorted and drained his glass.

'We spend most of our time in the country,' said Elizabeth Penny. 'When we did meet it was for business things.'

'How did your husband first meet him?'

'Oh . . . it was business. Do you see? In business one can't avoid people like that. Not these days.'

Royce said, 'I'm damned if I can see what this has got to do with anything. Isn't it time you left her alone?'

Elizabeth Penny raised one hand to hush him.

I said, 'What about Bates?'

She looked up at me. 'I didn't know things like that could happen . . . people getting murdered. Of course he wasn't a very *nice* man.'

'What did your husband think of him?'

'He put up with him. One has to.'

'What did he tell you about the murder?'

'Nothing, really . . . We talked about the widow. Whether there was something one ought to do.'

Her voice lurched suddenly when she said widow. She had never thought, when they discussed it, that two days later she'd be a widow herself.

'He was a good man,' Royce said angrily. 'He looked after people. He'll be missed.'

I stood up. I needed time to think about this, and about a lot of other things. I didn't think Elizabeth Penny had much more to tell me.

I said, 'I'm sorry to have disturbed you again.'

She shook her head. She was back in control, doing her duty. 'Is there anything else?'

'Yes,' I said. 'Did anyone telephone last night? Before he went out?'

'I don't think so.' She frowned. 'Our son, Nick, but that was later. There was a call during dinner. My husband took it.'

'Did he say who it was?'

She shook her head. 'It was very short. He finished his dinner and went straight out.'

Her eyelids drooped. The gin, or adrenaline, was wearing off. It was time for me to go. I thanked them again and got a scowl from Royce. Elizabeth Penny nodded. She was thinking about her husband the way she wanted to remember him: big, bluff and dependable, a kind man, a man with a sense of duty. Quite soon she wouldn't even remember what he was really like.

I left her looking into the middle distance with her blue eyes squinting and opening again as if the middle distance wouldn't keep still. The Spanish maid showed me downstairs.

Outside a taxi was drawing up. A man in his thirties got

out. He looked like a younger version of John Penny. Tears streaked his face; without a word he hurried past me into the silent house. The door closed behind him.

## 26

The receptionist at Hill Properties was crying again. It had been a bad week. At typing school they'd taught her spelling, punctuation and what to do when your boss puts his hand up your dress, but they hadn't warned her about death.

When I pushed through the doors she was on the phone. Her voice had butterflies in it.

I stood and waited, wondering how much Dick Hill knew of what had happened the night before. I needed badly to talk to Dick Hill about Penny's death. The risk was that someone had told Matthew Hill how I had forged his confession, and he had told his father. He already knew that there was no case against him: he knew that as soon as Mason released him. And he knew that I had been behind his arrest, which was why my head hurt every time I moved. It would take time, though, before he heard I had been suspended.

The receptionist hung up. She tried to raise a smile for me. It was the sort of brave smile you give when people die. She was getting good at that.

'Is Dick Hill in?'

'I'm afraid there's been a tragedy in the company.' It was a speech someone else had prepared for her. 'Mr Hill's in a meeting.'

'That's what I want to see him about. The tragedy in the company.'

The make-up around her eyes was caked where she'd tried to paint over tears. She made a stab at another smile, but her heart wasn't in it.

I said, 'Could you call up for me? Tell him it's Chief Inspector Havilland. I was here on Monday.'

She looked doubtful but pulled the phone towards her and dialled a number. Somebody said something at the other end.

'He won't be available for some time.' She was looking expectantly at me.

'Tell them it's about John Penny's death,' I said.

That seemed to help. She put the phone down, pushed back her chair and led me upstairs to a small meeting room on the first floor.

The room might once have been a study. There was a mahogany table down the middle and some leather books which no one had ever read. On the walls there were photographs of housing developments in Docklands. The pictures showed shiny kitchens and carpets the colour of mushroom soup: the taste of people who know where they want to go but can't remember where they came from; or maybe don't come from anywhere at all, just walk in one day with their suitcase and three new suits and start living. The taste of the market.

I looked at the photographs for a while, then sat down and looked out of the windows. A phrase from a Gerry Mulligan track had swum into my mind; just one phrase, a sax line repeated over and over. Across the street scaffolding had gone up and rubble was pouring down a chute through one of the windows. Old walls, carpets, ceilings torn out to be replaced by something that looked old but wasn't. In a few months' time it would be a photograph in a developer's meeting room. In a couple of years it would be torn out again for something else that didn't look like what it was; a succession of fakes, carnival masks worn all year round because nobody knew what the truth looked like any more.

After quarter of an hour the door opened and Mary Fane came in. She was wearing a neat black dress with a round collar. I wondered how many black dresses she had.

'I'm sorry about the delay.' She gave me a commiserating smile. 'Mr Hill says he'll be with you as soon as he can.'

I gave the smile back. Mine didn't mean any more than hers did.

'Did Jenny offer you coffee? She's very upset, you know.' She said it as if I was Jenny's father. 'Can I get you anything?'

I said, 'A coffee. Thanks.'

Her dark golden hair had been brushed loose, making an odd contrast with the sober dress.

'Mr Hill's awfully hurt by this.' There was a pause, then she added, 'We all are.'

'Did you know Penny yourself?'

'Sir John? Only a little. When he came into the office.'

I found myself wondering whether Mary Fane's voice was natural, or whether she'd bought it, like the tan and the expensive clothes. It was impossible to tell where she came from, or even how old she was: she might have been anywhere between twenty-five and forty. I wondered who paid for the tan and the clothes; who had paid for the voice.

She gave me another smile. 'Mr Hill will only be a minute,' she repeated.

He was about twenty minutes, two coffees and a lot of trying to forget what people had been doing to my body the night before.

He came in quickly, with his hands pressed tight together. There was something tense about his eyes. He didn't try to shake my hand.

'Chief Inspector Havilland.' His voice was cold.

The door stayed open behind him. His son appeared in the opening.

Hill was dressed just like an ordinary person, in a city suit and a tie. You'd never have known he'd spent the evening before banging my head against a wall. He didn't show any sign of it in the way he greeted me, either. The beating was to be a secret, something between the two of us. If that was how he wanted it, then – for the moment at least – I wasn't going to complain. I wanted to know first why he needed secrets like that.

Dick Hill went to the other end of the room and sat down, drumming his fingers on the table. I wondered which of us it was that made him so nervous.

Hill said, 'How are you, Chief Inspector. Haven't seen you since they let me go.'

I didn't say anything to that. Hill sat down at the end of the table and pulled a crumpled packet of Marlboro out of his suit pocket. He reached over and dragged the ashtray towards him. While he lit the cigarette he kept his green eyes on my face.

'All right.' Dick Hill's voice was too high-pitched, as if someone had hold of one end of it and wouldn't stop pulling. 'What's it about? What do you want?'

'To ask you some questions.'

'More questions?' Hill was smiling.

I said, 'It's too bad about John Penny. You'll need to find yourselves another director.' I nodded at Hill. 'Is that why he's here?'

Hill didn't stop smiling. He reached forward and knocked ash over the mahogany table-top.

'What business is it of yours?' Dick Hill was still drumming his fingers on the table-top.

'I didn't say it was my business. I said it was sad.'

'It is.' He cracked his knuckle joints together. 'Too right it's sad. Known John Penny for twenty years. A tragedy's what it is.'

'He died on one of your building sites, didn't he?'

'How did you know that?' Hill's eyes were two green slits.

I said, 'His widow told me.'

'What were you doing there?'

'Trying to ask him some questions.'

Hill said, 'It's a shame.'

Dick Hill got up from his chair again. 'We don't have time for this.' He was talking to his son. 'We've got things to do.'

'Like finding another director?' I said.

Hill laughed.

'I don't know why you came here.' The older man was on the edge of losing control. 'I knew you were going to try and pin Bates on Mattie. I knew it on Monday. You give up that one, now it's John Penny. I don't see why you can't –'

Hill said, 'Shut up.'

There was silence in the room. Deliberately, Hill reached over and ground the butt of his cigarette into the ashtray. His mouth looked cruel.

'All right,' he went on. 'Why did you come?'

I said, 'When John Penny went out last night he was going to meet you.' I was talking to Dick Hill. 'He told his wife. The next time anyone sees him, he's dead. Are you surprised I want to talk to you?'

Dick Hill pressed his thin lips together. Something inside him kept moving, rocking him back and forwards over the table. 'I never saw him.'

'That's not what his wife says.'

'There was going to be a meeting. That's true. But he cancelled it. Called up himself to cancel.'

Out of the corner of my eye I saw Hill picking another cigarette out of the crumpled box.

'What time was that?'

'Don't know. My secretary took it. Sometime after six.'

'How do you know?'

'Because I wasn't there. I was at another meeting, wasn't I?'

I said, 'What other meeting?'

'There's some people . . .' Dick Hill's voice was angry again. 'There's some people would say you weren't the right man to be asking me questions. There's some people —'

'Shut up.' Hill's voice was harder this time. He blew out smoke and shook the flame off the match. 'Havilland can ask all the questions he likes. There's nothing I've got to hide.' He turned and looked at me. 'I told you that two days ago. You should have believed me.'

Dick Hill said, 'All he wants is to pin something on you. Doesn't matter what it is, does it?'

Hill ignored that. He kept looking at me. 'Penny was going to have a meeting with my father, then he cancelled. Then he went and killed himself the easiest way he could think of. That's what happened.'

'Why would he kill himself?'

He shrugged. 'It happens.'

'Not without a reason. Penny was happy at home. He had money. What would have made him kill himself?'

Hill said flatly, 'He drank. You know that.'

'Mattie . . .' Dick Hill had stood up again. His voice was outraged.

'Don't call me that.'

There was a silence.

I said, 'Do you mean he killed himself because he had a drink problem?'

'Maybe.' Hill shrugged. 'Maybe whatever made him drink made him do that as well. Maybe his wife found out something as well. Maybe he liked little boys. How should I know?'

'Mattie . . .' This time his father's voice didn't expect to be heard.

'Maybe it really was an accident,' Hill went on. 'You don't want to be climbing round a scaffold when you're pissed.'

'Why was he climbing round the scaffold?' I asked.

Hill smiled. 'How should I know?'

'Wasn't it locked?'

Hill kept smiling. He didn't say anything.

I turned to his father. 'Aren't the sites locked?'

'Of course they are.'

'So how would he have got in?'

'I don't know.'

'Did he have keys?'

'Must have done, mustn't he?'

I said, 'Normally. Did he normally have keys to the building sites?'

Dick Hill shook his head. His son drew in smoke and breathed it out slowly.

'Who does have keys?'

'Better ask the contractor that. Site security, that's their problem.'

'What about you?'

'Sometimes we do.'

I said, 'What about this time?'

Hill laughed. He said, 'You keep scratching around, don't you?'

Dick Hill's expression was bleak. I kept talking to him. 'Where were you going to have the meeting?'

'Here.'

'What was it going to be about?'

He shrugged. 'Don't know. Johnny said there was things he wanted . . . things he wanted to go over. Wouldn't tell you even if I did know, probably.'

'Company business?'

'What other business is there?'

I said, 'What's wrong with the company?'

Dick Hill grimaced. 'You're right on the blasted edge, you are. I told you that before.'

'Nothing's wrong with the company,' said Hill. His voice was impatient. 'Why don't you just tell him?'

'I don't have to answer his questions. He doesn't have a warrant, does he?'

Hill said, 'He's a policeman.'

There was a silence. Hill wasn't smiling any more. He looked angrily at his father.

I repeated, 'What's wrong with the company?'

Nobody said anything.

'So Penny cancelled the meeting,' I went on. 'What did you do instead?' I was talking to Dick Hill.

'Went home. What do you want me to do?'

'Alone?'

His eyes were hard. 'No.'

'Go on.'

'Mattie was with me. And my housekeeper.'

Hill was tearing the brown paper off the filter of his cigarette.

I said 'What time was this?'

'All evening. I was home all evening. Mattie got in about seven. After your boss let him out. You can ask my housekeeper.'

'Why did he go to you?'

I kept my eyes on the old man's face. He looked at Hill.

Hill said, 'Go on.'

'Company.'

'I didn't think he was ever short of company.'

'Maybe he thought the coppers would be watching his place. People like you. Trying to pin something else on him. Stay with me again tonight, I expect.'

I kept staring at him. He didn't blink. I could feel Hill's green eyes on one side of my face.

'Did you try to call Penny?' I asked.

Dick Hill shook his head.

'Your son thinks he killed himself because he was fucked up and drank too much. Is that what you think?'

Suddenly the old man's eyes were hurt. Nothing else in his face changed. 'It was an accident.' He stood up, scraping back the chair. 'Must have been. Stands to reason. Climbing the scaffold at night.'

'When did you see him last?'

'Last week.'

I said, 'Was he drunk then? Did he tell you anything he was worried about?'

Dick Hill shook his head. 'If he had I wouldn't tell you.' His voice was aggressive.

'What did Penny do here?'

'Director. Backbone of the place, John Penny. I've known him for twenty years.'

I said, 'You already told me that.'

Hill said abruptly. 'Is that it?' He was looking at me.

Dick Hill moved around the table. His hand was out-stretched. He said, 'Sorry we can't help you more, Mr Havilland.'

His son stood up. The jacket of his double-breasted suit was unbuttoned. He nodded, turned and walked towards the door.

Dick Hill let him go ahead, then walked slowly downstairs behind me to the reception.

I said, 'Have you spoken to his wife yet?'

'Got a call from her this morning. Before I left home.'

'Is that how you heard?'

He nodded.

I said, 'What did you think, when you heard John Penny was dead?'

Dick Hill's eyes were black holes in a face the colour of dust. 'What do you want me to think? He was a friend of mine.'

'Did Elizabeth Penny ever tell you what she thinks of you?'

'I can guess.'

His tone wasn't even bitter. He had got used to living with people who looked down on him. A South London boy on the streets of Mayfair; Johnny's partner, a bright-eyed boy from the wrong side of the river who was allowed in because he had Johnny's arm round his shoulders and because of what he had in his pocket.

I said, 'Do you know what she told me . . .?' I stopped. Dick Hill wasn't listening to me any more. There was a fixed smile on his face.

Mary Fane was waiting in reception. Hill was standing next to her, leaning towards her. She was laughing at something he had said, her head thrown back and golden hair hanging loose.

Dick Hill said, 'What was that?' The smile was still on his face.

I remembered the way he had looked at his secretary the first time I had come to his office: indulgent, perhaps a little possessive. Maybe it was Dick Hill who paid for the dresses and everything else. I wondered if he got anything in return.

'It doesn't matter,' I said.

By the time I reached the reception desk Hill had disappeared. Mary Fane was filling something in on an official form. The receptionist wasn't there.

I said, 'You're right, he is hurt by it.'

She shook her head, smiling vaguely as if it was the first part of a joke.

I left her smiling and went out into the street.

## 27

Outside the office, traffic was tailing back down Deanery Street. I started walking past it into Mayfair. Suddenly I heard my name being called. When I turned round I saw Jill Cowans looking at me through the windscreen of an old Ford Escort.

I walked slowly up to her. The car was covered in dents and scratches where different colours of paint showed through. She regarded me warily as I came up. I couldn't work out if her expression was hostile or friendly.

'What have you been up to?' she asked. 'Poking your nose into something?'

I didn't say anything. I wondered whether Clare had told her about my suspension.

'Cat got your tongue?' She laughed contemptuously. 'Want a lift?'

'Are you going over the river?'

She nodded.

I said, 'Thanks. I've got to go back to the station.'

She pushed open the passenger door and I got in. The car behind hooted.

'Bastard. What's he in such a hurry about?'

Jill let in the clutch and the car moved forwards with a jerk. She drove sitting upright, with her hands high up on the wheel. She was wearing dark glasses and a black dress with a low collar. The glasses made her look younger.

'What are you staring at, dear? Seen something you fancy?'

I said, 'What were you doing in town?'

'Fucking copper.' She bit her lip. 'I was seeing a friend . . .'

We were taking the corner into Park Lane. She glanced up in the mirror. 'Dick Hill, if you really want to know.'

'I wondered.'

'Coppers are always wondering. That's all they ever fucking do.'

'What were you seeing him about?'

'Nosey bastard, aren't you?'

'It's my job,' I said.

There was a pause, then Jill said, 'I didn't think it was, any more.'

I looked out of the side window. We were just turning into Park Lane. Coaches were parked along the far side. The trees above them were covered in dust.

'How did you know that?'

'Clare told me.'

'Did you tell Dick Hill?'

She shook her head. 'We had better things to talk about.'

'Like what?'

She laughed rudely. 'Wouldn't you like to know?'

'I thought you hadn't seen him for years.'

'I hadn't. But he's all right, Dick. Money coming out of his fucking ears, but he's all right.' She went on quietly: 'It's what you said yesterday. I wanted to make sure his son doesn't bother Clare again. Now she doesn't have anyone to look after her.'

'Has he been in touch with her?'

'He's only been out one night.'

'Can his father stop him?'

'Maybe. It's worth a try. Hill's got enough on his plate trying to keep his nose clean for the moment.'

There was a pause. I said, 'What is it between Dick Hill and his secretary?'

'Mary Fane?' Jill snorted. 'Class act, she is. Out of my class.'

'Is she more than a secretary?'

'Why do you want to know?' Her face was wary.

'Interest.'

She shook her head. 'There's no fool like an old fool.'

'Does she sleep with him?'

'Aren't you the nosey one?' She laughed crudely. 'I bet Dickie'd like her to. She's too smart, that one. You won't find a woman like that tying herself to an old man.'

I looked out of the window, wondering why she had wanted to talk to me.

I said, 'Do you think Fred James could have killed Joe?'

'He said he did, didn't he?'

'People say a lot of things.'

She shrugged. 'He was a funny guy.'

'Everybody told me he wouldn't hurt a fly.'

'Who said that?'

'Your daughter, for one.'

'If Clare wants to think someone's a nice guy, she will. I wouldn't listen to her. Anyway . . .' She paused at Hyde Park Corner. 'I thought it was an accident. They were having a fight and the gun went off. He didn't have to do anything.'

'That's what Fred says.'

'There you are, then.'

We were passing along the side of Green Park. Couples were lying under the trees, eating ice-creams, throwing sticks for dogs.

I said 'I've just been in with Dick Hill. Does his son always treat him like that?'

'Like what?' Her voice was wary.

I said, 'Like shit.'

She took a long time to answer. 'Dickie can take it.'

'Does he mind?'

'What do you think?'

I didn't say anything.

'Anyway, he's not . . . it hasn't always been like this. Hill's changed.'

'Since when?'

'Since that business with the old drunk. He was softer before that. Did what his dad told him. If his dad ever did tell him anything.' We stopped at the lights on Parliament Square. 'If he was my son . . .' She shrugged.

'Has he ever talked to you about it?'

'You ask a shitload of questions, don't you?'

I said, 'Aren't you interested – in why Hill's the way he is?'

'Not much. I don't give a toss what Hill does. As long as he doesn't do it to me.'

We pulled off again.

Jill said, 'Why are you still chasing after this?'

'What else can I do?'

'Sit tight. Mind your p's and q's. They won't kick you out.'

'I wish.'

'Coppers?' She wrinkled up her nose. 'Stick together like fucking glue.'

I said, 'The police believe Fred James's confession. That leaves Hill outside. He's dangerous.'

'Particularly to you. After what you did. You ought to watch out for yourself. Can't be long before he hears you're on suspension, either.'

I told her what had happened the evening before.

Jill said, 'He must like you.'

'Why?'

'You can still walk.'

We rose up on to the bridge. The Thames gleamed either side of us; palaces on the north; on the south, a strip of grand buildings with wasteland behind them. We turned into grimy streets lined with offices and council estates, passed under a railway bridge, looked down rows of grey brick tenements and boarded-up shops. This was where Dick Hill had escaped from and Hill had made his way back to, burrowing into it with an animal's instinct for its own home. We passed bomb sites surrounded by hoardings, odd rows of Georgian houses trying to ignore what was going on around them.

At the Kennington Road Jill turned left.

'I said I was going to the station.'

'You can come and have a drink first.'

We drove the rest of the way in silence. Outside the Blue Corner we pulled up with a jerk. Jill looked over her shoulder to park.

'Why are you still doing this?' she asked again. 'It'll only make trouble for you.' She wasn't looking at me. There was a slight jolt as we hit the car behind. 'When they find out you're still doing it . . .' She switched the engine off and looked at me. 'I bet you told Dick it was a police investigation.'

'Yes.'

'What did you want out of him?'

'To find out what he knew about Penny's death.'

'I thought it was an accident.'

'You mean you know about it?'

'Dickie told me.'

I nodded. 'Everybody will think he killed himself. Maybe he did.'

'Sounds like he had reasons.'

We got out and I followed her into the pub. The Blue Corner had the remains of a lunchtime crowd: two lads playing darts, a benchful of old men, some jocks in tracksuits at the bar. The kid with greased hair and earrings was pulling pints. He nodded at Jill when she came in. She led me upstairs. The door to the gym was closed and grunting noises came from behind it. On the top floor she took me into a sitting room.

Jill said, 'Make yourself at home.'

She disappeared. I shoved a pile of records off the sofa and sat down.

The room was like her bedroom only not so tidy. There was a photograph of a man on the side table. I picked it up. A London face, slightly battered, as if someone had squeezed their fist around the temples like a child modelling clay. He had a long uneven nose and kind eyes. The eyes reminded me of Clare.

There was a step outside. Jill came back into the room.

She wasn't wearing the dress any more. She wasn't wearing anything. Her lips were freshly made up. The bush of hair between her legs was thick and black, contrasting oddly with her blonde head. She came across the room and straddled me. Close to she smelled of musk and something sweet, a tart's scent. She put her hands either side of my head and raised it until I was looking into her eyes. They weren't seeing me.

Slowly she bent forward and pressed her mouth against mine. When I didn't respond she gave a long aroused sigh and moved upwards from the hips, pushing my face into her heavy breasts.

'My horoscope warned me about a blue-eyed man,' she whispered.

I said, 'That's corny.'

I pushed her away and put my arms between us. Her thighs gripped my legs. All of a sudden the sex had gone out of her eyes. It was replaced by hatred, a black hatred flaring incongruously through the bedroom make-up.

'What's the matter, are you a pansy?'

I shook my head. 'It's the wrong time.'

'Time of the month?' She snorted. 'That's a girl's line.'

'Just the wrong time. I'm sorry.'

'Is it me?'

'No.'

'What do you think of my body?' She pushed her breasts up towards my face, posing like a page three model.

'You don't need me to tell you that.'

'Don't you want me?'

I said, 'Right now I don't want anybody. Not even you.'

The 'even' did something for her pride. She sat back and regarded me dispassionately, as if she'd never seen my face before. That was probably the way she looked at a lot of men: faces on her pillow, bearded faces, black faces. Just men. The smart ones would play the game with her and know when to walk out. The others, she would know how to deal with. I almost admired her. She was sitting with a man who'd just rejected her but she wasn't going to let that put her at a disadvantage. Even the fact that she was naked didn't seem to worry her. She used it against me: it made me keep my eyes on her face.

I said, 'Have you forgotten what Hill did to me last night?' I was trying to turn it into a joke.

'Kick you in the balls, did he? Poor dear!' She laughed crudely. 'Want me to kiss it better?'

She ran a hand experimentally over my chest. I picked the

hand up and held it for a moment. It was warm, soft. I almost weakened. It seemed a long time since anyone had offered themselves freely, without strings or complications.

Except that there were complications. This was Clare's mother. Clare's mother sitting naked on my lap with her thighs pressing my knees together.

'Thanks anyway,' I said.

'Prick.'

She got up and wrapped an overcoat round herself, lit a cigarette, sat down at the far end of the sofa. She blew a cloud of smoke into the uncertain space between us.

I found I was still holding the photo of her husband. Jill caught sight of it and made a wry face.

'Don't you mind?'

'Why should I?' She inhaled and blew twin jets of smoke through her nostrils. 'He's dead, isn't he? Anyway . . .' She tapped ash on to the floor. 'What does he think I'm going to do? Widow at thirty-six . . . the bastard.' She sat for a moment looking at the photo. Then she gave me an odd smile. 'You see? I don't even lie about my age.'

'You don't look it.'

'Don't bother.'

'I mean it.'

'I don't give a shit whether you mean it or not. What difference does it make? They all say they mean it. When they stop coming I'll know it was bullshit, won't I?'

There was silence for a moment. Jill drew on her cigarette with her eyes on the ceiling. It felt almost as if we really had made love.

Then her eyes slid back to my face. 'Are you after my daughter?'

I didn't say anything.

'Do you fancy her? What's the matter with you – cat got your tongue?'

I didn't want to lie. I said, 'It's too early for that, isn't it? For her?'

'Don't.' She crushed the cigarette on the stem of a lamp behind the sofa.

'Are you jealous of her?'

'I don't want you to. You leave her alone.'

'Is that a warning?'

'She told me you were sniffing round there last night.' She shook her head. 'As far as I'm concerned you're still just a copper. I may fancy you, but that doesn't change anything. I don't want you chasing after my daughter.'

I stood up. 'I'm not chasing after anything,' I said. 'Except who killed Joe Bates.'

'Clare's a fool.' Jill went on as if she hadn't heard me. 'She always needs someone to look after her. That's why she fell for Joe. That's how Fred James got in. Right now she's looking around for someone to lean on. You understand? But it's not going to be you.' She broke off and looked up at me. 'Going somewhere?'

'Did you bring me here for anything else?'

'No.' She shrugged and looked away, her lips pursed. I started moving towards the door. Jill didn't do anything to stop me.

As I reached the door she said, 'Stay away from Clare. Remember that.'

I left her sitting wrapped in a blanket on the sofa, staring at the photograph of her dead husband.

## 28

It was quarter to six. Mason wouldn't be out before six-thirty and I didn't rate my chances of bluffing my way past the entrance desk. I didn't suppose that he would actually want to see me.

I made my way towards the Kennington Road and found a sandwich bar behind Waterloo station. The day's trade was over. The owner, a balding Italian with his shirtsleeves rolled up, was putting bowls of food away in the refrigerator. I ordered a coffee and a stale-looking roll and sat down at the back.

On a shelf above the door the television was playing an Australian soap opera. A man and woman were having an argument about something I didn't understand. Maybe he'd had an affair, or their kid had stolen something from another kid. It looked like an ordinary domestic crisis, bad enough to keep the viewers hooked, not so bad that they'd switch channels. No one had killed anybody.

The screen vomited gaudy emotions, fake anger. Somebody was crying; somebody else stormed out of a room slamming the door. There were close-ups of happy faces, sad faces, people receiving good news and bad. Like a clockwork doll going through its movements, soap life clicked from one scene to the next: indoors, outdoors, in the pub, by the pool. It was about as much like real life as a toy doll was like a real person. It left out all the bits in between, when people didn't know what to think, or when they thought two things at once. It left out the main sensations of being alive, which were uncertainty, loneliness and fear.

The owner was backing around the shop with his mop,

trying to keep his eye on the screen. Every now and then he chuckled, and shook his head as if he was remembering a joke. The credit music came up. He stooped to sweep the mop under a table.

'I love it,' he said, pointing at the screen. 'It's funny.'

'You think it's funny?'

'My daughter's in Australia.'

'Lucky girl.'

'She watches it too. They get it three months before we do. I have to make her promise not to tell me what's going to happen.' He laughed and pushed the mop back behind the bar. 'She lives in Melbourne.'

'Have you ever been to visit her?'

'Once.' He looked out into the street. A garbage truck was rolling slowly along the market, picking up debris. Men in overalls were walking alongside it, slinging cardboard boxes into the back. 'She has a nice house. It's a good life there.'

'Why don't you go and live there?'

'Me? I'm too old. Besides, I've got my mother. It's nice to visit, though. In summer they go hiking in the bush. Every summer for two weeks. Her husband's a teacher, teaches English.'

I took a bite of my roll. It didn't taste of anything. I could have sat there for a long time, listening to someone else's stories about a place I'd never go to.

Instead of which I had to find Mason. I had to persuade a man who knew I was a liar that he'd made a mistake himself – more than one mistake. I had to go to him and say, 'You may not have any reason to trust me, but this time I'm telling the truth and you've got to believe me.'

The Italian came out from behind the counter and started stacking chairs upside down on the tables.

'You want anything else?' he said. 'I got to close.'

I told him I didn't want anything else. The clock above the door said quarter past six. I left some money on the table and went out. The market street was wet where the dustcart had been past. A man was walking behind it with a brush, sweeping up a debris of vegetable leaves, cardboard boxes, newspapers. I might have been walking to a night shift, just like a normal day. Except it wasn't a normal day, and I didn't have any night shift to go to.

I saw the photographers from a hundred yards away.

There was a group of them by the police station steps. I stopped. It was just possible that something else had happened in Kennington that day, and that was why there were photographers outside the police station. But it wasn't a risk I wanted to take.

I walked past the station without looking at it, then doubled back across the traffic lights. A side alley took me to the boundary fence of the station car park. There was nobody about. The barred windows of the station looked down at me. I had to take the risk that somebody might be looking out.

The fence was a wire net strung between steel posts, with cross-wires at every metre. I was hardly in the best condition for mountaineering. With an effort I got my foot on to the bottom cross-wire and hauled myself up. My legs started to complain. They wanted to be lying on a bed somewhere, with someone rubbing cool ointment into them. I rested a moment, then gripped the top of a post and swung myself over the netting. It dipped and swayed, but I was over. I dropped down on to the tarmac. No sound came from the station building.

Twenty to seven. If the reporters outside meant anything, Mason could be in there for hours. I stooped low and ran between the rows of cars until I found his, a blue Granada. It was parked with its back up to the building, not far from the door where people came out. I crouched down on the far side, close up to the wall, and started my wait.

Time passed. My legs went to sleep, but at least that stopped them from hurting. I struggled against sleep myself. Two officers came out laughing and drove off. Helen Rodber came out, her footsteps tapping fast across the tarmac. Two days ago these had been my colleagues, my equals. I'd been a part of a network, not a part that anyone liked much, but a member all the same; I was somebody. Now that had all changed. With a sickening lurch I'd fallen off the high wire. I'd been spun off the carousel and landed bruised on the grass outside its wheel of lights. In the distance I could hear the roar of London. It was a big, loud, untidy system, and I wasn't a part of it. People bought their groceries, rented flats, sued each other, died and were buried by other people. Somehow they all needed each other, but they didn't need me. I'd broken the rules.

Somewhere I'd read about Amazon villages where they punished people by exile. They didn't beat them or lock them up; they just took them outside the village at dusk and left them there. In the morning they'd be gone, taken by animals or defeated by the fear and loneliness of the jungle.

Night started to fall. The station lights came on, casting slatted shadows over the roofs of cars. I sat with my back to the wall and wondered which would get me first: solitude or the wild animals.

At half past seven the door opened and I heard a solid tread coming along the wall towards me. I ducked down and looked under the bumper. Feet approached the other side of the car, stopped; keys jangled. When I stood up he had his back to me.

I said, 'Mason.'

He swung round. His face was scared until he saw who it was.

'What the hell do you want? How did you get in?'

Maybe he was angry just because I'd surprised him, or maybe I would always make him angry.

I said, 'I had to see you.'

'You had to see me,' he mimicked. He kept unlocking the car. 'Couldn't you have made an appointment? If you've got anything worth saying.'

'Would you have seen me?'

He looked at me. There were lines of strain around his eyes.

He said quietly, 'I've had journalists on my back all day, baying for blood. You know why? Some prick tipped them off that a copper in my squad had been caught rigging evidence. I've spent six hours lying through my teeth for you. You know what I was thinking all the time? I was thinking, why am I doing this? Why don't I just throw him to the lions?'

I didn't say anything.

'Well – why don't I?' He swung open the car door. 'Here's the story. A businessman living in South London, member of the local community. Policeman has a grudge against him – no one knows why – so he frames him for a murder he can't solve. They don't know names or anything. But they know there's a bad smell and it's coming from my station. What do *you* think I ought to do?'

I said 'Who tipped them off – Hill?'

'It could have been Hill.' He shrugged. 'For all I know it could have been someone indoors. Some copper who'd put up with you throwing your weight around for too long and wanted to get his own back. Someone you snubbed. Someone you put down because no one could be as clever as George Havilland. Frankly I wouldn't blame them, if it wasn't me who had to clear up the mess.'

He threw his briefcase on to the passenger seat and started to get in.

'What are you going to do?'

'I haven't decided. That's the only reason I'm saving your skin.'

I said, 'Fred James didn't kill Bates.'

Mason stopped and looked at me. 'That's funny,' he said. 'He thinks he did.'

I shook my head. 'He can't have done. You can see that. There are too many problems with his confession. He didn't even know how many shots had been fired.'

'Tell me about it, Havilland.'

I came round to his side of the car. 'What about the motorbike? Do you think Fred James just forgot to tell us? Joe Bates was killed cleanly, three shots in the neck. There was no struggle.'

Mason shut the door. He pressed a button and the window rolled down between us. I could see lights on the dashboard.

'So maybe there wasn't a struggle. Maybe he killed him in cold blood. We haven't ruled that out yet. The old woman might have heard the bike in her dreams. You know what they're like. Anyway, if he didn't kill Bates, why did he say he did?'

'Someone forced him.'

'Who?'

'Hill,' I said.

Mason looked at me coldly. Slowly he shook his head. 'You would say that,' he said. 'Wouldn't you?'

He turned the ignition. The engine cleared its throat. I raised my voice to talk over it. 'What about Penny?'

'What?'

'Penny,' I shouted. 'Did Fred James kill him too?'

'Not related.' He was turning the wheel. I wasn't going to make him listen. 'We've had the experts in, Havilland. It was a straightforward accident. Tragedy, really.'

The car was moving. Mason was checking his mirror.

He said, 'I'd be careful getting back, if I were you. They might recognize you.'

'Do they have my name?'

He shrugged. 'I didn't give it to them.'

It was too late. Mason raised one hand; I stepped away from the car. His tail-lights were blinking at the entrance to the car park.

For a long time I stood watching the space where his car had been. Mason was gone, and he'd taken with him my only chance of getting back inside the system. I was out in the jungle, with the village lights twinkling behind a wall I could never climb.

Suddenly I heard a clatter of steps behind the exit door. I pressed myself back into the shadows. Three men came out. One of them was Cayman. They were laughing, carrying sports bags, on their way to a game of squash and a pint. Cayman was telling some joke he'd heard in the canteen. They threw their bags into the boot of a blue Astra and drove off.

Silence descended around me, and with it came fear. There

were reporters waiting for me at the door of the building. I no longer had the protection of a uniform; I no longer had the assistance of Mason, or Cayman, or anyone. I was alone in the jungle.

The wire fence sagged where I had climbed over it. I hauled myself back up and dropped down into the alley on the other side. At the end of the alley I turned left and started walking.

## 29

The flat hadn't tidied itself up since that morning. I switched on the light and surveyed the chaos. If anything it seemed worse. I picked up a few records. They were scratched beyond repair, with razor-slashes across each side. The sleeves were torn. On top of one pile I saw a familiar label: *Louis Armstrong's All-stars*. I'd bought it at home with my brother, one of my first jazz records. We'd taken it back to the attic and played it together, Satchmo's trumpet splitting the grey Midlands afternoon in half. I was just fifteen. That record would never play again. A crooked line cut across it from one edge to the other.

I picked up some more. *Mulligan meets Monk*, a CD bought from Ray's Jazz Shop a couple of years ago; *Sketches of Spain*, played so often it had started to jump; *Django Reinhardt*, an import I'd found in Pie's shop just a few months before. I'd been with Mary. That was before she decided that a lifetime alone would be better than one day married to me.

These records were my memories, my past. Every important moment of my life was stored in them. Through them I could travel anywhere: I could be a boy going on his first date; I could be looking at London for the first time; I could be making love in a student bedsit with the sounds of a party beating against the window. Or I could be staring down an empty sidestreet in a Midlands town, trying to make sense out of a blank pavement. Not all of the memories were happy, but that wasn't the point. Now I didn't have them any more I felt naked. It was as if I'd just been born that minute, a man without a past, into a ruined apartment with London humming and roaring outside. I felt empty.

The hi-fi lay in pieces on the floor, cases burst, wire entrails spewing out on to the carpet. I gave the flat another chance to do its own dirty work and walked down to the Blue Moon Café for something to eat. They gave me a plate of cannelloni and a mug of thick coffee. It was the first proper meal I'd had in days. I stopped on the way back to pick up a bottle of wine. At home I poured myself a glass and started to tidy the flat up. Most of the records I threw out. There were sleeves I almost wanted to keep but I made myself throw them out too. Suddenly I found that I was humming. It was a melody by W. C. Handy, from the dawn of jazz. I picked up the wrecked hi-fi and dumped it into the bin. Slowly the room was getting back to the way it had been before Mary and I moved in. One by one my possessions were thrown out, or piled up in the corner. The broken glass and debris were swept into the middle of the room and Hoovered up. The sofa was pulled upright. In the kitchen I went through everything, throwing out old cans and chipped plates, scooping up the glasses Hill had thrown on the floor. At the end of it I dragged two full bins out to the front area and went back indoors.

The flat was empty, cold, uninhabited. It wasn't mine any more, but nor did it belong to anyone else. It looked like a safe place to spend the night.

I went to the phone and dialled Clare's number. It rang a long time but no one answered, and the machine didn't cut in.

I sat on the sofa for a moment, just thinking, then went over to my case and dug out an address book. Andy Laing was a college friend of mine who was struggling as an architect in cheap offices in Camden Town. I hadn't seen him for more than a year. I dialled his number and got a machine playing Wagner.

I said, 'Andy, this is George Havilland. I need to see you about something.'

I left my number, hung up, then poured another glass of wine and lay down on the sofa.

There was something I had to think about. I didn't want to —

I'd been avoiding it for two days – but if I didn't turn round and face it now I'd have it on my heels for the rest of my life, a monster stalking through the jungle behind me. I had to face the confession I had faked for Hill.

I was sitting in my office at the station. Outside Cayman was talking to someone. Miles looked down at me from the pinboard; I didn't look him in the eye. I felt light-headed, almost drunk. My hands, rolling the statement form into the machine, were clumsy. I felt as if I was in a race, or panicking to get out of a burning house. I didn't have time to think about what I was doing, I just had to go ahead and do it . . .

No, I couldn't allow myself that. I didn't *want* to think about what I was doing. The idea had flashed into my mind, and at that point something had cut off. Conscience, habit, all the things that would have saved me from it – they were like a crowd pressing against a barrier. And I didn't let them in. That was conscious: I was standing at the barrier, blocking them out, and giving myself time to do something I should have known was wrong. I knew I didn't have much time – that was what gave me the feeling of panic. I knew that if I took too long, ordinary feelings would break down the door. They would tear the paper out of the machine, tell me that I was a fool, slap me about the face. But for ten minutes, half an hour – for as long as I didn't *think* about it – I was free to write my lie.

Something had set me free: anger, Hill's mocking face in the interview room. Maybe arrogance as well. Maybe it went back further than that, and for some time I'd been adrift from my moorings without knowing it. Because I no longer felt shamed by what anyone else thought, Cayman or Mason; and shame is, in the end, what keeps most of us trudging along the same pavement. I'd lost the habit of caring about their mockery or their condemnation, because I'd built another habit around me instead: the habit of despising them. I'd walked off into a world in which I was the only player who mattered. It was like skiing blind, or walking down a dark corridor: there was nothing around me to give me my bearings. Then Hill had appeared in front of me, Hill who had taken the rules of the game, torn them up and laughed. If he could step outside the game, commit a crime without punishment, then why shouldn't I? How could I catch him if I didn't tear up the rules myself and follow him out into the jungle?

At one point the door had opened. Cayman, asking for some detail on another case. I had leaned forward over the typewriter, covering it with my elbow – that had been instinct. But as soon as I'd done it, then the lie had beaten me. I had tried to protect it: I'd become its slave. It was too late to go back. The words had formed themselves easily enough in my mind: *It was because of his wife . . .* They were almost the same as the words he had used in the interview room. I could hear his voice whispering in my ear. Another few moments and the thing was finished: three extra paragraphs tacked on to the last page of the interview report which Hill had already signed. A confession neatly filling the half-page gap between his last statement and the signature scrawled at the bottom of the sheet.

That was the most dangerous moment, the moment when the truth should have reasserted itself. My head had been swimming. I felt as if I'd been taking drugs. There wasn't any time to lose. I had put it in a folder, walked – run, almost – to Mason's office and dropped it on his desk. He wasn't there. The folder lay in his in-tray. I turned away and went out. Sitting back in my office I heard his footsteps coming along the corridor, the door of his room opening. Then it was too late.

Suddenly, lying on the sofa in the flat, I realized that my face was wet. I was crying like a child, with my shoulders heaving and breath coming in agonized bursts. In ten minutes I had thrown out everything I'd been working for since leaving college ten years before; everything I had dreamed of on those grey afternoons at home, when I pictured robbers caught and villains sent to justice. I swung my legs on to the floor, sat up, leaned my elbows on my knees. I pressed the heels of my hands into my temples, took a few deep breaths and got it under control. I was back in the flat again; for the moment it was over. I didn't think it would ever really be over.

Shakily I stood up and went to the kitchen to refill my glass with water. I stood there by the sink and drank glass after glass, until my breathing was normal again.

Back in the sitting room I sat down with my shoulders against the wall. I didn't have time to linger too long on what I'd done; I had to work out what to do next. There were too many hunters outside: Mason, Hill, the press. I knew what I wanted. I wanted evidence against Hill, good evidence this time, that would put him inside despite what I had done. That way I would, in a manner of speaking, be proved right. Mason might be able to smooth over the charges against me – particularly if he owed Hill's conviction to me. The world would be turned the right way up again.

It was the best solution, by far, but I knew that I couldn't rely on it. I'd tried working backwards from a solution once, and it hadn't helped me. No, there was only one thing for me to do. I had to find the truth, whatever it was. I was almost certain that Fred James had not killed Joe Bates. If I could prove that Hill had, then I was in the clear. If not, then I would be sending myself down. It wouldn't be much of a reward. But finding the truth was the only way to untie a knot that I had tied – wherever it left me. The truth was in there somewhere, a narrow thread weaving through smoke. I had to discover it.

I tried to call Clare again and got the machine. I didn't leave a message, then I rang back and said that I had called. I imagined the yellow living room, Clare tidying the child's toys. I could happily spend time in that flat; time with the blue curtains drawn to hide what was outside, with Clare sitting on the blue and white sofa. I wondered what she would be like to come home to in the evening: the place cleaned up, toys tidied away – the sort of thing most men are dreaming about most of the time. I couldn't pretend to be original. The thought of her listening to my voice on the machine was comforting, somehow.

I went back to the living room. There were a lot of

questions to be answered, but I didn't have anything to throw at them. I had too little to go on – any number of questions, not enough answers. My mind was like a disengaged motor, chewing up air. About ten o'clock I went to bed to try and repair some of what Hill had done the evening before. It didn't work. Somewhere in the middle of this was a pattern, a melody that made the rest fall into place. I could catch snatches of it but not enough to reconstruct the tune.

About half past eleven the phone rang.

'George?' The voice sounded tentative. 'I got your message.'

'Andy.'

'I haven't heard from you.' He didn't say anything about Mary but we both knew that was why he hadn't heard from me. 'Am I calling too late?'

'No. There's something I want to ask you about. Is that all right? It'll take maybe an hour.'

He said, 'I've got all the time in the world.' His laugh sounded thin.

We made a time for the following morning, then couldn't think of anything else to say.

He said tentatively, 'I'm sorry about it. You and Mary.'

I said, 'Yeah.'

We didn't know how to say any more than that. Or maybe it was my fault, or the fault of all men who blame themselves for the end of something. After another pause we said goodbye and hung up.

I spent the night being sorry about Mary.

## 30

At eight o'clock the next morning I was sitting in a café opposite the building site in Old Brompton Road where John Penny's body had been found the day before. It was a sunny morning. The office workers trooping past the café window looked happy and eager, as if today was going to be a big adventure: they were going to make a fortune, fall in love, find a dream job. Yesterday it had been overcast and the future had looked bleak. All it took was a little sunshine.

I looked down at my newspaper. Penny's face stared up at me from half a column of obituary. It was a younger, sober Penny, blinking out of a stiff khaki collar and greased-back hair. I ran my eye over it: Eton, the army, a father in politics in the thirties. Penny was the kind of man who'd built the empire and won the war, but now there weren't any more wars to win, or colonies to conquer, and all he could think of to do was drink and front other people's property companies. It wasn't that much of a life. He'd been brave in the war but never climbed higher than captain. There were lists of charities he'd supported. I remembered Penny's nervous smile, the old woman's eyes watered down by drink. He'd looked the part, but didn't have anything to go with the looks. If he'd been born anywhere else his obituary might have been a memorial tankard at the back of the bowls club bar, or a couple of old medals sent down to the antiques shop. He hadn't got much out of his birth except the face of a duke, half a column of obituary in *The Times* and a nagging sense that everyone was expecting more of him than he was going to be able to give. It wasn't enough to keep him off the bottle. Maybe it hadn't been enough to keep him away from the scaffold sometime late on Tuesday night.

I took a sip of coffee and looked out of the window. A hoarding on the building site across the road said Hill Properties. Behind it was a stone façade held in place by steel girders; behind that was nothing but empty air. For some reason that made me think of Penny. Not just of Penny, but of everyone like him: stuffed shirts and noble faces, firm handshakes, public-school voices; and behind that nothing at all, just a lot of rubble where the empire had been.

The door opened and a crowd of men came in wearing builders' overalls. They sat down at a long table at the back. One of them opened out a newspaper. A long-faced woman came out from behind the counter, wiped a dirty rag over the formica table-top and took orders for breakfast without writing them down.

The man with the newspaper said, 'There's nothing here about the old man.' His voice was Irish.

I glanced out of the window again. Across the road a uniformed guard was standing in the site entrance, looking up and down the pavement. There was no sign of work on the scaffolding.

One of the other men at the table was lighting a cigarette. He shook out the match and said, 'There wouldn't be, would there? Geezer like that. Never touches the paper, they keep it private.'

'How can they?'

Someone else said, 'There's no reason to put it in anyway. An accident on a building site, it happens the whole time, like.'

The long-faced woman came out from behind the counter with plates of food that smelled of grease. She said, 'Sausage, two eggs, bacon and fried, no beans.'

The Irishman put his hand up like he wanted to answer a question at school, then folded the paper and propped it between the salt cellar and a bottle of vinegar. After a moment he said, 'Did anyone see Tommy this morning? Didn't think he'd come to work, after yesterday. Thought he'd call in sick.'

'He was sick, yesterday,' said the man with the cigarette. 'Fucking everywhere. When he saw the old man.'

'Can't blame him for that,' the Irishman said. 'I nearly lost it myself. Blood all over his head.' He shook his head.

The other man ground out his cigarette and said, 'Site I was working on once, guy put his hand in a fucking bandsaw. Blood fucking everywhere. You could see the bone where it took the hand off. A few of us picked up the hand, gave it to the ambulance man. They sewed it back on in the hospital. Fucking wonderful.'

A black guy at the end of the table said, 'I heard that story before.'

The café door opened. A boy in working clothes and a woollen cap came in wiping his hands on trousers that were dirtier than his hands were. The men at the table shuffled along to make room for him.

'All right, Tommy?'

He went up to the counter and spoke to the long-faced woman, then went and sat down.

One of the men said, 'Feeling better, Tommy?'

He said, 'I'm all right. It's just the flu. I had it all last week.' The men at the table laughed. He blushed. 'It's true. You ask Scotty, I told him about it Friday. Nearly didn't come in. My brother had it. I was heaving my guts out all weekend.' He looked around to see if anyone believed him.

The long-faced woman came over to the table with a mug of tea and put it in front of the newcomer. She started clearing up empty plates.

The Irishman said, 'Ought to be getting back. You'll be all right?'

The boy was warming both hands around the mug of tea. 'Scotty told me half past. Can I have your paper?'

The men got up from the table and began to move towards the door, digging in their pockets for change.

When they were gone I stood up and walked to the back of the café. The boy in the woollen cap didn't look up. He was sitting with the paper in front of him, reading football scores.

I said, 'Must have looked pretty nasty. It can do, when they fall from high up.'

His face was pinched and narrow. He looked wary.

I said, 'Do you mind?'

'What do you want?'

I pulled back a chair and sat down opposite him. He looked towards the door, then back at me. He didn't say anything.

'You work across the road, don't you?'

He looked suspiciously at me. 'Are you from the papers?'

'From the police.'

There was a pause, then he said, 'You weren't there yesterday.'

'I wasn't on duty yesterday.'

The boy took a sip of his tea. His eyes darted towards the newspaper.

'Was it you who found him?' I asked.

He looked back at me and nodded. 'With Scotty. It was Scotty, really. I was with him.'

'Who's Scotty?'

'Foreman.'

'What time was it?'

'I told them yesterday.'

'You can tell me again.'

He put the mug down. 'I don't want any trouble.'

'You're not in trouble,' I said.

His eyes darted back over the newspaper but without seeing anything. 'What are you doing in here?' There was a faint crease between his eyebrows.

'Same as you.'

He said, 'My brother's a policeman. Was. Works for Securicor now.'

'What's your name?'

'Wilson.'

'Your first name.'

He thought for a minute, then said, 'Thomas,' formally, the way he'd say it to a bank manager.

I said, 'I'll be asking you questions when I go up to the site, anyway. Isn't it easier if we do it in here?'

He shrugged. 'All right.'

The long-faced woman came over and put a plate of eggs in front of him. He stared at it as if he didn't know what eggs were for. He didn't pick up his fork.

I said gently, 'The first week I was on duty, after police college, there was a guy killed himself in his flat. I had to pick up the pieces, then we went to the canteen and everyone was playing with their food and making jokes about the way his head had looked. They thought it was funny.'

He nodded dumbly. 'My brother said it was like that.'

'Is that why he left?'

He shook his head. 'Couldn't take the hours. It was his girlfriend made him. His wife. My mum wanted me to go in, too.'

'You're better where you are.'

He sniffed, picked up his fork and began to play with the eggs.

I said, 'So what time was it you got to work yesterday?'

'Normal time. Just after eight.' He said it with his mouth full.

'Were you the first in?'

He nodded. 'Scotty picked me up. He lives just by us.'

'Is that how you got the job?' I asked.

'Friend of my dad's.'

'Is Scotty always the first there?'

'He has to open up.'

'You mean, unlock the gate?'

'And switch the power on.'

'When did you know he was there . . . Penny?'

The boy stopped eating and frowned at his empty mug. 'Went up to the power switches, up on the first stage. Saw his feet sticking out.' He looked at me, focusing not on my eyes but somewhere underneath them. 'Sticking out, like . . . not moving. We thought there'd been an accident.'

I said, 'There was an accident.'

He ignored me. 'Scotty started shouting and ran towards him. I . . . I kept behind him. I didn't want to. I wasn't feeling good.' The frown had turned into an expression of pain. 'Went after him and looked over his shoulder. Saw a guy lying there, all . . . He was in a funny position, and his head was . . .' He choked. His voice went on gasping, as if he couldn't get enough air in. 'He didn't have a head, just a . . . all covered in blood and . . .' He looked up at me. 'Bits . . .'

I said, 'All right. What did Scotty do?'

There was a pause. When the boy spoke again his voice was more normal. 'He started swearing. Never heard him swear like that. He said, "They've been fucking around on the hoist again." We didn't think who it was, that it was . . . He thought it was one of the guys . . .' He shivered. 'You wouldn't have recognized him from his face anyway.'

'Did you know who he was afterwards?'

'Yes.'

'When?'

'Larry came in. The Irish guy, the old one. He said, "It's Penny." From the clothes.'

'You all knew who Penny was?'

He nodded. The eggs were cooling on his plate.

'Did he visit the site often?'

'The whole time. Tried to talk to us.'

'What did he talk about?'

He shrugged. 'Nothing.'

There was a pause.

I said, 'What happened then?'

'Then Scotty told me to call an ambulance. 999 . . . I've never had to, before. They said, "What service do you want." I said, "An ambulance, what do you think I fucking want . . ."' He stopped.

'Where did you call from?'

'The site hut. When I got back they'd put a bit of sheet over his head, a bit of damp-proof.' He pushed the plate to one side and looked at his watch. 'I ought to be getting back. I'm past my time.'

I said, 'It's all right, I'll come with you. I'll tell them I wanted to talk to you.'

He nodded vaguely and fished in his pocket for change. The frown had stayed between his eyebrows.

I followed him out of the café.

At the site gate a lorry was backing off the road with the driver leaning out of the open door to look backwards. The guard in uniform was waving directions from the pavement.

He scowled when Tommy came up.

Tommy nodded towards me. 'He's from the police. He wanted to talk to me.'

The man looked at me. He stayed scowling. 'You weren't here yesterday.'

I said, 'That's right.'

Somebody shouted and the lorry's brakes squealed. The driver jumped down and disappeared towards the back of the site.

I said, 'I want to see where they found him. And talk to Scotty.'

'Scotty's busy at the moment.'

'Get him for me.'

'He'll be down soon. He's in the site office.'

I said to Tommy, 'Where's the site office?'

The man in the uniform said, 'They were here two hours yesterday, asking their questions. What's it for? If you ask me –'

I started walking towards a ladder that led up into the scaffolding above. Tommy followed me.

The man in the uniform said, 'You shouldn't go up without a pass, anyway. I don't know what good it is. It's not as if you can bring Sir John back.'

I turned round. 'Did you know him?'

The man stuck out the chest of his uniform. 'Sir John always had a word for me,' he said. 'Any time of day. Always had time for a chat. Nothing fancy about Sir John. Sir John used to say to me –'

I said, 'It's true, we can't bring him back.'

I started climbing the ladder.

Above me rose the back of the façade; I was looking up through where the floors had been. Immediately over the site entrance a scaffolding walkway extended out through one of the empty windows. At the first staging was a narrow timber catwalk leading to a Portakabin at the back of the site.

Tommy led me towards the Portakabin. Inside, two men were leaning over some plans on a table. There were plastic chairs behind the table and a row of yellow hard hats on the wall.

One of the men turned round when I came in. He was short and dark, with anxious blue eyes. He said, 'Yes?' He had a strong Glaswegian accent.

Tommy said, 'He's from the police. He wanted to speak to you.'

The foreman looked harassed. 'They came yesterday.' He put one hand to his eyes.

'Was it you who found him?'

'With Tommy.' He nodded towards the boy. 'Can't it wait?'

I told him it couldn't, and watched while he folded up the plans and said something I didn't understand to the other man. Then he put on a hat and led the way out on to the scaffold.

Builders stripped to the waist were joking over bags of tools. We followed a walkway just behind the façade. There were holes in the stonework where floors had been. Suddenly, about halfway along, we came out under a shaft that ran up through the galleries above. Beyond the shaft the loading walkway projected out over the pavement.

The Irishman I had seen in the café was unhooking a pallet from a cable which snaked up to a hoist somewhere above. Out above the pavement another man was shouting instructions to someone below.

'Half a minute, Larry.'

The builder nodded, grinned at me and stood aside.

I stepped out into the middle of the shaft and looked up.

'He was lying just there, where the pallet is.' The foreman's voice was trembling. 'Right in front of you. I tell you . . . Had the shock of my life when I saw him. Nearly lost my . . . Actually I didn't recognize him at first . . . just a fellow lying there. I nearly fainted.' His anxious eyes darted about him.

They were clear blue, a child's eyes that couldn't cope with what they had been forced to look at. 'Looked like a dummy from a shop window. I thought one of the lads had been playing a bit of a joke on me.'

'What time was this?'

'Twenty-five to eight. Soon as I got to site.'

'What did you do?'

'Oh . . .' He gulped. He was seeing it again, his eyes flickering over the empty planks. 'I went up to him slowly. The back of his head was all mashed in . . . like . . . like . . . Didn't know who it was at first. He had eyes open, looking right up at me. Haven't seen anything like that since . . . It was like something in the pictures.' The builder sucked air through his teeth and shook his head. I wondered how often the story had been told.

'What was he was wearing?'

'Normal clothes. A suit.'

'Did you notice his shoes?'

'No.'

I looked down at the platform. Two of the boards were new, paler than the others. The boards to either side were faintly darkened, as if someone had spilt oil on them.

I said, 'Did the policemen yesterday find where he had fallen from?'

'Up there.' He pointed up the shaft. 'The only place it could be.'

'Show me.'

He led me up a series of ladders, passing gloomy spaces lit by the glare of welding torches. A constant hammering reverberated through the frame. At the top we came out into the sunshine on a platform between the chimneys of the neighbouring buildings. Two lads who had been sunning themselves on a pallet scrambled up when we emerged and hurriedly started stacking bags of cement. The foreman ignored them.

At the top of the shaft was a steel frame with a pulley suspended from it. An electric motor was clamped to the scaffold behind. A man with his back to us was standing by the motor, peering down the shaft with one hand on the frame. The din of hammering echoed up the shaft from below.

'They said he was up here,' the foreman shouted.

'Do you know why?'

He shrugged. 'It's what they said. It's the highest he could have fallen from.'

'Isn't there a guard-rail?'

'There's a gate. It swings open to let gear through.'

He led me over to the frame and demonstrated. The man working the motor looked at us and shook his head solemnly.

I leaned over and looked down the shaft. Forty feet below Larry was hooking up a pallet of cement. For a moment I saw John Penny's body lying there, aristocratic head flung back, eyes staring at a tiny square of stars above him.

I said, 'Why would he have been here at night?'

The foreman's eyes widened. 'That's what the lads have been saying.'

'He often came on site, didn't he?'

'That's right.'

'Was there any reason for that?'

He shrugged. 'Bloody pain, to be honest with you. Always asking the boys what they were doing. Could have done without it.'

I said, 'What sort of state was he in, when he came?'

The foreman blushed. 'I think . . . to be honest with you . . .' He spread his hands out and shrugged again.

'Was he often drunk?'

'I wouldn't want to say.'

'You already did say.'

'All right.' The Scotsman wouldn't catch my eye. 'To be honest with you, I think he liked his glass. Let's say that, shall we?'

I said, 'You can put it however you like.'

Scotty looked at his watch.

I kept looking down for a moment longer. The steel cable swayed in the middle of the shaft. At every level were gates and piles of building materials. The sounds of work, hammering, whistling, drifted up from below.

We climbed slowly back down the scaffold. At the entrance I turned to the foreman. 'Did Penny have his own keys?'

'To the site? No, only me and the guv'nor.'

'Who's that?'

'Contract manager. From our firm. Kept a spare set at the office.'

'How often does he come down here?'

'Never unless he has to. Site meetings every week.'

'How many keys does it take?'

'Just the one. A Yale.'

I said, 'Who locks up at night?'

'I do.'

'You locked up two nights ago?'

His eyes went anxious. 'The other fellows kept asking me that.'

'Did you?'

'Yes.' His voice was defensive.

'Scotty wouldn't forget a thing like that,' the guard interrupted. 'Never has done. Not while I've known him. And that's a few years now –'

I said, 'Does the key look like this?'

I took a small brass key out of my pocket. It was the one we'd found on Joe Bates's body.

Scotty drew a key out of his own pocket and held it up against mine.

'That's the one.'

'Where did you get this?' the guard asked suspiciously.

I said, 'You've both been very helpful.'

From the other side of the road I looked back. On the hoarding was a picture of executives getting out of sports cars outside the building. They were smiling, shaking hands, making deals. Beneath it was the name of a firm of architects. I took down the name and turned towards the tube.

## 31

At Camden Town a drunk was sitting on the steps of the tube watching the traffic sullenly, as if it was all their fault. When I walked past he flung one hand out and drew it back again almost at once, as if he knew no one was going to give him anything.

I crossed Camden High Street and turned right into a dark side alley lined with old warehouses. Through windows I could see people staring at computers in brightly lit offices. I stopped at a narrow door halfway down with a row of buttons alongside it. I pressed a button near the top and waited until the machine buzzed at me. The brick walls of the staircase were painted pale green, the colour of prisons, hospitals and police stations. On each landing were doors with porthole windows showing modern offices behind them. Andy Laing's name was written in black metal letters beside a door on the third floor. I pushed it open and found a girl sitting behind a desk with her feet on a chair next to her. Her hair was dyed red and she wasn't wearing any make-up. Her feet were wearing Doc Martens. She gave me a friendly smile and asked me what I wanted.

'Is Mr Laing in? I've got an appointment.'

'I'll just see.'

She turned round in her chair and shouted, 'Andy! There's a guy to see you. He's . . .' She looked back at me. Her expression was vaguely challenging. 'What's your name?'

'Havilland.'

She shouted that over her shoulder as well, then smiled at me and said Mr Laing would only be a moment. I spent the moment looking at photographs of a model made out of white plastic and perspex with white plastic people looking happy on the pavement outside it. Somewhere a radio was playing jazz – maybe Coleman Hawkins, I didn't recognize the tune. A man came through from the office behind reception. He was in his early thirties, wearing a baggy white shirt with the tie tucked in between two buttons. He had long hair tied back in a ponytail and a face that was too chubby to wear hair that way. Since I'd first met him Andy's hair had gone up and down with every tide of fashion. There were two dark spots on his ear which had once been earrings.

I said, 'Hello, Andy.'

'George.' He gave me a broad smile. 'It's been too long. Where have you been hiding? I tried to call a couple of times.'

I said, 'I've been busy.'

'I heard about you and Mary,' he said. He shook his head, then he didn't know what else to say.

'Do you have an office?' I asked. 'Somewhere private?'

'You can come into our meeting room.' He smiled ruefully. 'That's what we call it, anyway.'

He turned and led me through a room full of drawing boards and long tables. Only one of them was occupied, by a girl with headphones on. Her head moved rhythmically as she drew. Andy opened a door at the back and led me into a long room that was too narrow for the table in it. There was a projector set up at one end, pointing at the window. He squeezed past chairs and sat down under the projector. Sketches were strewn haphazardly over the top of the table.

'So what happened?'

'What do you mean?'

'Between you and Mary.'

I said, 'She decided she didn't like me any more.'

'I'm sorry.' He put a hand to the back of his head and undid the ponytail. 'What's she up to?'

'Singing.'

'Jack said –' He stopped. He didn't tell me what Jack said. Instead, he said, 'You should have called. We could have . . . I don't know. Had a drink or something.'

Andy started playing with the elastic band that held his hair back. He smiled at me suddenly. 'I saw Phil Clarke the other day. You remember Phil Clarke?' Phil Clarke had been the person at college that everybody else laughed at. 'Works for a big commercial firm. Makes . . .' Andy's hand made big numbers in the air. 'It's the ones you never suspect, isn't it?' He laughed good-naturedly. 'I don't grudge him. Even if he is a talentless, scheming bastard.'

I said, 'That's good of you.'

Andy laughed again. 'Why don't you stay in touch?' he asked. 'Do you think I'm worried you're a cop now?'

'No.'

'You always said that was what you wanted, anyway.'

'I told you, I've been busy.'

'Don't knock it.'

I thought of the empty drawing boards next door. 'Has it been like this for long?'

'Too long. Some bastard needs to pick up the phone and dial my number.' He flicked the elastic band towards the window, then got up and bent over two chairs to pick it up. 'It's all right for you. People don't stop killing each other.'

'Tell that to the ones who get killed.'

Andy went back to winding the band around his fingers. 'What I need is a sheikh with a new town to build in a desert somewhere. Or somebody's daughter. Someone who owns a chain of supermarkets, and their daughter wants to open a trendy restaurant, money no object . . . you know? That would do me a treat, designing a hip restaurant for someone. Or a nightclub.' He flicked the band towards the window again and let it fall under a chair.

I pointed at the sketches. 'What's this?'

'Competitions.' He shrugged. 'You can't say we don't try. Three of them in the last six months, no places, no prize money, one lousy picture in a trade magazine no one reads except other architects with too much time on their hands.'

'So why do you keep going?'

He gave me an odd little smile and bunched the hair behind his head in one hand. 'Because it's fun.' He laughed, picked up a sketch and crumpled it into a ball. 'The same reason Mary keeps singing. I mean, she sings great but she's never going to be big. You do it because it's fun.'

He pitched the crumpled sketch towards the window and looked at me with the same odd little smile. 'Are you seeing anybody else?'

I didn't know how to answer that. 'Maybe. I don't know.'

'Early days?'

'You could say that.'

'Anyone I know?'

I shook my head.

Andy laughed. 'Have it your own way.'

'I don't have it any way,' I said.

He laughed properly at that and leaned forward over the table. 'What was it you wanted to see me about?'

I said, 'There's a case with some property mixed up in it. I wanted to find out how it worked.'

'What's the company?'

I looked at him. I could trust Andy because he wouldn't care about what I said anyway. All he cared about was architecture, and more architecture, and a few friends he'd had so long he didn't have to think about them any more. I hoped I was still one of them.

I said, 'Hill Properties.'

Andy nodded.

'Did you ever work for them?'

'If only.'

'What do people say about them?'

'You mean, are they straight?' He shrugged. 'As straight as anyone. They've been around long enough. Half the developers that appeared in the boom went under in the first six months.' He waved one hand. 'Big offices on credit, developments paid for out of city loans and the whole thing folding up if they couldn't sell within four months. They used to be able to get away with that. Everyone thought it was going to last for ever. Same as last time round.'

'What about you?'

'I'm not in that game.'

'You mean you don't work for developers?'

'I did once. He sacked me after four months and didn't pay me a penny. I was talking about ... houses and cities, good design – you know what I mean – and he was talking about money. It took us four months to realize we were both serious, that was when he sacked me and went off with some city boys who charged half as much and did everything he told them to.'

'Who does the Hills' work?' I asked.

Andy frowned. 'Firm called Benson Smith Hodge.'

That was the name I'd seen on the hoarding outside the building site where John Penny died.

'What are they like?'

'They're what you'd expect. Worse than some, not as bad as others. It depends who's employing them.'

'Where would I find them?'

'In Charlotte Street. I had a friend who worked there a few years ago.'

I nodded. 'Can you explain something to me? What happens when a developer goes to an architect – what's the procedure?'

Andy grinned. 'How long have you got?' He took a deep breath. 'To start with the architect draws a building that he thinks is the best thing ever designed by anybody. It's got style, beautiful details, everything. Then he shows it to the developer, and the developer says it costs too much and doesn't have enough rental space in it. So the architect goes back, cuts out his favourite bit and sticks another floor on top. It doesn't look quite as good, but it's still enough like what he started with. A week later the client calls back and says, "I love it, Andy. Just put one more storey on top, and a pediment on the front like the one I saw on my holiday in Greece. Give it a bit of class."

'Now the architect can see where it's leading, but he has his rent to pay, so he says, "All right, we'll put on the extra storey. But I'm not sure about the columns. Don't you think they're out of place on a building made out of glass?" And the client thinks for a bit, then he says, "Now you mention it, I never did like that glass."'

I laughed. Andy was grinning.

'So the architect says, "I thought you wanted something dynamic and modern?" And the client thinks some more and says, "Dynamic and modern, but with columns and a pediment." So the architect looks at his rent cheque, and the kids' school fees, and he draws on columns and a pediment. And he's thinking, This is the last time I ever do it. But by now it's two months since he got his last fee cheque and if he doesn't keep going he'll have to sue the client for his money, and it'll take two years, and anything that comes out will go to the lawyers. That's when the client rings up and says, "I met this interior designer at a cocktail party last night" – meaning he picked her up – "and I've told her she can do anything she likes with the inside." And an eighteen-year-old girl with Gucci jewellery walks through the door carrying curtain samples and some drawings that look as if they were done by a three year-old, and . . .'

I said, 'All right. All right.'

Andy was laughing now. 'Now do you understand why I don't work for developers?'

'Sure.'

'Is that what you wanted to know?'

I laughed with him. 'No.'

'What, then?'

I traced a pattern on the table-top with one finger. 'I wanted to know how much you find out about the developer. Whether they come to you before they buy the site or after . . . How the planners fit in, that sort of thing.'

Andy nodded. 'The answer is, you know as much about the developer as they want to tell you. No one has so much work they can walk away from it.'

'Do they tell you who else is putting in money?'

'Never.'

'What about the planners – how does that work?'

'Every new building needs planning permission. If it's in a conservation area – which is most of central London – it's harder. You take sketches to the planning officer and argue about it. When you've more or less agreed, you put in an application, then sit back and wait for it to come through.'

'Is the planning officer elected?'

'A Councillor? No, he's just an employee. They do all the dog's work, then they write a report recommending the application for approval – or not – and the Councillors make their decision.'

'Do they always follow what the planning officers say?'

'Nine times out of ten. Normally they'll only turn it over if someone's been getting at them.'

'Meaning?'

'Meaning a pal of theirs rings up and asks them to block something that's going to block their view.'

'Or the other way round?'

'Exactly.'

I nodded.

Andy said, 'And somewhere in all of that mess there are a few people trying to make something good. Like me.'

There was a moment's silence. Andy was frowning at the pile of sketches in front of him.

I stood up. 'I didn't mean to take so much of your time. Thanks.'

'That's all right.' He smiled. 'It's a while since I last got it off my chest.'

Outside in the office, the girl at the drawing board was crooning along to some song we couldn't hear. The receptionist was talking on the phone, cradling the receiver under one ear.

I pointed at the white plastic model by the entrance. 'What's that?'

'A competition. Do you like it?'

'I don't know.'

'Nor do I. Sometimes I think it's great. Then I wonder why I bother.'

I said, 'I don't know anything about it. You know that.'

I held out my hand. Suddenly Andy was awkward again.

'We should get together properly. Will you call me?'

'Soon.'

'Have a drink or something.'

I smiled. 'Soon,' I repeated.

I left him staring at the white plastic model by the reception desk.

## 32

It took me a long time to dial the number of Kennington police station. Traffic was roaring past on Camden High Street. A man with a briefcase was waiting outside the phone box. He looked stressed; he kept making gestures for me to hurry up. I wondered if he could tell anything from my face. Maybe there was a look you got when you asked favours from people you used to walk on. Maybe it stayed with you, like the marks of a disease. Maybe in thirty years I'd look as beaten as he did.

A voice whined in the earpiece. The coins dropped.

I said, 'I want to speak to Bob Cayman.'

'Can I say who's calling?'

'It's his brother.'

There was a long wait. There would be a long wait: Cayman's brother had been in New Zealand for four years.

'Mark?' Cayman's voice sounded puzzled, tentative.

I said, 'It's George Havilland. Don't hang up.'

There was a pause.

'Cayman?'

'Yes.' His voice had hardened. At least he was still there.

'I need your help,' I said.

I didn't much like saying it. Outside, the man with the briefcase was looking at his watch, a harassed little man who needed everybody's help, the picture of what anyone could be like if they crawled far enough.

'You need my help.' Deadpan.

'I need to talk to Fred James,' I said.

'Who the fuck do you think you are?'

His voice was twisted with dislike. That wasn't just for

now, it was for four years of rivalry and pent-up irritation. It was for the years he had spent checking parking tickets in Kennington Lane while I drank in a student bar somewhere, for the council flat he grew up in, for the nights I'd shunned gatherings in the police canteen.

I leaned my head against the cold glass of the kiosk.

I said, 'Fred James didn't kill Bates. He couldn't have. Joe Bates was shot in the back of the neck, not killed in a struggle. Besides, Fred James isn't the type. He's got a fast line in talk and nothing else. He wouldn't take on Bates, or if he did it wouldn't be like that, by himself at night. He'd get help.'

There was a long pause. This was the turning point. If Cayman kept talking now there was a chance I could persuade him.

He cleared his throat. 'He had a reason,' he said.

'So did a lot of other people. Joe Bates was dealing drugs for Hill, using his job driving Penny as a cover. One of his customers was drinking with them in Babylon that night, a man called Poole. He also had an argument with John Penny on the day Bates was murdered.'

'You're trying to drag Penny in?' he interrupted.

'Why not? Hill could have killed Bates over drugs money or it could have been someone further down the line. I'm not saying it was Hill.'

Cayman snorted. 'So why did Fred James burn his shop down?'

'That could have been Hill, frightening him into making the confession. James is weak enough for that. How do you know he did it?'

'He told us.'

'That's what he would say,' I said.

'Only if his confession was another lie.'

I winced at that, but it wasn't the right time to pick a fight. I needed him.

I said, 'Have you tested the gun they found there?'

'Yes.'

'And?'

'It was the same gun Bates was shot with.'

That was a set-back but I couldn't give up now.

'What about Penny?' I asked. 'He dies two days after Bates. Are you still calling that an accident?'

Cayman sounded cautious. He lowered his voice; someone must have come into the office. 'I'm not going to help save your neck.'

'It's not about that,' I said. I didn't expect him to believe it. 'I think you've got it wrong. I may have got it wrong too, but that doesn't make it any better.'

'You didn't get it wrong,' he said. 'You made it wrong.'

I swallowed. 'I know that.'

'Why?'

'You've got to help me, Cayman.'

'No. You tell me why, first. Why did you write that confession for Hill?'

He sounded angry and hurt, like a child whose parents have betrayed him.

I looked at the man with the briefcase outside. There was a jogger behind him now, running marathons on the balls of his feet. I didn't think I could tell Cayman why. I could tell myself why, but even I wasn't sure I believed it. To say it out loud, bring it out into the air – I didn't think I could do that. It would sound like an excuse, a pathetic self-justification, and that was probably all it was.

'I don't know,' I said. 'Paddy Moran . . . Because I didn't want Hill to get away twice. I don't know.'

'You know we're all going to suffer for it?'

'Yes.' There didn't seem any point in saying more.

There was a long, long pause. For a while I thought he must have hung up. I kept gripping the receiver, praying for him to speak again.

His voice, when it came, was reluctant. It didn't hold any anger any more: it was as if he'd forgotten he was talking to a traitor.

'Everybody thinks Penny killed himself,' he said. 'Apparently he had a drink problem. The widow won't have it, nor will his friends. They'll get the coroner's verdict their way. We're not stirring it over.'

'It went in as . . .?'

237

'Accidental death.'

'And no one's saying anything?'

'What difference does it make?' Cayman's voice was defensive, angry again, but for different reasons.

I said, 'It's not true.'

'Do you know how funny that sounds, coming from you?'

'That's not the point,' I said. 'The point is, Penny didn't fall off that scaffolding. Either he jumped because of the drink, or it has something to do with the argument he was having with Poole. In that case Bates is connected. And Fred James doesn't have anything to do with it.'

'*If* they're connected.' Cayman sounded weary.

'The trouble is, no one's trying to find out whether they are or not. Except me. That's why I need your help.'

Another long pause. The counter on the telephone marked time. I could hear voices talking behind Cayman.

'What do you want?' he said.

'I want to get to Fred James.'

'You've come to the wrong place.'

'What do you mean?'

'He's been bailed. They took his manslaughter plea and let him out yesterday afternoon.'

'Who stood bail?'

'Nobody knows.'

'Do you have an address for him?' I asked.

'Yes, but you won't find him there.'

'Where is he?'

I knew the answer before he said it. 'He's with Clare Bates.'

I said 'Thanks, Cayman. By the way, there's one other thing . . .'

'Yes?'

'What time did Penny die?'

'Just after ten o'clock.' He sounded reluctant. 'We got the medical report this morning.

'Thanks,' I said again.

'You could have found out anyway.' He was trying to justify speaking to me.

'Will you let me know if anything else happens?'

'No.'

'It matters.'

'I've got to go now.'

'All right, Cayman.'

Suddenly something occurred to me. I said, 'By the way, I thought you were on leave. What happened to your mother-in-law?'

I shouldn't have said it, but asking favours was new to me and it didn't come that easy.

Cayman's voice was tight with anger when he answered.

'She died,' he said.

## 33

By the time I came out of the tube at Kennington the early evening paper was on the stand. The headline was a story about police corruption in South London. I bought one from an old man with a scarf around his head and read it standing on the pavement. It was hot air, mostly. They didn't seem to have names or details, but someone was putting out rumours as fast as they could.

There were black rings under Clare's eyes when she answered the door.

'Can I come in?'

'No.' She wouldn't look at me. 'I don't think you should.'

'I know you've got Fred here,' I said.

'That's not why.'

'So you do have him here?'

She almost smiled. 'Bloody policeman.' She looked back into the flat, holding the door protectively in front of her. 'Yes, he's here. He won't see you, though.'

I said, 'What did your mother tell you about me?'

Tears filled her eyes. She leaned her forehead against the edge of the door. 'She said . . .'

'I know she doesn't want me around you. She told me that. She told me why as well, but I'm not sure I believed her. Was that it?' Clare didn't say anything. Her eyes were screwed tight shut. 'Or was it worse than that?'

'Just go away . . .' Her shoulders were heaving, now. It was taking all her self-control not to break down completely.

'She said something more than that, didn't she?'

The back of Clare's head moved up and down.

'Did she tell you I went to bed with her?'

'You bastard.' It was hardly audible. The knuckles of her hand on the door were white.

I said, 'That isn't true.'

There was no answer.

'It isn't true,' I repeated. 'She wants me to stay away from you because I'm a policeman and because she doesn't trust me. Maybe some other things. I met her at Dick Hill's office yesterday and she took me home. We talked.' I paused. What could I say that would persuade Clare to see me without destroying Jill? I took a deep breath and went on. 'She tried to seduce me. I said no as nicely as I could, but she doesn't like men saying no to her. After that she warned me off you. For all I know, that's the real reason she wants to keep me away from you.'

'Because she's *jealous* of me?' Her grey eyes were scornful.

'It's not impossible. Or she just hates the thought of you getting someone who didn't want her. Maybe it makes her feel old.'

'I didn't know I'd *got* you,' she said witheringly. 'Am I supposed to be flattered?'

'I didn't mean it that way,' I said.

'Do you think you've *got* me? Do you think women can't resist you – everyone falling over themselves, and fighting each other for you . . .?' Her voice was rising.

I said, 'That's not it. How well do you know your mother?'

Her shoulders drooped. 'Well enough. I know she sleeps with men, if that's what you mean.'

'Well, then.'

'Well, what?'

'So you know she's capable of asking a man to go to bed with her – any man. I'm not saying there's anything special about me.'

She didn't say anything. She rested her forehead on her arm.

'Yes?'

'Yes.' Her voice was muffled.

'In that case,' I said, 'you know I could be telling you the truth. Don't blame me for it.'

'I don't think my mother would lie to me.'

'Has she never done it before?'

'Go away.' She twisted her face away from me. She didn't close the door.

I said, 'Let me speak to Fred.'

'He won't.'

'He will if you ask him.'

'Why should I?'

'It might help him.'

'It might help you, too.' She sounded bitter.

'Yes,' I said quietly. 'It might. Is that so terrible?'

She turned suddenly and walked away down the corridor, leaving the door open. I followed her.

The yellow living room smelled of whisky. Fred James was sitting on the sofa. The dandy suit was gone. In its place he wore jeans and a shirt that didn't fit him. I wondered if it had been Joe's. He looked as if he hadn't slept for a week. His eyes blinked constantly at a point somewhere near the coffee table. He seemed to be carrying on some violent internal dialogue: his hands were twitching and his eyebrows rose and fell as if he was in the middle of an argument. An incessant low gasping sound came from his lips.

Clare said listlessly, 'He's been like this since he came out.' She disappeared into the kitchen.

I said, 'Hello, Fred.'

'What do you want?'

I didn't think he'd noticed me come in. His voice was loud, on the edge of hysteria.

'I want to talk.'

'No . . .' He screwed up his face. The words came out with an effort, as if he was vomiting them, not speaking them. 'No . . . more . . . questions . . .'

'All right.'

I left a pause. Carefully I moved towards the armchair, sat down opposite him.

'I don't need to ask you any more questions,' I said. His eyes never moved from that point just by the corner of the coffee table. 'I'm not a policeman any more. They suspended

242

me.' Sweat was beading his forehead. I raised my voice. I wanted Clare to hear. 'You know why? That confession of Hill. I forged it. Maybe you didn't know Hill had confessed.'

'Hill?' It was more than he could take in.

I noticed that his arms were bruised. The cells had not been kind to him.

'That's right.'

'He confessed?' His voice was full of confusion.

'Just like you.'

'He did it, then.'

I leaned forward, with my elbows on my knees. 'You tell me.'

'No!' He shook his head. He whispered: '*I* did it. *I* killed him.'

I sat back again. 'Everyone thought Hill had confessed,' I said, 'but he hadn't. I wrote it for him. It was a lie. Just because you say you did something, it doesn't mean you did it.'

A frown seemed to have settled like a heavy weight between his eyes. His brows twitched as if they were trying to throw it off.

'What about your confession?' I said softly. 'Was that a lie too?'

'Why would I lie?' He jerked it out violently, as if I'd just insulted him.

'To save your own skin.'

'No. I did it.'

'They threatened to kill you if you didn't take the blame for Joe Bates's death. When you refused they set fire to your shop, just to show they were serious. They nearly killed your mother. You couldn't take it – I don't blame you. So you owned up to the whole thing.'

I stood up. Fred James seemed to shrink back into the sofa.

'You couldn't have killed Joe Bates,' I said scornfully. 'You couldn't tread on an insect.'

'I did it!' It almost sounded as if he was pleading with me. He cast around for something else to say. 'What about the gun?'

'Anyone could have planted it.'

'And . . .' His head was shaking, now, as if he was looking for a way out of the room. I crouched down in front of him. He smelled of whisky and stale sweat, of fear. His skin was ivory yellow.

'You couldn't have killed him,' I whispered. 'You got all the details wrong. They'll work it out sooner or later. It's too late.'

'Is it true that you lied?'

I nodded slowly. 'Yes.'

'You forged Hill's confession?'

'That's right,' I said. 'So we've both done it now. We're just the same.'

I took hold of his face, leaned forward, hissed in his ear, 'Who did kill him?'

'I don't know.' His voice was hardly more than a breath.

'Did you?'

His head moved under my hand, moved from side to side. 'No.'

'Are you going to take back your confession?'

'No.'

I sank back on my heels, raised his chin until I was looking into his eyes. 'Are you telling the truth?'

His eyes were the colour of dirty glass. Softly he whispered, 'I don't know.'

His eyes closed. Slowly, like a balloon deflating, his whole face puckered up. He started to sob silently, a dismal, defeated sobbing that came from somewhere deep inside him.

Clare came back into the room. She took a look at Fred and turned accusingly towards me. 'What have you said to him?'

'I asked him if he was telling the truth.'

'Was he?' she asked quickly.

'He doesn't know.'

Clare went down on her knees in front of him. 'Fred?' She spoke the way she'd have spoken to the child. 'Freddy?'

He wasn't in the room with us. He was back in the police cells with the bullies and the iron bars; he was in the interview room with Mason's voice rising and falling in his ear; he was in the burning shop, listening to the crackle of flames.

'I thought it was all over,' I said.

'What?'

'Between you.'

She shook her head angrily. 'I haven't told him yet.'

'Is he staying?'

'Is that any business of yours?'

I started to walk towards the door. Clare's voice said, 'Don't go.'

I turned round. She came towards me, pushed me into the hallway, closed the door.

She said, 'I'm sorry.'

'What for?'

'What I said earlier.'

'That's all right.'

'I don't know who to believe anymore.' She sounded tired; her face was tired.

I said, 'This won't last for ever.'

'It feels as if it will.' She shook her head. 'Fred has to stay here. You must see that. There's nowhere else for him to go. Besides . . .'

'Yes?'

'I owe him a lot.'

'What do you owe him?'

'Keeping me sane while Joe was alive.' She didn't make a meal of that. She said it straight, and even, not bothering to pretend she was mourning for Joe Bates.

I looked at her wide, frank forehead. I wanted to put my arms about her, kiss her, but it wasn't the right time.

I said, 'Can I come back and see you?'

'If you like.'

She gave me a brief smile. There wasn't anything else to say just then. She turned back into the sitting room and closed the door.

## 34

Benson Smith Hodge worked from a nondescript office building next to a Greek restaurant on Charlotte Street. There were wide, uncomfortable-looking chairs in the lobby. At the far side of it a man was scowling at a photocopier. He didn't pay me any attention.

I waited a couple of minutes, then asked him if this was Benson Smith Hodge.

'Of course it is.'

He didn't ask me what I was doing there. He had a narrow face with a long jaw and lips firmly clenched together. It took me a moment to remember where I'd seen him before: in Dick Hill's office on the day after Joe Bates was killed.

I said, 'I want to talk to the partner who works for Hill Properties.'

'We all do.'

I looked at him for a moment. He stabbed angrily at buttons on the machine. It didn't do anything in return.

'Are you Benson, Smith or Hodge?'

He looked up at me as if he was surprised I was still there. 'Benson's dead,' he said.

'So why do they keep his name on the company?'

'Don't know. Bloody stupid if you ask me. Died last year. Cancer of the throat.' He looked up at me again. 'I'm Willis.'

'Are you the new partner?'

'I'm an associate.'

'What difference does that make?'

'I don't get so much money and I work harder.'

'Do you work for Hill Properties?'

'I told you, we all do.' He lifted the cover of the machine

with a snort of rage. 'Why don't these bloody things ever work? Two jobs to go out this afternoon and the bloody machine doesn't bloody –' He broke off and shouted 'Jane!'

A voice from somewhere shouted something that neither of us could make out.

He said to me, 'I told her last week. Does she do anything about it? Jane!'

Jane appeared through a door at the back of the lobby. She had a lot of yellow hair, red lipstick and the sort of pretty face that would be gone by the time she was twenty-five.

'What is it?'

'The bloody machine. How many times have I told you –?'

I interrupted them. 'Are Smith or Hodge in the office?'

Jane gave the man by the photocopier a triumphant look. She said, 'Excuse *me*, Alex.' She gave me a big red smile that was halfway to a come-on. That was probably the only way she knew how to smile. 'Mr Hodge is in. Do you have an appointment?'

I said, 'I'm from the police.'

'That's all we bloody need. The photocopier's broken and the bloody police are raiding the office and I've got two jobs . . .'

Jane rolled her eyes to the ceiling and picked up a phone on the reception desk. 'What's it about?'

'I'll have to talk to Mr Hodge about that. Tell him it isn't serious but I'd appreciate some of his time.'

She waited until someone answered the phone, then told him what I'd said. Alex had given up on the photocopier and disappeared back into the other room.

She said, 'He can only manage a few minutes.'

'That'll be fine.'

She gave me another smile and led me through into a big drawing office with windows down one side. Alex was shouting at somebody in the corner. At the back of the office was a corridor with doors off it. Jane knocked at one of the doors and ushered me into an untidy room with drawings spread out on a meeting table. A man was sitting behind a desk. He had grey hair that was thinning at the temples and a badly pressed suit.

'The police?' He was frowning.

I said, 'Are you Mr Hodge?'

'Simon Hodge, that's right. What's it about?'

Jane disappeared and I sat down on a stack of files which were sitting on the only free chair. 'Do you work for Hill Properties?'

'That's right.' He looked suspicious.

'Have you worked for them a long time?'

'We developed the relationship ten years ago.' He spoke in the careful tones of a company brochure.

'Do you do all their work?'

He thought for a moment, then said, 'We do a lot of it.'

'Does that mean other people do some?'

'I don't believe so. We've got a good relationship.'

I said, 'I'm interested in any recent developments they've begun in London. Maybe not even started building yet, just applied for permissions.'

The grey-haired man was shaking his head. 'Why don't you ask them?'

'We can't do that.'

He stood up and looked out of the window. Nothing was happening outside. 'Where did you say you were from?'

'The CID. Detective Chief Inspector Havilland.'

'Are the Hills in trouble about something?'

'Nothing you need worry about.'

He sat down again. 'I don't have to tell you, do I?'

'No,' I said. 'But it would be helpful if you did.'

'Dick Hill's my oldest client. There's such a thing as loyalty.' He frowned at his in-tray, then added, 'Client confidentiality.'

'You're not a lawyer.'

He looked up at me. His grey eyes were hostile now. 'It doesn't make any difference.' He shook his head. 'I can't help you. I'm sorry.'

I said, 'One day you might have to help us.'

He shrugged.

I stood up. 'Thank you for your time, Mr Hodge.'

'I'm sorry you had a wasted trip.'

I went out of the office. In the drawing office Alex was bawling at a small Chinese girl who was doing her best not to cry. Jane was varnishing her nails at the reception desk. I smiled at her, went out and crossed the street. Twenty yards down there was a pub with a wooden sandwich board advertising meals. I went in, ordered a coffee and took a seat in a corner by the window. It was just after five o'clock. Two men at the bar were arguing office politics, something about a man who'd spent all his time in the pub and lost his job.

At half past five Jane came out of Benson Smith Hodge in a tight black overcoat and started walking towards the tube. A couple of men on the far pavement turned to look after her. The pub started to fill up with a crowd of office workers and media types from the television studios further down Charlotte Street. The juke box was playing Roy Orbison. Simon Hodge came out of his office and walked off in the same direction as Jane. There were still lights on in the drawing office. I pushed my way to the bar and ordered another coffee. When I got back to my table it had been taken by three secretaries who were pressed tight together on the bench, talking about somebody's wedding. I apologized and squeezed back into my corner. One of the secretaries moved their pile of coats and gave me a fleeting smile when my leg brushed against hers. Six o'clock. I peered out of the window again. A group of men and women were coming down the steps of Benson Smith Hodge. The Chinese girl I'd seen earlier was among them. They lingered on the pavement for a moment. One of them, a man, also Chinese, gave two fingers to the window behind them, then the group split up and they drifted off in different directions. Another half-hour passed. The juke box played Ike and Tina Turner, then the Vandellas. The secretary was watching me out of the corner of her eye, wondering what I was doing by myself. She was no longer taking part in the conversation of the other two.

I said, 'Excuse me.'

She turned too quickly and gave me a brief smile. I pushed past them and went out into the street.

Benson Smith Hodge was on a corner where Charlotte Street met a narrow alley leading towards Tottenham Court Road. I took the alley. There were still lights on in the drawing office but I couldn't see anybody through the windows, which were only just above my head. At the back was the goods entrance to the television studio, then a row of garages. The street beyond was deserted.

Just beyond the drawing-office window was a door which must lead to the corridor I had been in earlier. Across the alley from it was a small piece of waste ground which somebody had filled with trees and benches and tried to call a park. The gate was unlocked. I went in and settled down against one of the trees. I spent the time trying to think about Hill, and Fred James, and other things like that, but couldn't keep my mind on them. I had a snatch of tune going through my head: Betty Carter singing 'Round Midnight', with the weird way her voice rose up the melody and faded away at the top. It wasn't the whole song that stayed with me, just the first part of the melody rising, dying, starting again at the bottom. I wondered if Clare Bates liked jazz, or would ever start to like it.

> It begins to tell 'round midnight, 'round midnight.
> I do pretty well till after sundown.
> Suppertime I'm feeling sad,
> But it really gets bad 'round midnight . . .

I hadn't ever seen her, yet, without that tired crease between her eyes. That or, worse, the way she looked at Fred James as if he was no longer a person any more, just a weight she had to carry. Was that how I was? It didn't take long to lose your place in the crowd. It had taken my father just long enough for boots to drum together into a fast roll he could no longer hear; Joe Bates just long enough to register another person's footsteps and what they were holding in their hand; Fred James two days; John Penny perhaps his whole life. And me, the time it took to roll a sheet of paper into the typewriter and stamp a lie on it.

None of them had found a way back. I still wasn't sure if I would.

The drawing-office lights went out at nine o'clock. I waited another hour, then stood up, straightened out some limbs that had gone to sleep and crossed the alley to the back door of Benson Smith Hodge. There was nobody coming. I pulled a penknife from my pocket, opened out the blade and slipped it under the doorframe, just opposite the lock. The first heave did nothing at all except pinch my fingers against the frame. I dug the knife in deeper and started a rocking movement that lifted the door back from the keep of the lock. It didn't take me long. At the fourth or fifth pull the lock caught on the frame. I threw my weight against it, and it swung open into the corridor.

Immediately a high-pitched whining filled the air. Two red lights were glowing somewhere above me to my right.

I snapped the knife shut, slipped it back into my pocket and walked away, around the building to the front. By the time I got there the alarm was shrilling, its din filling the whole street. Nobody seemed to be paying much attention. I went up to the front door and rattled the handle. It was locked. A red light was flashing inside the lobby.

Car tyres screeched behind me and a door opened. A young copper with broad shoulders and a red, anxious face got out of the car. He wasn't wearing a helmet.

I said, 'Chief Inspector Havilland. CID. I was walking past and heard it go off.'

He looked relieved. His companion got out of the car the other side and walked round the bonnet towards us.

'Do you know whose building it is?'

The copper took a step back and looked up at the dark windows above, as if something would be written on them.

The second policeman said, 'Firm of surveyors or something. Sorry, sir.' He pushed past me and rattled at the front door. 'Probably just an alarm fault. Keyholder be here in a minute.'

'Do you know who that is?'

'Usually the alarm company. Offices don't usually have anyone living near enough to be any good.' He pushed a switch on his radio and said something into it.

I said, 'Maybe there's a door round the back.'

The young policeman nodded and disappeared round the side of the building. His friend kept talking into the radio. A red van with the name of an alarm company painted on it pulled up behind the police car. A man in a T-shirt and jeans got out. He was carrying a mobile phone and a large bunch of keys.

I said, 'Hello, Bob.'

He looked surprised. 'Hello, George. Off your patch, isn't it?'

'I was just passing by.'

'Taking some time off?'

I said, 'Seeing a friend.'

He nodded to the policeman with the radio and began fumbling with keys.

'They probably set it wrong,' he said. 'Offices are all the same. Leave it to some secretary who wants to get home to her boyfriend. Puts in his phone number by mistake.'

The policeman said, 'In that case it wouldn't set at all.'

Bob laughed.

There was a shout from around the corner and the young policeman came back running.

'Door open at the side. Looks like someone tried to get in.'

Bob pushed open the door and led us into the lobby. The alarm pad was high up on the right. He punched three buttons. The whining stopped abruptly and there were two satisfied bleeps, then silence.

'Better take a look round.' The second policeman's voice sounded too loud.

We switched on lights and went into the drawing office. It was as I'd seen it that afternoon: drawings out on the tables, dirty coffee cups, half-finished models. The door to the corridor was standing open. Through it came the distant sound of traffic.

'That's how they got in.' The policeman turned to Bob. 'Have you got a number for anyone?'

I left them talking and wandered towards Hodge's office. I opened a few doors before that one, looking casually into each room as if I was checking for signs of theft. When I got to Hodge's door I glanced behind me. The policeman was talking into his radio again, Bob tapping buttons on the mobile phone. The other copper had disappeared. I slipped into the office and let the door swing shut behind me.

The light was on the desk, which was still covered in piles of papers: Simon Hodge was not the sort of man who tidied up before leaving work. On the right, against the wall, was the big drawing chest I had noticed earlier.

I went down on my knees in front of it and started to go through the drawers from the top. The sound of voices still came from outside. Projects seemed to be stacked together: coloured sketches, presentation drawings, then mounted photographs of marble lobbies and balconies over the Thames. The whole top drawer was full of a housing development in the Docklands. I pushed that drawer in and tried the next. There were smaller projects in it, most of them out of town. I flicked through drawings of phoney cottages, trees, a golf clubhouse. In the third drawer were photographs of an office building with St Paul's in the background. Beneath them were a sheaf of sketches: apartment blocks, offices, a shopping mall in Reading. Nothing that made the sort of sense I was looking for. The fourth drawer was empty.

I found what I was looking for between a converted warehouse and a photograph of Simon Hodge smiling in front of some revolving doors. The drawing label was in the bottom right hand corner: 'Proposed Office Development'. There was a drawing number, date, and an address – and Hill Properties' logo stamped under them. I started to note it all down.

Suddenly footsteps sounded outside. I kicked the drawer shut and turned round.

Bob was smiling at me. 'What are you up to?'

I said, 'I always wondered what architects do for a living.'

'Fuck all, as far as I know.' He laughed. 'I can't raise anyone tonight. We'll have to board it up and deal with it in the morning. Probably ran away when the bell went off.'

I said that was probably what had happened.

The two policemen were standing in the middle of the drawing office. One of them said, 'Find anything gone?'

I shook my head.

He said, 'We won't trouble you any more, sir. Thanks for your help.'

'That's all right.'

Suddenly the light went on in the lobby. There were footsteps. Alex Willis was standing in the doorway.

His long face looked aggressive. He stood a little unsteadily, as if he'd been drinking. 'What the bloody hell's going on?'

One of the coppers said, 'Attempt at a break-in. Do you have anything to do with the property, sir?'

'Do I have anything to do with it?' He laughed as if that was a stupid question, but couldn't find anything to say. Instead, he pointed at me. 'I know him.'

My smile was tight, the kind of smile you give customs officers, schoolteachers and policemen. I said, 'Mr Willis has been helping us with an enquiry.'

Willis advanced across the drawing office, looking furiously around the empty desks. 'What the *bloody* hell's going on? I go out to get a bite to eat, come back ... the place is crawling with bloody *policemen*.' He came up to the younger copper and pushed his face close up against his. 'I'm going to do something about this,' he shouted.

I said, 'There's a door open at the back. Someone's tried to get into the offices.'

The young copper shot me a grateful look. Alex Willis took a step back and looked at me. 'What the hell have you got to do with it?'

'I was walking past twenty minutes ago,' I said. 'I heard the alarm go off.'

The second copper said to Alex Willis. 'We'll need you to check the premises, sir. See if anything was taken.'

'Of course nothing was taken.'

I nodded to the two coppers. 'I'll leave you to it, then.'

They thanked me for all the help I'd been. I turned and started walking towards the door. Behind me I heard voices.

It was Bob's that got through to me: 'Havilland. Works in Lambeth.'

I kept walking. There was nothing I could do about it now.

## 35

I dreamed that I was on the run.

I was running down dark streets, unlit, with tower blocks above me. I had been running for a long time. My legs burned; my ears were filled with the roar of a motorbike. I ran down a narrow alley between dustbins. The motorbike kept following me, crashing the bins aside. When I looked over my shoulder I could see Hill's silver-white head, unhelmeted. I knew I couldn't go on for much longer. Suddenly I was in an alley surrounded by high walls. There was a door at the end. Fumbling, I pulled out a screwdriver and started to prise up the lock. Exhaustion made me clumsy. It gave suddenly, with a crash, and I fell forward into a large square.

I was in a market. It was full of people but no one seemed to notice me. In an open space trestle tables had been set up, some of them covered with awnings. People were walking in silence around the market, picking things up, examining them, setting them down again. No one seemed to be speaking to each other. I got up and walked over to the nearest stall. It was selling apples. I picked up an apple and asked the stallholder the price. He didn't seem to hear me. He kept gazing into space just past my shoulder. Putting down the apple, I went on to the next stall. The man behind it had a thatch of white hair and a puffy face. I turned in panic. Suddenly I realized that the market was full of people I knew: Mason, Cayman, John Penny. Moving away from the man with white hair I found myself at a record stall. It was selling jazz records: Miles Davis, Stan Getz, Keith Jarrett. I picked one up and slipped it out of its sleeve. Someone had cut their initials across the grooves: GH. I looked up at the stallholder to complain. It was my brother. He didn't recognize me. He was smiling to himself, his lips moving, crooning a song I couldn't hear. I called his name, but nothing seemed to get through to him.

The silent market was beginning to frighten me. I walked away from it, shouldering my way through the crowds, and found myself on a patch of grass. I lay down with my head pillowed on my arms.

While I was lying there someone came up and sat down on the grass beside me. I turned to look at her. She had blonde hair and wide-apart grey eyes. She was naked. She smiled at me but didn't say anything. In one hand she was holding a photograph in a frame. Still smiling she held it out so that I could see it. It was a picture of a man lying on a pavement, his head in a pool of blood. She felt in the grass beside her and pulled out a revolver.

Suddenly I felt cold stone under my fingers. I was lying on a pavement. I could feel nothing at all; all I could see was the denim sleeve of my jacket. It was night. Close to my head was the wheel of a car. I could read the legend around the tyre: 'Goodyear'. Somebody had been with me but now they were gone. I could remember pain, but that was gone too. I felt something tugging at my leg. I tried to twist round to see what it was, but I couldn't move. A man's panting breath was coming closer to me, working round towards my head. At last he came into sight. A puffy-faced man with a thatch of white hair, stooping down so that he could touch the ground. He was red in the face. I couldn't tell what he was doing until his hand passed right beneath my face. Then I realized: he was drawing a chalk mark around my body . . .

When I woke up the phone was ringing. It sounded tired, as if it had been ringing too long. My ears were still filled with the panting breath of the man in the dream. I shook my head, swung my legs out of bed and hobbled through to the living room.

'Hello?'

'It's Cayman.' His voice was flat, neutral, neither friendly nor hostile.

I pinched my fingers into my eyes. I had to be awake. 'What's happened?'

There was a pause. I could hear voices in the background. Cayman must be waiting for them to go away.

His voice returned, hushed. 'It's Fred James. He was beaten up late last night, near Kennington Lane. Two guys on a motorbike.'

'What?' I struggled to clear my head. I could still see the bike in my dream, always following me. 'Is he dead?'

'Not yet. They've got him at St Thomas's.' Again there was a pause before his voice came back. 'He's in a coma.'

'How did it happen?'

'Nobody's sure. An old woman found him this morning. Clare Bates says he left her flat about midnight, wanted a walk to clear his head. When he didn't come back she thought he must have gone to friends. They'd had an argument.'

'Did she say what it was about?'

'She wouldn't. Maybe she wouldn't let him sleep with her.'

'Why the hell do you say that?' I snapped.

'Just a hunch.'

'Did she say anything to make you think it?'

'No. She was funny about him. Told us she'd broken up with him a long time ago. Said she was just helping him out as a friend. Funny to take in the man who says he's killed your husband.'

'He didn't –' I started.

'I know. He didn't kill him.'

There was a pause.

'Do you believe that?' I asked.

'I don't know. This makes it . . . I don't know.'

'What about Hill?'

'What do you mean?

'Have you heard anything from him? Is anyone keeping an eye on him?'

'No reason to. Officially he's in the clear. We've got Fred James's confession and that stands.'

'What does Mason say about the attack on James?'

'Bad luck.'

'It's a bad week for luck,' I said.

Cayman didn't say anything.

'Were there any witnesses?'

'Yes. That's how they know it was a bike. Student in a bedsit near there was looking out of the window. Said the bike mounted the pavement to cut him off. Guy on the back got off, knocked him down. Said they were kicking his head for five minutes. Got away on the bike.'

'Why didn't he report it?'

'She. She didn't want to get involved. African student, scared of the police.'

'How did you find her?'

'Door-to-door. It could just have been a mugging. They do happen.' He didn't sound like he believed it.

I said, 'I didn't tell you. Hill worked me over on Tuesday night. Hill and one of his gorillas.'

'You should have reported it.'

'Would anyone have done anything?'

There was a short pause.

'No.'

I said, 'What else?'

'Nothing. Journalists sitting on the front steps here.'

'What about Fred James?' I said. 'Do they think he's going to come round?'

'Nobody knows.'

'Can I get to see him?'

'I wouldn't if I were you. Mason's up there.' He paused. 'I'll let you know if anything happens.'

'Is Clare Bates with him?'

'She was earlier on. I've got to go now.'

I said, 'Have you thought about Penny?'

'Yes.' He sounded cautious.

'And?'

'I don't know. I just don't know. It could be you're right. I don't know what I'm supposed to do about it.'

'You don't have to do anything,' I said. 'Just help me if I need it.'

'I've got to go.'

I said, 'Thanks, Cayman . . . thanks for calling.'

The phone buzzed in my ear.

I got up, made myself a coffee, showered.

Fred James was in a coma. Someone had put him there, probably the same person who had killed Joe Bates. Someone whose face I would never see. Fred James's last sight on earth had been the same as my father's: an oblique view of running feet and the roots of buildings, then nothing. Paddy Moran had ended up like that, and so had Joe Bates. Maybe I would end up out there myself: out there with the feel of cold concrete at the back of my head, and nothing else. I shivered.

I had picked up my case and was on my way out when the phone rang again.

It was a woman's voice, well-spoken and precise. The last time I'd heard it, it had told me to ask Fred James about Joe Bates's death. Now it had some other instructions.

The voice said, 'Do you know the café outside the National Theatre?'

I said I did.

'Be there at half past twelve.'

There was a click. The line went dead.

## 36

Westminster Council kept their planning department eleven
floors up an unmarked office building off Victoria Street. A
sign in the lobby said 'Caring for the Community'. Behind it
were a dozen yards of dirty linoleum and a glass kiosk with a
metal speaker grille in the middle of it. Posters on the walls
told the community to use pelican crossings, check for breast
cancer, pay their television licences and never to share needles.
There were statistics for numbers of parking spaces, and more
statistics for how many children were killed on the roads.
The whole place smelled of disinfectant, disinterest, frustration. It smelled of small people sweating in long corridors,
waiting in the wrong offices, trying to push their lives over
obstacles they were too weak to move. It smelled of hopeless-
ness, of panic. An Indian man was standing in front of the
kiosk, leaning over the counter. He was moving one hand up
and down, palm down, the way people do in government
offices all over the world. Meanwhile he was talking into the
metal speaker, trying to stand on rights he didn't have. As I
came up he shook his head and drifted away. Someone
should have told him that the council weren't there to put
you back up on the high wire. They just broke your fall with
a safety net of petty legislation, NI numbers, official forms,
and left you wrapped up in them. Anyone who knew how
London worked wouldn't have to stand on their rights,
anyway. Rights were for losers.

The kiosk was half covered with handwritten notices taped
to the glass with sellotape. Most of them told you about
things you shouldn't have done, the rest about things you
should have done but no one had told you about. Through

them I watched a young black kid trying to push a frayed lace through an eyelet on his shoe. He didn't move when I came up. The other shoe was up on the desk with his foot inside it.

'Hello?'

He raised his chin and looked at me through the glass. He looked at me the way he'd look at people in a television set with the volume turned down: distant, wildly gesticulating characters with whom he couldn't communicate.

I said, 'Planning offices?'

He grimaced and tried to nip the end of the frayed lace from the other side of the eyelet.

I could think of a dozen things to say to him but there was no point. If I got too rude he'd take a coffee break or go out and buy himself a new shoe.

With a snort of disgust he threw the shoe aside and looked up at me.

'Yes?'

'Planning offices.'

'Eleventh floor.'

'Is there a lift?'

He nodded vaguely towards the far side of the lobby and picked up his shoe again. I left him at it.

The lift was full of seventies formica and people carrying files from one office to another office. The Indian man came up with me, maybe hoping I knew something about the labyrinth that he didn't. A poster on the lift wall showed a crowd of multi-ethnic schoolchildren showing their teeth at each other.

I got out at a long corridor which smelled of bleach. Somewhere, about a mile away, a woman was pushing a mop towards me. A door halfway between us said 'Planning Office'. The planning office was a grey-carpeted waiting room full of the plastic chairs you only find in waiting rooms. On the walls were architects' drawings of parks, playgrounds and dazzling housing blocks. Scattered around the chairs was a public library crowd of old men and women with nowhere better to go, a couple of young men in garish suits, two girls in leather jackets with their heads shaven. An old black guy was shaking his head over a file; a smart looking woman in a headscarf was staring at a big map of Westminster on the wall as if she'd never realized she had to share it with so many other people.

No one looked up when I came in. I crossed the room to a reception desk at the far side where a girl with lacquered hair was watching her nails grow.

'Can I help you, please?' She didn't make it sound like helping me was going to be fun. It didn't even sound like that was her job.

'I want to find out about a planning application.'

'An application you've already made, or an application you propose to make, please?'

It sounded like I should tick one box and hand the question back.

'Someone else made it,' I said. 'I don't know who. I want to find out.'

She rolled her eyes. I was one of the awkward ones.

'Also,' I went on, 'I want to know who's dealing with it. Which planning officer.'

'I'd have to go and ask.'

'Go and ask, then.'

'What's the address, please?'

I gave her the address. She stabbed buttons on a desk phone and checked her nails for growth while she waited. Her eyes stared past me into the grey middle-distance of bureaucracy.

'Thank you.' She put the phone down. 'He's not in today.'

'I didn't say I wanted to see him.'

Her mouth opened and shut again. Armour-plated glass went up over her eyes.

'What's his name?' I said.

'He's not in today, sir.'

'Is he on holiday?'

'He's off sick.'

'Since when?'

'I'd have to ask.'

'Just tell me his name,' I said.

'Serra.'

'How do you spell that?'

She told me, and gave me his first name.

'All right. I want to see the file on this application. Is that allowed?'

I waited while she asked if that was allowed.

'Someone will have to get it for you.'

I waited for that, too. The two men in bright suits had been gathered up by an official in a grey suit and ushered into a meeting room. The lady in the headscarf had gone back to Mayfair. The old women kept on staring at the drawings on the walls as if they were willing them to come to life: trees that hadn't been killed by vandals; balconies with the sun shining on them; staircases that no one had yet covered in graffiti. The drawings showed the world the way it should have been; the way it would be if real people never got their hands on it. A clean city, newly painted, with no crime, no dirt, no old age, poverty or disease, no soul. I wondered if the drawings ever fooled anybody.

A man came round from behind a screen and dropped a thick file on the reception desk. He was a young man with the top button of his shirt undone and the knot of his tie loosened. He spoke to the receptionist; she nodded and called out the name of the development. It had taken her all of five minutes to forget who I was.

The young man watched me as I approached the desk. 'What's your enquiry relating to?'

'I want to see the plans.'

'Are you a resident?'

I told him I was.

'Mr Serra will be back soon. Or you can write in, if you want to lodge an objection.'

'Would it make any difference?'

'It's your right.'

'That's not what I asked.'

He shrugged.

I said, 'How long has Mr Serra been off sick?'

'All week. There's a thing going round.'

'Do you work with him?'

'No.' He nodded at the file. 'Bring it back to the desk when you're finished.'

I took the file to a plastic table in a corner and opened it out. There were a couple of inches of letters and forms, some loose sheets, and a thick wad of drawings at the back, held by a rubber band. I took out the drawings and opened them on the table. They showed a big office building with glass walls and a sign over the door. They were the same as the drawings I had found in Simon Hodge's office the night before, apart from one detail: these copies weren't stamped with the Hill Properties logo.

The drawings smelled of ammonia. I folded them up again and turned to the file. It started with letters from the architect to an unnamed planning official. The letters were signed by Alex Willis. There was nothing of interest in them: a lot of jargon about net areas and habitable space, some off-putting replies from the planning official. Serra's name was first mentioned about halfway through the file. Near the top was a batch of forms, crookedly photocopied, that someone had marked with a red date-stamp. The date was about a month before. The first seemed to be the planning application form: the name of the architect, the development, a list of accompanying plans. There was no mention of Hill Properties; the Applicant was listed as a company called Central Developments. Beneath it were a dozen identical forms in blurred photocopy. I read through them one by one. They seemed to be notifying a number of different property companies that an application had been made to develop land they owned. The companies had the sort of nondescript names that could mean anything from airlines to tampons: Western, Regal, Connaught. Again, there was no mention at all of Hill Properties. If I hadn't seen the drawings in Simon Hodge's filing cabinet, I would never have known there was any link to Dick Hill at all.

The two men in bright suits were coming out of the meeting room. They looked disappointed. The man in the grey suit came out behind them. He looked the same way he'd looked when he went in. I gathered the file together, picked it up and took it back to the desk. The girl had disappeared. I waited a few minutes then knocked on the surface of the desk.

The young guy with the open collar came out from behind the screen. 'Yes?'

I gave him the file back.

'Was there anything else?'

I said, 'Do you keep a list of Councillors here?'

'Only the planning committee.'

'Where could I find out about other committees?'

He shrugged. 'In the other departments.'

'Isn't there a central list? Some kind of reference book?'

'I don't know. I'm a planning officer.'

'Where could I ask?'

'You could try reception.'

I said, 'Thank you for all your help.'

He rolled his eyes, as if sarcasm wasn't new, and disappeared behind the screen.

The black kid in the glass kiosk had been replaced by a fat man in a T-shirt who was eating potato crisps. Wafts of salt and vinegar filtered out through the metal speaker. Through mouthfuls of crisps he directed me to a third floor office where a woman told me to try the information department on the top floor. The information department was a tired-looking Indian woman in a brown sari. She took my name, disappeared between two filing cabinets and came back with a dog-eared sheet of yellow paper covered with names.

'Thank you.'

Her smile was almost human. She had dark rings under her eyes.

I said, 'Is there a telephone I can use anywhere? A pay-phone?'

'There is, but it's always broken. The kids do it.' She smiled again, a brief, tired smile. 'You can use mine if you want.'

I borrowed her phone book as well and made two calls,

one to a solicitor I knew, the other to a number I got out of the book. Both, after a good deal of bullying, promised to fax me answers to my questions the next day. Then I picked up the phone book again.

It was lucky he wasn't called Smith. There were only nine Serras in the phone book, and only one R. Serra.

I took down his address and headed for the lift.

## 37

Outside, the cars were grinding along Victoria Street in a constant stream. It was twelve o'clock, half an hour before my meeting at the South Bank. I started to walk east, towards Parliament Square. New Scotland Yard rose up on my left. Bored policemen in flak jackets loitered on the pavement outside. Secretaries lay sunning themselves on the patch of dirty grass the other side of the street.

I left the office workers behind, pushed through crowds of tourists photographing Big Ben, turned left along the Embankment. There were tramps dozing on the benches by the parapet. Beyond them the Thames slid past, wide and brown, and eddied around the piers of the bridge. Wind tugged at banners outside the GLC building on the far bank. A police launch pushed its way fussily upstream, kicking up spray from the bow. I passed a crowd of tourists getting out of their coach.

My brother had once asked me why I lived in London. He'd asked it in a patronizing way, as if only a fool would tie themselves to smog, high rents and danger on the streets. I told him London was like a jazz song: it was big, and unpredictable, and you heard something different every time you listened to it. It wasn't tidy or symmetrical; no one had ever worked out how to put it together. Instead, it made itself up as it went along, using whatever people it could find, jamming, taking you, every time you walked through it, into backwaters you never knew existed before. It was a city without a beginning or an end, just a middle which kept on going without reaching anywhere.

My brother hadn't been impressed. He thought I'd been living there too long.

I climbed steps and crossed the river by Waterloo Bridge. From there I could see the terrace outside the National Theatre. I couldn't see anyone I recognized. Kids were skateboarding on the podium, jumping over a board they'd set up on a pile of bricks. There was a tramp huddled against the parapet, begging the pavement for money. I hurried down steps to the wide walkway along the river. More kids on skateboards, strollers, art lovers on their way to the Hayward Gallery. The bridge rumbled as cars went over it. The last time I'd been there I was with Mary. We were going to hear Wynton Marsalis play at the Festival Hall. It had been a cold night, I remembered. Mary had wrapped her arm through mine and plunged both her hands into my pocket to keep warm. That was before. Before we stopped going to concerts or to anything else. Before our relationship soured. Before Hill.

I wandered towards the parapet some way away from the café and looked over the crowd outside. A dozen tables, half of them filled. Couples, groups of students, an old man by himself: no one I recognized. Probably the unknown person I was meeting was standing off, too, waiting for me to show.

I strolled over to a free table and sat down. There was no earthquake; Joe Bates didn't pop up from the manhole in front of me; nothing happened at all. A waiter came, a slim man with a shaven head. I ordered cappuccino and glanced back down the terrace. Plenty of people, but no one I knew. A drunk in an old sheepskin coat was moving from table to table. He was reciting bad poetry, doggerel about a life of drink, women who left him and police cells. Nice-looking women were digging into their bags. If he wanted poetry-lovers with a social conscience he couldn't have come to a better place. His eyes flicked over me. I looked away, back down the terrace, and after a moment heard his footsteps going back in the other direction. The waiter brought me a cup of dishwater with white froth on it. I sipped it and watched tourist boats passing along the river, cameras winking in the sunshine. On the far bank the tall buildings of Whitehall rose high above the trees. Twelve-forty; still no sign of anyone I knew.

He came at one o'clock, a man in dark glasses with a thatch of blond hair that was almost white. He was walking fast, with his hands in the pockets of his jacket, coming from the direction of the Festival Hall.

Hill pulled back a chair next to mine and sat down. He said, 'It was good of you to come.'

I couldn't read his eyes behind the shades. The voice might have been mocking or conciliatory.

I didn't say anything. The waiter came. Hill looked at my empty cup and said, 'Two coffees.'

The waiter nodded and disappeared. There was a pause.

I said, 'Did you hear about Fred James?'

Hill frowned. 'Nasty accident.'

'It wasn't an accident,' I said. 'He was beaten up. Funny thing, that happened to me the other night. I was lucky. I didn't end up in a coma.'

'People make their own luck,' said Hill.

'You mean it was Fred James's fault?'

He shrugged.

There was another long pause. The waiter brought our coffee and took away my empty cup.

Hill sipped at his coffee and said, 'I didn't come here to argue.'

'What did you come here for?'

'To talk to you.'

'What do you want to talk about – Joe Bates? Fred James?' I turned towards him. He was looking out over the river. 'John Penny?'

Hill took off his glasses, folded them, put them in his pocket. His eyes were bloodshot.

He said, 'I was talking to my lawyer this morning. He wants me to press charges for wrongful arrest. Do you know what you get for that? He told me he'd find out.'

'So let him find out.'

'It's not just the court case.' It sounded like he was thinking aloud. 'It's what the press would do to you.'

'They've already tried.'

'No good if they don't have your name. What if they

had your name? It shouldn't be hard for them to find out.'

I said, 'It depends who they're talking to.'

'"Bent Copper Forges Confession",' said Hill, 'Can't you imagine it? I could almost write it for them.' He laughed. 'I found out about it yesterday afternoon. I knew you were going to fit me up but I didn't know it was that bad. You're on suspension now, aren't you? What if that got into the papers?'

I said, 'It works both ways. If they get my name they'll want to know yours. Your name means Paddy Moran ... They'll enjoy that almost as much.'

'So would I.' Hill leaned across the table suddenly. He smelled of sweat covered by expensive aftershave. His voice was tense. 'Do you know something? The week after the trial ended every woman I met wanted to fuck me. There was something about having a killer balling them – it turned them on. They were coming up to me at parties. I guess they could boast about it afterwards – "You know Matt Hill? The murderer? I went to bed with him." Being fucked by a killer, that's exciting. You could see it in their eyes.'

He sat back just as suddenly, his voice lazy again. 'Someone they thought was a killer,' he added.

I said, 'You're sick.'

'Am I sick? Or are they?' He laughed.

'The whole damn lot of you.'

'It doesn't sound so good now,' he commented. 'Not from you. A week ago you could tell me I was sick and you were a saint, Saint George Havilland killing the dragon in the streets of London. The trouble is, you've come down to my level now. There's nothing between us. Look at them.' His eyes flicked towards the group of students larking at a nearby table. 'If they knew what I've done and what you've done, do you think they'd say there was any difference?'

I tried to keep my face still. I said, 'Is that a confession?'

'It's what you want it to be. You see how this changes everything? I even could confess to you – I could even do it. And it wouldn't matter any more. You'd go along to Mason and say, "Hey, Hill confessed to me again." You know what he'd say?' He laughed, a soft dangerous laugh. 'What was it knights used to have in children's books? Magic swords, invincible shields – well, you've lost them. No one believes in you any more.'

I didn't reply. For a moment we sat in silence, watching the passers-by on the terrace. Then Hill said quietly, 'I didn't kill Joe.'

'Is that what you came here to tell me?'

'Part of it.' He swivelled his eyes towards me. 'I didn't kill him and I don't know who did.'

'Not Fred James?'

'Maybe.' His eyebrows flicked up. 'Maybe it was Fred. He told you so, didn't he?'

'Do you think Fred James could have killed Bates?'

'Stranger things have happened.'

I said, 'Fred James was a coward. He was enough of a coward to confess to a murder he didn't do if someone was putting pressure on him.'

Hill was watching one of the girls at the other table, a slim girl in a T-shirt. 'You may be right.' He looked back at me. 'I always thought he was a pansy,' he said. 'Until someone told me he was getting it from Clare Bates.'

'Is *that* why you torched his shop?'

'What do you mean?' His eyes were hard.

I said, 'You tried it with her yourself and she told you there was nothing doing. It must have hurt to find out she was sleeping with a man like Fred James.'

His gaze wandered away again, towards the girl in the T-shirt. 'Women have odd ideas.'

'You mean they don't all find murderers sexy?'

He shrugged. 'Who understands what they find sexy?'

The girl had noticed she was being watched. When her friend made a joke she laughed too loud and swept her hand through her hair.

Hill said, 'I never cared about Clare Bates. I just wanted to see what it was like . . .'

'To sleep with a nice girl?'

'To see if she would.'

'She would,' I said. 'But not with you.'

He pursed his lips suddenly, involuntarily. It was almost a wince. Clare had hurt him in one of the few places where he could hurt: in his sexual vanity. Hill would certainly want someone to pay for that.

Musingly he said, 'I offered to set her up – did she tell you that, too? I told her she could leave Joe and I'd set her up in a flat in Kensington, send the kid to a good school.' He turned towards me. His face was puzzled. 'It's what she wants, isn't it?'

'Probably,' I agreed. 'The price must have been too high.'

He pursed his lips again. 'It's not as if she ever cared for Joe.'

'Did anybody?'

He looked at me. 'He was a friend of mine.'

I shook my head. 'You don't have any friends. There are just people you use and people you don't use.'

'Maybe.' He cocked his white-blond head. He liked that idea of himself.

After a pause I said, 'What did you use Bates for? Just drugs, or other things as well?'

'You keep forgetting, Havilland. You're not a copper any more. You're one of us.' He took his eyes off the girl at the next table and smiled briefly at me. 'Anyway, this isn't what I brought you here for.'

'Why did you bring me here?'

He was grinning nastily. 'I want to save you,' he said.

'Save me?'

'From the journalists. From having your name dragged through the mud. From doing time with a lot of hard men who'll tear you to pieces the moment word gets around you used to be on the force.'

I didn't say anything. His green eyes were fixed on my face.

'None of that needs to happen,' he said. 'Does it? Not if I don't pull the trigger.'

'It's not up to you,' I put in. 'It's up to Mason.'

273

'Mason!' His expression was scornful. 'He'll look after his own. If I hold off – no charges, no complaint – if the press get bored because they run out of details . . .' He lifted both hands, spread the palms. 'You'll be back on duty in a month. Rap over the knuckles, no promotion for a year or so, then they'll forget it. Coppers always look after each other . . .'

He leaned across the table. I could smell his breath.

'I want you to go back on duty,' he said. 'I want the whole thing to be dropped. But if that happens . . .' His smile widened. 'I want you to remember how much you owe me.'

I looked at him. The white eyelashes were narrowed.

'Every time you go into court, every time you help a little old lady across the road, you remember who you have to thank that you're still inside the charmed circle, not rotting up at the Scrubs with all the local hard men taking it out of you because you used to be a copper.'

'Are you trying to buy me?'

He sat back and folded his arms.

'I'm trying to save you. You think I'm going to do it for nothing?'

There was a long pause. He knew what I wanted, all right. I would have given almost anything for what he described: for the past to be forgotten, and the doors of the charmed circle opened to me again. And here was Hill offering me all of that.

But it wasn't for free. I had to keep remembering that, otherwise I would start to be tempted. If I said yes, I'd spend the rest of my life paying him back. Friends he wanted acquitted, charges he wanted dropped. I'd be his tame copper, a dog on a lead. I'd look like a copper and sound like a copper, but inside I'd be rotting away. What he was offering me looked right, but it didn't solve anything because it wasn't the genuine thing. The price was too high.

I wanted time to think. I said, 'Who told you Fred James was going to retract?'

Hill drew in a long breath through his nose. He said 'Are you saying no? I thought you were smarter than that.'

'Did he tell you himself? He was far enough gone.'

'Let it rest, Havilland.'

'Or did the boys who worked him over ask questions first?'

'Let it rest, Havilland. I've told you what I'll do if you don't take my deal. Did you think I wasn't serious?'

I didn't say anything. I knew he was serious.

'He's being a hero,' Hill said mockingly. 'They're going to take him away and flay the skin off him and he isn't even going to scream.'

'What they'll do to me is quick compared to what you'll do.'

He shook his head. 'It's not that quick. Do you think you'll ever get a job, with this behind you? One look at your face and they'll be slamming the door. People walking down the street will look at you and say: "He's familiar – isn't he that bent copper who did time for fabricating evidence?" He leaned over the table. 'It's for life, Havilland.'

A lifetime of faces turning away from me.

The beggar poet was coming round the tables again, reciting his doggerel. Is that where I'd end up? A fairground sideshow, or a recluse hiding in a basement somewhere, not daring to show his face out of doors. And instead, I could be back in the police canteen, back where I wanted to be. In time they really would forget about it – or at least put it down to too much zeal. I could eat humble pie, keep my nose clean, move to another station.

But then the calls would start. Hill's voice, calling in his deal, demanding payment. He knew what I wanted. He always knew what people wanted – that was the secret of his success. He'd known what Clare wanted: a leg-up out of the world she was born into. But the price was too high for her, and it was too high for me. Suddenly I saw Paddy Moran's face lying on the pavement: shocked in the moment of death, pleading, defeated. When we rolled him over there were dust stains on the knees of his trousers. Someone had made him beg for mercy before they cut his hands off. That would be my paymaster.

Hill's mouth was open. The tip of his tongue rested on his

lower lip. If I hadn't been there he'd have gone over and chatted up the girl at the next table. I could almost see him calculating his chances.

I said, 'Why did you come back south? You could have gone on from where your father left off. You could be in the City somewhere ... You could be one of the nice guys.'

'What's your answer?' He wasn't looking at me.

I said, 'No.'

He turned slowly to face me. His mouth was still open. Behind his head the Thames flowed past; on the far side, the glittering prizes his father had always yearned for: money, power, a place at the top. And Hill had rejected it, choosing instead the power he had over women, over junkies – maybe over me.

His eyes were flat, expressionless.

He said, 'You should have taken it.'

All of a sudden he was gone, walking swiftly away towards the stairs with his hands in the pockets of his jacket. I saw his blond head bobbing above the top of the parapet, then he was out of sight.

I sat on for a while outside the café. The students picked up their bags and departed, the girl glancing at me on her way past. A group of German tourists came and sat down where they had been. I finished my coffee, fished some change out of my pocket. Still I couldn't bring myself to go.

Further down the terrace a young busker was just getting ready to play. She opened the case in front of her and pulled out a tenor sax. She handled it lovingly, as if it was alive. A few passers-by had begun to gather. She hooked the sax on to the cord round her neck, tested the reed, began to play. It was a melody with nothing behind it, a thin sound spread out against the din of cars and the London sky. An Ellington tune, 'Jack the Bear'. She didn't have much of a tone. I stood up, paid and started walking towards her. I knew that I could never have accepted Hill's bargain.

As I passed the busker I dropped two coins into the instrument case; she acknowledged it with her eyes. The sound of the melody stayed with me all the way to the bridge.

## 38

Up on Waterloo Bridge I hailed a taxi and gave the driver an address in the City. It was just after two o'clock. The traffic was nose-to-tail up Cheapside. There were crowds of men in suits standing in the sun outside wine bars. They were talking big, laughing loud, flirting with groups of secretaries. Young men hurried along the pavements with attaché cases under their arms. They were hurrying because that was the way the City worked – it was what they were paid for. You could almost hear a hum rising up from the crowded, tall buildings: the drone of money being made, the drone of half a million office workers rubbing their back legs together to look busy.

The taxi dropped me outside a pair of revolving doors off the London Wall. On the other side of the doors I found myself in a lobby full of brownish marble and rubber plants. It was like being in a fish pond with no water. At the far end lifts rose up into a glass atrium with galleries around it.

A man in a uniform raised his eyebrows at me. I went up to the desk. 'I want to see Mr Poole.'

'Do you have an appointment, sir?'

'No.'

'There's someone with him now. He won't be able to see you without an appointment.'

'Will you call up?'

He ran his finger down a list of phone numbers and dialled one of them. Holding the receiver against his ear he said, 'What name?'

'Tell him Joe Bates wants to see him.'

He could see Joe Bates without an appointment. He could

see Joe Bates any time. The receptionist pointed to the lifts and told me seventh floor.

The lifts were glass boxes tracking up the side of the atrium like bubbles rising through a goldfish tank. I watched the fake plants at the bottom recede. A faint hum rose up the atrium: voices, machines, footsteps clicking on the marble floor below. The seventh-floor gallery was lined with modern paintings. I stopped a girl in high heels who pointed to an office at the corner of the gallery.

The door was open. Inside was an ante-room with two leather armchairs and a secretary in headphones tapping a keyboard. She took the phones off when I came in and smiled a standard-issue smile made of teeth and lipstick. 'Mr Bates?'

I told her I was Mr Bates.

'He'll be free in a minute.'

As she spoke the door opened and a man came out. He was large, clumsy, with bushy eyebrows and red, coarse cheeks. He didn't look at me. Around him there seemed to be an invisible barrier, the barrier that comes with power and privilege and people to look after you. The secretary jumped up to help him with his coat.

'Get me a taxi.' His voice was deliberate.

'Yes, Mr St Aubyn.'

I stood back to let him past.

Poole was standing in the door of the office. His eyes looked murder. He said, 'You'd better come in.'

He was taller than I remembered, an athlete or a nightclub bouncer dressed up in pinstripe and shoehorned into a City office. He held himself like a boxer, neck tensed, standing on the balls of his feet.

'What are you doing here?'

I said, 'Let's call it a social visit.'

'Why did you call yourself Bates?'

'You don't know my name.'

'I don't want to.' His voice was cutting.

'I want to know some things,' I said. 'I want to know who killed Joe Bates.'

He looked at me for a long time. Then he turned and

looked out of the window. We were on the penthouse floor. Outside there was a terrace and the back of a stone pediment.

He said, 'Why?'

'Isn't that obvious?'

'No.'

'I took over his job. I don't want the same thing to happen to me.'

'You'd better give it up, then.'

'In that case,' I said, 'who'd bring cocaine to your wife?'

Poole turned towards the desk. He fished in a box and brought out a big cigar. Lighting it took time. I waited.

At last he shook out the match and said, 'Are you trying to blackmail me?'

I didn't answer.

He flicked out his hands and shrugged. 'Sheila has a problem. It's no secret.'

He went round behind the desk and sat down. The brown fringe fell over his forehead. Again his gaze reminded me of an animal's. He looked like a foreigner, as if he was thinking in some language I wouldn't understand; but he wasn't a foreigner. I wondered where he did come from.

He shrugged. 'What would you do? Either I warn her off the stuff and she does it in secret, or I sanction it.' His eyes pretended to look for sympathy. 'That way at least I can keep control of the problem.'

'How did she start?' I asked.

'Oh . . .' He took a puff of his cigar, blew out smoke. 'Sheila started buying four years ago. I don't know who put her on to it. I came back one day and she was out of her head, really' – he shook his head – 'like a wild animal. When she calmed down she confessed to me. I made her promise never to use it again, but . . .' His chin had sunk down into his chest. 'That's the worst thing about addicts. They lie to you.'

'You found some cocaine?'

'A packet of it, in her things when we were on holiday.' He raised his head. 'Why am I telling you this?'

'Because you're scared I'll stop bringing it.'

He gave an unconvincing smile. 'That was when I made her promise to do it in the open. So that I could know how much she used, and so that I could pay for it.' There was a veil of smoke between us. 'She'd been selling things.'

'Has it done any good?'

He shrugged.

'How did Bates get involved?' I asked.

'Somehow he spotted she was a – a drug user.' He'd been about to say junkie. 'I suppose a pusher will always know. She told me that he was bringing it to her during a scene.'

'Did you know who was behind it?'

'Not to start with.'

'That must have been a surprise,' I said.

'It was. I didn't know Mattie Hill dealt in drugs.'

'Do you have anything to do with his father?' I asked.

He didn't answer that. He watched the ash growing on the end of the cigar. We both watched it.

'You know I'll tell Mattie you came here?' His voice was sharp.

'Yes.'

'Did he send you?'

I shook my head.

'So why did you come?'

'I told you, I want to find out what happened to Joe Bates.'

He crushed the cigar suddenly into the ashtray. 'I've never met Dick Hill. I've heard about him from John.'

'John Penny?'

He said, 'Your employer.'

'John Penny died,' I said. 'You know that?'

'Yes, I know.'

There was a pause.

'How did you meet him?' I asked.

'We're on the Council together.'

'How well do you know him?'

He looked at me. 'I don't have to answer your questions, you know. You can get out now.'

I said, 'You haven't told me anything yet. Did Penny know what Bates was doing?'

'John Penny? Good Lord, no!' He laughed, almost scornfully.

'So what were you arguing about last Sunday afternoon?'

There was a long silence. Poole took the cigar out of the ashtray, turned it round, replaced it. He sucked in air between his teeth. 'If you do want money, I'd prefer it if you made your demand now. I'm a busy man.'

'I told you why I came here,' I said. 'I want to find out what happened to Joe.'

'Was he a friend of yours?'

'You could say that.'

His lip curled. 'John Penny has nothing to do with it, if that's what you think.'

'That's fine,' I said. 'I just thought, maybe John Penny found out his chauffeur was selling drugs out of his nice motor car. Maybe he kicked up a fuss about it and someone got annoyed with him.'

Poole's eyes didn't waver. He said, 'I don't like what you're suggesting.'

'I don't expect you to,' I said.

For a moment we stared each other out. Then his eyes dropped. 'No,' he said. 'John Penny never found out. We were arguing about something different . . . politics. Who told you about it?'

'Your wife.'

He laughed ruefully. 'Sheila ought to keep her mouth shut. Not that it matters. If I were you . . .' He stood up. 'If I were you I'd look for a reason closer to home. If you want to know why Bates died.'

'What does that mean?'

He came round the desk. Gently he was pushing me back towards the door. 'People in his world must know some pretty unpleasant people. Surely I don't need to tell *you* that.'

I didn't move back. He advanced until he was standing right in front of me. His boxer's shoulders were tense, his hands swinging by his side like a streetfighter ready for a scrap. His brown eyes looked into mine.

'You probably know some pretty unpleasant people yourself,' he said.

'Maybe.'

'How long do most pushers last?' His voice was provocative, as if he was pushing me into fight. 'A year? Two years? It's a dangerous game. Don't ask me to feel sorry for you.'

I said, 'Did Joe Bates know he was in danger?'

'I wouldn't know. I hardly ever spoke to him. He came round during the day, when John didn't want him.'

For a moment we stared at each other.

Then I said, 'John Penny wrote a letter.'

'A letter?' His voice was in neutral.

'On his desk,' I said. 'I saw it there. A letter to you.'

'That's not interesting.'

'You must have made an offer to him. The letter said no. It said what you wanted and it said why not.'

Poole's brown face stayed unmoving, as if I hadn't said anything at all. He said, 'And you read this letter?'

I nodded.

He shrugged. 'There wasn't any letter.'

'Big risk,' I said.

He shrugged again. 'Not for me.' There was a moment's silence. 'I haven't got anything to be worried about.'

'Are you sure?'

Poole's expression didn't flicker. He said, 'I've dealt with petty blackmailers before. Small men. I know how to do it.'

'Are you saying you'll go to the police?'

'I'm not saying anything.' He made his voice bored. 'I'm saying you don't frighten me.' He waved a hand. 'There are people like you and people who know what to do with you. It's a bluff. I'm calling it.'

His brown eyes were steady on mine. Like an animal's, they looked almost friendly, the eyes you'd want your big brother to have, or a favourite uncle. I hadn't dented his self-assurance at all.

He was playing with the cigar again. I turned towards the door.

'Don't go to my house again,' his voice said. 'If I were you

I'd move away. A long way away. Hill can get pretty nasty when he wants to. So can I.'

'Did he kill Bates?' I kept my back to him.

There was no answer. Papers rustled on the desk. I walked out of the door and closed it behind me.

## 39

St Thomas's was full of sick people, dying people, people whose relatives were dying. It smelled the way hospitals always smell: a thin covering of disinfectant to keep out the stench of death. In the lobby old people sat shaking on battered rows of seats, waiting for doctors, or for patients, or maybe just waiting for someone to come and take them away. A flowerstall in the corner spilled garish pot plants out into the corridor. Nurses pushed trolleys to and fro, walking fast so that no one would be able to stop them. The noise of their shoes was the only noise. From a pedestal on the wall somebody's bronze head watched it all impassively, as if he was trying to think of a cure.

I gave Fred James's name at the main desk and waited while a stern-looking woman made calls and checked ledgers.

Eventually she pointed to the lifts with her biro and said, 'Sixth floor. John Holland ward.' Her voice had the sharp metallic tap of a typewriter.

I shared the lift with people who hadn't thought it was going to happen to them. A man with a white, shocked face was squeezing the shoulder of a woman. He wasn't saying anything, just squeezing her shoulder. The woman kept her eyes tight shut. Her lips were moving.

I got out at the sixth floor and followed signs to John Holland ward. Outside the ward was a row of orange plastic chairs with an old woman crying in one of them. I went through swing doors. The ward was a long windowless corridor with numbered rooms off it.

For some reason it made me think of the ward they'd taken my father to. From behind my mother's skirt I'd looked out at a figure with his head wrapped in bandages. Ralph had been holding my hand. The face on the pillow didn't look like my father's: it wasn't smiling. I'd asked Ralph if the bandages were supposed to make him better. Ralph hadn't said anything. He was older than me, and he knew the bandages were there to hide things, not to heal them.

A nurse was walking along the corridor carrying a clipboard. She smiled when she saw me.

I said, 'Fred James?'

'Number thirteen.' She kept walking. 'I'm afraid there's still no consciousness. Are you a relative?'

I said I was.

'You'll find Mrs Bates at the end.'

Her heels clicked off down the corridor. I went to the room at the end. The door was open. Clare was sitting inside.

She didn't see me at first. She was sitting on a plastic chair, cradling a mug of tea. The room had no bed: it was used as a waiting room. A trolley loaded with oxygen cylinders was stored in the corner.

She looked up. 'Hello.' Her face was white and bleak.

I said, 'Hello.' I came and sat down beside her. 'You look tired.'

'I am tired.'

'How is he?'

She made a face. 'No change.'

'What does that mean?'

'No change.' She shrugged.

'Will he come out of it?'

'Nobody seems to know.'

All of a sudden she was crying, pressing the back of her hand into her eyes. I put my arm about her shoulders.

'No . . . don't. It's all right.' She sniffed. 'I'm fine.'

She wriggled her shoulders. I took the arm away.

'It's just . . .'

'You think it was your fault.'

'No, I know that's stupid. It's stupid.' She wiped her eyes again and took a sip of the tea. 'They'll get you a cup if you ask them.'

'I'm fine. Where's Patrick?'

'With my mum. She's been great. She'll keep him overnight.'

I said gently, 'What happened?'

It took a while for her to answer. She sat still with her eyes shut. I didn't think she was crying, but when she spoke her voice sounded as if she was. 'He went out about midnight last night. We'd been arguing. He wanted . . .' She shook her head violently. 'He wanted to sleep with me.' Sleep came out as a high squeak but she recovered quickly. 'I told him it was over. I had to tell him – didn't I?' She didn't wait for an answer. 'He said in that case he didn't want to stay. He said . . . Oh, he said all sorts of things.'

'Did he tell you where he was going?'

'Friends. I knew he had friends. I thought it was for the best. I didn't know' – her voice became muffled again – 'he was in *danger*.'

'How could you?'

'Then the police came this morning. That man who was with you the first day . . .'

'Cayman.'

'He said Fred had been found in an alley on the estate. Somebody had beaten him up and he wasn't talking.' She took a deep breath through her nose. When she went on her voice sounded almost normal. 'He was nice, your man. He was kind.'

'He's all right,' I said.

'They drove me here. They said he was here. None of them . . .' She gave a rather wild laugh. 'None of them know what I've got to do with it. The doctors. I told them I was a friend. They all looked at each other, like, "Oh, *yes*." I've been sitting here all day, waiting for someone to tell me what's going on. They won't tell me. Your . . . a policeman was here half the morning, the older one, questioning me. They think I . . . I don't know what they think. Two of them. In a week. Both dead . . .'

I said, 'Fred's still alive.'

'He might as well not be,' she burst out. 'They took me in

287

to see him. One eye open and his mouth open, making noises
. . . like a baby . . .'

She put her face in her hands and her shoulders started to
quiver.

'There were all these tubes coming out of him. The
doctor said nobody can tell whether he'll come round or
not. We just have to wait. They haven't even told his
mother yet. She's still in shock from the fire. I keep thinking, What if I hadn't made him go away? What if I'd let
him stay?'

'You couldn't,' I said. 'It was better to have it out with
him – to be honest. You couldn't know he was in danger.'

'Of course I would have, if I'd thought about it. Look
what happened to his shop. I just didn't think. When he said
he had friends he could go to, I just . . . I was *relieved*.' She
sobbed again but soon had it under control. 'I was so relieved
not to have him in the flat. There! I wasn't even thinking that
somebody might be after him. I was just thinking about
myself. As always . . .'

'Stop it,' I said.

'Thinking that now I was free of him, and I didn't have to
feel guilty any more, and –'

Her voice was rising. I gripped her firmly by the wrists
and pulled her round to look at me. She stopped talking. Her
eyes were wide, scared. Slowly her shoulders relaxed.

She said, 'Thank you.'

'Listen,' I said. 'He shouldn't have gone to you in the first
place. He knew that. That was why he wanted to leave. It
would have been worse if he'd stayed. They might have
come for him there – whoever they were – and then Patrick
might have been hurt. My guess is, he knew that. You
mustn't blame yourself.'

She thought about that. Then she said simply, 'He trusted
me.'

'He was caught in something he couldn't control and
didn't know how to fight. If he'd stayed with you he would
have dragged you in, too.'

'Aren't I in already?' she said bitterly. 'Just about as deep as anyone could be? My husband. My . . . *lover.*' She said the last word angrily and turned her face away.

I said, 'He wasn't that any more. You told me. You told me yourself it was over.'

'Yes.'

'And as for doing it . . . No, it's better to look at it straight on. As for having a lover in the first place, it's not surprising with a husband like that. Don't forget what Joe was like. He mistreated you. How could he ask you to show him any faith? It isn't your fault.'

She gave a short laugh. 'Joe dead,' she said, 'and Fred in a coma. And it isn't my fault.' She shook her head. 'I'm tired,' she said. 'I want to go home.'

There were footsteps in the corridor outside. A young doctor appeared in the doorway. He was carrying a clipboard and had a stethoscope looped into the pocket of his coat.

'Mrs Bates?'

'Is there any news?' Her voice was eager. I felt a pang of jealousy.

The doctor shook his head. 'It's a waiting game, I'm afraid. I know how difficult it is.'

'Is he any better?'

'Just the same. It's what I told you earlier. He could stay like this for . . .' He shrugged. 'For a long time. I'm awfully sorry.'

'Are you keeping him alive?' I asked.

'Yes. We tried taking him off the ventilator but his heart wouldn't do anything.'

'What about other injuries?'

'Oh . . .' The doctor looked down at his clipboard. 'Broken leg, fracture of the skull. There's certainly damage to his spine but we can't test how severe.'

'What did you come here for?' Clare asked angrily. 'If there isn't anything to tell me?'

The doctor sank down to a squatting position. He spoke very slowly, the way you'd speak to a hurt child. 'There really isn't anything else you can do tonight,' he said. 'Don't you think it would be better if you went home now?'

Clare's eyes moved dully across his face. 'I don't know,' she said. 'I don't know what to do.'

I stood up. 'I'll take you home.'

She rose obediently and allowed me to drape her coat around her shoulders. The doctor showed us to the door of the ward. Outside the main entrance there was a queue of taxis. I gave Clare's address. She sat far away from me in the cab, looking out of the side window. It was almost dark.

The flat seemed empty, silent. She switched on lights, checked the answering machine. I stood behind her in the entrance to the sitting room, watching her move about the room.

'Sit down,' she said. 'I don't want to be by myself.'

I sat on the sofa. Clare disappeared into the kitchen.

'I'll make you something to eat, shall I? I'm starving.'

I looked at the framed prints on the wall, fantasies from another age. Clare's dream of a nice life was in ruins now, lying in a police mortuary, lying in a hospital bed surrounded by tubes.

She came back in with a tray of sandwiches and two mugs, put them down, sat on the sofa next to me. I was glad she was sitting next to me. Her face was drawn, tired, but no longer afraid.

For a moment we ate in silence. Then I said, 'Do you want to talk about it? Tell me if you don't.'

'No. We have to. It's . . . better to.' She sounded resigned.

'Did he say anything else before he went out? Anything about Joe, or . . . What was his state of mind?'

Clare thought for a moment with her face buried in her mug. 'He was very confused,' she said at last. 'Not just last night. Ever since he . . . since he came back. He couldn't focus on anything. He kept crying. Whenever we talked he'd keep contradicting himself. He'd fly off the handle at the least thing. I think . . .' She looked straight at me. 'I think killing Joe must have done something to his mind.'

'You think he *did* kill Joe?' I tried not to show my surprise.

She shrugged. 'Who else?'

'But . . .' I tried to put it into words. 'Didn't you mind him being here?'

'When I think about it now. But to start with I was sure Fred hadn't. I didn't think he could have. It's only now . . . afterwards . . .' Her brow wrinkled. 'The funny thing is, I think he thought that I *knew*. He thought it was something we'd done together. Killing Joe so we could be together.' She shook her head. 'He was terribly sick,' she said.

'Why are you so sure it was him?'

'Who else? And he was so confused, so different. Something must have happened to make him like that. More than what happened to the shop. He was like another person.'

'Did he tell you he'd done it?'

'Sometimes he said he hadn't, then he'd tell me it was him and he was sorry. Once he wanted me to telephone the police to make sure that they believed him.' She passed a hand over her eyes. 'I didn't know what to think.' She looked at me. 'You mustn't think I'm sad about Joe. It was hell, living with him. I've tried to feel sorry, but I can't.'

I said, 'That's all right.' I wasn't sure what I meant.

'Now . . .' she began.

'Yes?'

'Oh, I just want it all to end. I want . . .'

Suddenly she leaned her head against my shoulder. It was light, cool; her eyes were closed. We sat like that for a long time in silence. Then she said, 'Why can't we just miss out the next two months? Just go ahead, go a year ahead and see ourselves then . . .'

I let that settle. After a bit I put my arm around her shoulders. She didn't tell me to take it away. I thought about the way she had been after Joe Bates's death: sitting across the table from me in the police interview room, trying not to cry. She was a brave woman who didn't want anything that most people didn't want: a decent home, someone to love. Somehow she'd managed to cling to that despite everything. I thought of the place she'd been brought up, with the sound of men fighting downstairs and voices raised in the bar. She'd overcome all of that, or tried to. Somehow she had managed to stay decent, not to be hardened by it, to stay human. Some of that rubbed off on me. Being with her I felt fresh again, the way I hadn't felt for years. I felt as if life had possibilities, not just penalties to exact.

After a bit more I bent down and kissed the top of her head. Her hair smelled fresh. It gave softly under my lips.

'Is that all right?'

For answer she twisted her face up towards me. Her eyes were grey and clear, full of a longing to be released. I could feel my heart beating, a double pulse like the start of a familiar song. I kissed her on the lips. She had soft lips which yielded, responding to the pressure. I felt her body against me, strange, the way a new body always is. Her hands were about my neck.

I pulled back and said, 'Are you sure?'

She shook her head and kissed me again, almost angrily. 'I don't want to think about it. I don't want to think about anything. I want to forget.'

Later we went through into the bedroom. The sheets smelled clean. There were fresh flowers on the table, whose scent gently permeated the darkness. I felt her light, muscular body moving against me, her voice murmuring in my ear. She clung to me as if I was her only hope of escape from a burning house. At the final moment she made a sound which could almost have been weeping.

For a while, both of us managed to forget.

## 40

I was in my bed at home, in the lower bunk with my brother's mattress close above me. Ralph's steady breathing floated down from above. It was early morning: I could hear the sound of voices outside, and the first traffic; downstairs my mother was moving about in the kitchen. The curtains moved faintly in the draught from the open window.

I was not awake but I knew that I was waking. It felt like rising, rising through water towards a silver membrane which undulated gently above me. This must be what it felt like to be born. I rose faster and faster, rising towards the light. Soon I would break through the surface, feel cool wind on my cheek, and the warmth of sunlight. Soon I would be awake.

I lay for a moment without moving. The calm sensation of my dream was still with me. Someone was revving a car engine outside. There was a warm light glowing through the orange curtains.

Clare was lying next to me, sleeping peacefully with her face at rest. One arm was curled underneath her head. I rolled on to my back. The memory of childhood was still with me. I could remember the creak of my mother's footsteps along the corridor, the sound of Ralph stirring in the upper bunk. We had shared a room until he left home. At night we lay talking about music, about his future. Life had seemed simple. There were good guys and bad guys and we would be on the side of the good. He would cure the sick; I would right nameless wrongs. With enough time and enough like-minded souls the world would surely become a better place.

Suddenly knowledge of the past few days came flooding back: Joe Bates's body lying on the pavement; the building site where Penny died; Hill's mocking face. I opened my eyes; the calm feeling I had woken with was gone.

When had things become so complicated? In childhood they'd equipped me with simple truths, simple choices. Later I'd gripped those weapons and ridden out like some medieval knight errant into a world of shadows and half-truths, of compromises, of transactions where my crude armoury was worth nothing at all. There weren't any heroes and villains, just some people you'd trust more than others. There weren't any solutions. There was no book of rules, just a slender melody, somewhere, wreathed about by smoke.

Somewhere, a long way away, a phone started to ring. I looked at Clare. She stirred a little but didn't wake up. I wondered if there was any chance that we would both come through this and make something together. More likely I'd soon be hiding from reporters and Clare . . . what would she do? Find a man, probably – someone she could trust, and who would look after her. Someone who wasn't going to get themselves shot or wind up in a hospital bed with his mouth drooling over the sheet.

I sat up and swung my legs over the side of the bed. The phone was still ringing. Clare was lying motionless again, her breathing regular. I stood up and tiptoed through into the living room. Sunlight was pouring over the yellow walls. Our plates from the night before were lying on the carpet. The phone rang shrilly, persistently, refusing to take no for an answer. I stood and looked at it for a long time, willing it to stop. It didn't stop.

'Hello?'

'Who's that?' It was Jill's voice. I recognized it at once.

I didn't say anything.

'Who is that? Fred?' She sounded shocked.

I said, 'No.'

There was a long pause. When she spoke again her voice was hard, full of venom. 'You *bastard*.'

I said, 'Talk to Clare first.'

'I'm talking to you. Didn't you hear what I said before?'

'I heard it.'

'And you thought you didn't have to listen.'

'What Clare does,' I said, 'is for her to decide. Isn't it?'

'And what has she decided?'

'Why don't you ask her?'

She interrupted me, speaking fast and low. 'Get out, copper. Get out now. Pick up your filthy clothes and go. I don't want you in my daughter's life, do you understand? And I don't want you in her bed. You'll only bring trouble.'

'What has anyone else done?' I said. 'What have you done?'

'I'm not even going to talk to you about it.' She sounded ugly. 'I'm not talking about anything. I'm just telling you to go. You don't touch Clare and you don't touch her baby either. I want you out.'

There was a click and the phone went dead.

I went back to the bedroom door and looked in. Clare was still asleep. I picked up my clothes from the floor and took them into the living room to dress. By the phone I found a pad and a biro. I wrote her a note and left it on the coffee table, where she couldn't miss it. I read it through twice, then wrote a note under it telling her where she could find the key to my flat.

Outside it was colder than it looked. A cold wind was chiselling between the tower blocks. I wrapped my coat about me and walked towards the bus stop.

The bus was a long time coming. When it arrived it was filled with a Saturday crowd: men in jeans, children on their way into town. I got off at Westminster and took the tube to Notting Hill Gate. At Notting Hill people were drifting towards Portobello Road. I fell in with them. It was a good-natured crowd of punks and tourists, hippies, middle-class couples looking for birthday presents. Music blared from shop fronts. At the stalls people were turning over old cutlery, clothes, books. A fat man in an orange T-shirt was shouting out the price of vegetables. There was a smell of grease from a burger van, the acrid smell of a fish shop. The blind man with the accordion was playing old music hall numbers to the darkness.

Halfway down the market someone called my name. Pie was standing in the door of his record shop the other side of the street.

I crossed the road.

'Come on in. I got the kettle on.'

I said, 'I can't.'

'Why not?'

'I'm working.'

Pie laughed big, the way he always laughed. 'Working?' he said. 'So am I working. Everybody's working.'

I started to move away. I wanted to say yes, and spend a day leafing through old records and listening to people talking in the shop; a day thinking about Clare.

I said, 'Another time.'

'Make it soon.'

'All right. Soon.' I didn't believe that.

'Hey, how's Mary? She hasn't been in.'

'I don't know. I don't see her.'

He lifted one hand in a motion that said more than anyone else had managed: tough, but not so tough that it stops everything; not so tough that you don't come back alive.

I raised one hand and turned away.

A hundred yards beyond the motorway bridge I took a turning to the left. It was a long, narrow street of ill-kempt houses with net curtains in the windows and too many doorbells. Somewhere further along a car motor was straining. There were kids sitting on the front steps, two women talking over the railings. I felt their eyes on my back as I went past.

The noise of the car motor grew louder. It came from an old Rover chocked up at the front with a man's legs sprawled out from under it. The bonnet was up. An electrical cable snaked across the pavement and disappeared into a basement window. In front of it a little girl stood with her thumb in her mouth, staring into the engine.

The number I wanted was right behind the car. It was a narrow house of four storeys which looked smarter than its neighbours. The curtains were drawn; it had a dead look.

I climbed the steps and rang the only bell. I rang long and hard. The noise echoed indoors. I took a step back and waited. Nobody came; there was no sound inside the house. I rang again. The little girl was watching me now. She stared at me without embarrassment. I smiled. She stuck her finger back in her mouth and pirouetted, twisting her body away from me. The tone of the Rover engine suddenly rose a note, then fell again. I put out my hand and rang the bell a third time.

Almost immediately the door opened, snapping violently back on a chain. A woman's face appeared in the gap. She was white, in her mid-fifties, with straggling grey hair. Her eyes were wild.

'What do you want?'

'Mrs Serra?'

'Yes.'

'I want to see your husband.'

'You can't.' Her voice was only one notch away from hysteria. 'He's sick. He can't see anybody.'

She jumped back and slammed the door. I leaned on the bell until she opened again.

I said, 'I'm from the police.'

'Oh, *God*.' Her mouth was hanging open. Without realizing it she was making little whimpering noises, like the noise of a frightened animal.

'Let me in.'

'I can't.'

'Why not?

'He's gone away. I don't know where he is, do you understand? Just leave us alone!'

Her voice rose to a shriek. She slammed the door in my face. I heard footsteps inside running away from the door and up the stairs.

I rang again but there was no sound inside the house. It didn't matter any more. I knew all that I needed.

I turned and went back down the steps. The man in overalls had emerged from under the Rover. He had a thin beard and a woollen cap clinging to the side of his head. He grinned at me through smears of oil.

I stopped on the pavement next to him. The little girl was looking up at me wide-eyed. 'Is there a Texaco service station near here?'

'Sure.' He had a lilting Jamaican accent. 'At the end of the road. Ladbroke Grove.'

I nodded towards the old Rover. 'Is it yours?'

'No.' He made a face. 'Heap of junk. I do 'em for friends.' He patted the bonnet affectionately.

'Do you always work here?'

'Sure.' He laughed. 'This is my garage.'

'Were you working here last Sunday?'

He nodded.

'Did anyone come to visit them?' I indicated the silent house behind me. 'A big car, Rolls-Royce.'

He whistled. 'Don't get too many of them down here. Big green motor . . . I saw it.'

'Was there a man driving it? A man in uniform?'

'Tried to keep the kids off his bonnet. Gave Rosie a crack over the ear.' He grinned at the little girl, who came and draped herself over his leg.

'How long was the other man inside?'

He shrugged. 'An hour, maybe. Long time.'

I thanked him. He disengaged himself from the girl and sprawled himself out on the road. His head disappeared under the car. The noise of the engine rose again.

I had been right at the very beginning. John Penny hadn't been where he told me on the day Bates died. He'd come up to North Kensington, and stopped to fill up with petrol, and Bates – the way he always did – had put the receipt in the glove compartment where I'd found it two days later.

But I'd been wrong about the reason for his visit. John Penny hadn't been seeing a mistress. He was there on business.

## 41

In South Audley Street a man in a tailcoat was standing in the road, looking vainly up and down for a taxi. His wife was snapping at him from the pavement. She kept saying, 'We're late, Charles. I *told* you we'd be late.' A drunk was watching them impassively from a doorstep. Either he didn't care that they were late, or he didn't care about anything. There weren't many other people around. Anyone who lived in South Audley Street had better places to go for the weekend.

I rang Hill's doorbell. The entryphone crackled but there was no answer. I rang it again and waited. After a while the dome-headed porter came out on to the doorstep and stood watching me.

I said, 'Have you seen Mr Hill this morning?'

'They both went out.'

'What time?'

He shrugged and turned his back on me.

I crossed the road to a coffee bar and settled down to wait.

Half an hour passed. The waiter, a young Italian, stood behind the bar with his chin on his hands, gazing out at the street. A cassette recorder was playing Italian opera. An old woman went by, towed along the pavement by a fat Pekinese with no legs. The music stopped and the barman reached up lazily to flip the tape over. Another half-hour passed.

Then I saw Mary Fane.

She was walking along the far pavement, dressed in a cool cream suit. She looked as if South Audley Street belonged to her. Her dark golden hair was brushed loose.

At Hill's doorway she stopped and fumbled in her bag for a key.

I dropped five pounds on the table and ran out of the café. The door was just closing when I reached it. Mary Fane swung round with a gasp. Her face showed fear, then froze into an expression of cool contempt, the one she used when men were too familiar with her.

I closed the door behind me and leaned against it.

I said, 'I didn't think you got on that well with your boss.'

She gave me a cold little smile. It wouldn't have warmed up an ice cube. She said formally, 'Matthew Hill is my fiancé.'

The porter came out of his office and watched us suspiciously. He didn't say anything, or go away.

'You're a lucky girl,' I said.

She didn't bother to answer that.

'Where is he?'

'Why?'

'We need to talk.'

'What about?'

'You know what about.'

Her beautiful face was still, giving nothing away.

'Is he upstairs?'

'No.'

She turned away, began to climb the stairs. Over her shoulder she said, 'I'll tell him you called.'

'Will I find him at Babylon?'

'Maybe.'

'Why did you tip us off about Fred James?' I said. 'The phone call and the notes to the station. You know he didn't do it.'

She turned at the half-landing and looked down at me. Her face didn't give anything away. 'I don't know what you're talking about.'

I wasn't sure that I knew either.

'You must have been desperate to call me yourself. Why was it so important to get Hill out of the lock-up?'

'You're ridiculous,' she said. 'Why should I waste my time talking to you? Who would ever take *your* word for anything, anyway?'

'Is this love?' I said. 'Or is he paying you?'

She didn't answer.

'Or maybe this is the price,' I went on. 'Is that it? You don't want money, you want a husband. Do you know what you're taking on?'

'Frankly, I'm not interested in your opinion of my personal affairs.'

'I thought you were too tough to be impressed by Hill.'

'Please don't be coarse,' she said.

The porter grunted and took a step towards me. Mary Fane was moving away, climbing on up the stairs.

I said, 'What does the old man think?'

She stopped. 'He's not an old man.'

'Does he know yet?'

'Of course.'

She wasn't looking at me. There was a pause, then she started walking again.

'You won't change Hill,' I called.

Her voice floated back down to me: 'You can think what you please.'

There was a rattle of keys, and a door slammed.

I found a taxi in Park Lane and told the driver to take me south. I spent the journey wondering what I would do if he wasn't there. I needn't have worried. From the pavement outside Babylon I could see his white head at the far end of the bar.

I paid the taxi-driver and pushed open the door. The place was crowded. People were eating bar snacks at the little tables along the wall, passing drinks over shoulders from the bar. The talk was subdued. Most of the people in there were men.

Harry saw me coming in and his face went scared. I pushed through the crowd until I was standing right behind Hill. He was leaning forward over the bar, talking to a thin black guy with a heavy necklace.

Very clearly I said, 'You killed John Penny.'

It was like dropping a stone into a pond. The people

standing around us went silent; then the silence spread out. Someone laughed incongruously at the back of the room.

Hill's head turned towards Harry. 'Find Peter. I want him out.'

He didn't look at me.

I took a step closer. The whole bar was staring at me now. Something made me go on. It was a kind of rage, a knowledge that this was the only way I was likely to reach him. Maybe he would never pay for anything he did. But at the very least I wanted him to know that I knew the truth.

'It was Mary Fane who cancelled Penny's meeting with your father. She told your father Penny had sent her a message. That kept him at home. Then she rang Penny and told him your father wanted to meet him at the building site. When he got to the site you were waiting for him.'

Hill turned round slowly. His eyes were bright, unfocused, as if he was turned on. He was holding a knife.

Suddenly everybody else was looking away. The bar was a row of backs. I was aware of people spilling out on to the pavement behind me. There must have been fifty people in the bar, but there weren't any witnesses. I had come to Hill's castle and had my say. Now he would get rid of me.

He moved fast, but his face had given him away. I twisted to one side and got a grip on his right wrist, the one that was holding the knife. Bodies reeled back from us. I fell against a table which slid back, then Hill's weight was on top of me. I was using both hands to keep the blade away from me. My arms were shaking: they were still weak from Hill's beating four days before. I knew I couldn't hold him for long.

I rolled, and jumped off him as the knife went past. Hill scrambled to his feet. He was panting, bent double, his lips drawn back over his teeth. When he came at me again it was with a full-armed swing of the blade. I ducked, felt it snag on my collar, and charged him. My weight took him over backwards. I had both hands on his upper arm now, forcing the arm up and back to prevent him stabbing at me. He was grunting, purple-faced, his jaws snapping. A trickle of saliva ran down his chin.

I could feel his left hand tearing at my ear. Shaking free, I rammed my head into his face. I did it again and felt something wet on my forehead. He gave a low grunt of pain. His heels were drumming on the wooden floor. I relaxed, then realized all of a sudden that his right arm was free. I felt a blow on my left hip, as if he had hit me, and pushed myself back across the floor. My left leg didn't want to help any more. Hill was crawling after me, slashing at my hands, too crazed to work out what to do next. I grabbed hold of a chair and put it between us. That gave me time to stand up. There was something running down my leg, inside my trousers. I tried not to think about that.

Hill pushed the chair aside, closed on me and we went down together. Drinks crashed on to the floor. A woman was screaming. Hill's face was close against mine, now. His nose was a red blur. My fingernails dug into his right hand, tearing at the skin. Hill's mouth opened and he spat into my face, again and again, his throat uttering inarticulate noises of hatred, noises that came from before language; the noises of a killer trying to finish his prey.

Suddenly I became aware of footsteps and shouting. A leg pushed against me: we were no longer the centre of attention. A woman's voice was shouting roughly, using words I couldn't make out. People were moving around us. Hill's face seemed very close to mine.

Abruptly it was plucked away as if someone had pulled a puppet-string from above. I felt hands on my shoulder. They tore at my jacket, dragging me to my feet. My left leg suddenly came to life and pain stabbed through it. I opened my eyes.

The bar seemed to be full of uniforms. Two men in uniform were holding me by the arms, twisting my arms back so far that I could hardly stand. One of them had his mouth open: he was shouting at me. I could see Hill standing two yards away, his arms pinned in the same way. There was a smear of red where his nose had been.

A strange cloudiness seemed to be drifting through the room. A red face pushed itself up against mine and bawled something I couldn't hear. Voices came and went. The woman was still screaming hysterically. Outside someone was swearing loudly and repeatedly: 'Fucking Bill. Fucking Bill'.

I squeezed my eyes shut and opened them again. The hand gripping my shoulder was covered in blood. I wondered if it was my blood. A siren came from outside, louder and louder, then stopped. Harry was crouched against the bar, his face the colour of his white shirt. Two men in bomber jackets ran into the bar, looked around, focused on me. One of them seemed familiar.

'George fucking Havilland . . .'

The policemen were manoeuvring Hill out through the door, lifting him almost off the ground. His white and red face was twisted with pain.

The man in the bomber jacket came up to me and shouted 'Thanks a million!' I wondered what he meant by that, or if it meant anything at all. He turned to one of the men holding me. 'Take him out.'

People were milling in the doorway, women in gaudy dresses, the moon faces of a crowd. A policewoman was talking into her radio. Dimly I wondered what was happening, where I was being taken. It felt familiar, as if I had done it before.

A hot voice snarled in my ear, 'You can stop struggling now.'

It said something else but I lost the end of it. They were twisting me out through the door: I felt cold wind on my forehead. I knew why this was familiar: I was being arrested. In front of me was the open door of a police car. The man in the bomber jacket was holding it for me. I felt a hand squeezing my head, and my head was forced down. Someone pushed me face forward into the car.

The door slammed. The man in the bomber jacket was sitting next to me. White faces peered through the window. He turned towards me a hard, hairless face with a battered nose.

'You look a fucking treat, you do.'

I tried to say something but my voice wouldn't come. The

pain in my leg seemed to be rising, as if there was a plant growing under my skin.

'What the fuck do you think you were up to? We'll throw the book at you for this and you fucking deserve it.'

His name was on the tip of my tongue. Wilson? Wilkins? It was as if I had met him a long time before, when I was a child.

The car was moving, now. I could feel the pain in my leg rising up towards my chest. I wanted to press my hand against it to stop it. But I couldn't move my hands. I wondered why. Something was constricting my wrists, holding them in an iron grip.

The man in the bomber jacket was sneering. 'Violent Disorder,' he said, 'I'm taking you in.'

I looked down. He snapped the handcuffs shut on my wrists.

## 42

It was a long night, and the day that followed it was even longer. I didn't enjoy much of it. They'd sewn up my leg and given me painkillers, but the pills ran out of steam around midnight, and from then on it was long, sleepless grind through to dawn. I made it by thinking about Clare.

They'd taken me to a station in Borough and amused themselves by putting me through all the things you have to do when they arrest you. They photographed me two ways, rubbed my finger in ink, spelt my name wrong and asked endless questions which didn't have any answers. I knew how it worked; I'd done it myself. Somewhere along the way you stopped being a person, stopped believing in your own freedom, handed over just enough of yourself to them. By the end of it you were grateful when they pushed you into a bare cell with two tramps and a drunken football supporter. By the end of it you could hardly remember what your own bed looked like.

The charge sergeant knew me from before. He knew me just well enough to make me repeat my name three times and then spell it out slowly at the top of his voice. I could hear laughter from the room next door.

'Age?'

I told him.

'Occupation?' He leered at me across the desk.

'You know that.'

'It says, "Occupation",' he bellowed.

More laughter from next door.

'They won't send you up until Monday morning. Anyone you want us to call?'

There wasn't any point fighting it. I gave him the answers as straight as I could and tried not to show that I minded. There wasn't anyone I wanted to call. Through the glass porthole in the door I could see faces peering in at me. I could have raged; I could have clowned for them, if I'd been another person; or I could have thrown myself on their sympathy. Instead, I tried not to look too hurt, or too bored, or too much of anything. There were only so many questions on the list; there were only so many ways to spell my name.

They put me in with an old man and a pimply kid on a drugs charge. The old man spent the night groaning in the corner with his face to the wall. The kid paced up and down, jittered, swung his arms. In the darkness I could see his eyes glinting, moving wildly around the walls of the cell. I stretched out on the bunk, and lay on my back, and tried not to think about the leg. That meant I had to find something better to think about. For a long time I pictured Clare, tried to remember some of the things she had said to me the night before. It lasted for a while, but it couldn't last for ever. In the end I gave up and let the pain sink its teeth into me. It gnawed on my body while the grille over the window turned to grey shadow, then to a rusty steel mesh.

About nine o'clock they took the kid away. I could hear a woman crying outside the cells. The old man was sitting on his bunk with his head in his hands. For breakfast they brought painkillers and cold tea. I knew when the shift changed because the flap in the door opened and eyes looked in. Afterwards I could hear laughter.

Sunday went on for ever. Sometimes I managed to think. I thought about Joe Bates and Hill, about John Penny standing over the shaft on a building site; I thought about Sheila Poole with her crazy, unfocused smile; I thought about Fred James. At other times my thoughts drifted. I found myself walking along a street at home. There were trees at the end of the street; I was a child. A man was leading me by the hand. When he looked down at me he was smiling. Then I was in Clare's flat. I seemed to be at home there. I was sitting on the sofa in the yellow living room. A child was playing on the floor. Clare came in from next door and put her arms around me, twining her fingers in my hair. I buried my face in her neck.

The pain in my leg throbbed fitfully. They brought bowls of soup in the evening. The old man ate his, then retched thinly into a bucket in the corner. A drunk was dragged noisily into the cells and locked up next door. His voice snarled abuse at the locked door until it was overcome by sobbing. The grille over the window darkened again.

About ten o'clock the next morning they loaded us into a van with long benches along the sides. The old man swayed against my shoulder. There was more waiting in a cool room below the courts, then I was taken into a windowless room with a table and two chairs. A woman was sitting behind the table.

'Mr Havilland?'

'Yes.'

'You asked for legal aid. My name is Belinda Grieg.'

She was younger than me, nervous, with an intense look. Her hair was tied back in a severe ponytail. I could imagine her at political meetings and discussion groups. She probably thought her job was making the world a better place; maybe she even felt sorry for us. When I told her I was a policeman she frowned. Something was wrong here. The policemen were the bad guys who baton-charged striking miners and murdered black men in their cells. She had a whole mythology worked out and I was wandering in from another story.

I told her I was on suspension.

'Why?'

'Is that relevant?'

'Not if you don't want to tell me.' Her voice was crisp, businesslike.

'Do you need to know?'

She looked at me. 'I think I'd better not.'

I didn't tell her. She took notes, explained a ritual I knew too well already, and sent me back to the cell. They took me up at about half past eleven. The court was an echoing room in dark oak. Above the bench there was a royal shield with the gold paint fading. It must have impressed somebody, but no one in the room looked as if they could remember who. The clerks watched me disinterestedly as I came in. Up in the gallery bored local reporters were eating sandwiches and talking in whispers across the back of the seats. The chief magistrate was a middle-aged woman with the kind of face that should have been passing round the collection tray in a church.

Belinda Grieg was shuffling papers on a desk below me. She reached up towards me and whispered, 'Someone's offered to stand you bail. If we can get it.'

A man in a wig hit his desk with a hammer and stood up. He read out my name and details in a single stream without pauses, hurrying to push another name through the machine, knowing that no one would be interested. When he read out my occupation a stir ran through the press gallery. That would be one for the papers the next day. I set my face. There were questions, answers, some brief muttering between the magistrates. It was routine stuff. Belinda Grieg said something about bail and there was more whispering on the bench. I could hear excited laughter up in the gallery. The man in the wig stood up and hammered his desk again. Someone pulled at my sleeve and led me out of the court.

Belinda Grieg met me out in the main hallway.

'That went well,' she said brightly.

'Did it?'

She gave me a severe look. 'They could have refused you bail.'

'Who's offered to stand it?'

'A friend of yours, I suppose.' She looked at her notes. 'A Mr Richard Hill.'

'Are you sure?'

'Of course. Is he a friend of yours?'

I said, 'I don't know.'

She ran through some more details, gave me a brief, professional smile and left me on the steps. A week ago I'd come to hearings like this and despised them: the self-important officials, the lawyers, the thugs dressed up in ties to look

309

like model students. It was a machine designed to grind the waste of London into something small enough to swallow. It was the system which had betrayed Paddy Moran. Now I wondered what else could have done any better. Someone had to deal with it – the petty theft and aggression, the heat of endless friction between six million souls. It wasn't the law, it was just a machine to sweep up the mess the law left behind. By the time anyone reached that courtroom the law had already failed.

I went home, showered, put some coffee on to brew. The light was winking on the answering machine. I pressed the button and Clare's voice filled the flat. It sounded fresh and eager. 'I got your note. Please call me. I . . . I'll stay in until you do.' There was a tone and then her voice again, more anxious this time: 'Where are you? I was calling all last night.' A pause. 'Call me.'

Under the fax machine there was a roll of paper on the floor. I tore it off and took it back to the sofa.

There were two messages. One of them was on official notepaper headed HM Land Registry. It gave me details of the most recent purchase of six properties in Greycoat Place, SW1. The other was from a lawyer I knew who worked out of a shoebox in Brick Lane, and specialized in company searches.

I read through the letters twice. Then I lay back and started to think.

I thought a lot of things. Some of them were good; others made me wish I hadn't thought them. At one point the phone rang. I didn't answer it. There was a click, then the message, then Clare's voice: 'I don't know what's happening. It's been two days. Please ring me.' She sounded desperate.

I thought about Duke Ellington, about Webster, about Miles; about the little shop in our town where I'd started to buy records fifteen years ago. I thought about Belinda Grieg labouring over the dispossessed of London; about Mason; about the hurt in Dick Hill's eyes whenever I mentioned his son.

The phone rang again: an embarrassed message from

Cayman, hoping I was all right. The daylight was starting to go, but I kept thinking. Everything was making sense now. I knew what had happened: I had reached the truth. It didn't matter whether I liked it or not.

At half past seven I swung my legs off the sofa and dialled Dick Hill's number.

It rang only once before his quick voice answered. 'Yes?'

I said, 'It's George Havilland. I want to speak to you. Can I come round?'

'It's not convenient.' His voice was tense.

'Why did you pay my bail?'

'Don't want to discuss it. You can call my office in the morning.'

'No,' I said. 'I'm coming round now. You need to be there.'

'Why?'

I could think of a dozen reasons why he needed to see me. I gave him one of them and hung up.

## 43

Dick Hill's address was a steel door in the wall of a red brick building on Park Lane. Beside the door was a video entryphone. When I pushed Dick Hill's name a light came on and the door opened on to a narrow corridor panelled with mirrors. At the far end was a lift. I got into the lift and pressed a button; it moved up without a tremor. I looked up at the ceiling of the lift and found my own face looking down at me. I looked scared.

The lift took me to a wide lobby full of plants. Through a glass wall in front of me I could see a roof garden lit by concealed spotlights.

A large black door on the left was standing ajar. I pushed it open. Inside I was overwhelmed by the smell of flowers. I was in a dimly lit hallway with carpet underfoot. Flowers, huge lilies and foxgloves, waved at me from the shadows. The pool of light from a table lamp lit up a telephone and somebody's glasses.

Footsteps were coming along a corridor on my right. A Filipino woman appeared, wiping her hands on a cloth. She might have been in her fifties. She was wearing a neat housecoat.

I said, 'George Havilland.'

She nodded and disappeared again. I looked around me. The whole place felt as if it had been polished too much, hoovered too often, as if one lonely man couldn't make enough mess for one housekeeper to clear up. The rugs and pictures were straight, a stack of letters on the side table neatly aligned. From outside, very faintly, I could hear the sound of traffic.

More footsteps. Dick Hill was padding towards me down the corridor. He was wearing an open-necked shirt and a brown cardigan. He held out his hand to shake mine. His eyes were cautious.

'Nice place,' I said.

'You like it?' He shook his head. 'Out of date now. Nineteen-seventies . . . my time.' He gestured vaguely towards a dark corridor running away on the left. 'Too big for me, really. Old man by himself. Do you want to see around?'

He led me up the right-hand corridor. Plate-glass windows looked over the roof garden I had seen before. A constant flow of cool air came from grilles in the floor.

'Share the garden. Arab chap, hardly ever here. Gives me a free rein. Are you a gardener? Me neither. Leave it to the professionals. Got a man, Australian chap. Does it for me.'

He was talking just to stop me talking. He opened doors on to dark, quiet rooms, all immaculately tidy. Large windows looked out over Mayfair. Through an open door I saw the Filipino woman sitting on a bed, sewing.

The passage opened out into a dining room: a modern glass table that could seat twelve but probably never had. I imagined Dick Hill dining by himself every night with the housekeeper bringing him elaborate courses; sipping his expensive wine, listening to the silence of the flat. A man with all the money he needed, but no one to share it with, and his past a long way behind him. He must have built it in the first rush of enthusiasm for his new life, his Mayfair life – certain that it would be filled with the great and the good: the Pennys and people like them coming to dine with their friend Dick Hill. Now he was shrinking inside it like an old man in a jacket that had become too large for him. His footsteps barely made a sound on the thick carpet.

Dick Hill opened a door at the end of the corridor and ushered me into a vast living room. It was furnished with leather sofas, a modern rug, big abstract pictures that the architect had probably chosen for him. A rack of records covered one wall. There was a low coffee table made out of glass.

'Drink?'

He pressed a buzzer low down in the wall. The Filipino woman appeared, took our orders and left. He dithered for a minute, then bustled off behind her. Maybe he didn't want me to start talking, or maybe he was always like that: unable to leave anything to anybody else, always having to find something to spend his energy on.

While he was gone I looked about the room. It could have been anybody's room, mostly. It was too tidy, too empty, stylish but not with his style. The heavy smell of flowers saturated the air. I ran my finger along the records. The records told me something more personal. There were sentimental hits from the forties, Broadway shows, band music, a lot of Glen Miller and Mantovani. That would have been the music he danced to in his youth, back in the Old Kent Road when he was just a smart young man with a quick brain and too much energy to stay put. On the desk there were photos, neatly arranged: Hill as a child, and as a teenager with long hair; a studio shot of a woman smiling over the photographer's head; a holiday snap of a couple. The couple were slightly familiar. Then I recognized the man: it was Clare's father, the face I'd seen in a photograph in Jill's flat. The pretty blonde woman with him, her face slightly blurred, must be Jill.

There were footsteps in the corridor. I put the photo down and turned round. Hill came in, carrying a tray with a bottle and two glasses. Clearly he wanted to keep it civilized.

'Sit down. Sit down. Anywhere you like. Music? Better not. Have a drink.'

He handed me a glass and sat down himself. The sofa looked too big for him. He looked around. There was no way he could put it off any more.

'All right, then. Spit it out. What is it you want to tell me?'

I said, 'Your son killed John Penny.'

He didn't even blink. He took a sip of wine, held it in his mouth, swallowed. 'That's quite an accusation, Mr Havilland. Quite a mouthful.'

'When did you find out yourself?' I asked. 'On Wednesday morning? Or did he come to you on Tuesday night and tell you straightaway?'

He sat forward with his elbows on his knees. His expression looked almost like a smile. He didn't say anything.

I said, 'Hill was planning to kill Penny from last weekend. Poole was in on it and I don't know who else. For a while I thought you were too, but I don't think they trusted you enough to bring you in. They thought you might turn soft on them. Your son was behind it.'

He turned his glass round by the stem. His eyes, normally so quick, almost seemed dulled. 'And why,' he said, 'would I have any reason to hurt John Penny? Why would Mattie?'

I said, 'That was what took me so long to work out.' I closed my eyes. He didn't interrupt. 'Some time ago your company started buying plots of land in Greycoat Place, just behind Victoria Street. Your son was behind it. I don't know when he told you about it. The purchases weren't made by Hill Properties but under different names, all of them companies you happened to control. I had a friend carry out searches on them, and you – or people connected with you – appear on all of the company boards. They were buying the land from Westminster Council. The prices they paid' – I shook my head – 'were ridiculous. Peanuts for some of the most valuable building land in London. Why?'

Dick Hill opened his mouth as if he was going to answer the question. I didn't give him a chance.

'Because the committee responsible for selling Council land was chaired by a man called Gerald Poole. He was cut in on the whole deal. So was the head of the Planning Committee, a man called William St Aubyn. I don't know how many others – enough to get the majorities they needed. The Council employees who put the sale through didn't question it because the land wasn't all going to the same purchaser. By the time a planning application went in showing the land developed as a single lot it was too late. And the chief planning officer – a man called Richard Serra – was in their pocket.'

Dick Hill was smiling. It was a noncommittal smile, a holding operation to save him coming up with any other expression.

'To start with I don't think you knew much about it – except that your son had some project going in Victoria and the figures looked good. When you realized how good the figures were you must have begun to suspect. John Penny didn't know about it either. But even so, he was the key to the whole thing. It was through him that your son met and recruited the Councillors he needed. Penny was just a pawn, a sleeping partner in the game. Sooner or later he was bound to find out – probably later. But by then he would be in too deep. Your son assumed he would be able to bring him round.

'But somehow he found out about it – maybe through some loose talking by Bates. That happened last weekend. He spent Sunday afternoon going to see Poole and the others to find out what was going on. They were nice chaps – chaps like him. He didn't think people like that did things like that – he thought it was only people like you and your son. But here were his oldest friends, men like himself, telling him that his own company had pulled off the biggest property fraud he'd ever heard of. And he'd never known a thing about it. He went to see Serra, and Serra confirmed it. All of a sudden he was in the middle of a scandal. And he didn't have any idea what to do about it.'

I paused. Dick Hill was gripping his glass with both hands.

'What Penny hadn't realized,' I went on, 'is that Bates was reporting everything he did back to your son. That was why Hill recommended him for the job in the first place. Bates, Poole and your son met that night to work out what to do. Their answer was simple. Penny had to be killed before he could blow the whistle. They made an attempt to pay him off, but Penny wasn't having any of that. He was a drunk and a failure, but when someone hung temptation in front of him, he still remembered to say no . . .'

I paused. Dick Hill's chin had sunk down on to his chest. He held his untouched glass perfectly still.

'They paid Bates to do it – twelve hundred pounds in cash. Penny would be lured on to the building site and Bates would be waiting there – I found the key to the site in his pocket. But that was when things started to go wrong.

'When Bates was killed that same evening, your son had lost his assassin. To make matters worse, I arrested him for the killing. Suddenly, at a crucial moment, the key player was out of circulation. There wasn't much time to lose. The next day Penny might come out with the whole story. It was my fault that he didn't. I think he might have told me about it if I hadn't pushed so hard to find out where he'd been the day before. And I didn't think hard enough because all I could see was Hill. I had it in my head that Penny was worried about a sex scandal, that he'd been seeing a mistress . . . If he'd told me more it could have saved his life. But Poole and the others knew Penny wouldn't accept whatever they'd offered. It was only a matter of time before he blew the whistle.

'Meanwhile Mary Fane was doing all she could to get your son out – she'd started as soon as he was arrested. The funny thing was that they all knew he was innocent: he was the last person on earth who'd kill Joe Bates just then. But they didn't know who had killed him. What they needed was a scapegoat, someone they could pin the crime on so as to free your son.

'Fred James was the perfect candidate. He'd been having an affair with Bates's wife, he'd already been paying protection to some of your son's friends, and he was an easy target for threats. Mary Fane rang me to start the process, and sent in the anonymous letters tipping off the police to his affair with Clare Bates. The next morning someone arranged for the arson attack on his shop. The attack worked better than they could have hoped. Someone else had already had the same idea, and planted the gun under his desk. Under that sort of pressure James caved in. He confessed the same evening to the murder of Joe Bates – just like Mary told him to. And your son was free.

'Immediately they decided to put their first plan into

effect. Mary Fane found out that Penny had planned a meeting with you that same evening. She told you that Penny had cancelled it. Then she rang Penny – she was your secretary, after all – to tell him you wanted to meet him on the building site. He thought it was odd but he didn't question it. He went to the site and found your son waiting for him. Your son killed him.'

Dick Hill raised one hand in an involuntary gesture of protest, then dropped it back into his lap.

'From there he went on to my place. He knew my case against him had fallen apart and he wanted to scare me. Everything was falling into place for him. Penny was gone. Fred James seemed to be taking the rap for Bates's murder. The police seemed to be buying everything – including the idea that Penny's death was an accident. In fact, the police thought Penny had probably killed himself, but it didn't make enough difference to matter. It still left your son in the clear. The only possible source of trouble was me. He needed to have me sewn up.

'He made a start at that by playing games with me the same night Penny was killed. But fear wasn't going to be enough to muzzle me for ever. Without knowing it, though, I had played into his hands. Sometime on Thursday he found out that I had been suspended. Forging his confession and being caught for it put me in a perfect position to be blackmailed. Either I knuckle under and play his game, or he goes public and has me ruined. He knew that without that pressure the police probably wouldn't bother to punish me themselves. He put the deal to me on Friday. I hadn't quite worked out, then, why it mattered so much. Now I know. If I can charge him with the murder of John Penny, then he isn't going to be in a position to blackmail anybody . . .'

Dick Hill stirred suddenly on the sofa. He seemed to shake himself out of a kind of lethargy. He said, 'Why are you telling me this?'

'You mean you're not interested?'

He shook his head. 'Why don't you go straight to your boss? If you're so sure.'

It took me a long time to know how to start. This was the hard part, but somehow I had to do it.

'A year ago,' I said, 'your son murdered Paddy Moran – no, don't bother pretending he didn't. He was acquitted; he can't be tried for it again. But we both know what happened, whatever you've tried to pretend to yourself ever since . . .'

Dick Hill's eyes held the same hurt I'd seen in them before. He looked very old, suddenly, and tired.

'I don't know when he started to go wrong,' I said. 'I don't just mean stealing. I mean when he showed that he wasn't like you – that he was cruel. Probably it was the same time he turned his back on what you'd given him and started hanging out in the sort of places you left twenty years ago. I don't think you've ever understood that – I don't think anyone could. You thought when someone crossed the river it was for good. You had money and that would buy everything your son would need: the clothes, the friends, the school. The trouble was, you never knew how the system worked. You never realized you could be as rich as you liked and still people wouldn't invite you to their dinner table. Your son knew it. He played with them – people he met at school or in the nightclubs. But he wasn't one of them and he knew it. You thought your only son would marry some-one with a title and raise horses in the country, become what you would have wanted to be.' I shook my head. 'At some point you lost him. He fell in love with the dirty side of London, places you'd left behind when you were a young man. He wasn't interested in dinner parties and titles. He wanted real power over people, the kind you only get from pain and from fear. That's why you're afraid of him yourself.'

Dick Hill shook his head slowly, as if to clear it of a headache. He repeated, 'Why are you telling me this?' His voice had lost its crisp vigour. It was an old man's voice.

'Why am I telling you? Because I've had Hill on the hook once and he wriggled off it. He did that with you behind him, and the best lawyer money can buy. This time I don't even have as good evidence as before. And no one will believe what I say – not after what I did over Joe Bates. I need your help.'

He opened his mouth. His expression was almost comical. 'You want me to sell my own son?'

There was a long silence. A door closed somewhere else in the flat; neither of us moved.

Dick Hill said, 'You're off your blasted head.'

I tried to keep my voice calm. 'Did Hill tell you what he was doing with Poole and the others?'

There was no answer.

I said, 'He put your whole company on the line, everything you've worked for twenty years. And he never even told you. He's probably been moving in on the company for years. What happened after Penny died? Did he ask you to make him a director? This deal was part of something bigger. If you let him get away with this, then he'd be in control. He knew that.'

Dick Hill's face was twitching, as if whatever held it together was no longer strong enough for the effort required.

'The worst thing is, it wasn't just for money that he did it. I think you could have understood that: you've done enough for money yourself, in your time. But your son doesn't need money. He did it for something else, something you don't understand. I don't understand it myself.'

I paused. The old man's mouth was hanging open, as if he'd frozen in the middle of saying something.

Quietly I said, 'Maybe he did it to hurt you.'

There was no sound in the flat except the faint hum of the fans under the windows. I kept my eyes on Dick Hill's face. Without my noticing it his brows had creased into a frown, as if he was trying to remember a name from a long time ago.

'And then he killed John Penny,' I went on. 'Did he tell you he was sorry about that? Or did he just come to you and say he needed your help – that he wanted you to lie for him, say he'd been at your place all night?' I shook my head. 'He probably didn't even ask, just told you what he wanted. Because you've always given him whatever he wanted in the past. Even if it's an alibi for murdering your friend.'

Dick Hill wasn't looking at me. He was looking at the

circle of golden liquid in the top of his glass, as if he'd never seen such a thing before in his life.

I leaned forward. I said gently, 'You've got to let go of him.'

There was a long pause.

When Dick Hill spoke his voice was confused. 'Where I come from . . .' he said, and stopped. I let him take his time. 'Where I come from you look after your own. Get me? Everyone else is a mug. You can take them for a ride . . . let 'em look after themselves . . . to hell with 'em. But you look after your own.'

He paused, looked at me. He didn't go on.

I said, 'So why did you pay my bail?'

There was no answer.

'It can't work that way,' I said. 'Or if it does work that way, then it's up to you to keep Hill under control. You can't do that any more. He's broken loose.'

He raised his glass suddenly and tipped it back down his throat.

I said, 'You told me he was with you on Tuesday night, when Penny was being killed. He wasn't. I know that because it was on Tuesday night that he beat me up. And you know it. You and your housekeeper are Hill's only alibi. I'm not asking you to give evidence against him. Just don't lie for him.'

There was a long pause. I couldn't tell what Dick Hill was thinking. I remembered the way Hill had treated him when I saw them together after Penny's death: the contempt in his voice; the old man's pleading expression. I remembered the way Dick Hill had looked at Mary Fane when she was standing next to his son in the lobby of their office.

Quietly I said, 'Did you know Mary Fane's engaged to him?'

It hurt to look at his face. I remembered what Jill had said about him: 'There's no fool like an old fool.'

He nodded.

'When did you find out?'

'She called up earlier.' His voice almost died halfway through.

I said, 'Is he doing that to hurt you as well?'

321

He shook his head.

'If your son goes down,' I said, 'she'll go with him. An accessory. She set the whole thing up. Maybe that's why he wants to marry her. He thinks you'll hold the line for her sake.'

Dick Hill didn't answer. He looked away, staring fixedly at the long shelves of records on the far wall. I was holding my breath, willing him to make his decision. My only hope was that his fear of his son, and hatred of him, had grown strong enough to break the ties of a father's love.

When Dick Hill turned his face back to me it was spiteful, the face of a cornered animal.

He said, 'I've still got some decency in me.'

I didn't say anything.

'We're not in the blasted jungle. I know what the jungle's like. I was born in it. I've left it.'

I said, 'No, you haven't. Not until you let Mattie go.'

Dick Hill stood up. He was shaking with rage, now, his whole body trembling, arms rigid by his sides. 'Who the hell do you think you are? You come here and tell me to sell my own boy ... Who the *hell* do you think you are?' The veins were standing out on his forehead. 'Get out!' he shouted. 'Get out or I'll bloody tear you apart ...'

He didn't move. The words had come out automatically and meant nothing. There were running footsteps and the housekeeper appeared in the doorway. She stood there wiping her hands on a dishcloth, eyes flicking nervously between us.

I stood up. I said, 'It's your choice. Think about it.'

Dick Hill couldn't speak any more. He was blinking rapidly. Sweat poured from his forehead. His eyes looked spiteful, angry; but most of all they looked bewildered. I had peeled back the corner of something he had always tried to hide from himself. He knew what his son was, but for all this time he had looked the other way. Now I had dragged it into his own home and left it on the carpet in front of him.

I crossed the room. The housekeeper didn't even look at me. I walked down the long corridor, past the empty rooms that no one had come to stay in. At the front door I looked back.

Dick Hill was standing in the open doorway with his face pressed against the woman's shoulder. His shoulders were heaving. As I closed the door behind me I could hear an old man crying in the empty flat.

## 44

I went home across the park, walking slowly to try to control myself. Dick Hill's voice was still with me, drowning out every other sound.

As I approached my flat I saw a light in the window. I froze. I was standing at the top of the steps; the curtains were drawn. I got out my key as quietly as I could and went down the steps on tip-toe. The door was not locked. I pulled it towards me and eased it open.

The hallway smelled of coffee, and something else unusual which I couldn't place – something which hadn't been there for a long time. The sound of running water was coming from the bathroom. I kicked the door shut behind me and dropped the key on to the window ledge with a rattle. My heart was beating.

Clare came out of the bathroom.

She was wearing jeans and a big white shirt with the sleeves rolled up. She looked too beautiful to be there. She came up to me, put her arms round my neck and kissed me. Her eyes were smiling. I held her against me for a moment.

'What have you been up to?' She pushed me away suddenly. 'I'm supposed to be cross with you. You disappear before I'm awake and then don't even call me for three days. I promised myself I wouldn't even ring up after the third message.' She laughed. 'It didn't work. So here I am. I thought maybe . . . Oh, I thought up all the excuses for you. You can't tell me anything I haven't already thought of. I kept saying to myself, "You've got to play it cool, Clare."' She turned, smiled, kissed me again. 'I bet you've been with another woman, haven't you? Just like a man.'

I said, 'It isn't like that at all.'

Suddenly she looked concerned. 'You're limping. What's happened?'

'I got into a fight with Hill.'

'Oh God!' Her face was white. 'Are you . . . are you all right?'

'I'm fine,' I said. 'I couldn't get to a phone.'

'Why not? Where were you? You should have called and I could have come . . . Oh God, I sound like a wife already . . .' She blushed, put a hand over her face and disappeared into the kitchen. 'Go and sit down.' Her voice was muffled. 'I've just made some coffee.'

I went into the living room. The room seemed different, somehow. Maybe it was the smell of her, or just the prospect of her presence enlivening all those dead objects. I sat down on the sofa. Paradise beckoned, but I couldn't go in. I wished there was some way I could avoid saying what I had to say to her. Afterwards the flat would be empty again: as empty, cold and impersonal as my own life. I could hear Clare moving about next door. Maybe I could put off speaking to her for a day – give myself just one evening of happiness before opening the door to reality. But that was too dangerous a bargain: one I couldn't promise to keep.

Clare came in holding two cups. 'I've got some food for later,' she said. 'You need to do something about your kitchen. There's hardly even a knife.'

She began to move about the room, tidying things, straightening up. I watched her slim back. It was a nice glimpse of heaven but it wasn't for me – or for her.

I said, 'I know who murdered Joe.'

She froze, her back still to me. 'It was Fred, wasn't it?'

Her voice was uncertain. She was no good at lying. She had deceived just about everybody, me included, but she was no good at lying. That was why I could have loved her.

'Your mother killed him,' I said.

She swung round. Her face was very pale, the grey eyes staring out of it like two stones on a white sheet. Her mouth was open. The way she looked at me was almost enough to make me stop. But it was too late for that.

'You knew all along.'

'I *didn't*.' Her voice was desperate, the voice of a little girl denying that she'd broken something.

'Yes.' I put my hand over my eyes. 'I thought it must be Hill for a long time – long after Fred confessed. I was obsessed with him: it stopped me seeing anything else clearly. I thought, He was a killer, and Bates knew him, and they'd been seen arguing together. It had to be him.' I shook my head. 'It was what I wanted to think. First because I wanted to get him, then because I didn't want to see the truth. I should have listened to Harry Freeman – the barman at Babylon. He told me right at the start that Hill was in the bar when Joe died. And now I know that Hill was the last person on earth who would have killed Joe just then. He was planning to use him to murder John Penny.'

Clare was standing before me. Her arms hung at her sides as if she had forgotten them. All of a sudden she collapsed on to the floor, hunched up with her arms wrapped tight about her legs, hugging herself as if to ward off cold. Her lips moved but no sound came out.

'I assumed all along that they were connected – Joe's death and Penny's death. There was enough to connect them: working together, Hill, the drugs – did you know Joe was acting as a pusher for Hill? But I was wrong. It was the exact opposite. Joe's death was the last thing Hill had expected, and I played into his hands by trying to pin it on him. No . . . someone else killed Joe Bates. Someone with a much better reason than Hill would ever have. Someone whose daughter was being destroyed by him, and who had always been brought up to look after her own. I think the final straw was when he started to hit the baby. You know the bruise I saw on the first day? That was Joe, wasn't it? He'd started to beat Patrick when he was drunk. You told Jill about it, and she did what she thought was right.' My voice was ready to give up. I'd spent too long, now, telling the truth to people who didn't want to hear it. 'Where she comes from that was justice. Isn't that right? You don't go to the police, you sort it out for yourself. Isn't that how your father died?'

Clare's lips moved again, working furiously as if they were summoning up the breath to speak. 'No!' It was more a wail than a word. She repeated it in a whisper. '*No!*'

'You did know, didn't you?'

Slowly her head moved up and down.

'She telephoned me afterwards.' She looked up at me. Tears were streaming down her face. Her voice was indistinct. 'She told me . . . told me . . .' The rest was lost in a storm of sobbing.

'I didn't notice almost until now how what you said to me kept changing. First Joe was a model husband and you were happy together. Then he was a monster who beat you, and you were really in love with Fred James . . . You thought you were safe then. Hill had been arrested and you were getting rid of two birds with one stone. Then Hill was let out and Jill picked up word that it was being pinned on Fred. Hill never even knew that she was the murderer – it would have been too dangerous for her to tell him. All of a sudden Fred was in the past. Your affair with him was finished. You let Fred make his confession. Then he gets beaten up – Hill had that done – and you changed your tune again. Suddenly you believed that he was the murderer.' I shook my head. 'Four days ago you told me he couldn't kill a fly.'

Anger was starting to rise through the tears now. Her face was hardening.

'So what are you saying?' She pushed herself up on to her knees. 'Are you saying I'm a liar?'

I took a deep breath.

'Not quite. I'm saying you can make yourself believe in anything. You've had to – it's the only way you've got by. You made yourself believe Joe Bates was the knight in shining armour, then Fred James, then me. All the time you've closed your eyes to what was really going on. You've never seen what you didn't want to see. Instead you've lived on fantasies – that one day everything would work out all right, and you'd live in a nice house with a nice man . . .

327

You've had to be tough to keep hold of those dreams. Joe Bates went easy enough. When Fred James was getting in the way you let go of him, too. You closed your mind to him, moved on to the next thing. Deep down I think you're almost as tough as Jill. It was the only way to be, where you grew up. No one else was going to look after you except your mother, and she didn't understand what it was you wanted – to get away from her and the pub and live somewhere decent . . .'

I put my hands over my face. I couldn't go on.

Clare's voice said 'You hate me.'

'No.'

'You think I'm a liar.'

'No,' I said again.

I took my hands away. She was leaning away from me, looking at me almost with fear.

'Yes. You've just told me that I said things that weren't true.'

'What I'm saying is that you didn't know the difference – or that the difference didn't matter to you. Other things mattered more.'

'Is that so wrong?'

'It's not unusual, if that's what you mean. Nearly everybody has something that matters more than the truth.'

'Except you.' Her voice was bitter.

I didn't know what to say.

Clare's voice was high and fragile. 'I thought I mattered to you.'

'You do.'

'So?'

She crawled towards me across the floor.

'So?' she repeated. Her hands were on my knees. She forced my chin up so that I had to look at her. 'What difference does it make?' she said.

I could have told her that it made all the difference in the world. I could have pointed out that even now she was still only thinking of herself. She hadn't mentioned her mother once: she was getting ready to leave her behind as well.

But that wasn't what she meant.

'What difference does it make?' She spoke low, quickly, trying to persuade me. 'Don't you see? What difference? Fred's ... the doctors say he may not come round ever. He made that confession. It doesn't make any difference to him now.' Her voice was getting stronger. 'My mother isn't – oh, you know what I mean. She's not dangerous, or a criminal, or ... Joe – you know what he was like. He deserved it, almost. Why can't you just leave things as they are? Fred won't suffer for it – not any more than he already has. No one will. It's our only chance!'

In thirty seconds she had convinced herself of it. Already she could see the future. A smile was starting to break out through her tears.

'Why can't you leave things as they are?' she whispered. 'Let Fred take it. He wouldn't mind.'

I hadn't even thought of it that way. It took someone with Clare's genius: a genius to cover over the ugly bits, to forget what you wanted to forget. It was tempting: everything was so neat. Hill charged with Penny's murder, and Bates's quietly forgotten because the man who'd confessed to it wasn't in a fit state to point out that he hadn't done it. Jill would stay free. Clare would be free to ... what? To marry me? She'd already thought of that. I imagined coming home every night and finding her there, warm and loving. She would love me; there was no doubt about that. She deceived other people but she was even better at deceiving herself. And all the time Fred James would be lying in St Thomas's with his mouth open and tubes coming out of his nostrils: the gigantic, silent, living lie at the foundation of our fairy castle.

As if she knew what I had been thinking, she said tentatively, 'Do you think I've been making it up with you? I haven't, you know. I do love you.'

'I know.'

It was true. I was there. I was the right person to fall in love with at the time.

'Do you believe me?'

'Yes.'

'Well, then!'

She jumped up. Her eyes were bright. She put out her hands to me.

I shook my head. I said quietly, 'No.'

'What?'

'No.'

I looked up at her. Her face was shocked.

'Why not?'

'Because it's not true.'

'What difference does it make to anyone? You said your-self . . .' She was backing away from me. 'You said yourself, everybody has something . . . something that matters more to them . . . I thought you loved me!' She was backing towards the door.

'It makes a difference to me. In the end it will make a difference to you, too. At the start of this I tried to make up my own justice, rig things the way I wanted them to be . . .' I shook my head. 'It doesn't work. It can't work. One day we'd start to blame each other, for lying and for being lied to. Even if you get away with it to start with, it's always there behind you. I won't do it again.'

'Don't you care about me at all?' Her chin was high. 'Did you just want bed? Are you like the rest of them?'

'No,' I said. 'It wasn't like that.'

'What was it like? If it matters to you, then . . .'

I said, 'It doesn't matter enough. We don't have so much behind us that we can't let it go.'

It hurt to say it. What we had behind us wasn't the point: it was everything we could have had in front of us that I was letting go.

'You *do* think I'm a liar.'

'It's not a matter of true or false,' I said. 'It's what people believe, what they want to believe.'

'Please . . .' Her voice was a whisper.

I looked away. I was too close to saying yes, embracing the lie, living with it.

She gave a gasp. I thought she was going to say something but no sound came.

When I looked round the room was empty.

I sat for a long time without moving. The flat had died around me; I felt as if I was in a coffin. I thought about Joe Bates and Hill, about Paddy Moran, about Clare and about a lot of other things. But most of all I thought about the truth.

After a while I picked up the phone and dialled Mason's number. His wife answered. In the background I could hear a television and voices – the sounds of an ordinary family going about its business. It was ten minutes before he came to the phone.

We talked for a long time. It took a long time to make him believe what I said, but in the end he had to believe it. We discussed arrangements that needed to be made. Mason said he would take care of certain things. Then we agreed to meet at his office the next morning, and he hung up.

I sat for a long time with the receiver in my hand. When I put it down I was alone. Clare had gone. I closed my eyes and felt the loneliness flood over me.

## 45

Nothing seemed to have changed at Kennington police station. Another old lady was reporting another lost pet; there was still somebody whistling at the far end of the office corridor. Business was going on as usual: the ordinary everyday business of persuading six million strangers to live together in peace.

The desk clerk ignored me. I climbed the stairs to the office. A few people turned their backs. Cayman stood up. He looked anxious.

He said, 'The old man's waiting for you.'

His expression didn't tell me anything more. He was biding his time.

I knocked on Mason's door. His voice told me to walk in. He was sitting behind the desk with the photographs of the red-faced woman and the adolescent boy. There was a pile of papers on the desk but Mason wasn't looking at them. He didn't look at me, either.

He said, 'All right, George.' With one hand he flicked a switch on the telephone and leaned forward to talk into it. 'Send her in as soon as she comes. If she comes.'

Then he sat back in his chair. He sat back gingerly, the way an old man would.

I said, 'Well?'

'Am I going to apologize, you mean?' He said it sharply.

'No.'

'If you mean . . . what we discussed . . . yes, it's all done. We'll have to wait and see.'

There was an awkward silence. Mason scratched his ear with the end of his pen. I wasn't going to say anything. I didn't know what to say.

'You've done good work, George,' he said. 'These last few days. I should have done some of it for myself.'

I shrugged.

'What are we going to do with you?' He tried to laugh but it ended up as a sigh.

'Has Dick Hill called you?' I asked.

Mason's eyes fixed on the end of his pen. 'Yes.'

'And?'

'We'll have to see.'

'What does that mean?'

'It means what I always told you, George. It isn't simple. You ought to know that by now.'

'So what are we doing?

'Waiting.'

He scraped back his chair, walked over to the window, looked down at the pavement below.

'I've spent more time waiting in this job than anything else,' he said. 'Waiting for villains to confess, waiting for evidence to come in. Sometimes I think patience is all it takes.'

He wasn't saying any of what needed to be said. Something lay between us, filling the room, making any subject pointless. We were both waiting now.

'Will he protect Hill?'

'That's what we need to find out.'

I said, 'I'm not expecting it to help me . . .'

Mason raised one hand in a dismissive gesture. He didn't answer.

'It's like I told you before,' he said. 'We just make the case and send it on up the line. Sometimes they go down and sometimes they get away. It isn't our business.'

'Have you taken Hill in?'

'Not yet.'

There was a silence. The strain between us – the strain of things unsaid – was almost unbearable.

Suddenly the telephone on the desk shrilled. Mason picked it up and snapped, 'Yes?'

A voice spoke at the other end. He put it down and turned

to me with a smile. Outside in the corridor we heard the sound of cool footsteps.

A policewoman came in and held open the door. Mary Fane walked into the room behind her.

She walked in calmly, quite in control, the way she'd walk into a cocktail party. If they'd been taking her away to hang her she would have put on her best dress and smiled charmingly at the executioner. She brought into the room a smell of rare and expensive flowers.

She smiled at Mason as if he was an old friend.

'Hello, Chief Superintendent.'

'Please sit down.' Mason was businesslike. He looked at me. 'Perhaps you'd better go through it, George.'

'Do I need to?'

The question was directed at Mary Fane. She kept her charming, bland smile.

'I should think so, shouldn't you?'

I said, 'Stop me if you've heard it before.'

I took her through it step by step, not bothering to go easy on her. Either she knew what I was going to say or she knew how to hide surprise: with Mary Fane it was impossible to tell. She sat with one leg crossed elegantly over the other until I was finished.

There was a moment's silence. I could feel my heart beating. This was the key to it. What had Dick Hill said to her? I was working in the dark. I couldn't tell how deep was the father's bitterness at his son's betrayal – that betrayal of everything he valued himself, everything he had given Hill. Or else, as usually happened – as had to happen – families would protect their own. Hill would be safe again behind a web of loyalties no law could penetrate. The only worthwhile evidence we would ever find against him would be the testimony of the cool woman sitting in front of us.

She turned her beautiful eyes towards Mason. They betrayed no glimmer of emotion.

'What can you offer me?' Her voice was the practised voice of a mercenary.

Mason looked back at her. He was good at this. He wouldn't be charmed or sidetracked. He would keep his cards close to his chest.

'Immunity from prosecution.'

She didn't say anything. Somewhere behind her eyes there was a calculation going on. It had a lot to do with herself and something to do with whatever Dick Hill had told her. I didn't think it had much to do with her fiancé.

'If I may say so, Miss Fane . . .' Mason leaned forward over the desk. 'You're in a bit of a tight spot. Any jury would call you an accessory to murder.'

Two dimples had appeared in Mary Fane's cheeks. It was as if Mason was halfway through a dinner-party joke and she was getting ready to laugh.

'We can trace the tip-off notes back to you, no problem. That's nothing. But it was you who arranged the meetings on the day Penny died. You set up Penny for Hill to kill him.'

'You'd have to prove that.'

'We would.'

'So why do you need me?'

Mason smiled grimly. 'You're our insurance policy. Hill's got off things in the past.'

'Without me you don't stand a chance . . .' It was as if she was weighing up the price of something in front of her.

'I wouldn't be too sure about that. You don't know what we might still find out. Even if we lost, your name would be put about everywhere. It would be unpleasant. Hill wouldn't mind that, but I think you would.'

'Yes.' She nodded, accepting the point.

'Well?'

Mary Fane's eyes narrowed just for a moment.

She said, 'I'll take it.'

Her voice was as cool as if she had just made a decision to buy a new dress, not to betray her fiancé. I realized suddenly that my nails were digging into my palms.

'You'll make a full statement?' Mason asked.

'Yes.'

She looked towards me. Her eyes were mocking. 'Second time lucky,' she said.

She stood up. Mason pressed the buzzer on his desk again and a woman police constable came in. 'Will you show Miss Fane to a waiting room?' He turned to her. 'I won't be a minute. Will you excuse me?'

She snapped a smile at him, turned and followed the policewoman out. She'd only ever had one loyalty and she hadn't betrayed it. She was a mercenary who knew when to swap sides, and she wasn't going to punish herself. Hill's bid was too low. What we had offered her – whatever Dick Hill had offered her – was the better price.

The door closed behind her. We were alone.

'Well?' Mason said.

I didn't answer.

'You've got him. You should be pleased. He won't wriggle out of this one, not with her evidence.'

'You're sure she won't back down?'

He shook his head. 'Not her. She'd worked it out before, otherwise she wouldn't have come. That was just playing hard to get.'

I sat down. All of a sudden my legs felt too weak to carry me.

'What made you think she'd come over?'

'Dick Hill wouldn't let her come to any harm,' I said. 'Once he'd decided to let Hill go, the first thing he'd do was warn her to jump clear. This was her only way of saving herself.' I shrugged. 'Maybe that was why he did it – for her sake. Maybe he wants his son out of the way.'

Mason nodded. There was a pause.

I said, 'What about Jill Cowans?'

I wasn't looking at Mason when I said it. He took too long to answer. I looked up quickly.

Mason said, 'We went to pick her up last night, after you called me. Someone had told her we were coming.'

'She got away?'

'You could say that.' He sighed. 'There was a note up in

the flat confessing to it. The river police found her down by Tower Bridge this morning. She had guts, that one.' He looked at me more closely. 'You had something going with the daughter, didn't you? I'm sorry.'

Jill Cowans had not run away when she realized it was over. She could have gone to jail and come out an old woman with ruined looks; she had taken the easier way out. In the whole case Jill might have been the only truly honest person involved – honest according to her own rough system. But she was also a murderer, and now she was dead.

Mason was fumbling in the drawer of his desk. He pulled out a sheet of paper. There was typewriting on it. He passed it across the desk.

I picked it up. It was a letter addressed to him, and it said that Detective Chief Inspector George Havilland should resume his duties immediately.

I looked up at him. His grey eyes were smiling.

'You've earned it,' he said. 'I don't suppose you'll make a mistake like that again. I owe it to you for Hill.'

I said, 'There's something you're not telling me.'

'No.' He raised his hands in a gesture of denial.

'What about the others – Poole, St Aubyn, the other Councillors – have they been picked up?'

'What for?'

'I told you what for.' I stood up. I knew now why Mason had been so soft on me. 'Are you letting them off the hook?'

Mason's voice was almost pleading. 'What are you complaining about? You've got Hill. You've solved the Bates case. What's the problem?'

'These are more important than Hill,' I said. 'They're bigger than him, and they do more damage. Just because it happens quietly and no one gets killed doesn't mean it's all right.'

Mason said, 'Most people would reckon you weren't in much of a position to argue.' He gestured towards the letter lying on the desk between us.

'Is that it?' I asked.

Mason nodded slowly. He didn't want to look at me. 'I

had a call this morning,' he said. 'At home. My boss had had the politicians on him. No move on Poole or the others.'

I stared at him. I couldn't say anything. Mason shrugged.

'I asked him about you at the same time. He authorized me to go ahead and reinstate you, *provisionally*.'

I nodded slowly. 'On good behaviour. As long as I don't make a move against the people at the top. Did you accept that?'

'It's not for me to accept it. It's just the way it is.'

'You can't!' My voice was rising despite myself.

'What option do I have?' His voice rose over mine, silencing it. There was a pause.

I said, 'I could go to the press.'

'They own the press.'

I didn't say anything.

'You're not really in a position to complain, are you?'

I looked at Mason. He seemed to have shrunk, somehow – shrunk under the weight of too many compromises over too many years.

He said, 'It's a game of percentages, Havilland. You win some, you lose some. We've got Hill – it ought to be good enough. It's like I told you before, we don't make the rules, we just play the game. It's not about justice, Havilland. That's where you went wrong all along. We're just part of a system . . .'

He didn't sound as if he thought I'd believe it. He was rambling now.

'Some of them are good men, in some ways. It's not a simple picture. William St Aubyn for instance – the head of the Planning Committee. He gives money to charity, owns businesses. What would happen to all the people he employs if he was taken away? You have to weigh these things up, Havilland. Or somebody does. Not us. We just do our job.'

I stood up. Mason looked at me. His grey eyes were flecked with rust.

He pointed at the letter. 'Won't you take it? Please, George.'

Maybe we all had to compromise; and maybe simple ideals

couldn't survive in a crooked world. But somewhere, I knew, the compromises had to stop. There was no sharp line, no boundary you crossed. Every decision we made was a bargain struck in a giant market where loyalties of all kinds were for sale. Mason had wandered too far into the market. He had got used to the dealing and forgotten what it was he was dealing in. He had forgotten that the one thing you couldn't sell was the truth. That was the currency we all needed to trust, the thread running through everything – however slender and confused – without which music was just noise and Hill was no different from any of us.

Mason pointed towards the letter on the desk.

'Won't you take it?'

I looked at him. His grey eyes were tired, corroded. What he was offering me was another compromise, another bargain like the one Hill had offered me before. And the price was too high.

I said, 'You can sell your own soul.'

Outside it was raining. Rain washed the pavements, the roads, the windows behind which six million Londoners struggled to live in some sort of peace and decency; struggled to find the threads of their lives, to make out a weaving melody through the all the din and chaos of a city.

I didn't have a home to go to or a thing to do. In all of the miles of streets around me there wasn't a soul who would take me in. I felt empty, like a bucket that had been tipped out into the gutter. I looked up and down the Kennington Road. Rain soaked down on the trees, on traffic lights, on a pile of builders' rubbish. It was deserted except for a woman scolding her child.

I started walking towards the river.

# Visit Penguin on the Internet
## and browse at your leisure

---

- ◆ preview sample extracts of our forthcoming books
- ◆ read about your favourite authors
- ◆ investigate over 10,000 titles
- ◆ enter one of our literary quizzes
- ◆ win some fantastic prizes in our competitions
- ◆ e-mail us with your comments and book reviews
- ◆ instantly order any Penguin book

### and masses more!

---

'To be recommended without reservation ... a rich and rewarding on-line experience' – Internet Magazine

## www.penguin.co.uk

# READ MORE IN PENGUIN

In every corner of the world, on every subject under the sun, Penguin represents quality and variety – the very best in publishing today.

For complete information about books available from Penguin – including Puffins, Penguin Classics and Arkana – and how to order them, write to us at the appropriate address below. Please note that for copyright reasons the selection of books varies from country to country.

**In the United Kingdom**: Please write to *Dept. EP, Penguin Books Ltd, Bath Road, Harmondsworth, West Drayton, Middlesex UB7 0DA*

**In the United States**: Please write to *Consumer Sales, Penguin USA, P.O. Box 999, Dept. 17109, Bergenfield, New Jersey 07621-0120*. VISA and MasterCard holders call 1-800-253-6476 to order Penguin titles

**In Canada**: Please write to *Penguin Books Canada Ltd, 10 Alcorn Avenue, Suite 300, Toronto, Ontario M4V 3B2*

**In Australia**: Please write to *Penguin Books Australia Ltd, P.O. Box 257, Ringwood, Victoria 3134*

**In New Zealand**: Please write to *Penguin Books (NZ) Ltd, Private Bag 102902, North Shore Mail Centre, Auckland 10*

**In India**: Please write to *Penguin Books India Pvt Ltd, 706 Eros Apartments, 56 Nehru Place, New Delhi 110 019*

**In the Netherlands**: Please write to *Penguin Books Netherlands bv, Postbus 3507, NL-1001 AH Amsterdam*

**In Germany**: Please write to *Penguin Books Deutschland GmbH, Metzlerstrasse 26, 60594 Frankfurt am Main*

**In Spain**: Please write to *Penguin Books S. A., Bravo Murillo 19, 1° B, 28015 Madrid*

**In Italy**: Please write to *Penguin Italia s.r.l., Via Felice Casati 20, I–20124 Milano*

**In France**: Please write to *Penguin France S. A., 17 rue Lejeune, F–31000 Toulouse*

**In Japan**: Please write to *Penguin Books Japan, Ishikiribashi Building, 2–5–4, Suido, Bunkyo-ku, Tokyo 112*

**In South Africa**: Please write to *Longman Penguin Southern Africa (Pty) Ltd, Private Bag X08, Bertsham 2013*

# READ MORE IN PENGUIN

## A SELECTION OF CRIME AND MYSTERY

**Paper Doll**  Robert B. Parker

Olivia Nelson had almost been a candidate for sainthood – perfect wife, perfect mother with a perfect home in the best part of Boston. Too perfect, perhaps. Because someone murdered her. But when Spenser sets out to solve the case, nothing – least of all the life and death of the victim – is what it seems . . .

**Simeon's Bride**  Alison G. Taylor

In the North Wales village of Salem, beauty and poverty, suspicion and superstition, walk hand in hand, and police and criminals know each other only too well. But nobody admits knowing anything about the woman found hanged in the woods.

**Under My Skin**  Sarah Dunant

Castle Dean health farm caters to the rich and wannabe beautiful, but when someone starts putting nails in the massage head, it's just the beginning of trouble. 'A complex murder investigation cunningly plotted to keep you riveted to the very last page' – *Independent*

**V. I. for Short**  Sara Paretsky

In these irresistible, entertaining stories, Vic uses her skills, her judge-ment, her intuition – and sometimes her Smith & Wesson – to get the better of her adversaries. 'Feisty private eye V. I. Warshawski grows more interesting, quirky and admirable with every story' – *The Times*

**Berlin Noir**  Philip Kerr

Ex-policeman Bernie Gunther thought he'd seen everything on the streets of 1930s Berlin. But then he went freelance and with each case he tackled he became sucked further into the grisly excesses of Nazi sub-culture. And even after the war, amidst the decayed, imperial splendour of Vienna, Bernie uncovered a legacy that made the wartime atrocities look lily-white by comparison . . .

# READ MORE IN PENGUIN

## A SELECTION OF CRIME AND MYSTERY

**Ripley Under Water**  Patricia Highsmith

Tom Ripley's past would not bear too much close scrutiny. But he has carefully covered his tracks as far as murder and forgery are concerned. Or so he thinks. 'Ripley is back, as polite and lethal as ever . . . he does what he wants and gets away with it. That's why we like him' – *Time Out*

**No Night is Too Long**  Barbara Vine

Tim Cornish, a creative writing student, sits composing a confession: an admission of a crime committed two years ago that has yet to be discovered. 'A dark, watery masterpiece . . . suffused with sexuality, which explores with hypnotic effect the psychological path between passion and murder' – *The Times*

**The Malcontenta**  Barry Maitland

Detective Sergeant Kathy Kolla, seconded to the provinces and sidelined to mundane duties, leaps at the chance to investigate the unnatural death of a physio at the exclusive Stanhope House Clinic. 'Maitland has a sure touch, and the storyline is complemented by a serious look at the issues of sexism and corruption in the police force. An engaging read' – *Sunday Express*

**The Complete Richard Hannay**  John Buchan

From Scotland to Constantinople, rural England and the bloody battlefields of France, Richard Hannay's adventures in the pursuit of justice are classic, compelling reading. Collected here are: *The Thirty-Nine Steps*, *Greenmantle*, *Mr Standfast*, *The Three Hostages* and *The Island of Sheep*.

**Riding the Rap**  Elmore Leonard

'A great read . . . his underworld remains a bizarre but strangely accurate funhouse-mirror of America-at-large. His petty thieves, gamblers and con-men are just trying to get a leg up the precipitous ladder of American life. Who can really blame them if they skip a few rungs when nobody is looking?' – *Sunday Times*